Hallowed Be Thy Name

BROOKE WINTERS

CONTENT WARNINGS

Mild child abuse (verbal & physical), homophobia, Christian and Bible references, trauma, alcoholism, nightmares and traumatic events, mental illness, death, murder, cults, attempted exorcisms, demonic imagery, blood, gore, body horror and graphic violence.

To all those fighting demons no one else can see.

PART I

PROLOGUE

I murdered my mother.

Her ghost now haunts the House on North Lane. It is called the House on North Lane because it is the only one on the street—a tall, timbered structure hidden beneath an overgrowth of grass and vines, a single shattered window its only breath of life.

Armed with bare, razor-edged branches, a skeletal tree guards the entrance, long limbs outstretched as if to ward off intruders—or to keep something in.

A young boy lay buried within the walls, time eating away at the flesh that had once enveloped his bones. Abandoned, forgotten—the House shielding his cries from a saviour that would never come. Or so the story goes. That story, anyway.

The children in town speak of another. Of a witch entangled with the Devil, condemned to the House for all eternity. Her thin, pale form stood by the window every night, hands clasped together in prayer as she begged for a salvation that would never come.

My personal favourite? A clawed monster, imprisoned by God, powerless to leave due to its hunger for revenge. It howled in the night, thrashing against the door, mourning a salvation that would never come.

There are many stories about the House on North Lane, but the one I am about to tell is not one the children whisper around a campfire on a cold night. It is about Augustus Saint. And I am just a man. A man who murdered his mother, a man now entrapped in the House on North Lane.

The first night of my imprisonment was quiet. And it was cold, the evidence of every exhaled breath a white mist drifting through the darkness. Goosebumps crawled along my arms, hairs upright, standing to attention like obedient soldiers preparing for battle.

An icy breath caressed the back of my neck, sending numbing shivers straight down my spine as I crouched to retrieve a long, blood-stained crucifix abandoned on the empty floor.

The second night bore me no mercy. Nausea enveloped me in its arms, the air thinning to the point it was like breathing in through a straw. I scrubbed blood, ash and dust off the wooden floorboards, vision blurring and replaced with a static screen.

Footsteps echoed on the floor above me, the only sound other than my laboured breathing and thundering heart. I ventured up the old, winding staircase, a flickering candle in my hand to fend off the darkness. The empty hallway glared back at me as a rat scurried from one crack in the wall to another. There was no one there. At least no one I could see. But I felt her. Taunting me. Waiting for the right moment to exact her revenge.

By the one hundredth night, I'd grown accustomed to the creaking floorboards and the whispering walls, the heavy breathing and the dancing shadows. The House and I were in an endless waltz. It despised me, and yet it had no intention of letting me leave, twirling me around with no respite. My sin entrapped me here, as did hers.

I want nothing more than to leave this prison, to escape this wicked nightmare, but there are phantom hands wrapped around my throat, imprisoning me here among the many stories of the House on North Lane.

CHAPTER ONE

By now, you are probably wondering why I did it. Or, perhaps, you are just here for the ghost story. Either way, I shall start from the beginning.

It all started with a mirror. A long mirror, taller and wider than I had been when it greeted me at four years old, locked out on the front porch of the House on North Lane.

With my back pressed against the door, knees secured to my chest, I watched the mirror drift closer until it paused in front of me, hovering above the ground as though it were a ghost unable to touch the Earth.

I had been banished outside for not finishing my supper, throat still aching from the meat that had been forced down with rough fingers and sharp words. The screaming, the crying, the begging—it earned me a night spent in darkness, with only a pair of black shorts and a thin grey singlet ruffled around the neckline from where I had been yanked to my feet.

"If you're going to behave like the Devil," my mother hissed, throwing my thrashing body out into the cold autumn night, knees meeting the wooden deck with a sickening crunch, "then you will be treated like the Devil."

The mirror's thick, golden frame was arched like the entrance of an old church, decorated with angels sharing baskets of fruit, one reaching for a single apple dangling from a thin tree branch. Scenes of merriment and delight were juxtaposed with golden feathers that fell from angel wings, their bodies descending to an Earth they would never reach.

My reflection peered back at me with red-rimmed eyes, a mess of untamed brown curls, and a swollen cheek. Dry tears stained my pale skin, cracked lips spattered with blood. I turned my head, but the mirror followed.

"Go away," I whispered.

The mirror stayed.

I opened my mouth to confront it again, prepared to raise my voice, if necessary, but words evaded me as pools of darkness corrupted the mirror.

The reflection that once shared my hazel eyes now stared back at me with black ones, darkness eating away at the white circling the iris. Slowly, they sank into my skull, leaving nothing but blood pouring from my empty eye sockets.

The Devil, I thought to myself, *he's got me.*

Children were inherently evil. They were born with the original sin—a sin shared by all of humanity when Adam and Eve devoured the forbidden fruit, disobeying God's command.

I had been baptised, cleansed of this sin, but my mother had always said I had the Devil inside of me. And she was right.

My lips parted in a scream, yet I made no sound. In silent horror, I watched my mouth open wider, jaw dropping lower, until a deafening snap resounded in my ears. There was no pain, only untamed terror as my jaw dangled at an inhuman angle.

Insects crawled out of my disfigured mouth, snakes slithering over my shoulders and down my body to form a puddle at my feet. Spiders, cockroaches, beetles—they choked me, smothered me, ate away at my flesh.

A faceless shadow materialised behind me, clawed hands wrapping around my throat. It leaned down to whisper in my ear, my name pouring from its lips in a menacing hiss.

I willed myself to scream, to alert someone, *anyone*, of the danger I was in. The sound that erupted from me instead was laughter. Cold, wicked laughter. As my body shook, drops of flesh melted from my face, devoured by the hungry creatures crawling at my feet.

I wanted to cry, I wanted to scream, I wanted to *breathe*. But air no longer ventured into my lungs, and my voice had long since abandoned me. This was the end.

The mirror vanished when I awoke. In its place, darkness glared back.

The dark and I had never been friends. In the dark, the Devil hid in the shadows, waiting to plunge his teeth into flesh and bone. The light drove him away, but there was no light when I sat up on the front porch, locked outside just as I had been in the nightmare I escaped from.

North Lane was surrounded by trees, and in the endless black, they morphed into leering monsters threatening to tear me limb from limb. One tree stood guard by the entrance, shielding me from its hungry brothers while I stood to slam my firsts against the door.

"Mumma!" I cried. "Mumma! Let me in!"

The gentle whistle of the wind was the only response.

Punishment upheld, alone in a darkness threatening to consume me, I slid down the door and turned to the one being us Christian children were told would never abandon you. God.

"In the name of the Father, the Son and the Holy Spirit," I signed the cross and clasped my hands together in prayer, straightening my posture just as I would in church.

The Lord's Prayer had been ingrained in me from the moment I said my first word, as familiar to me as breathing in through my nose and out the mouth. And so, without a second's hesitation, I recited, "Our Father, who art in Heaven, hallowed be Thy name..."

The prayer spilled out of me, desperation lacing each and every word as my gaze lifted to the heavens, pleading for salvation. Stars winked back, a lone cloud sailing past the pale glow of the moon. The Devil's cold grasp was near, and God's warmth so, so far away.

"Please," I whispered, "I'm...scared. I want to...to go inside. Please help me. I didn't mean to be bad for Mumma. I will be good. I promise. Please help me."

The problem with being raised on the belief that God was an all-powerful, omniscient being, was that when your prayers went unanswered, you knew He had abandoned you. Why wasn't He listening? Why would He not save me?

"Please," I repeated, "I don't want to be out here all alone."

An owl hooted, a bat landed on a tree, and a cool breeze caressed the hair out of my eyes. But still, no response from God.

"I don't want to be alone anymore," I continued. God may not have been listening, but maybe *someone* was. Maybe an angel was sitting up in the clouds, my voice carrying through the wind that drifted up to Heaven. "I want a baby brother or sister. Someone to be with me when I'm out here on my own."

I wanted someone to face the shadow monsters, a brother or sister to stand by my side as we fought the Devil, sharing the burden of being *good*.

God did not answer my prayer that night.

I remained out in the cold, haunted by tree monsters and sinister shadows until the sun rose, its light finally banishing the darkness.

But He answered my prayer nine months later, delivering a baby boy—his piercing wail hauling me from my slumber, my paper aeroplane falling to the floor to be crushed by a nurse hurrying into the maternity ward.

Dressed in a pair of dark green dinosaur pyjamas that barely fit, I shifted upright, blinking repeatedly to adjust to the waking world. I didn't know where I was, or how I got there, only that my wrist ached and that the metallic taste of blood assaulted my tongue.

I had been in a hospital once before, and recognised the distinct, bitter scent of antiseptic and chemicals. As I slipped off the bench where I slept, my gaze drifted to a door on my right, open just enough to reveal my mother holding a white bundle in her arms. There were muffled voices all around her, drowned out by the beeping of machines and alarms from other sections of the ward.

I approached the door, lured in by the faint, yellow glow around the newborn. Everything in the room was a blur of motion as people scurried in and out, but my attention remained fixed on *him,* as if there were nothing and no one else in the world.

"Hey, baby," my mother greeted me with a small, tired smile, her untied hair drenched with sweat, "come meet your baby brother. Isn't he just a precious little gift from God?"

I risked a step closer, avoiding the tubes connecting my mother to the machines beside her bed, slithering up her arm until they disappeared beneath her gown. The baby cried, and I barely saw a wisp of dark hair before I was scooped up and settled on the edge of the bed, my father holding me up to secure a better view.

"Why is he sad?" I asked.

Despite my mother's attempts to soothe him, his cries did not cease. I was not allowed to cry. The second I did, I would be threatened with something to *really* cry about. And so, I avoided the tears, knowing it would not grant me the same compassion or sympathy it granted others.

"I think it is because you haven't introduced yourself yet," my father said.

My mother cracked a smile, though it did little to hide her distress as she rocked the baby back and forth in her arms. I waited for my father to offer his help, but he didn't.

"Hello," I said, reaching for the baby's small, fisted hand, "my name is Augustus. I am your big brother."

The newborn, of course, did not respond. His crying did, however, cease. And when he opened his eyes, a sea of ice blue peered up at me. In those eyes, I saw the two of us galloping through a field of flowers with sticks for swords, drawing together by the lake behind North Lane, and reading under the stars, writing our own stories of heroes and villains. Finally, *finally*, I wouldn't be alone.

But it didn't feel as though we were meeting for the first time. He was not a stranger; more an old friend that had finally found his way home. This was indeed God's gift, and I would never forget it.

"What is his name?" I asked, a small smile growing on my lips as the baby's hand curled around my index finger, grip tight.

"Auden," my mother answered.

"Au-den," I tested the name. "Au...it sounds like Au-gustus."

"Yes," my father chuckled. "You already have something in common. Isn't that great? Are you going to be a good big brother?"

I nodded without really knowing what the role of big brother entailed. But I was determined; determined to protect him, to love him, to guide him.

I hadn't known then, as I held his small hand, that I was meeting the second half of my soul. I hadn't known, as his fingers curled around mine, that I was meeting my salvation. I hadn't known, as his eyelids fluttered shut, that I was also meeting my doom.

CHAPTER TWO

We are all born sinners.

To be purged from sin, Catholic children are anointed with oil, blessed, and cleansed with holy water. Provided these children grew into adults who upheld the word of the Lord, baptism guaranteed their entry into the Kingdom of Heaven.

It was why Auden, at little over six-months-old, was draped in a white gown to be christened by our parish priest, Father Andrej. It was, in my mother's words, a necessary ritual to ensure Auden was sinless and accepted as a child of God.

I did not understand why such initiation was necessary. Were not *all* children...children of God? He was the creator of *all*, was he not? What sin could a six-month-old possibly commit that would alienate him from God before he could even talk?

Questions like *that*, however, earned you a slap on the wrist, for how *dare* you question the Almighty Father?

I waited in the living room while my parents finished preparing for the ceremony, my white trousers too short and my white collared shirt too tight. There was not a lot of money to spare, so clothing, especially ones worn on such rare occasions, were not a worthwhile expense. The clothes I wore belonged to a boy from church, several months younger than me, while Auden wore my old christening gown, the white silk loose around his shoulders.

"There is something wrong with him."

I lifted my head, gaze landing on my mother who stood in the hallway with my father. She wore a long, white linen skirt and a pale pink blouse, auburn hair rolling down her back in gentle waves. Lines of worry creased her forehead, light makeup bringing colour back to her pale cheeks. Her hands trembled in front of her, only pausing when my father reached out to clasp them with his own.

"All babies are different," he said. His dark hair, the same shade as my own, was combed neatly to one side, a single curl falling over his forehead. Hanging from his neck was a golden crucifix, the white collar of his shirt unbuttoned as though granting Jesus a window to the ceremony.

"I know that, Marcus. I am not stupid!" my mother insisted. "But there's something *wrong*. He doesn't cry, he doesn't smile, he doesn't even look at me."

It was true that Auden rarely cried. Not for food. Not for a nappy change. Not even for attention. The last time he cried was the day he was born. You barely got more than a sniffle or a squirm out of him.

My father said that made Auden the perfect baby, but my mother disagreed. It made her anxious. She feared that she was a terrible mother, unable to determine the needs of her baby.

I overheard many discussions in the middle of night when my mother would cry, the word failure falling from her tongue in breathless sobs. If my father was there to reassure her, he wasn't successful.

"Mumma?" I spoke up, daring a step toward her. I hated seeing her upset. I had deemed it my responsibility to comfort her when my father could not, yet I had not mastered how to do so without escalating things further. The only solution, in my young mind, was to take on the role of big brother and ease her burdens. "Do you want me to help Auden get ready for you?"

"Not now, Augustus," she waved me away, massaging her forehead as though I were causing her pain.

A heavy weight pressed down on my chest. Guilt, perhaps? No, it was fear. A selfish safeguard. For I knew that if I failed to resolve my mother's problem, to ease her burden, it would become *my* problem. The only way to protect myself was to protect her.

"I can help," I tried again. "I can—"

"I said NOT NOW!"

I flinched at the raised voice, backing away before the shout became a punishment.

My father shot me a look that said *go away.* And so I did.

***

Clothed in white, feet blistering in shoes that did not fit, I followed my parents to the front of the church to greet the parish priest of St Augustine's.

Father Andrej was a middle-aged man born of Polish immigrants, his ash-coloured hair shaved close to the scalp and his thin framed glasses magnifying his wide, grey eyes. His parents moved to England after the Second World War, though it wasn't until he was ordained as a priest that he arrived in the small town of Rose Chapel.

He shook my father's hand, and then my mother's, greeting Auden with a warm smile only to be met with a blank expression. When he stepped forward to ruffle my hair, I hid behind my father, his long legs a shield.

Apologising for my shyness, my father followed the priest toward the front row of pews, my mother scolding me quietly as she adjusted Auden on her hip.

I sat between my parents, legs swinging back and forth as more people piled in, floral perfume and incense filtering through the air. Auden remained still on my mother's lap, his light brown hair combed neatly out of his blue eyes, just as bright as the day he'd first opened them.

Strangers approached our pew to greet Auden, making faces in an attempt to draw out a smile. He rewarded them with nothing but a slow blink, his blank expression unwavering.

I grinned, satisfied with the disappointed expressions on the strangers' faces. I did not like them very much, but after my disrespectful behaviour with the priest, I was not permitted to ignore them. I let them pat the top of my head and pinch my cheeks, swallowing back my words of protest. I could bear it all if it drew them away from Auden.

St Augustine's was the only Catholic church in Rose Chapel, standing solemnly with an ensemble of moss, ivy and algae crawling along the weathered limestone, indiscriminate in their invasion. Sunlight poured through its tall, arched windows—many of which were stained with various depictions of Jesus Christ, the Apostles, and Virgin Mary, casting an array of colour onto the worn marble floor.

The majority of Rose Chapel's population were followers of the Church of England, but a small number were Catholic, and they were all piled inside the church to welcome the newest member of their community.

A soft hymn announced the start of the ceremony, Father Andrej leading the procession toward the large, dark oak altar draped in a gold and white cloth.

My gaze lifted toward the light fixtures above me, a stark contrast to the 15th century architecture. There were artworks lining the top of the walls to my left, scenes of Jesus' crucifixion painted in vivid detail, blood dripping from his crown of thorns. This obsession with Christ's brutal and agonising death were everywhere, with a large sandstone sculpture of Jesus on the cross displayed behind the altar, a confronting reminder of his eternal sacrifice.

"Why did Jesus die for us?" I had asked my mother once.

"To save us from our sins," my mother answered, "and to restore our relationship with God so that we can have eternal life in Heaven."

Guilt ensnared me, forcing my gaze down to my feet in shame. Jesus died and suffered for my sins, yet I was a sinner. I owed it to Jesus to do better, but the Devil lingered inside me, claws buried deep in my flesh.

There were no images of the Devil inside the church. No snake slithering into Eden. But I could feel him, hiding in the shadows, waiting to devour those whose thoughts strayed.

It was said the Devil was not welcomed in a place of worship, that he was forbidden entry. Though if all of God's creatures were welcome, would that not include the Devil? Was he not one of God's creations?

A nudge from my mother snatched me from my wandering thoughts, gaze sliding to Auden instead. He was fiddling with the hem of his christening gown, blissfully unaware of the Devil and his presence in the church.

Father Andrej recounted the origins of sin—of Adam and Eve's disobedience in the Garden of Eden, the consumption of fruit that deemed all of humanity sinners.

I did not understand why their sin was now Auden's to bear. Why did *he* need to be absolved of a sin that wasn't his own? He was innocent. Blameless. And yet he was carried to the basin of holy water by his godparents anyway, two members of the church who hadn't even met him until this moment.

I watched the scene unfold from the pew, wincing at the scream that erupted from my brother when the water rolled down the back of his head. I wanted to eliminate the water then and there for making him cry, envious of the sun and its ability to evaporate water with its heat. The heat of my anger only resulted in my father's hand on my shoulder, warning me to behave.

Following the ceremony, we attended a small church-held event to celebrate Auden's official entry into the Catholic church. It was in a small, modern hall behind the church, and everyone who attended was invited.

There were far too many people, all of whom I wanted to avoid, so I remained glued to my mother's side, listening to her conversation with a middle-aged woman with short black hair and smoke on her breath.

My mother was a small, thin woman with freckles painted across her nose and cheeks, hazel eyes hidden beneath long lashes.

Auden shared her bow-shaped lips and small round nose, though his eyes were so clear and bright, you could see yourself reflected as though peering through a mirror. My eyes were my mother's, a blend of green, brown and gold.

"I heard Joanna's daughter…" The black-haired woman lowered her voice as she leaned closer to my mother, looking around wearily as if to ensure she would not be overheard. "I heard she had an abortion last week."

A gasp was my mother's response.

"I know," the woman said as I busied myself with colouring the picture of John the Baptist that had been distributed to all the children. "How tragic. The Devil got to her. Joanna is a mess."

I flinched at the mention of the Devil, dropping my pencil in the process.

"Is that why she hasn't been to mass?" my mother asked. I reached down to retrieve the pencil, sliding off my chair and crawling under the table. "Augustus, sit still."

I abandoned the pencil and climbed back onto the chair as the woman said, "That's right. Embarrassed, no doubt. Horrified. I would be too. A daughter like that? It's just not right! That poor child!"

"It's awful," my mother agreed, reaching to wipe the dribble off Auden's chin, "we must protect our children and keep the Devil far, far away."

I winced and shifted in my seat. For two women who claimed to worship God, they sure seemed to talk about the Devil more than Him.

Noticing my unease, the black-haired woman studied me for a long moment before suggesting, "Augustus, sweetie, why don't you go play with some of the other children while Mummy and I talk?"

The suggestion was so mortifying that I deigned to respond. It was not that I did not *like* the other children. There were some I played with at school, joining a game of hide and seek or a round of handball. But, if given the option to approach strangers or sit alone drawing, I would always choose the latter. I preferred my own company—other people did not always act the way I wanted them to. It was easier to be alone rather than learn to contain them.

"It's alright," my mother said, fingers gently raking through my curls, "he likes to stick by me when there are lots of strangers around."

"Ah, a little bit of a Mumma's boy, is he?"

"A little bit, yes," my mother mused.

I finished colouring while they chatted away, their conversation turning to other women in their circle, some whose husbands were cheating on them, some who hadn't attended a recent wedding, and some who they simply did not like.

Their voices became senseless muttering as my mind fixated on which colours to select for different sections of the drawing. I wanted the water to be blue, but I needed a darker shade in the deeper part of the river and a lighter one where John the Baptist stood with Jesus. Once satisfied, I held up the paper to my mother.

A small smile spread across her face as she examined it. You could never quite predict what reaction you would get, what mood she would be in, so it was a relief to receive her approval. She leaned down, kissed the top of my head, and told me to draw on the other side of the paper.

"How is the little one doing?" the woman asked, her gaze settling on Auden who watched me draw from our mother's lap.

"Oh," my mother's smile faded, "I don't know...it's hard to tell. He's a good boy, but..."

"But?"

"Well," my mother lowered her voice, and I strained to hear her over the sound of chatter all around us, "he's not really... meeting any of his milestones. He doesn't respond to his name, won't look me in the eye. He won't even *smile*. I'm worried. I don't know if he's comfortable, if he's sick, if he even... if he even likes me."

"Oh, sweetie, all children are different," the woman said gently. "My second was a lot slower than my first."

"I know. I just...I feel like he's *really* behind."

"If you're really worried," the woman said, placing a hand over my mother's, "attend mass more regularly and pray for God's guidance. Trust in Him. Only he can help you and your beautiful little boy."

My mother did pray for God's guidance, but it was the Devil who answered.

CHAPTER THREE

Church became our home every Sunday.

Rain drummed against the rooftop, flashes of lightning illuminating the stained-glass windows as Father Andrej addressed the morning congregation. I sat in between my parents, picking the lint off my charcoal trousers as candlelight flickered with every gust of wind sneaking in with a late parishioner.

"Psalms 9:17 warns that *the wicked go down to the realm of the dead*. And in Matthew 25:46, the wicked are condemned to eternal punishment while the righteous go to eternal life with our Heavenly Father."

I shifted uncomfortably in my seat, struggling to fend off the yawn that had been lingering since the moment I sat down. The last thing I, at six years old, wanted to do was endure a lecture about Hell.

Auden had grown restless, too. He was nearing two years old, recently mastering the art of walking. A late walker, my mother said, but he'd gotten there in the end. Being trapped in my mother's arms was torture when he had a new found skill to refine.

"Sin, no matter how small, is sin," Father Andrej went on. "And without God's guidance, even the smallest of sins condemn us to *Hell*."

A flash of lightning lit up the room, roaring thunder following close behind. The rain fell harder, and an altar boy handed the priest a microphone to prevent his voice from being drowned out.

"And so, Mark 9:13 says *if your hand causes you to stumble, cut it off*." Father Andrej's voice was as dark and brooding as the clouds that rolled above us, shedding rain with unyielding force. *"It is better for you to enter life maimed than with two hands into Hell."*

Thunder bellowed at the word *Hell*, God himself emphasising the priest's warning. I sank lower in my chair, heart pounding as though I would be swallowed into Hell's eternal flame at any moment. I did not want to cut off my own hand. Nor did I want to spend eternity in Hell, condemned to the Devil's wicked games.

And so that night, as I prepared for bed, I kneeled before God, hands clasped together in prayer. The priest's words echoed in my head like a broken record. I turned to God, begging that He repel the Devil who lay claim to my soul.

But it was the Devil who answered, a wicked hum in my ear, phantom claws curving over my shoulders. His presence cloaked the room in darkness as I prayed for God's light.

"Our Father, who art in Heaven, hallowed be Thy Name," I recited the prayer from memory, the words spilling out despite my mind succumbing to distraction. I was not praying hard enough. The Devil was still there. There were doubts circling my mind like a fish debating a hook. If God was an all-powerful, omniscient being, why did He not answer my prayers? With all the death and destruction in the world, it almost seemed like he wasn't answering *anyone's* prayers. Was there even a God at all?

The Devil laughed—a cruel, taunting sound.

Closing my eyes, I resumed my prayers, desperate to ignore the Devil and summon God in his stead.

But no matter how hard I tried, no matter how many nights I spent on my knees, calling out to God, he was always too far away, somewhere I could not follow.

***

"Ma-Ma. Say Ma-Ma."

The grandfather clock chimed seven times, its song dancing down the hallway and into the living room where I sat cross-legged in front of Auden, his Winnie-the-Pooh security blanket clutched firmly in his hands. Colourful building blocks were scattered all around him, the play mat beneath us decorated with black and white roads for toy cars to drive down. My Batmobile was parked next to Thomas the Tank Engine, surrounded by Auden's smaller Hot Wheels cars.

"Ma-Ma," I repeated, sounding out the word slowly in the hopes that Auden would say it back to me.

He didn't.

Despite nearing two and a half years old, Auden was yet to say his first word. I had mastered 'Mumma' and 'Dada' at nine months old with little prompting, hence why my parents were concerned when at twenty-eight months old, Auden was yet to speak.

I did not share these concerns.

Auden may have been quiet, but he was curious. His eyes would often track my movements as I played with my toy cars, built Lego, or reached for a book to read. He would sit on my lap, point to the characters on the page, and clap his hands when the hero won the battle. Sometimes he would even reach for my superhero figurines as I flew them around the room, as if he too wanted to fly. He was always watching, learning, taking everything in. His silence was not an indicator of his intelligence. He just needed some encouragement.

"I just don't know what I am doing wrong," my mother told a friend on the phone earlier that week. "I'm doing everything I'm supposed to. I talk to him, I read to him, I play with him. What am I doing wrong? It just seems like I'm... I'm failing as a mother."

Guilt pooled in the pit of my stomach. It was overwhelming, threatening to surge up and spit my lunch out onto my math homework.

I hated the thought of my mother blaming herself for something out of her control. I wanted to do something, *anything*, to ease her concerns and make everything okay.

If Auden started talking, if he just said the word 'Mumma', then maybe our mother would stomach more than just a few bites of food and sleep more than just a few hours every night. Maybe she would smile again, tuck me into bed, tell me she loves me. If Auden could just say *one* word, maybe we'd all be okay.

That was why I dedicated every morning before school to encouraging Auden to say that one single word.

Although he would watch my mouth, and sometimes even move his own, no words came out. But he was trying. And that was enough.

"Come on, Gus," my father said, shrugging on his jacket as he wrestled to unlock the front door. He was dressed in his usual work attire—tan cargo pants, a yellow high visual shirt, and a navy jacket with his company logo on the back. "Let's get you to school before it rains."

I leaned down to kiss the top of Auden's head, promising to return the second school ended for the day, and reached for my bag to follow my father out the door.

St Augustine's Primary School was attached to the church. It had only two-hundred and three students from reception to year six, most of whom attended Sunday mass and Wednesday youth group. My year one class had eleven students, the other only had nine. Small classes meant we all knew each other quite well, but we were not necessarily friends.

At six years old, I was already an avid reader, face buried in a book when given the opportunity. In the highest reading group, I read novels written for nine to ten-year-olds, my report card delivering an A in every subject except mathematics, which glared at me with an unflinching C.

My favourite subject was art. While my peers spent their Friday afternoon art class flinging paint at one another, I dedicated mine to perfecting my drawings, experimenting with water-colours and acrylic paint to decide which felt more comfortable on my paintbrush and canvas.

The classroom was decorated with many of my artworks—some of which my teacher submitted to Rose Chapel's youth art competitions. I didn't win, but I came third place for my painting of the Nativity Scene.

Academically, I was successful. Socially, not so much. I didn't avoid making friends. There were some days I would join a game of football on the grass or a game of tag, but I preferred to play on my own terms where I could control the narrative.

Having endured one hour of spelling and another hour of mathematics, I was itching to spend recess alone. There were stories in my head I wanted to play out—stories I hadn't yet written down.

I found a long, sharp-edged stick in the woodland that divided the playground's grass field from the school gates, the dirt littered with fallen leaves and twigs of all sizes. Weapon in hand, I swung it at enemies only I could see, a sword worthy of slaying a wraith, a goblin, a wicked king. I battled each one, the hero of a story I conjured in my head.

Laughter infiltrated the battle scene. Four boys, arms folded over their chests, eyes crinkled with humourless smiles as they watched me. They were a few years above me, but I recognised them from Sunday mass.

"Who are you playing with?" one of the boys asked. His mother was in the choir and his father organised the charity bowls. James was his name. It was muttered by his friends who snickered and shoved him forward.

"I'm not playing with anyone," I stated the obvious.

James leaned down to retrieve a stick of his own, longer and sharper than mine. "I can play with you," he said. His friends laughed. "You were playing... swords, right?"

I nodded, oblivious of the torment to follow. Although I preferred my own company, I would be lying if I told you I didn't find the idea of a real opponent, a real playmate, appealing. Since Auden was still too young for games like these, I had no one to play with. Given the rare opportunity, I could not refuse.

Our sticks collided gently. I imagined that I was a gallant knight combatting a cursed warlock; a hero entrusted with saving the kingdom from his evil grasp. It was fun, but James played the role of 'cursed warlock' far too well. His advances grew in strength, our sticks connecting with a force so strong it snapped mine in two.

I staggered backward, losing hold of my weapon as James aimed his sword at my chest. Fear flooded through me, their laughter circling me like vultures, hungry for the kill.

James grinned, drinking in the fear that poured from me like a raging waterfall. "Scared?" he taunted, raising the stick higher with both hands, a soldier prepared to land a fatal blow.

The laughter ceased. His friends drew closer. My gaze locked on the sharp end of the stick, breath evading my lungs as time slowed, the weapon falling lower and lower.

I rolled at the last second, James' stick landing inches to my left with a loud snap. There was a collective gasp as I stood, leaves tangled in my hair and dangling off my jumper, a smudge of dirt on my cheek.

Take his sword and slam it into his throat.

The voice was soft, coaxing, almost melodic. It was not a voice I had heard before, but the presence was familiar. The mirror flashed behind my eyelids.

Black eyes, the flesh melting from my face, the pool of insects devouring me. It was the Devil. He was here.

I ran. I ran without looking back. I did not stop until I reached the library, safe amongst the shelves where I could hide from James and, more importantly, the Devil.

It was there, where I sat between two shelves, that I realised I was not the hero I liked to pretend I was. I was only a coward.

***

I was weary of the Devil returning that afternoon when I entered the House on North Lane. He did, but not in the way I had anticipated. The moment I stepped through the door, I was greeted by earth-shattering screams and distraught, violent sobbing. The former my brother, the latter my mother.

Alarmed, I dropped my bag in the entryway and followed the sound of my brother's distressed wails. He was on the floor of his bedroom, in only a diaper, his face and chest covered in what was either food, vomit, or both.

My mother was on the other side of the room, back against the wall, knees hugged to her chest. Her shoulders shook, hair spilling over her hands that clawed at her swollen eyes.

This time, I could not run. This time, I had to be the hero.

I scooped Auden up into my arms and carried him into the bathroom, carefully removing his nappy before lowering him into the small tub to fill it with warm, soapy water.

"Shh, Auddie, it's okay," I tried to soothe him, reaching for a clean cloth to wipe the food—or vomit—off his body. He flinched at the sensation, threatening to release another scream when I reached for his bath toys to distract him. It worked, giving me enough time to clean him up and dress him in a red and yellow Winnie-the-Pooh romper with a honey pot stamped on the back.

His crying ceased, but his eyes remained red and swollen. With his security blanket hugged to his chest, I carried him to his bed and set him down, stroking the hair out of his eyes as he watched me with big, unblinking eyes.

"Are you feeling better now?" I asked him.

He dipped his head in a nod as his eyelids fluttered shut, his face softening, all tension fleeing his body. With Auden settled, it was time to face my mother.

Her shoulders had stilled, though her face remained hidden beneath her untamed hair. I approached her, slowly, and reached for one of her hands. She flinched, as though scorched by flame, and lifted her head to look at me, tear-stained face twisted in anger.

"*Demon*," she hissed. "Do not touch me!"

I withdrew, hands falling at my sides as I whispered, "It's me, Mumma. Augustus."

"Augustus?" my mother repeated. "How dare you say his name, *demon!* I know what you are!"

Dread carved into my chest, the memory of the Devil's melodic voice replaying in my head. "What are you talking about?" I asked.

A cold laugh escaped her throat, eyes wild as she reached for my wrist, fingernails digging into bone as she rose to her feet.

"Do not act a fool!" she snapped, hauling me toward the door as Auden stirred in his sleep. "You have no place here! No place!"

She threw me out into the hallway and slammed the door shut in my face, her footsteps shuffling toward the bed where she scolded Auden for waking.

I stood there, outside the door, massaging my wrist as I tried to process the words my mother spat in my face. What had I done wrong? How did she know about the Devil inside my head?

Knowing I would not get an answer until this strange mood passed, I sulked toward my own bedroom, peeling off my uniform in preparation for a shower. It was only as I reached for a comfortable pair of grey sweatpants and a long-sleeved t-shirt that my gaze fell upon the crucifix above my bed. It had been turned upside down.

***

Silence was the punishment for my unknown crime. My mother refused to speak to me, and although I scoured my brain, replaying every word that rolled off my tongue, I could not determine what I had done to deserve the label 'demon'.

Guilt hung over me like a storm cloud, shadowing me in darkness with the threat of lashing rain. I was desperate to end the days of silence, to make my mother smile again. But that meant I had to apologise, even if I did not know what for. And I had the perfect idea.

Crayons lined my bedroom floor, a piece of white paper gradually transforming with colour as I prepared the 'apology gift' for my mother. I drew often—sometimes animals, sometimes a knight on his noble steed, sometimes my favourite superheroes. But, more often than not, I drew my family.

Evidence of these drawings were scattered on my desk, special ones selected to hang on the refrigerator for a week before they were thrown away.

Satisfied with the drawing of my mother and I holding hands, I slipped it under my parents' bedroom door, hoping that once she laid eyes on the two of us smiling, she would open the door and welcome me back into her arms. She never did.

I waited, and waited, and waited. But the door never opened. Instead, I heard the sound of paper tearing in two, my heart tearing along with it.

The following day, as I stood in my bedroom, bottom lip between my teeth, I decided that in order to return to my mother's good graces, I needed something more *powerful* to express my love and remorse.

My gaze darted from wall to wall, searching for inspiration. Those said walls captured my attention, birthing an idea that would show my mother how much I loved her, how much she meant to me. And maybe, just maybe, she would look upon me with fondness once more.

The idea was disastrous. Naturally, I did not realise this until it was too late. As I reached for my crayons and approached the blank wall, I thought of my mother and everything she loved—everything that would make her love *me* again.

An hour of drawing resulted in a wall decorated with St Augustine's church, my parents hand-in-hand as they stood in their finest Sunday clothes. A row of red roses—my mother's favourite flower—led to Auden and I swinging on the old tire that hung from the tree beside the statue of Mary. We all wore identical smiles. A picture-perfect family.

I studied my artwork, proud of what I had been able to create with nothing but an eight-pack of crayons. It was not my best work, but it was from the heart.

Crayons abandoned, I emerged from my bedroom, eager to announce the surprise I had for my mother. She was seated at the dining table, wrapped in a brown cardigan with a cup of tea in her hands, eyes glued on her computer screen.

"...and it is important you emphasise that everything, *everything*, in your home is yours, not theirs," a voice said from the computer. A man in a black suit spoke to my mother through the screen, a wooden cross swinging from his neck as he paced back and forth. "Your child is living in *your* home, under *your* roof, and they must obey *your* commands. Just like we are living in God's creation and must obey His commands."

"Mumma?"

She paused the video and turned to appraise me with suspicion. "What?"

"I have something to show you!"

She waved me away dismissively, attention returning to the video on her screen.

"It's a drawing!" I added, "a present!"

With a long, drawn-out sigh, she shut down her computer and followed me toward my bedroom.

I pushed open the door with a wide smile, confident I would be praised with a 'Wow! This beautiful' or an 'Augustus, you have made Mummy very happy.'

You could probably guess what I was met with instead when my mother's eyes landed on the drawing. What you probably did not anticipate, however, was that the drawing I had left the room with was not the drawing I now walked into.

The church was engulfed in flames. My mother, my father, Auden—all gone as though scrubbed clean. In their place, I dominated the scene, eyes as black as night, a crimson river pouring from my eyes.

There was a gasp, a lingering silence, and then...chaos.

"AUGUSTUS SAINT!" Knuckles met the back of my head with a loud crack, two crayons snapping beneath my bare feet as I stumbled forward. "WHAT IS THIS?"

My bottom lip trembled as I scratched the back of my head, vision blurring with unshed tears. "I... I don't... I don't know. I didn't draw this!"

"How dare you lie to me?!" my mother snapped, raising her hand to strike me again, only to lower it at the last second. "You are going to clean this up right now!"

Tears rolled down my face freely as I glanced in between my mother and the drawing that was not mine. I had wanted to make her happy, but instead I had made everything worse.

"Stop crying!" She gripped my face in one hand, fingernails stabbing into my cheeks as she forced our eyes to meet. "Are you a baby? No, you're not. Stop crying. Clean this up!"

Sadness twisted into anger, a howling beast with its teeth sinking into my thundering heart. It needed to be released, its heat burning through my veins.

My mother's grip loosened, and without a word, I reached down to collect my crayons, throwing them against the wall with a cry of frustration.

I regretted it the moment the Devil's laughter infiltrated my mind, sharp talons clawing at my skull.

"Mumma I'm sor—"

Her hand met my cheek, silencing my apology before it could leave my tongue. She dragged me out of the room with a bruising grip around my wrist. I screamed, I cried, I thrashed around wildly in an attempt to tear free. But it was no use. We reached the kitchen where she threw me to the tiled floor, the back of my head smacking against the drawers with a sickening crack.

Dazed, I watched my mother open and shut cupboard doors, muttering incoherently as she pulled out a bag of cable ties.

The Devil crouched beside me, his expression hidden behind blurred features.

Is that it? he asked with that same melodic voice he'd used when James attacked me. *Is that all the fight left in you?*

My mother hauled me to my feet, shoving me into the linen cupboard amongst towels, bed sheets and bathmats. She restrained my wrists together with a cable tie, its teeth biting into my skin.

There was barely enough space to breathe, yet alone stand, but the door clicked shut in my face before I could utter a word of complaint.

The walls were too close. Crushing me. Breath evaded my lungs. Panic spread. I tried to get out, but the scraping of a chair indicated I was enclosed in.

"Let me out!" I cried. "Mumma! Mumma! Let me out!"

"Not until you spend some time reflecting on your behaviour."

"Mumma! Please! I'm sorry! Mumma!"

I sobbed. I sobbed until I exhausted myself, collapsing onto one of the shelves, curling into a small ball to fit amongst the sheets.

I don't remember how long I was confined in that small cupboard for, but it felt like an eternity. And as I drifted off into a fitful sleep, a voice right next to my ear whispered, *You deserve this.*

CHAPTER FOUR

Summer leaves danced freely along the treetops, a barrage of green armour guarding us on our journey deep into the woods behind North Lane. Sunlight poured through the cracks in the armour, painting speckles of gold along the path toward the lake.

Ducks disappeared beneath the calm blue ripples, birds soaring from branch to branch as my mother guided Auden closer to the water's edge.

In nothing but a pair of swim shorts, I followed my father into the water, gliding past lily pads and tangled weeds until my feet no longer touched the bottom.

"Hey," my father nudged me with a grin. "Race you to the island?"

The 'island' was a green mound in the centre of the lake, with two tall trees and long, untamed grass. It was about a thirty-metre swim, and when I attempted to race my father the previous summer, he had to carry me back when I swallowed too much water. But I was older this time. And more determined to prove my strength.

Returning a grin, I launched myself under water, my father granting me a ten second head start before he soared past, his long limbs disappearing in the dark depths.

My arms cut through the water, legs aching as I pushed through the exhaustion threatening to drown me. I gasped for air with every resurface, water splashing into my eyes as I watched my father reach the island with ease.

He was an excellent swimmer. Throughout his secondary schooling, he'd been captain of the swim team, winning gold medals in the one hundred metre freestyle sprint and the longer eight hundred metre butterfly. Olympic level, if he'd taken his training more seriously.

It was quite clear, even from a young age, that I did not inherit my father's athleticism. I was not a *terrible* swimmer, but it was obvious I would never win a medal or compete in any national competitions. And although he never blamed or criticised me for my swimming failures, I could tell he was disappointed that he would not be able to fulfil his life-long dreams of being a professional swimmer through me. And I was disappointed too, for not being able to perfect the one thing my father and I could bond over.

By the time I made it to the island, panting and gasping for air, the sun had dried the wet droplets off his shoulders.

"About time, kiddo," he chuckled, hauling me up onto the slippery, moss-covered rocks beside him. "You okay?"

"No."

"No?"

I coughed, water dribbling down my chin.

"Ah," my father clicked his tongue. "Drinking up the whole lake again?"

I shot him an unamused look.

He laughed in return—a deep, pleasant rumble that shot through his entire body, his grey eyes betraying nothing but fondness. It was a rare sound, even rarer that he would playfully tackle me to the grass, pretending to fight like we were a pair of wolves battling for the last bite of food.

My father and I didn't spend a lot of time together. Not alone, at least. He was always at work, or out drinking with his mates, or watching a game of football that I wasn't allowed to interrupt.

But in these moments, laughing in a tangle of weeds, feet splashing through puddles of water, my father and I felt closer than ever.

We swam back to shore fifteen minutes later, my father leaving me to sit in the shallows with the ducks and the dragonflies while he helped my mother set out the picnic blanket, water dripping from his brown curls.

"Audie!" I called my little brother who stood alone under a large pine tree, his bottom lip jutting out in a pout. "Come here!"

He shook his head, determined to stay far, far away from the water. The lake, for reasons unknown, was his enemy.

With a sigh, I climbed to my feet and reached for a towel to dry off, my mother handing me a sandwich and a bottle of water to scoff down.

Just as I raised the bottle to my lips, she snatched it off me with a disapproving click of her tongue. "You need to say thank you, Augustus."

"Thank you, Mumma."

Once we'd finished eating, Auden and I raced around with sticks for swords, setting off on a quest to find the wicked witch of the forest. We soldiered through endless rows of trees, climbing over rocks and crawling beneath large, fallen logs. Dirt stained our clothes, but we ventured on, determined to play the heroes.

"Over here!" I called Auden. "The witch went this way!"

Wet leaves clung to our bare feet as we followed along a small brook, our reflections shimmering up at us between moss-covered stone. I avoided my own gaze, afraid of what might glance back.

Spearing my stick through the water, I dragged it along behind me as I listened to the gentle rustle of leaves and the collective humming of crickets.

The brook led us to an open field of blood red hellebores, green stems swaying in the light breeze.

"The witch is on the other side of this field!" I told Auden.

The long grass swallowed his sword as he trudged toward the rose-like flowers, hand outstretched as though entranced. He reached to tear off the petals, but I stopped him, a gentle hand on his wrist.

"Poison," I warned, "the witch may have set this as a trap."

He paused, lowered his hand, and opted to run his fingers through the long grass instead, lips spreading into a wide, carefree smile.

A smile from Auden was as rare as my father's laugh. I savoured it, following him through the flowery field, laughing and stumbling with nothing but the wind in our hair and our wild imaginations. It was at this moment I was reminded of why I had asked God for a younger sibling. My adventures were no longer my own. I had Auden. And he was ready to follow me into the very depths of Hell, all with a bright smile.

Broken twigs lured us back into the woods, small droplets of rain falling into my curls as I pushed them out of my eyes. The sun had disappeared behind dark clouds, cloaking the woods in darkness. I reached for Auden's hand to keep him close, but I was met with only air.

"Auden?!" My head whipped from side to side, scanning the trees for my brother's small frame. "Auden!"

Twigs snapped and leaves crunched beneath my feet as I ran deeper into the woods, my brother's name on my tongue. Panic spread through me like wildfire, flames licking at my heels, urging me to run faster.

"Auden!" I shouted. "If you can hear me, use your sword to make a sound! Hit it against a tree or... or the ground!"

I waited, but there was no sound. The leaves had stopped rustling. The crickets had stopped humming. Birds were nowhere in sight. It was just me and the soft patter of rain, standing alone in the woods blanketed by shadows.

Augustus.

My name whistled through the air, a soft whisper that would have brought comfort if it had come from my brother. But Auden did not speak.

Goosebumps spread over my arms and legs, breath evading capture as I slowly turned my head.

The Devil wore a face cloaked in shadow, horns protruding from a nest of brown hair, his body blending in with the dark woods looming behind him.

"Where is Auden?" I demanded, voice cracking.

Who?

He drifted closer, but his features remained hidden beneath a veil of darkness. Snakes slithered at his feet, long ribbons of black scales threatening to swallow me whole.

"My brother," I answered, fighting the instinct to flee. "Auden. Where is he?"

A heavy silence hung in the air as the Devil watched me. No one moved—not a single breath shared between us. The hunter and the prey.

I opened my mouth to repeat my question, but the words died in my throat the second my feet lifted off the ground and my back slammed against a tree. Pain burst through my spine, vision blurring as the loud crack of bone against bark echoed in my ears. I anticipated a drop, but the earth below grew farther and farther away as my body lifted high into the treetops.

Tendrils of smoke slithered up my body, curling around my neck in a tight embrace. I gasped. Choking. Withering.

You don't need Auden, the Devil whispered in my ear, *I am right here.*

"I... don't... want... you..."

I couldn't see the Devil's face, but I knew he was smiling when he said, *You will.*

"AUGUSTUS!"

My mother's voice cut through the darkness, the Devil loosening his hold. Warm sunlight chased away the shadows, air slowly returning to my screaming lungs.

"Augustus, what are you doing up there?!"

I glanced down at my mother, her fingers interlaced with Auden's as they both peered up at me with wide, unblinking eyes.

That was when I realised I was at least twenty branches high in a pine tree, my hands covered in dirt, leaves and splinters.

Confused, I climbed down carefully, my heart thundering as I replayed the last few minutes in my head.

"I lost Auden," I explained, "I… had to climb the tree to look for him."

"Auden was right here when I found you," my mother said, reaching down to pick a leaf out of my hair.

"What?" I looked at Auden, but his eyes were on the tree. Had he really been there? Had he seen the Devil?

"Come on," my mother said, "let's get you cleaned up."

***

A scream tore me from sleep's warm embrace.

Disoriented, I sat up, fingers massaging my eyes to prepare them for the waking world.

I thought I imagined the scream. But then I heard it again, the sound crawling up to the second floor, bursting into my bedroom with ferocity.

Wood groaned beneath my feet as I stumbled into the hallway, the faint glow of the moon peering through the windows my only guide. Hand on the railing, I descended the staircase, squaring my shoulders to prepare for the scene below.

Auden was on the couch, sandwiched between my parents. Tears poured from his red-rimmed eyes, mouth wet with dribble as he released a river of screams, fingernails tearing through the pale flesh of his arms.

My father restrained his wrists behind his back to stop him, but Auden thrashed around like a wild animal caught in a net, a trickle of blood rolling down his arms.

"What's going on?" I asked in alarm.

"Go back to bed," my mother said, fingers raking through the knots in her hair as tears nestled on the dark patches under her eyes.

"But what's wrong?" I demanded. The idea that I would simply return to my bedroom while Auden screamed in distress was ludicrous. That was just not going to happen. It was my job to protect him when my parents couldn't. And clearly…they couldn't.

"We don't know," my father said, voice dripping with exhaustion. With each blink, it seemed harder and harder for his eyes to reopen. "He came into our room and when we sent him back to bed–"

"He became a nightmare," my mother finished, shaking her head.

"Nothing will calm him down," my father sighed.

"I think I can help," I offered, taking a tentative step toward the couch.

"And what could *you* possibly do?" my mother scoffed, her tone as cold as the breeze that entangled itself around my bare arms and legs.

"He wants his chocolate drink," I answered.

Chocolate drink, or hot chocolate, as we all call it. Not only was it Auden's favourite drink, but it was a critical part of his morning routine.

Adults had their coffee, Auden and I had our chocolate drink. We could not start our day without it. But for Auden, this break in routine was a broken limb that would not heal.

"It's not even four am," my mother said. "He's not having his chocolate drink."

"Yes, but–"

"Chocolate drink is for morning. To have with breakfast. Not at three am after waking up in the middle of the night," my mother cut me off.

"I don't think he understands that it's too early," I argued. "He's so used to waking up and getting his drink that he's probably just confused as to why he isn't getting it now. Maybe he can just have a little bit?"

My mother looked as though I had just asked her to shave off all her hair. "No, Augustus. No. He cannot just have a little bit. If we give in to his demands, he'll expect chocolate drink every time he wakes up in the middle of the night and throw a tantrum when he doesn't get his way!"

"You're not listening. He's just confused and–"

"YOU ARE A CHILD!" my mother snapped. "You do NOT get to tell me what to do! You do not get to tell me how I should parent!"

"I know," I whispered, fighting off the instinct to lower my gaze in submission. My eyes drifted toward Auden. He was rocking back and forth, head shaking from side to side as tears streamed down his face. He couldn't defend himself, it was my job to do it for him. And I was failing.

I looked to my father, but he averted his gaze, leaving me alone and unarmed on a battlefield where my opponent had the upper ground. But even facing an army of soldiers, I would stand by Auden.

"Please," I said, "he's upset. He doesn't understand. If we could just give him a little bit to calm down and then we can explain–"

"I SAID NO!" my mother shouted. She struck my face, head whipping to the side so fast that my neck cracked, pain shooting down my spine. "I am so SICK of you always talking back!"

My father stood. "Mary–"

Tears rolled freely down my cheeks as I clutched my neck, legs trembling to the point I had to crouch down so as not to fall.

"I can't do this anymore, Marcus!" my mother said. "I can't do this! I can't do it! I can't–"

My father pulled her into his arms, comforting her the way I wanted him to comfort me, to comfort Auden. But he barely spared us a glance as my mother sobbed into his chest.

Punish them, the Devil's voice whispered, *strike them back.*

I reached for Auden, securing him in my arms without sparing my parents a second glance. They might have had each other, but I had Auden. And that was all that mattered.

I carried him upstairs, away from the chaos, and carefully settled him into bed.

Once his cries shifted to gentle snores, I walked toward the small window overlooking the driveway, compelled by an untamed rage that flooded through my veins. It was overpowering. All-consuming.

My fist slammed through the window, puncturing a hole as glass shattered, blood seeping from my sliced knuckles. I expected pain, but the only thing I felt was relief.

Good, little monster, the Devil said, *let it out.*

CHAPTER FIVE

Darkness enveloped the House on North Lane, the air thick with rot and decay. It was as though the House had been abandoned, even with the four souls living inside.

Silence followed me down every corridor, broken only by the groan of shifting beams and the creaking of floorboards.

The Devil's eyes followed me through the portraits on the walls. Watching. Waiting. For what, I did not know.

While my father worked, my mother barricaded herself in her room, shutting Auden and I out like we were the Devil's children, not hers.

She emerged only to attend church, dragging Auden and I along with her. Neither of us dared make a sound in fear of punishment.

We sat in the front row of pews, heads bowed, and hands clasped together in prayer. Our mother sat with Father Andrej on the pew across the aisle to our right, a rosary in each of their hands.

I could hear her shaky voice, the sharp intakes of breath, the quiet slap of her hands against her thigh every time she dropped them into her lap. She was discussing Auden. And me.

My attitude.

His silence.

My disrespect.

His tantrums.

Not wanting Auden to overhear, I directed his attention to the statue of Jesus on the cross. I told him how much Jesus loved him. How much *I* loved him.

"You'll never be alone," I whispered, "because you have Jesus to pray to. And you have me. I'll always be here. Always."

His lips spread into a small smile, eyes on mine as he took in every word. My voice seemed to calm him enough to nestle closer, his head resting on my upper arm.

I ruffled his hair gently, forcing a smile of my own as my mother complained about how difficult we made her life. We weren't the perfect children she felt she deserved as a loyal servant of God. Father Andrej didn't dispute her, telling her that God would not have entrusted her with us if He didn't believe she could guide us to Him.

"I am not who He thinks me to be, then," my mother sniffled, "I wish I had never had children."

A blade through the heart would have hurt less. I swallowed the pain, keeping my eyes clear of tears for Auden's sake. Unlike my mother, I would not give up on him. He was not a burden. He was the light I would follow out of the darkness. The light I would protect when the shadows tried to drown him out.

The drive home was quiet except for the radio. Auden was asleep, security blanket glued to his chest in a warm embrace. I glanced past him, gaze on the row upon row of trees that followed us to North Lane, a blur of green, brown and grey.

I thought about what my mother had told Father Andrej—about how much of a burden Auden and I were. Auden was battling through his inability to communicate, and I had the Devil in my head. I needed to be good. Be better. Make my mother's life easier.

That will never happen, the Devil hummed.

"What did Father Andrej say?" were my father's first words as we stepped through the door.

"He thinks we should see a doctor," my mother answered.

"A doctor?" my father frowned. "Why?"

"It doesn't matter. Because he's wrong. A doctor isn't going to heal our children from sin." She dumped herself onto the couch while Auden and I approached the staircase. I let Auden climb up, but I remained, listening as my mother added, "I need God's guidance, and Father Andrej has sinned terribly for suggesting we turn to earthly means for a solution."

"What? Mary, no. Father Andrej is right. If there is something wrong we need to–"

"God is testing us, Marcus, don't you see? We're failing. Augustus is disrespectful. He resorts to violence when he's upset, he always talks back and thinks he knows it all. And Auden..." Her voice trailed off as she glanced toward where I hovered by the staircase. I slipped away before I could endure a scolding, heart hammering in my chest as I went.

I didn't get to hear the rest of the conversation, but by the following Sunday, we were attending a new church.

***

Our new church was a small building with a large cross plastered on the front door, floorboards cracked and splintered with age. Our new priest was a man with self-appointed authority to speak on God's behalf, his allegiance not to the Pope, but to himself.

My father did not approve. He had been hesitant to leave the St Augustine community—a community that had welcomed him in Rose Chapel when he was freshly nineteen, looking for work in a small, honest town.

My mother disagreed. She believed St Augustine's had betrayed her, that Father Andrej was no longer a trustworthy advisor. That was why we joined the God's Soldiers Church. Here, she said, we would be saved.

But it didn't feel like we were being saved. My mother had lost a lot of weight, blue veins protruding from her pale skin. Sleepless nights darkened the circles around her eyes, bottom lip speckled with dried blood from her incessant picking.

Religion became an obsession. It controlled her every waking moment. While she grew closer to God, we all grew further apart.

"You have the devil in you," she'd tell me whilst securing rope around my wrists, the rough fibres biting into my skin. "This is for your own good."

She'd then throw me into the linen cupboard, slamming the door shut.

Blood soaked into the rope's frayed strands, droplets falling one after the other as I blindly reached for a towel to control the bleeding. This earned me further punishment when my mother opened the door hours later to find two towels soaked with blood.

Dragging me into the kitchen, she removed the rope and poured lemon juice over my open wounds, a scream ripping from my throat at the burning acidity.

I spent more time locked in that linen cupboard, fighting through panic attacks, than ever before. If this was what being saved entailed, then I did not want to be saved.

Another Sunday rolled around, red, orange and yellow leaves crunching beneath our feet as we piled into the car.

The gentle patter of rain fell against the windshield, blurring the multitude of trees that followed us to the God's Soldiers Church. Upon arrival, we hurried from the car to the house, ducking beneath our coats as a fine mist chased us up the steps.

Joseph Kade—or Joe, as my mother called him—stood at the front of the dimly lit room, black hair combed away from his forehead, light stubble grazing his sharp jaw. He spoke slowly, deliberately, each word casting a spell over the small congregation in attendance. Heads tilted, eyes widened. They were starving and his words were theirs to devour.

"We are called to spread the word of God," he said, colourless eyes meeting mine for a fraction of a second before drifting to the entranced devotees digesting his every word, "and to silence those who speak against it."

My mother had a small notebook on her lap, thin fingers curled around a pen to record each and every word that rolled off Joe's tongue.

"God delivered you all here, to me. It is our mission to save the world, to repent, to free one another of sin," he went on.

"Man thinks he's Jesus," my father mumbled under his breath.

I barely suppressed a smile.

It was no secret my father disliked Joe. He thought him to be arrogant and prideful, a false prophet claiming to be divinely chosen by God. But my mother worshipped him, hanging off his every word.

"The Devil is among us."

Silence.

Not a cough. Not a whisper.

No one moved. No one blinked.

I held my breath, the Devil stirring at the threat. I closed my eyes, willing him to remain quiet, fearful of the consequences. My leg bounced up and down, a subconscious admission of guilt.

"You."

I opened my eyes, expecting a finger pointed in my direction, cold eyes condemning me for my sin. But there was no finger. At least not pointed at me.

Joseph's eyes were on a young woman in her early twenties. Trembling, she shook her head, the denial dying on her lips as all attention fixed on her.

"Come here, child," Joseph said, opening his arms.

The woman exchanged a glance with the young man beside her before slowly rising, the gentle tap of her heels drowning out the silence.

Biting my lip, I forced my leg to stop bouncing as Joseph placed a hand on the young woman's head, leaning forward to whisper in her ear. I don't know what was said, but whatever it was, it conjured a tear that rolled down her cheek.

"Tell us about yourself, Angela," Joseph said, one hand falling to her shoulder while the other gently wiped the tear from her cheek.

"I... I don't know what to... to say," she stammered.

"How about you start by telling us all why you are here?" Joseph suggested.

Angela nodded, brushing a single strand of honey-blonde hair behind her ear. "Okay. Okay, um. I... I was never uh... never religious. I mean... I believed in God and everything but... I didn't really go to church or pray or anything like that." She sniffled, a second tear rolling down her cheek. "And then a few months ago... I... I tried to kill myself. It was stupid. I was in a dark place. While I was standing on the edge, overlooking the Thames... I saw him."

"Saw who?" Joseph asked.

"The Devil."

A collective gasp filtered through the room, quickly silenced by Joseph's raised hand.

"And what happened when you saw him?"

"He taunted me... laughing about how humans didn't appreciate God's creation... how worthless creation was when we just... threw it all away," Angela said. "And that was when I realised... he was right. I wasn't... I wasn't *appreciating* the life God gifted me."

"I stepped away from the bridge… went home… and found your videos on the internet" she added, giving Joe a small, shy smile, "and that's how I found myself here."

"God brought you here, my dear," Joe said, "and I am so glad he did, because the Devil left that bridge, too. And he came here with you."

Members of the congregation exchanged worried glances, my mother leaning forward in her seat, notebook forgotten.

I inhaled sharply, holding my breath as Joe placed both hands on either side of Angela's cheeks, looking intently into her eyes.

"Brothers and sisters," he said, "let us pray for young Angela's soul."

Heads bowed, a chorus of prayers filled the room, my own lips moving despite my attention wavering. My gaze was fixed on the way Angela trembled, Joe's grasp firm as he led us through prayer, voice raised like a General leading his soldiers into battle.

Angela's knees slammed against the floor with a loud crack, a hush falling over the room. All eyes were on Joe as he tilted her chin up to meet his gaze, expression softening as he spoke in a language I did not recognise.

An endless stream of tears rolled down Angela's cheeks, candlelight chasing the shadows out from her dark brown eyes. The words Joe spoke wrapped her in a warm, protective embrace, something shifting in the air.

Her sobs quieted, her body stilling. A reverent look passed between them. And then she stood, a wide smile spreading across her tear-stained face.

"God is good," Joe said, placing a hand on Angela's shoulder as he looked out at his wide-eyed followers. "And when we fight in His name, we can drive out the Devil himself."

A river of applause flooded the room, my mother rising to her feet, a look of adoration and wonder in her eyes.

****

"Augustus is a quiet boy," Mrs Hadley said, lips spread into the inviting smile she often wore in the classroom, "but he is doing really well. He gets all his work done, he listens, and is always polite. He is an absolute pleasure to have in class."

"I wish he was like that at home!" my father laughed.

Mrs Hadley chuckled awkwardly while my gaze fell to the floor, the Devil stirring awake as shame and embarrassment flooded through me.

You're a bad kid, he said, *a monster.*

A snake slithering into the Garden of Eden.

Evil, wicked, full of sin.

The villain.

I wanted to scream at the Devil to be quiet, but he was right. No matter what I did, no matter how hard I tried to be *good*, I was marked forever by sin. In my parents' eyes, I was the devilish child who ruined their lives.

Disrespectful.

Disobedient.

Disgraced.

I wanted to be good. But was it all a lie? Mrs Hadley believed me to be an absolute pleasure, but my father was right, I wasn't like that at home. I wore a mask. I was a liar.

At home, I challenged my mother's parenting of Auden. At school, I obeyed Mrs Hadley's every instruction. At home, I punched holes through windows. At school, I scrubbed the windows clean at the end of the day. At home, I talked back. At school, I stayed silent. At home, I was the Devil. At school, I was an angel.

You're living a lie.

Panic spread through me like a ravenous plague. They were going to find out. Sooner or later, *everyone* was going to find out the truth. They were going to realise I was a wolf in sheep's clothing, a devil masquerading as an angel.

My parents and Mrs Hadley resumed their conversation, discussing my grades. This was normal for a parent-teacher interview at St Augustine's Catholic School, but I didn't understand why I needed to be present. I was eight years old, and what child of that age wanted to be in a classroom after hours, forced to listen to the adults around them discuss them like they weren't there?

"I am concerned about something I found in his school bag, though," Mrs Hadley said, dread pooling in the pit of my stomach.

She placed a drawing in front of my parents. I recognised it immediately, confused as to how it found itself in my year three teacher's possession.

A boy stood in front of a mirror. Inside the mirror, large black eyes spilled blood, wide mouth crawling with spiders. Clawed hands wrapped around his throat, a haunting shadow looming beside him.

Lying was a sin, but I sinned anyway, too afraid of the consequences of admitting the truth. "That isn't mine."

Mrs Hadley opened her mouth to speak, but my mother cut her off. "Of course it is yours. You draw all the time. I would recognise your work anywhere."

I might have been pleased with that statement if she wasn't looking at me with such disdain.

Chewing on the inside of my mouth, right hand wrapped around my left index finger, I sunk lower into my chair.

"I don't mean to overstep," Mrs Hadley said, "but a drawing like this... at such a young age... is quite unusual. Perhaps it might be beneficial for Augustus to have a one-on-one session with the school counsellor, Miss Lawrence. She is lovely, really, and she might be able to–"

"No," my mother said, snatching the drawing into her hands. "There is no need. He just watches too many horror movies when he knows he shouldn't. I apologise for any concern this has caused. It won't happen again."

The car ride home was unbearable. There was silence. Then shouting. And then silence again.

"If you draw anything like that again, so help me God, I will take away all your pencils, crayons, paint, *everything!* Do you hear me?" my mother demanded.

"Yes," I said quietly.

"What on Earth possessed you to draw a... a demon?!"

"It's not a demon," I murmured. "It's me."

My mother laughed as her gaze shot to my father. "See, Marcus? I told you he has the Devil in him."

"He doesn't have–Mary, come on. He's a damn kid," my father sighed. "Sometimes kids draw weird things. He probably had a nightmare or something."

My mother shook her head but said nothing further. She was quiet for the rest of the day, locking herself up in her bedroom, emerging only to eat dinner.

"It's your turn to do the dishes," were her first words to me since the car ride.

I glanced down at the cracked skin of my hands, red from scratching. They stung, itched. I wanted to tear off my skin and let the cold air kiss my flesh.

"Can I sweep up the kitchen and living room instead?" I asked softly. "The dish soap hurts my skin."

"Wear gloves, then," she said dismissively.

"The gloves rub against my skin and it hurts."

"Do you remember what Jesus suffered when he died for our sins, Augustus?"

I nodded.

"He was whipped, crowned with thorns, and forced to carry his own cross until he was nailed onto it, left to die," she went on. "Do you think he could just stop because it hurt?"

I shook my head.

"That's right. He could not. So you will do those dishes, and you will not complain. Do you understand?"

Ensnared by guilt, I nodded my head. She was right. How could I be so selfish? Jesus suffered. For me. A sinner. And here I was, complaining about soapy water and cracked skin.

But, the Devil spoke up, just as I rolled up my sleeves to fill the sink with water, *Jesus did not want to die. His Father condemned him to that fate. Just like your mother is condemning you to yours.*

"That is not the same," I whispered under my breath.

You're right. It isn't. Because you are not Jesus, and your mother is not God. So why should she control you as though she were?

I reached for the dishwashing liquid and poured it into the warm water, ignoring the Devil's words. He was just trying to get me into trouble.

I know you don't want to do it, Augustus.

My hands hovered above the soap, the instinct to avoid pain holding me back. The Devil was right. I didn't want to do it. I didn't want to be in pain.

Without uttering a word, I walked away from the sink. My mother called my name, but I ignored it.

"Mary–" my father started, but he was too late.

My mother's fingers found the back of my shirt, using it to throw me down onto the cold, tiled floor.

"You don't want to do as you're told?" she asked, a dangerous glint in her eye. "Very well. You leave me no choice."

She bound my arms and legs together with rope, dragging me along the floor toward the linen cupboard.

My father watched with a pained expression but did nothing to intervene when my mother poured lemon juice into the cracked skin of my hands, another scream tearing from my throat at the excruciating pain.

She shoved me into the cupboard, the towels and bedsheets familiar prison mates.

"I hate you," I hissed.

"I hate you more," my mother hissed back.

The door slammed shut in my face, and the last thing I heard was, "I am taking him to Joe tomorrow."

CHAPTER SIX

There was a room in Joe's house, with floor to ceiling mirrors on each wall. Not a single window, light reduced to the thin crack beneath the metal door.

In the centre of the floor yawned a small, sunken pool, the water motionless and black. There, in the water, I sat.

Iron chains snaked around my wrists, a cross dangling above my head. I screamed, and begged, and thrashed around. But my pleas went unanswered.

"The Devil is in him, Mary," Joe told my mother, their bodies huddled in the doorway, "you were right to bring him to me. God will save him. But we need to be strong."

"How long will it take?" my mother asked.

"I cannot say. It is God's will."

The door clicked shut.

I was trapped, swallowed by a vast ocean, lost to the ripples that danced in the mirrors all around me. Darkness crawled over my bare skin, leaving goosebumps in its wake.

It was worse than the linen cupboard, for when my eyes adjusted to the cruel darkness, I saw my own reflection all around me, the Devil wearing my face.

I closed my eyes.

My mother and Joe wanted to draw the Devil out, but I was too scared to face him. Hearing his voice was one thing, seeing him another.

Don't be a coward, Augustus, open your eyes.

My eyes remained shut.

What are you so afraid of? Yourself?

I did not answer.

I just had to endure him until God saved me, releasing me from this nightmare. He would come. He would free me from these chains.

Do you really think He is coming to save you? He has abandoned you. You are mine.

I had to pray. God would hear my prayers this time. He had to. He was the only one who could tear me from the Devil's grasp.

"Our Father, who art in Heaven, hallowed be Thy name," I whispered.

Laughter echoed all around me, but I dared not open my eyes. The Devil would not steal my soul. I would not let him.

"Thy kingdom come, Thy will be done on earth as it is Heaven."

The laughter grew louder. My body trembled like a leaf hanging from a branch, desperate to fend off the wind.

"Give us this day our daily bread; and forgive us our trespasses..."

A loud splash resounded to my left, as if the Devil had jumped into the water with me. My heart thundered wildly. I wanted to run, but the chains kept me in place. My only defence was prayer.

"...as we forgive those who trespass against us; and lead us not into temptation, but deliver us from evil, Amen," I finished.

The laughter ceased.

I exhaled. The Devil had his eyes on me, but he would not devour my soul. God was here. And I was saved.

My eyelids cracked open and the Devil's face hovered inches from mine, black eyes bleeding red, tongue dangling from his dislocated jaw. His skin was peeling, fungi sprouting from his flesh, spiders pouring from his ears. It was a nightmarish reconstruction of what I had seen in the mirror all those years ago. Me and the Devil. The Devil and me. One face. One horror.

I screamed, and screamed, and screamed. The Devil laughed, and laughed, and laughed.

God had forsaken me. I could not be saved.

***

I was a shaken shell of a boy when I emerged from that room. I did not speak, I did not eat.

I refused to look in the mirror when I brushed my teeth. The mirror was my enemy, I never knew who would be staring back. Would it be my own hazel eyes, or the Devil's black pits?

Without a mirror, I had neglected to notice the bruises littering my cheeks. I could see the torn skin around my wrists, but my face was a mystery only solved when my father applied cream or when my mother scowled with disgust.

I wore a long-sleeved sweater to school to hide my bruised arms. My face, however, was difficult to shield from unwanted attention. Despite the curls that had grown down my neck and over my forehead, the school had noticed the state I was in. They called my parents who told them I had been getting into fights with the neighbour's children.

Lying was a sin, and yet my parents lied with ease, scolding me for doing the same.

North Lane had no neighbours, but it was a believable lie since I had started getting into fights at school. Not the kind I had any chance of winning, but the kind that saw me on the ground, curled up in a ball, enduring the several pairs of feet striking my fragile body.

My year four teacher sent me home early on one autumn afternoon, my body aching from yet another fight I did not win.

I stepped up onto the front porch of North Lane and unlocked the door, stepping inside with an uneasy feeling in my chest. It was quiet except for the faint sound of music coming from my parents' bedroom.

Lowering my school bag and discarding my shoes, I made my way through the living room and down the hallway toward Auden's bedroom. He was asleep in his bed, one arm dangling toward the floor where his security blanket had fallen. I approached him with a fond smile, adjusting his arm so that it rested on his stomach, placing the security blanket on top of his thin body. Assured that he was safe, I kissed the top of his head and continued down the hall toward my parents' bedroom, the music growing louder.

I knocked on the door, but there was no response.

I should have walked away. I should have waited in my room, and then maybe my world would not have shattered because of one stupid mistake.

I entered the room without an invitation, words locked in my throat the moment my eyes landed on a man on top of my mother, their limbs entangled in a passionate embrace.

"Mum?" I asked in alarm.

Her eyes flew open and the man on top of her turned around. It was not my father.

Joseph Kade blinked at me in stunned silence as I backed away, left shoulder knocking into the doorframe in my haste.

My mother called my name, but I ran. I ran until I was out the front door and into the woods, until my legs ached and I fell to the grass, gasping for air. I didn't know where I was, but I was glad to be far from that bedroom.

My mother and...

...that monster.

It wasn't that I was naive enough to believe my parents had a perfect marriage. I knew they had their problems, like many did, but they were God-fearing Christians. Adultery was a sin.

My mother had accused me of being a sinner my whole life. And yet there she was, underneath a man who was not her husband. She was a hypocrite.

I glanced down at my bruised wrists, the evidence of the punishment for my sins. Would my mother confine herself inside the linen cupboard or in a dark pool of water, alone and handcuffed like a criminal?

Of course not, the Devil growled, *you will have to make her.*

I closed my eyes to shut him out. His thoughts were not my own. I would never lock my mother away. I couldn't, even if I wanted to. God was on her side.

I do not recall how long I remained in the long grass, sobbing into the dirt, but the sun had barely grazed the horizon when I rose to my feet, a thick morning fog swallowing the House on North Lane. A lone leaf drifted in the ice cold breeze, falling at my feet as I pushed open the door.

A darkness had settled inside the House, a poison that devoured its very heart. The air was thick with rot, a dampness that wouldn't dry out. Dust painted the dark oak furniture grey, cobwebs hanging from every corner of the ceiling. It was as though I had been gone years, instead of mere hours.

On the staircase, Auden coughed.

His arms were wrapped around his shivering body, dark circles under his pale blue eyes. I guided him up to the second floor, each step grunting beneath our weight. A dark corridor greeted us with a sinister hum, the walls pulsing with the sound of rats scurrying along the wooden beams.

Mold infiltrated my nostrils as my bedroom door creaked open, an ice-cold breeze from the shattered window lashing me like the sharp end of a whip.

I drew Auden close, securing him to my warmth as I wrapped him in a blanket. With his shoulders covered to fend off the chill, we ventured back out into the hallway and into the heart of North Lane.

The hallway light flickered as we neared Auden's bedroom, casting taunting shadows that followed our every move.

We stepped inside the room and sighed with relief, the biting cold confined to the hallway as we shut the door behind us.

"You look like you haven't slept," I told Auden as I guided him into bed, tucking him in beneath the sheets.

He shifted closer to the wall, leaving room for me. I debated returning to the darkness to find my mother, but Auden's pale cheeks and wide eyes convinced me to climb onto the mattress beside him, securing his back to my chest.

Warmth lured me to sleep, and I was standing in the woods surrounding North Lane, walking along the brook barefoot, a long stick glued to my hand. I was alone, with only the sun kissing my skin and the birds whistling from the treetops.

It was peaceful. Calm. Like the many summers spent venturing through the trees with an imaginary quest to occupy my time.

But the scene shifted the moment I slipped on a moss-covered rock, falling forward with my knees grazing the sharp spikes jutting out of the water.

Blood tainted the stream and darkened the reflection peering up at me. A red droplet rippled the water, twisting the grimace on my face into a wide, devilish smile.

Horns protruded from my nest of curls like blackened roots, dark eyes unblinking. It followed the movement of my hand, but where my fingers ended with shortened nails, the reflection wore monstrous claws.

You should wake up, Augustus.

I jolted awake, heart pounding. My treacherous brain would not grant me respite, even in sleep. The Devil followed me. I was his to torment.

It was cold, the absence of my brother's warmth sending alarm bells ringing in my head. I rose to my feet and looked around the room, emptiness glaring back.

"Auden?" I called out as I stepped into the hallway.

Unease trickled down my spine. The House was too quiet, as though it had devoured every soul and was now sated.

I descended the staircase, hand on the wall to safely guide me through the darkness. Wood groaned beneath my feet, the sound reverberating along the walls, frames trembling.

Upon reaching the bottom, a faint sob echoed through the House. My feet guided me forward, heart thundering inside my chest.

The living room was void of all furniture—no couch, no coffee table, not even a rug to warm the cold wooden floor. In their absence, a white chalked star entrapped within a circle centred the room, each corner of the star home to a flickering candle, red flames illuminating the darkened room.

In the heart of the circle was Auden, seated with his knees drawn to his chest, rocking back and forth as tears streamed down his face.

His name left my lips in a gasp, my feet moving toward the circle before I could even process what was happening. I crouched by his side and pulled him to my chest. He slumped against me, exhausted, skin glazed with sweat from the heat of the candles.

"Shh, it's okay, it's okay, I'm here," I tried to soothe him.

My mother stood beyond the circle in a long white gown, fringes soiled with ash and dust. A harsh breeze stirred the fabric, rippling like the wings of an angel. Her eyes were wide and unblinking, drawn to Auden's shivering form.

"Ma?" I moved in front of my brother, shielding him from the eerie sight. "What's going on? What are you doing?"

She raised a small, dark green bible, face flickering in and out of darkness as the flames cast shadows across the room. Incoherent muttering rolled off her tongue as she held a silver crucifix toward us, her voice rising as the wind grew in strength.

The flames closed in, heat bearing down on us without mercy. I reached for Auden's hand and started toward the circle's edge, determined to get him to safety before things could escalate.

"Halt, demon!"

And halt I did, gaze locking on Joe who emerged from the shadows to stand beside my mother, his body draped in a clean white suit with his hair slicked back neatly for the occasion. In his hands, a wooden crucifix hung like a blade between us, the mightiest weapon of one of God's soldiers.

"Why are you doing this?" I shouted.

Words spilled from his lips—words from an ancient tongue that my mother repeated, their crucifixes glinting in the candlelight. Together, they chanted their foregone language, eyes aflame with the spirit of God.

A scream shredded through my body as Joe knocked over a candle, sending flames along the chalk circle all around us. I lifted Auden up over my shoulder, intending to carry him away from the searing heat.

A wall of flames forced me back. Smoke poisoned the air, burning down my throat into my gasping lungs. Auden coughed, sweat dampening his hair to his forehead.

I staggered backwards.

Confused.

Scared.

Struggling to breathe.

Falling to my knees, unable to bear Auden's weight, I watched the flames crawl towards us, smoke smothering my lungs with the kiss of death. Auden whimpered beside me, oxygen evading him as much as it evaded me.

"Please, God," I coughed, arms tightening around Auden's trembling body, "save us."

Every breath was a stab of pain. Tears burned my eyes, ash painting my hair white. I squinted through the smoke, gaze landing on my mother. She looked the part of an angel, framed by a flickering golden glow, though her cracked lips were pulled up into a cruel smile.

I screamed for God, praise and worship pouring from my scorched tongue. I needed him to hear me. Just this once, I needed him to save me.

There was laughter. It circled me like the flames, but it had only one source. And she stood there, watching me, as if I were a demon and not her son.

A glint of a blade.

Demons dancing in the smoke.

Screams buried in the ash.

God had not come. Heaven had not sent their soldiers to save me. Their soldiers, instead, chanted to my destruction.

My eyelids fell shut, surrendering to Death's warm embrace, abandoning all trust in the Heavenly Father. He had chosen his side. And it wasn't mine.

Wake up, Augustus. You need to wake up.

The Devil's voice was loud. Urgent. He was angry. Afraid. There was desperation in the way he called my name.

Augustus. Wake up. Augustus, Auden needs you. Augustus. Augustus. Augustus!

I forced my eyes open, my shadow grinning up at me as I pushed myself up off the ash-covered floor.

Hell was born that night. And it remained burning ever since, a poison contaminating my veins.

I hauled Auden to his feet, dragging him through the flames, the Devil watching the scene through my eyes as I collapsed to the floor outside the circle, surrendering to the safety of darkness.

PART II

CHAPTER SEVEN

Lights flickered inside the dark, abandoned halls of the House on North Lane, wind howling as tree branches knocked menacingly on every window. Shadows crawled along the walls. Dust thickened the air. Rain pattered against the rooftop with bruising force, but oh how I longed to feel the cool droplets against my skin, to escape the damp Hell inside the House on North Lane.

It was nearing midnight on Halloween—a night where children paraded as monsters, as if being a monster was no more than a fun mask. At least they could peel off their costume at the end of the night.

Trick-or-treaters never ventured to North Lane, yet the hushed whispers carried by the wind proved there were children who had braved the journey.

"Shut up," a voice whispered. "There is a witch inside!"

"There is no witch," said another. "It's a monster."

"What kind of monster?"

The answer was drowned out by a lash of wrathful thunder.

I snorted as the children screamed, bodies shuffling closer to the door. There was a time when I too had been afraid of storms. But when a storm rages in your head every day and every night, you grow accustomed to its unpredictable ire.

The door would not open. I could not grant the children shelter. The House would not let me leave, for when it had the first time, I returned with a vengeance. But the children could open it, I was sure.

"Come on," I murmured, pacing back and forth in front of the door, *"open up."*

If they heard me above the roaring thunder, they gave no indication. There was only silence. And then arguing.

"What if the monster is waiting for us?" a third voice asked.

"It's probably sleeping."

"Do monsters sleep?"

The answer was no, for the record. If you were reading this with the intention of conquering a haunted house imprisoning a monster, you should enter with the knowledge that the beast inside never sleeps, and you will face it whether you want to or not.

"Let's just go in," one of the children decided.

The doorknob began to turn, hope building up from the pit of my stomach to my chest. I smiled, momentarily forgetting that the House on North Lane was an efficient jailor, and its prisoners could never leave.

Deafening thunder crashed the moment the door creaked open, three children in raincoats peering inside with their small bodies huddled together.

I cared little for them, my attention drifting to the haunting mist and torrential rain behind them. I could almost taste the freedom that awaited me.

I made it no more than three steps before tendrils of white mist snaked around my ankles and wrists, lifting me into the air only to slam me back down with a ruthless snap.

The children screamed, staggering backwards into the rain, eyes bulging and skin as white as the blanket of mist chasing them away.

I thought their fear was my doing. But as I rose on unsteady feet, sharp pain tearing down my spine, I realised the children hadn't seen me at all. Their eyes, instead, had found the mirror. The very one that had cursed me all those years ago, its golden frame now spattered with blood.

Nausea wreaked havoc in my stomach as I watched my face contort into the snarling demon lurking inside of me.

It laughed as blood spilled from the mirror, surging like an open wound, a red bath flooding the entryway.

My fist met the mirror with a shattering crack, the demon's low, guttural laughter only increasing in volume. Each shard of glass grinned up at me, the devil multiplying as droplets of blood fell from my knuckles and into the pool at my feet.

In the cold darkness, I turned my back to the mirror and limped toward the living room, massaging my bruised knuckles and lower back interchangeably.

A photograph lay abandoned on the floor, edges charred where flames licked at the corners before dying out. It was taken on my fifth birthday, my mother hugging me to her chest, both of us grinning from ear to ear. My father stood beside us, Auden in his arms, their smiles nearly identical.

Crouching down to pick it up, a stray tear escaped my blinking eyelids, the taste of salt on my tongue as I memorised the happiness pouring from our smiling faces. Happiness I would never see again.

I choked on a sob, biting down on my bruised knuckles.

Where had it all gone so wrong?

The House on North Lane, once a symbol of love and family and freedom, now stood as a haunting reminder of the fractured life I once knew.

I would never leave this prison. I was rooted in the very heart of North Lane, the House, the Ghost and the Devil my jailors.

CHAPTER EIGHT

I met the Devil on a Sunday morning.

He was kneeling by the altar, head bowed, hands clasped together in prayer. Flames crawled toward his bare feet, his white suit unblemished while the smoke swallowed everything around us.

Come, Augustus.

I stepped forward, weary. The Devil had only ever worn my face or a veil of darkness, but this version was uncloaked, his features that of a man instead of a distorted boy.

"Is this Hell?" I asked.

What gave it away?

I kneeled beside him, knees pressed against the polished marble floor. Flames danced all around us, an invisible barrier shielding me from its heat.

"The fire."

The fire, the Devil chuckled.

"Is that the wrong answer?" I asked, risking a glance at the strange figure beside me. His face was hidden beneath a curtain of brown curls, the small curve of his lips the only feature I could make out through the smoke.

No, but it amuses me.

"Why?"

Hell is so much more than just eternal flames.

"The Bible says—"

You humans need to find a new book to quote, that one is rather old.

"If this really is Hell, why are you praying in front of an altar?"

God is my father too.

"You rebelled against your father."

And you rebelled against your mother.

"She was hurting me."

Now we understand each other.

"God was hurting you?"

You sound surprised.

"God is good."

Not to me.

"But you're praying to him..."

No, you *are praying to him.*

His head whipped around to face me, and I was met with familiar hazel eyes, matured around the edges. Sharp talons curled around my throat, choking me as smoke slithered into my lungs.

Wake up, Augustus.

***

I awoke in a hospital bed.

The room pulsed with the low hum of monitors and machinery, white walls blinding as I adjusted to the fluorescent lights. An IV drip pumped fluid into my veins, its steady flow harmonising with the symphony all around me.

An oxygen mask covered my face, lungs and throat screaming with every intake of breath.

Quiet snores drifted from the chair to my left, my unfocused gaze landing on my father. Dark circles bruised the skin beneath his eyes, brows furrowed and lips twitching in distress.

"Dad?" I called out, voice barely a whisper.

I coughed, glass shards stabbing into my throat. Tears threatened to fall as I swallowed through the burning sensation, the taste of smoke lingering on my parched tongue.

"Dad?"

His eyelids flew open, and he straightened in his seat within seconds. "Hey, buddy," he said gently, "how are you feeling?"

"Throat. Hurts."

Reaching for the cup beside my bed, my father removed my mask and raised the plastic to my lips, showering me with praise as the cool water trickled down my throat.

"What...happened?"

My father hesitated, expression shifting from weariness to confusion as he lowered the cup. "You don't remember?"

I remembered the flames, the cursed symbol on the floor, my mother in her white dress. I was on my knees, holding Auden, choking on ash and dust. The Devil smiled and then...I was here. In a hospital bed.

"Augustus...your mother is gone," my father said, running a hand over his face as he looked in every direction but mine.

"Gone?" I repeated.

"She...disappeared."

"Where...did...she...go?"

"I don't know."

"She...was there. She..." I coughed.

My father shook his head.

"Is...she...coming back?" I asked.

A quiet sigh escaped my father's throat, defeat written on every line of his face. "She abandoned us, Gus. I don't think she is ever coming back."

My mother was gone.

I heard the words, I knew what they meant, but I couldn't seem to apply the meaning. It didn't make sense. She was gone...but where? Why? And without a goodbye?

I remembered the hatred in her eyes as she watched me through the flames, the word demon rolling off her tongue like a curse.

She left because of you and Auden.

Auden.

He was on the bed to my right, awake and seated upright in a dark blue hospital gown. His hair was dripping wet from a shower, the scent of aloe vera body wash wafting pleasantly through the air.

My shoulders sagged with relief. He was alive. He was safe.

With a sad smile, I extended my hand toward him, and he came, like a magnet, crawling into my arms without a second's hesitation.

I wanted to comfort him, to offer soothing words in response to our mother's absence, but the glass shards in my throat cut them off before they could reach my tongue.

His bright blue eyes were wide and unblinking when, in a small voice, he said his very first words. "Chocolate milk?"

CHAPTER NINE

Our mother's absence proved to be a sanctuary for Auden. Words poured from his lips as though he had been verbal for years instead of weeks. He was still quiet, but the words came out easy, practiced.

A little over a month had passed since we moved in with our Uncle Brady, my father taking time off work to lead the search for Mary Saint.

Black-suited detectives had ceased their questioning; their investigation reduced to mere posters painted around Rose Chapel. But no one had seen her since that night in North Lane.

Dishes piled up, floors went un-swept, and since Uncle Brady was in and out of jail, I adopted the role of housekeeper and caregiver while my father drowned his sorrows.

The stench of alcohol poisoned the air every night, empty bottles littering the living room floor while my father sat in his armchair, staring blankly at the television screen for hours.

My mother's disappearance hit him the hardest.

She had abandoned him, just like she abandoned us. I did not know the extent of his knowledge regarding my mother's affair with Joe, but I never spoke a word of what I had walked in on. There was no point adding salt to the wound.

Unlike our father, Auden thrived without our mother. Colour returned to his cheeks. His smile, once a rare sight, now brightened his features like sunlight infiltrating long-forgotten halls.

He missed her, though. You could see it in the way he flipped through old photographs, or waited by the door, hoping she would return as though she had never left.

I did not miss her.

My bruised wrists were finally healing, the skin able to breathe without the threat of restraints.

Fear was no longer my constant companion, though it was impossible to forget the cold hatred in her eyes as the smoke crawled toward us.

And yet, there were rare moments, as I lay in bed in the late hours of the night, where I yearned for her fingers to comb through my hair, for her voice to filter through the room as she read me a bedtime story. I missed her. But I was glad she was gone.

***

Auden started his first year of school with a vocabulary of a nine-year-old. It had taken me a while to adjust to a world where Auden could communicate his thoughts and feelings, but it was a world I had wanted for him since the moment he first opened his eyes.

Making friends, however, proved just as difficult for him as it had been for me. Despite no longer being non-verbal, he was certainly no chatterbox. He kept to himself in class, and spent his lunchtimes with me, glued to my side until the chiming of the bell.

We were on the way to our usual spot in the woodlands when a ball almost tripped Auden over. I steadied his arm and looked around, sighing as a group of boys from my class ran over.

"Kick it back, freak."

Jensen Loyd and I had been in the same class since year one. We had never been friends, but we'd been civil. He'd never been outwardly cruel. Not until my family left the church and rumours spread about my mother joining a cult.

"Who are you calling a freak?" I demanded.

"You. Your whole family."

Although we were the same age, Jensen towered over me, his curved lips directly in my line of sight. His friends hung back, not wanting to get too close to the 'freakish Saints'.

"We are not freaks," I said, hands curling into fists at my side.

"I heard your psycho mum tried to get a demon out of you."

"Shut up."

"Father Andrej says your family is crazy."

"Father Andrej is an old cow."

Jensen's eyes widened. "What did you say?"

"I said Father Andrej is an old cow."

"You're going to Hell for that."

"What would *you* know?" I scoffed.

Jensen's gaze slid to Auden who hid behind me, hands fluttering anxiously in front of his chest. "I know that you and that freak are the reason your mum went psycho."

Shut him up.

I acted without thinking, hands slamming into Jensen's chest with enough force to send him to the grass.

"Guses!" Auden's fingers enclosed around my wrist, pulling me away from Jensen as he rose with a snarl.

His fist struck my nose with a crack, the metallic tang of iron flooding my mouth, blood spattering on the white collar of my school uniform. I staggered backwards, ears ringing as a teacher intervened, sending Jensen to the principal's office before guiding me to the first aid room.

My father was quiet on the drive home, only speaking to tell me to keep the ice on my nose every time I lowered it. He didn't yell at me for getting into a fight, nor did I receive a physical scolding of any kind. Instead, upon returning to Uncle Brady's, he sat me down at the dining table and pulled up a chair to apply ointment to my throbbing bruise.

"He called mum a psycho," I said quietly.

Silence.

"Is she?" I pressed on.

"Is she what?"

"A psycho."

A sharp inhale was my father's response.

"Dad?"

"You need to learn how to defend yourself."

"I started the fight," I mumbled.

"All the more reason for you to learn how to do it properly."

"You *want* me to fight?"

"Of course not," he shook his head, "but if you are going to fight anyway, I'd at least want you to win."

***

It was early the following morning when we stepped onto the athletic field near Rose Chapel Public School, frost decorating each blade of grass.

Auden sat with a picture book while my father pulled out two boxing gloves, helping me tug them on before proceeding to arm himself with his own.

"Hit my gloves as hard as you can," he instructed.

I raised my fists in the air, hesitation circling me like a wolf assessing its prey. It didn't feel right. It felt like something the Devil would want me to do.

"What is it, Augustus?"

"Fighting...isn't it wrong?"

"Sometimes," my father nodded, hands dropping to his sides, "but if we want to protect ourselves and those we care about...it's necessary to learn the basics."

I must have looked unconvinced, for my father chuckled and ruffled my hair before gesturing for me to start throwing punches. I did.

"What do you know about the Sons of Thunder?" he asked, taking each of my blows without moving an inch.

"Like Thor and Loki?"

"Augustus!" He scolded me, shaking his head. "The fact that you know more about Norse Gods than your own God is concerning."

"Who are the Sons of Thunder then?"

"The Sons of Thunder," my father started, gesturing for me to strike his gloves harder, "were two of Jesus' disciples—brothers, actually. James and John."

"Why is everyone in the Bible named James and John?" I grumbled.

"There are plenty of other names," my father chided me.

"Okay," I shrugged, "so why were this particular James and John called the Sons of Thunder?"

"Well, when Jesus and his disciples were refused accommodation by Samaritans, James and John asked Jesus if he wanted them to call fire down from Heaven to destroy those who rejected them."

"What did Jesus say?"

"Jesus told them not to strike them down, of course."

"Why did the Samaritans refuse them anyway?"

My father waved a dismissive hand. "Jew-Samaritan tensions. That is beside the point. My point is...James and John were determined to defend themselves and Jesus. It shows us that maybe, when necessary, we should be like the Sons of Thunder."

I shook my head, confused. "But Jesus told them not to."

"Yes," my father agreed, "but he did not shame them for having that thunder inside of them, instead, he gave them that title. If he wanted to banish it, he would have, would he not?"

I hesitated, weighing his words before nodding.

We trained for an hour. Then again the next day, and the next. Sometimes before school, sometimes after.

Once satisfied I had the capacity and the skills to defend myself and Auden, he turned to the bottle once more, seemingly having nothing left to do, no goals to achieve.

Depression claimed him. And then the cancer did.

I was eleven when he got the diagnosis. Liver cancer. A malicious cell that spread through his body, swimming through the bloodstream to invade his blood vessels and lymph nodes. Their colonisation weakened him, but I was assured that once he received treatment, he would never pick up a drink again.

My father lied.

Bottles of whiskey littered the living room floor, the air heavy with a bitter stale scent that soaked into the walls. His chemotherapy was in the morning, and by the time I returned home from school, he was passed out in his armchair, dry vomit on his shirt.

Uncle Brady was released from prison a week before my father's condition deteriorated. He refused hospital treatment, no longer attending his chemotherapy sessions or doctor's appointments. He'd given up.

Although Brady was not the nurturing type, he supported his older brother by guiding him in and out of the bathroom, showering him, and organising his medications. It meant I had more time to prepare meals, clean the house, and raise Auden.

One afternoon, as the sun drowned in the horizon, Uncle Brady and I sat on the front porch, a comfortable silence drifting between us. He took a long drag of his cigar, releasing the smoke to disappear with the wind.

Brady looked a lot like my father. They shared the same dark brown curls, grey eyes, sharp nose and thin lips. The black ink decorating his whole left arm, as well the long, jagged scar on his right cheekbone, were the only notable differences between them.

There was a lot about Uncle Brady I did not know. My mother had never liked him, and since he was in and out of jail, he was never around for family holidays. But he was here now, and that was all that mattered.

"You doin' alright, kiddo?" Brady's question pulled me from my thoughts.

"Yeah," I lied. "You?"

"Fuck no."

We sat in silence for a long moment before I asked, "Do you think he will make it?"

"I dunno, kid. The cancer has spread," he sighed, "and once that shit spreads…it's harder to kill. Your father…might not be around for much longer."

The words plunged into me like a knife. It was not surprising, and yet, hearing it said out loud made it all the more real. My father was dying. And there was nothing I could do. I could not stop my mother from leaving, and I could not stop my father from dying.

"Okay…" I breathed out, hands clenching and unclenching into fists on my lap. "…we just…we need to pray harder. We haven't been to church for a while. Mum always said that if we turned to God he will–"

"Fuck God," Brady cut me off. "Fuck religion. People like your Ma...they think they're saints, God's obedient soldiers doing his bidding, but they're a bunch of god damn hypocrites."

A twisted grin spread across his face, and in that moment, he looked nothing like my father. He looked like a corrupted version—like my own face shifting to a demon in the mirror. "If there is a God...I'll always root for the Devil. At least he doesn't pretend to be something he's not."

Maybe Uncle Brady was right. What had prayer ever done for me?

That is right, little monster. God has abandoned you.

CHAPTER TEN

A sea of black proceeded through the arched doors of the church, a chorus of condolences filtering through the air.

Jesus eyed me from the cross above the altar, a crown of thorns shadowing the sadness in his eyes—a harsh reminder of the brutality of death, something not even the son of God could escape.

A hand rested on my shoulder, and I lifted my head. Father Andrej offered me a small smile, his eyes mirroring the sadness of the Lord.

It had been years since I had seen him, and in that time, the priest had lost the remainder of his hair, wrinkles creasing the skin around his eyes, mouth and nose. Draped in white, a gold crucifix around his neck, he guided me to a chair in the front row beside Auden and my Great Aunt Vera. I sat, like a programmed robot, staring blankly at the marble floor.

"Your dad is with God now," he said.

I could only nod, a numbness stealing my words and my thoughts.

My father was enclosed in a black casket decorated with a bundle of white roses secured to the top. He was carried by eight men—Uncle Brady leading the procession. Lowered onto a white marble table, flowers were arranged on the floor around him, a sea of white contrasting with the black.

Father Andrej greeted the congregation as we all rose to our feet. My gaze locked on Jesus instead of my father, for if I focused too much on the fact that he was dead and soon-to-be buried, I would completely unravel.

Despite my fragile relationship with God, I remained drawn to Jesus. Perhaps it was because he had once been a man. And as a man, he understood the fragility of life. He felt our joy, our pain, our suffering and our love. He would understand me.

Do you think Jesus was angry with his Heavenly Father when his earthly father died?

I was. I was angry. He'd already taken my mother, why must he take my father too?

Because he's the villain, the Devil purred.

A sniffle yanked me from my thoughts. Auden was wiping at his eyes with one hand, the other fluttering restlessly at his side. I mentally scolded myself for neglecting him during the ceremony, my hand reaching out for his, squeezing gently to calm him down. He shifted closer, my arm snaking around his shoulders as tears flowed freely down his cheeks.

Following the ceremony, we buried our father in St Augustine's Cemetery. Auden cried. I hung my head, fiddling with the small golden crucifix my father had given me only hours before he drew his last breath. He'd told me to always carry Jesus in my heart, that as long as I did, I would find him again in the next life. I'd asked him if he feared death. He just smiled, my unanswered question following me to his funeral.

Mourners gradually dispersed until only Auden and I remained, seated in front of my father's fresh grave.

He was dead. Really, truly, dead. Swallowed by the Earth, never to see the light of day again. He was gone, and I didn't know how to process that.

God takes everything from you. Your mother, your father...eventually Auden too.

***

He wore my mother's face, a crucifix trembling in her hand. It hovered inches from my face, manic laughter pouring from my mother's lips as the Devil wrapped a hand around my throat, pinning me in place. Her eyes bled black, the same colour as the spidery veins crawling along her pale skin, her hair wild and untamed.

Flames circled me like hungry wolves, smoke smothering my lungs. I gasped for air, every breath a stab of pain that cut through my throat, slicing all the way down to my chest.

God stood over her shoulder. He had no face, no more than a blinding pale light.

I called out to him, praise and worship rolling off my tongue. Just this once, I needed him to hear me.

Augustus.

Flames bit into my flesh, devouring me like a wild beast sinking its teeth into prey. I screamed in agony, screamed for mercy, screamed for my mother to end this wicked torment.

Augustus.

The voice was everywhere and nowhere. It was not my mother's, nor the Devil's. For a moment, I thought it might have been God.

"Augustus!"

My eyes flew open, jaw aching from being clenched in my sleep. Sweat drenched my bed sheets, heart racing as though I had been running in the woods behind North Lane.

I had hoped the nightmares would not follow me to Cambridge with Great Aunt Vera. But there was nowhere I could go—nowhere the House on North Lane would not follow. Even in my dreams, I surrendered to her cold embrace. Her claws were buried deep into flesh and bone, I no more than an animal on a leash. At her command, I always slithered home to her chains.

"It's okay, Guses, it was just a bad dream."

There was an arm wrapped around my middle, a head of hair on my shoulder. I glanced down, surprised to see Auden holding me the way I had once held him when he couldn't sleep. A stab of guilt slammed into me. I must have woken him up during my nightmare.

"I'm fine, Auddie, I'm fine," I assured him.

"You were calling for Mumma and–"

"I'm fine," I cut him off gently. "Are you hungry? Let's eat breakfast."

"Aunt Vera says no breakfast before seven."

"Aunt Vera can kiss my ass."

Great Aunt Vera lived in a large house—a mansion, if you will. Though I would not call it that in front of her. Four bathrooms, eight bedrooms, two kitchens, three living rooms, a two-storey library, a wine cellar and an indoor swimming pool—it may as well have been a palace.

In the heart of Cambridge, she lived close to public transport and beautiful public parks, the university mere streets away. She was a retired university professor, having written three academic books on the history of feminism and feminist epistemologies.

With nearly one hundred and fifty thousand people, Cambridge was a vastly different demographic than the small, sheltered population of Rose Chapel.

Before Auden and I moved in, Aunt Vera had lived alone with only a housekeeper and a gardener to share her grand hallways and luxurious block of land. Most of her time was spent travelling Europe with her wealthy, academic friends, the house left in the care of Mrs Brighton while Mr Leyton tended to the garden.

Although she wasn't thrilled to have been given the responsibility of our upbringing, she ensured we had everything we needed. She refused to even consider letting Uncle Brady raise us when his idea of child-rearing was sending a child into the wilderness to learn to survive a cold night alone. And besides, it was her name listed on my father's will, not his.

"I don't like children," she had said when she first brought us home, a displeased scowl on her face when Auden and I stood awkwardly in the doorway, coats and shoes still attached.

Uncle Brady told me of her struggles to conceive a child with her late husband Norman. Perhaps her dislike of children was a result of her inability to have her own.

Auden and I grew on her, though.

Once she learned of my passion for art, she had Mrs Brighton order me a mountain of art supplies, dedicating one of the spare bedrooms as my own art studio. Canvases, easels and paint palettes lined the floor, white sheets covering my unfinished work.

I was hesitant to pick up a paint brush at first. With my family torn apart, I had little inspiration to bring any form of art to life. But it was an itch I could not scratch, and my fingers wrapped around a brush with the eagerness of a frog snatching up a fly. I painted the only light in my life. Auden.

Other than his blue eyes and straight hair, Auden was becoming a mirror of me. Painting him almost felt like I was painting myself, but where I was all dark colours and rainy days, he was sunshine and warmth.

He adored the library. Aunt Vera made him his own little retreat where he could read in comfort, surrounded by a cushioned fort draped in expensive blankets with fairy lights hanging from the corners. It won him over, just as his smile of delight won Aunt Vera over in return.

A black cat meowed at the foot of my bed the second the clock chimed seven. Shakespeare, Aunt Vera's eleven-year-old cat, crawled toward Auden, nuzzling his face with contented purrs, requesting breakfast that Auden had adopted as his morning chore.

Shakespeare and Auden were inseparable from day one. I, on the other hand, avoided the cat, his yellow eyes eerily similar to my mother's hazel ones when illuminated by flame.

I climbed out of bed and groaned when one of Shakespeare's toys crunched beneath my feet. He was always shepherding toy mice into my room in the middle of the night, wanting to play with Auden who had snuck into my bed.

"Go feed that monster, and I'll meet you downstairs," I told Auden.

"He's not a monster," Auden pouted.

Shakespeare meowed in agreement.

"Could have fooled me," I mumbled as I entered the bathroom attached to my room, a white towel covering the mirror so I wouldn't catch a glimpse of the Devil when I brushed my teeth.

On the opposite side of the room was a walk-in wardrobe where my school uniform hung—a white-collared shirt, grey buttoned vest with matching grey trousers and a dark green tie.

My new school was a private one, much larger than St Augustine's, and enrolling five weeks later than everyone else had been daunting. My father's death, moving to Cambridge, adjusting to Aunt Vera—it meant I was far behind everyone else in my age group. Aunt Vera assured me I would catch up, but it felt like the end of the world to be the only one sitting in a classroom, not knowing what the teacher was talking about when she referred to the article they had read the previous week.

Auden entered year three with the same anxiety. His school was only two streets from mine, but he wasn't thrilled that we would no longer be in the same vicinity. I was worried, too. Who would he spend time with, if not me? The thought of him being alone broke my heart.

Dressed in my school uniform, hair tamed, and teeth brushed, I made my way downstairs to join Auden at the dining table, his own hair combed neatly.

Mrs Brighton was in the kitchen, humming to herself as she dished out three plates of food. Her ash-coloured hair was tied up in a loose bun, vanilla perfume overpowering the smell of bacon, eggs and hash browns.

Aunt Vera sat at the head of the table, a mug raised to her lips as she flicked through the morning's newspaper. Her dyed blonde strands crawled away from her greying roots, her straight ends resting just above her shoulders.

"Good morning," Auden and I both greeted her in unison.

Aunt Vera acknowledged us with a quiet 'mhm' without looking up from her paper.

"Good morning!" Mrs Brighton beamed as she carried a tray of food into the room, the smell of fried mushrooms reminding my stomach of its hunger.

"How are you liking your new school, Augustus?" Aunt Vera asked, eyeing me as Mrs Brighton placed a plate down in front of her.

It was only my third day, but I imagined that was more than enough time for most people to have formed an opinion. "It is very…clean," I said.

"I should very well help so," she said. "Anything else?"

I racked my brain for something, anything, to add, but nothing came. Shaking my head, I reached for my glass of water and took a long sip.

"Your father once told me you are quite studious, is that correct?" Aunt Vera asked.

"Oh. Um…yes. I like school. Learning."

"Secondary school is very different."

"Yes, ma'am."

"I expect you to remain on top of your studies. Nothing below ninety percent in any subject. This school is expensive, and I will not have my money wasted."

"Yes, ma'am."

"And," she added, more firmly, "I expect you to behave well in school. I will not tolerate any trouble. Is that understood?"

"Yes, ma'am."

"Good."

Walking through the school gates with my head down, I shoved my trembling hands into my pockets and darted straight toward my form room to wait for the bell. Chatter hummed through the corridors as students crowded around lockers and greeted their friends. No one spared me a glance except for a boy I recognised from a few of my classes. Light freckles painted his cheeks, dark green eyes blinking beneath long lashes as a smile curved his lips. Alexander was his name. He gave me a nod in greeting as he ran his fingers through his black strands, my own lips tilting upward before the Devil infiltrated my thoughts.

He's only smiling at you because he doesn't know what you are.

Tension shot through my body, the smile snatched from my face and replaced with a grimace. Not now. Not here. I closed my eyes, hands curling into fists at my sides.

The Devil laughed at my attempt to subdue him.

I am always here, little monster, you will not get rid of me.

Students poured into the classroom as Miss De'Lour opened the door, greeting every student with a warm smile and an enthusiastic 'good morning'. Some students returned the greeting, others just walked past as if she were a ghost they could not see.

I dumped myself into the seat beside a dark-skinned girl chewing gum, her twin braids decorated with silver starred clips. Despite it being my third morning seated beside her, I was still yet to learn her name.

She looked me up and down, slowly, and I stared back, challenging her to look away first. She won the battle, my eyes dropping to my desk.

We didn't say a word while Miss De'Lour did roll call and read out announcements. I sat stiff in my chair, one leg bouncing up and down while I glanced in between the clock and the door. As soon as the bell rang, I was the first to leave.

You're lost, the Devil hummed while I stood in front of a classroom that was not my year seven history class. Scratching the back of my head, I looked around wildly, trying to retrace my steps.

"Are you okay?"

I locked eyes with Alexander, his head tilted and eyebrows raised as he glanced in between me and the empty classroom.

"I'm...looking for D3," I said.

"That would be in D block."

I thought I *was* in D block. As if reading my mind, Alexander shook his head and stepped forward to pull me by my school bag.

"Hey! What are you doing?!" I asked in alarm.

"Taking you to D3, duh," he answered, shooting me an amused grin.

All I could manage was a quiet 'oh' as I followed him through the main yard and into D block.

"All the smart kids are in D3," Alexander said. "We had to take a test on our first day. When did you take yours?"

"Um...a week before I started," I answered, a little breathless from the quick pace he set. "Sent in the mail, I think."

"Cool. What did you get?"

"Huh?"

"In the test...what mark did you get?"

"Oh...um...forty-seven out of fifty."

Alexander paused in front of a classroom, green eyes wide as he turned to look at me. "Shit. Really?"

I nodded.

"You...beat me by two," he said slowly.

I stared at him, not really knowing if he was congratulating me or waiting for an apology.

The door to the classroom opened and Mr Singh glanced in between us with an unimpressed expression, handing each of us a booklet on the day's topic.

I dumped myself into a lone chair at the back of the classroom and avoided Alexander's gaze as he sat near the front, his jaw clenched and familiar smile gone.

In a classroom of high performing students, it wasn't difficult to determine who my academic competitors were. Every time Mr Singh asked a question, Alexander and the chewing gum girl from my form room raised their hands, fighting to be the first to answer. I knew the answers too, but I kept my hand down, not wanting to draw attention to myself.

At recess, my intention was to study in the library. I was five weeks behind my peers, and if I wanted to please Aunt Vera, I needed to be at the very top of all my classes.

To get to the library, however, I had to cross a battlefield of students in the main yard.

Drawing in a deep breath, bracing myself for battle, I took a step forward and walked as fast as I could with my head down.

A ball flew past my head, a sandwich crunched beneath my feet, a group of girls nearly collided into me and as I neared safety, Alexander crossed my path, a sinister smile contorting his once friendly face.

"Where are you going, new boy?"

I paused, weighing my route to the library.

"Have you forgotten how to talk?" he asked, head tilted to the side as his eyes roamed up and down my body.

I said nothing, my lips pursed as Alexander shifted from one leg to the other.

Good boy, the Devil praised me. *Do not say a word. Look at how uncomfortable your silence makes him. He is unravelling, and you don't even have to lift a finger.*

Alexander watched me, fingers running through his hair before risking a step closer. "Why won't you answer me, Saint? Do you think you're better than me?"

I shook my head.

"Yes, you do."

I shook my head again, longing for the quiet of the library I was yet to reach.

I was supposed to have a fresh start. And yet, no matter where I was, trouble followed. In Rose Chapel, I was the freak whose mother tried to exorcise him. In Cambridge, I was the new kid who supposedly thought he was better than everyone.

Alexander circled me slowly before snatching my bag, using it to yank me backwards until I stumbled to the floor, the sound of laughter flaming my cheeks. I stood, hands curling into fists, the Devil chanting *kill, kill, kill.*

"Why are you doing this?" I asked.

I did not understand what I had done to warrant such a response. The way Alexander looked at me suggested there was something I was missing.

"We're just playing," he shrugged.

"Well, I don't like this game."

"Too bad."

"Leave me alone."

Alexander placed a hand on my chest and shoved me backwards. "Or what?"

I used to run away from boys like him. The little boy from St Augustine's would have scurried to the safety between bookshelves. But my father had taught me how to defend myself, how to be a Son of Thunder.

Kill, kill, kill.

My fist connected with his cheek before my leg swung up to slam into his stomach.

Collapsing to his knees, Alexander groaned, arms around his stomach as he leaned forward, coughing.

Good boy, Augustus.

The praise should have felt good, but as I watched a single tear slide down Alexander's cheek, all I felt was empty.

Knuckles throbbing, I retreated toward the nearest bathroom, weary of entering due to all the mirrors above the line of sinks.

I entered with my head down, relieved to find the bathroom empty. Hands trembling, I reached for the tap, wincing as the cool water slipped through the small cracks of my skin.

The confrontation with Alexander was stupid. I did not understand what I had done to offend him. And Aunt Vera...what punishment would await me when I got home?

A light bulb shattered, the bathroom exploding in a flash of yellow before darkness swallowed the room.

My head whipped up in alarm, gaze falling upon the mirror as though drawn there by an invisible force. In the infinite pools of darkness, my reflection grinned.

Hello, little monster.

I splashed water onto my face, closing my eyes to shut out the Devil in the mirror.

His laughter filled the room, a symphony of terror flooding my veins. Why was he here? Why did he haunt me? Was I truly so evil that the Devil himself was attached to my soul?

I lifted my head to confront him.

Black eyes blinked through the droplets of water falling from my eyelashes, a sinister hum echoing along the bathroom tiles. It mirrored a lullaby, one my mother would sing as she cradled me to sleep.

My reflection opened its mouth with fanged teeth stained with blood. It trickled down my chin in endless streams, the tap, tap, tap of it filling the sink echoing inside my head.

I did not look away. I had to face him. There was only so much running a twelve-year-old boy could do.

"What do you want?" I whispered.

To help you.

I narrowed my eyes.

To guide you.

"That is a lie."

I do not lie.

I shook my head, but my reflection remained still. Like Peter Pan's shadow, it had a mind of its own.

"You need to leave me alone."

I am afraid that is not possible.

"Why not?"

Because we need to survive this.

"Survive what?"

You are a monster. And that monster needs to be nurtured.

I staggered back, as though the Devil had dealt me a physical blow. "I am not a monster. You are."

How quickly you forget that night on North Lane.

"I have not forgotten."

You have not thanked me for what I did for you.

"You did nothing."

You are a fool.

"Leave me alone."

Don't you want to protect Auden?

I froze at the sound of my brother's name on his cold tongue. He knew my weakness—knew that I would do anything for my brother.

You need me.

"Need you?" I echoed, shaking my head. "You are the reason my mother abandoned me! The reason my father is dead!"

No. You *are the reason, little monster.*

"Liar!"

Tendrils of smoke poured from the mirror and slithered over my shoulders, a black mist clouding my vision while the Devil's voice circled me like a storm cloud awaiting a downpour.

You know it is true.

"Shut up!"

You know that Auden will meet the same tragic fate if you don't–

"I said SHUT UP!"

Glass splintered around my fist, blood spattering over the jagged reflection peering back at me. The Devil had gone and there I stood in his place, eyes watery and lips grimaced in pain.

The lights slowly flickered on, the shattered bulb repaired as though it had never been broken.

Had the Devil even been there at all?

CHAPTER ELEVEN

"Mr Saint, please come in."

Principal Reid was a tall, curvy woman with warm, russet skin, her shoulder-length hair a crown of curls that hid the golden jewellery swaying from her ears.

"Take a seat."

I lowered myself onto the chair opposite her desk without a word, my knuckles aching.

We met three days prior when Aunt Vera finalised my enrolment papers. Just as she did then, she offered me a mint. Just as I did then, I declined.

"As I am sure you are aware," she started, leaning back in her seat as she appraised me with a calm, unwavering expression, "we have zero tolerance for violence here at Trinity College."

"Do other schools normally tolerate violence?" I asked, feigning innocence despite the sarcastic line of questioning. "Is Trinity College different in that regard?"

"Mr Saint," she sighed, "it is only your first week. I would have expected you to be making friends, not enemies."

"Can we just skip to the part where you expel me?" I asked.

"Expel you?"

"Yeah. That's what you're going to do, right? For breaking your zero tolerance of violence."

"I am inclined to be more lenient given the circumstances," she said, gaze softening. "I know it has only been a few weeks since your father's passing."

I said nothing.

"I want you to see our school counsellor, Mr Klarke Grayson," she went on.

No, absolutely not.

My leg bounced up and down erratically, sweat coating my hands that curled and uncurled on my lap.

"I assure you, Klarke is a useful resource available to you here at Trinity. He has helped many students in similar situations as you."

He will find out, the Devil said, *you can't let him find out*

"I...I don't want to," I spoke up. "I'm fine, I promise. I won't get into any more fights and I-"

"Augustus," she cut me off. "I understand it can be scary to open up. But this is an opportunity for you to get some support during this difficult transition."

No. No. No.

"I said no."

Principal Reid sighed and without pressing me further, I was dismissed.

***

Aunt Vera was displeased when I entered the library. She was lounging on her rustic armchair, Shakespeare purring on her lap.

I had changed into grey sweatpants and an oversized black X-Files sweater that had belonged to my father, the hood drawn up to fend off the cold. The scent of whiskey and cologne still clung to the fleece material, but I refused to wash it, my father's presence comforting in this new, unfamiliar reality I found myself in.

Exhaustion followed me toward the smaller armchair across from my aunt, a yawn threatening to stretch my aching jaw. All I wanted to do was sleep, but I knew a punishment awaited me, and the anxiety of not knowing kept me awake.

"Tell me about your day."

This question was not mere curiosity. I knew Principal Reid would have called Aunt Vera to inform her of the incident, so the question was a means of building up to my punishment. There was a linen cupboard waiting for me, no doubt. I massaged my wrists, remembering the way the rope sliced into my skin, lemon juice burning my raw flesh.

"I am a twelve-year-old boy plagued with an impenetrable forest of guilt and a fear that I will be discovered. Of what? I could not tell you. But once everyone knows, they'll bury me so deep into the Earth I'll sink down into Hell itself, consumed by dead souls who share my rotten heart."

There was a long silence as Aunt Vera and I appraised one another.

"Poetic, right?" I smirked.

"Did you steal that from somewhere?" she asked.

"No, the Devil told me to say it."

Another long silence hung between us.

"Augustus," she sighed, unperturbed. "Your day."

"Just tell me what my punishment is."

"Punishment?"

I barely suppressed an eyeroll. "I am not an idiot."

"Clearly you are, if you think I go around punishing children for express-ing their emotions."

"So...you're not...?"

"I'm disappointed," she clarified, leaning back in her seat, one leg crossed over the other, "but I don't believe a punishment would be beneficial at this moment."

"I'm sorry."

Shakespeare meowed and jumped off Aunt Vera's lap as she leaned forward to hand me a leather-bound journal.

"What's this?" I frowned, turning the journal over in my hands.

"It belonged to your mother."

Every muscle in my body tensed at those words, and it was a divine miracle I managed to keep hold of the journal instead of flinging it into the fireplace warming the room.

"It was amongst your father's things that Brady and I divided," Aunt Vera explained. "I think you should have it."

"I do not want anything from that woman."

Aunt Vera assessed me with an unreadable expression. "You don't miss her?"

"Why would I? She left."

"I met your mother only a few days after you were born," Aunt Vera hummed, leaning back in her armchair. "She looked so proud, holding you in her arms."

I rolled my eyes. "That pride died the minute I learned to speak."

"Do you really believe that?"

"You don't know what it was like," I said, leaning forward in my seat to glare at her. "She treated me like I was a fucking demon!"

Aunt Vera should have scolded me for my filthy language, but she didn't. Instead, rather calmly, she said, "You're right, Augustus. I don't know what it was like. But I don't want you spending your life believing your mother hated you when that simply was not the case."

"How would you know?!" I scoffed. "You weren't there. She said it. She said she hated me."

"And did you say you hated her?"

I fell silent.

She pointed to the journal in my hands. "I think you should read through it."

"I don't want to."

"Just take it," Aunt Vera said, a little impatient, "one day you might actually want to learn more about your mother."

"I doubt it."

"We'll see."

CHAPTER TWELVE

The House on North Lane haunted my dreams, summoning me to wander down its dark halls once more.

My mother's face, the Devil's voice, the flames—every night was the same. When I woke, my mother's journal called to me from under the bed, like a monster waiting to drag me down to Hell. I already had one Devil on my shoulder; I didn't need another.

School was an escape *and* a prison. My studies forced the Devil to the back of my mind, but there was little I could do to avoid trouble when Alexander hunted me down like I was a deer grazing in the woods.

Sanctuary was found in an unlocked classroom inside the art block. There, amongst the smell of wet paint and wooden easels, I could melt into my artwork, safely hidden from those who tormented me.

I pushed open the door, gaze landing on a familiar figure standing in front of an easel. It was the chewing gum girl from my form room, the girl who competed with Alexander to answer every question leaving Mr Singh's mouth. Her twin braids were pulled back into a single ponytail, a golden stud on each ear. White earphones silenced my entry, the tangled cord disappearing into the pocket of her dark green blazer as she appraised the black canvas in front of her. A paintbrush dangled between her teeth; her eyebrows furrowed with dissatisfaction.

I hovered in the doorway, unsure whether to find another empty art room or reclaim my territory. She lifted her head before I could decide, her expression shifting from disapproval to confusion as her gaze darted between my bruised cheek and my swollen lip—a result of another scuffle with Alexander.

"Can I help you?" she asked, slowly removing her earphones.

I shook my head.

"You're the new kid, right? Augustus...Saint?"

I nodded.

She set down the paint brush and scoffed. "You don't look very saintly."

"What does a saint look like?" I asked.

Her hands connected in prayer as she made a sound I assume was meant to resemble an angelic choir.

"I'll consider being saintlier, then," I mused.

She grinned. "I'm Ava."

"Nice to meet you," I nodded, gaze drifting toward the canvas. "What are you painting?"

"A nightmare I had last night."

I squinted at the artwork. All I could see was black. "What's the nightmare?"

"I am in a room. It's dark...I can't even see my own hand in front of my face," she recounted. "I'm walking around for a while, trying to find a way out, but the room doesn't seem to end. I am trapped. And there are...voices. Some are quiet, some are loud. They say such...cruel things."

That doesn't sound too bad.

"I can't seem to paint just how terrifying it was to be trapped in the darkness," she added with a sigh. "I'm painting what I saw but...it's just this vast nothingness."

Clearly a terrible artist, then.

My gaze remained locked on the canvas. "I see your problem."

"And?"

"You're painting what you're seeing, not what you're hearing. Or what you're feeling."

"No shit. I can't exactly paint sound or feelings."

"Art shouldn't always be literal," I explained, reaching out for her paint-brush. "May I?"

"Sure, but don't mansplain," she mumbled, "it's not very saintly."

Rolling my eyes, I dipped the brush in white, and added some light to the black vastness that stared back at me, the colour hauntingly similar to the black eyes of my reflection smiling in the mirror.

I outlined faces, ones you might mistake for a whiff of smoke or a distortion of light if you weren't paying attention. They wore smiles of razor-sharp teeth, their laughter flowing through the darkness as they danced along the artwork. A once empty canvas, now a nightmare.

Look at you, little monster.

Ava followed my every movement, stepping closer as her nightmare slowly came to life.

Wicked laughter waltzed all around us, darkness seeping in through the windows, pouring over us like cans of black paint. When I finished, she asked, "You're an artist?"

I stepped back, admiring the hideous creation like Frankenstein did his monster.

You are an artist, the Devil confirmed, the black ink bleeding red, *and you paint with blood.*

***

Ava was there the next day, a blood red apple in one hand and a thin paint brush in the other as she bent over her workbook. Her tangled earphones lay abandoned beside her pencil case, crumpled papers littering the desk.

I walked toward her slowly, sneaking a glance at the water colour paint she applied to a sketched dragon. She flinched when I dumped myself into the seat across from her, my school bag crashing to the floor.

"You know, this is usually where I spend my time *alone*," she said as a greeting.

"I didn't see a sign on the door saying no entry," I said.

"I'm not complaining," she shrugged, "but...why are you here?"

I pulled out a cheese and bacon roll freshly baked by Mrs Brighton, still warm thanks to my insulated lunch box. "I don't really have anywhere else to go," I admitted.

"Huh, so you haven't made any friends yet?" she asked.

I shook my head.

"We can be friends, if you want."

That is suspicious. Why would she want to be our friend? She barely knows us.

"Why?" I asked.

"Why what?"

"Why would you want to be my friend?"

Ava arched an eyebrow. "I don't know. You helped me with my art yesterday. Seems like we got that in common. Art, I mean."

You can't afford to have friends. If you let them get too close, they'll know.

"I...don't really have much experience...being a friend," I admitted.

"Well, you're in luck, because no experience is required for this role. We can just chill."

You're a monster, Augustus. Monsters don't deserve friends.

"Okay," I breathed out. "Cool."

"Got any art you can show me?" she asked before taking another bite of her apple.

I glanced down at my school bag and pulled out my visual arts book. It was already filled with unfinished work, most of it completed on the bus ride to and from school. "Yeah...some."

"Can I see?"

Swallowing the lump in my throat, I slid the book across the desk and watched as she flicked through, expression unreadable. She lingered on some pages longer than others, bottom lip between her teeth as her eyes took in every inch.

Feeling vulnerable?

I bit back a retort and busied myself with my lunch. It didn't matter what Ava, or the Devil, or *anyone* thought. If she hated it, that meant nothing.

Liar. You long for approval like a dog longs for a bone.

"Who's this?" Ava's question broke through my thoughts, holding up an artwork I had completely forgotten about. I tried to snatch it back, but she pulled it close to her chest at the last second.

"Why is she on fire? And what's in her hand?"

It was a crucifix, but I didn't say that. Instead, I made one last attempt to retrieve my book and when I succeeded, I shoved it into my bag.

"Looked like something out of a horror movie," she commented after a brief, tense pause.

"It was," I lied. "Just something I...I saw."

Ava nodded, though the way her eyes drifted toward my school bag told me she didn't quite believe me.

She knows.

No, she doesn't.

She knows. She knows. She knows.

The bell summoned us to our next class where Ava, to my astonishment, sat next to me. We didn't discuss the artwork. We didn't discuss anything at all. The silence was comfortable. And for the first time in my twelve years, I thought someone might actually be my friend.

***

A year had passed and October painted Aunt Vera's garden an array of red, orange and yellow as leaves scattered across the yard, some swimming in the bird bath and the fishpond.

In a maroon knitted sweater and plain black trousers, I sat with Auden on a red and white picnic rug, a basket of biscuits, cheese, and fruit prepared by Mrs Brighton shared between us. Auden was in a matching maroon sweater, though whilst mine was plain, his was stitched with Winnie the Pooh and Piglet catching autumn leaves with a net.

We had spent the morning feeding the fish, playing board games and counting how many leaves fell from the tree above us.

Auden wanted to explore Aunt Vera's maze, but I was weary. Years ago, I would have jumped at the chance. I would have made a quest out of it. But at this moment...the thought of getting lost in the hedges condemned my stomach to sickening nausea. Who knew what trick the Devil would play in there? How long before the tall hedges began closing in?

"Please, Guses!" Auden pouted. He crawled toward me and threw himself onto my stomach, trusting that I would catch him in my arms.

"But why?" I laughed to hide the anxiety soaring through my veins. "What do you think is in there?"

"Treasure!" Auden answered without hesitation.

"Treasure?" I raised an eyebrow. "What kind of treasure?"

Auden sat up and adjusted his new black-framed glasses before beaming, "Mumma!"

Everything inside of me shut down at those words. All traces of joy fled, leaving an emotionless ghost in its wake. Auden and I didn't speak of our mother. We simply didn't. I thought we had put her behind us.

"Why would…why would she be in the maze?" I asked.

"The witch put her there!" Auden answered, jumping up and down now as he glanced down the path leading to the dark green botanical nightmare.

"The witch?" I repeated.

It hit me, rather late, that Auden was playing a game. Just like the ones we used to play in the woods behind North Lane. The memory brought with it a harsh ache.

"Come on, Guses! We've got to find her!" he called out as he raced down the path.

I followed reluctantly, confining my trembling hands to my pockets. "Auden, wait!"

He paused by the entry, the hedges so tall they blocked out the light of the cloudless sky, all traces of warmth absent.

"Are you sure you want to go in there?" I whispered.

He nodded, unbothered by the dark gloom.

A quiet sigh escaped my throat and as I reached for his hand, I said, "You stick right by me, alright?"

We started forward, the soil beneath our feet a dark black void of fallen leaves and discarded twigs. It was soft, damp, as if it had recently been watered. But Mr Lenton had not been here this week, nor had it rained.

The hedges on either side of us were dark green, cut evenly to avoid stray vines. Not a single flower grew, though I heard Aunt Vera say that just weeks prior to Auden and I moving in, the hedges had been scattered with colourful flora. Mr Lenton was working hard to regrow them, but it seemed not one single flower was ready to blossom.

We turned left when the path forward came to an end, Auden squealing with excitement. He kept repeating 'find mumma, find mumma, find mumma,' and I was starting to question how much of this really was just a game for him.

He'd been very young when our mother abandoned us. And although things did seem to improve for him once she was gone, perhaps our father and I did a disservice to him by not talking about her, by not explaining what had happened. But the truth was, not even I was certain what happened.

"Okay, which way now?" I asked once we reached a crossroads in the maze.

"Let's go this way!" Auden declared confidently as he darted to the left, his fingers releasing from mine.

"Auden," I said warningly. "Don't get too far from me!"

He skipped ahead, but he remained in my line of sight, humming cheerfully as though we were on a fun adventure. Meanwhile, I was fighting off a panic attack.

You know that feeling, when you're walking and you think you hear footsteps behind you, but when you turn around, there's no one there? That was how I felt in this maze. Every time I turned, I was met with dark hedges and nothing more. But it didn't feel as though we were alone.

By the fourth time I turned around to find nothing there, I rationalised that it was all in my head. But when I turned to resume my way forward, my heart stopped.

"Auden!"

The only path forward was to turn right, but there was no sign of Auden's brown hair or maroon sweater. It was like he had been swallowed by the hedges. A fresh wave of nausea crashed over me, but I refused to stop searching. I had to find him.

I ran until I collided with his back, his body a statue staring into the darkness. Panting, I opened my mouth to scold him when my gaze landed on a figure half-submerged in an unfinished grave.

Shielding him from the grotesque sight, I pushed him behind me and squinted through the darkness to make sense of what I was seeing.

The moment I did, horror consumed me.

My mother's body lay buried in the dirt, her white dress covered with blood, soil and earthworms feasting on the thin material.

Cockroaches poured from her parted lips, her lifeless eyes staring right at us as brown rats feasted on her exposed scalp. Mushrooms grew out of her nose, spreading along the grass and soil beneath her. Maggots and grave flies crawled along her pale flesh, the scent of rot poisoning the air.

"What....the hell...?" I breathed out, backing up a step only for my back to slam into a hedge. I looked around, searching for a way out, but the entry we had ventured through had disappeared, and we were trapped inside this green prison.

Vines slithered out from beneath the hedges, entangling themselves around my limbs as I fought to get away. I'd lost sight of Auden again, and my panic grew. Before I had a chance to scream his name, a vine lodged itself down my throat, vision blurring as I choked.

I watched, breathlessly, as my mother's corpse crawled towards me, her black hole of a mouth opening wide in a blood curdling scream as she–

"Augustus!"

Mrs Brighton was in front of me, her hand flushed against my forehead as she worried at her lip. Auden hovered behind her, his eyes darting in between me and the housekeeper who was reaching for a bottle of water to splash over my face.

"You got yourself a fever," she said, shaking her head. "Why didn't you tell me you were unwell? Let's get you inside, sweet boy."

Confused, weak, and shivering, I leaned on Mrs Brighton as she guided me inside the house, gently lowering me onto a sofa with blankets and a cup of warm tea.

It took me several minutes to realise what had happened in the maze hadn't happened at all. I had hallucinated it, from the very beginning.

Auden sat beside me under the blanket, his head resting on my upper arm. He was fine. He must have had a fright, though, when he saw me shivering and calling his name.

"Get some sleep, Guses," he whispered gently.

When I looked at him to give him a small smile, I could have sworn I saw a mushroom in his hair.

CHAPTER THIRTEEN

Friendship with Ava McTavish was laughing until we couldn't breathe, paint fights, and finding new and inventive ways of getting out of PE. Ava used her period cramps several times a month to avoid the torturous exercise, and because Mr McCallum didn't want to know more about her monthly cycle, he never questioned it. I, on the other hand, wore a bandage around my wrist to feign a fracture. Unfortunately, Mr McCallum pointed out that I could still use my legs, and Ava would laugh from the benches as I fumbled through games of dodgeball and cricket.

It was late nights sharing memes, early mornings debating whether an education was worth waking up before the sun, and weekends spent browsing art supplies and bookstores. One night, she'd convinced me to attend my first ever concert and I was terrified. The Devil insisted on listing every single thing that could go wrong, and as the mosh pit crowded around me, the music blasting from the speakers and fluorescent lights dancing across my vision, I was seconds away from a panic attack. Ava reached for my hand, squeezed gently, and pushed people away when they got too close. I was safe with her, building up the courage to jump up and down alongside her when our favourite song came on.

Our friendship was bedroom doors wide open when we visited each other's houses because Ava was yet to announce she exclusively liked girls, and her parents did not trust that I wasn't lusting over their daughter.

We went from year seven to year eight, year nine to year ten. And then to year eleven, enduring dating rumours because of how inseparable we were whilst everyone else around us built steady relationships unlike the week-long relationships of previous years.

Although Ava had many friends, I only had her. I grew attached, perhaps more than I should have. Not a crush, though everyone seemed to think so. It was more—fear, jealousy. I only had Ava, and if she decided she liked her other friends more than me, I would be alone, and I was terrified of losing her. But things were good. Ava and I were two sides of the same coin.

And then came Eden.

We met her during an art gallery exhibition hosted by the school's visual arts department. It was a small event, though there were more people than I had anticipated.

Ava and I stood by our artworks watching people walk past, seemingly uninterested.

"This is so humiliating," Ava mumbled.

"It's because everyone is just here for their own kid's work," I told her.

"I hope mum and dad get here soon," she sighed, adjusting her canvas so it hung straight on the wall behind her. It was a self-portrait, face decorated with meaningful scenes from her childhood and early teenage years. There were moments with her parents swinging her in between their arms, moments playing board games with her cousins, and even a scene with me from last summer when we went to South End's Adventure Island. It was beautiful. Truly. Though a competitive side of me still wanted to take first place.

"Is your aunt coming?" she asked, fiddling with the gold chain around her neck as she looked around for her parents.

"No. She's in Rome."

"Rome? God, wasn't she in Florence just last week?"

"Uh-huh."

"What a rich bitch."

I snorted.

Moments later, her parents arrived. They were so proud, snapping several photos of Ava in front of her artwork. She complained when they fussed over her, but no matter how hard she tried, she couldn't wipe the smile from her face.

"Oh, Augustus, come, come! Let me take a photo of you both together!" her mother said, ushering me to stand with Ava in front of her work.

"Let me get one of you in front of your work too, sweetie!" her mother added, ushering me the other way toward my canvas.

My artwork was inspired by Shirley Jackson's *We Have Always Lived in the Castle*; an old, gothic mansion with a black gate at the entrance, dark greenery devouring the cobbled pathway toward the front steps. Inside the house was a young girl standing by the window, a solemn expression darkening her features as she stared right into the eyes of whoever beheld the painting. Behind her, an ominous shadow loomed, misting around her as though tightening its grasp.

"You're both so talented," Ava's father said, beaming from ear-to-ear.

Their praise and support meant the world.

Having no parents of my own to share in this achievement was difficult, but Ava's family never made me feel excluded. It was hard, though, knowing the photos they'd taken would be in *their* family album and not my own.

While Ava and her parents went to taste test some of the cakes baked by junior food technology students, I remained by my artwork, shifting from one leg to the other as more people filed in.

Mrs Brighton had promised she would try and bring Auden, but I didn't hold out hope. She was struggling with arthritis, and driving caused her all kinds of discomfort.

"Bit grim, innit?" a voice said to my left.

I silenced a groan as my gaze landed on Alexander, hands in his pockets as he observed my artwork.

"Fuck off," I said.

"Rude," Alexander pouted. "Shouldn't you be, I don't know, explaining your work or something?"

"Shouldn't you be, I don't know, terrorising local neighbourhood kids?" I bit back.

Alexander rolled his eyes. "Come on, tell me. What is your artwork about?"

"I will not entertain you, Parsons."

"Why not?"

"Because I am not in the mood."

"You're such a bore, Saint."

"Then go away."

"Or what?"

"Or I'll smash your face into the dirt and use your blood on my next artwork," Ava said, returning to my side with her arms folded over her chest.

"Ah, here she is," Alexander smirked. "Here to save your boyfriend, Mc-Tavish?"

"I like girls, dipshit," Ava said.

"You're too pretty to like girls."

"And you're too ugly."

Alexander shrugged. "At least I–"

"Wow," Eden Bexley cut him off, her flawless sun-kissed skin and emerald green eyes decorated with make-up. "Your artwork is absolutely beautiful."

Ava beamed at the compliment, my eyes darting in between Alexander's scowl and Eden's radiant smile.

"Thank you," Ava said.

Alexander walked away, my eyes tracking his movements to ensure he really was leaving.

"Can you tell me a bit about it?" Eden asked, pulling a stray blonde hair behind her ear.

Ava nodded enthusiastically and explained the meaning behind her work and the process, all the while I stood to the side awkwardly, unsure whether to leave or not.

Eden was in our year, though we didn't share any of the same classes except for history. She was a swimmer, and so she spent most of her time with the more athletic crowd whereas Ava and I were amongst the social outcasts. Not that I had a problem with that. I really didn't care for one's gym routine or the ingredients in a protein shake.

My gaze ventured toward Alexander who stood with his friends, one of whom was a food technology student with a table of pasta. He smirked as his eyes flickered toward Ava and Eden who were laughing, bodies shifting closer together.

If I had known anyone else, I would have left. But I didn't, so I played the role of an uncomfortable third wheel.

"Wow," Ava breathed out once Eden returned to her family who were waiting by the food tables, "I didn't know she liked art. She really knows her stuff."

"Not just a dumb swimmer, then," I mumbled.

An elbow to the ribs was Ava's response.

No longer were we spending our lunch breaks organising social justice school events—Ava was very passionate about the environment and inequality—or painting in the art rooms. There were no more concerts to plan or theme parks to save up for. Instead, we shuffled onto poolside benches to watch the girls swim team train. Or, more accurately, watch Eden train.

I missed the quiet of the art block, the familiar scent of charcoal and wet paint. The splashes of water, the cheering, the music—it was overstimulating. Even when I brought my art book to draw, concentration evaded me.

"God, she's so beautiful," Ava would sigh dreamily.

Everything was all about Eden. It was exhausting. I wanted to discuss art, music, books—Ava wanted to discuss Eden, Eden, Eden.

"I heard she's going to be at Jesse Somerton's party this Saturday," Ava said during one lunch break, her gaze locked on Eden as she climbed out of the pool, wet blonde strands slipping from her swimming cap.

I pulled a face. Jesse Somerton had been arrested twice for driving under the influence of drugs and alcohol, and he wasn't even eighteen yet. He was always smoking in the bathrooms, setting off the alarms until we all had to evacuate to the sports field. Somehow, he evaded expulsion, which I suspected had something to do with his politician father.

"We should go," Ava went on. "It will be our first real party! There will be drinks and music and heaps of people from school. Eden invited me. You should come!"

"To a party?" I repeated, alarmed.

Ava nudged me. "Why do you look so scared? It will be fun! And I need you there for support because...maybe I'll finally build up the courage to ask Eden out."

"But...you don't even know if she...you know..." I waved my hand around in a vague gesture.

"Likes girls?" Ava supplied.

I nodded.

"We've been texting a lot," she shrugged. "I'm not one hundred percent sure but I have to shoot my shot, right?"

"And what am I supposed to do while you're flirting with Eden?" I asked, rolling my eyes.

Ava wriggled her eyebrows. "Maybe ask a girl out yourself. I heard Elysse has a crush on you."

"Not interested."

"Okay, it doesn't have to be *her*," Ava chuckled. "But I mean...don't you want like...a girlfriend or something?"

"No. I'd rather just...hang out with you."

Ava frowned, gaze lowering to her hands as she turned so her body faced away from me. "We're friends, Augustus. Just friends."

Heat rushed to my cheeks.

"And I'm gay," she went on, "so I shouldn't have to explain to you that–"

"I don't like you like that!" I cut her off.

Ava paused. "You...don't?"

"No!" I said, shaking my head. "You're my *friend*, that's all."

An uncomfortable silence lingered between us.

"Okay, well, good," Ava said. "Sorry."

I shut my art book and climbed to my feet, bag swinging over my shoulder. "Have fun at the party."

"Augustus–"

I didn't hear the rest of her sentence as I walked away, tears of frustration threatening to roll down my cheeks.

Why are you crying, little monster?

I had no answer for the Devil. I didn't like Ava in any romantic capacity. At all. The fact that she, of all people, questioned that after everything just made me feel pathetic. Did she really think our friendship only meant something because I wanted to be with her?

It didn't matter, not really. Things were changing, and if I couldn't keep up, Ava would leave me behind.

CHAPTER FOURTEEN

Sleep maintained its distance, lingering in the shadows to ward off the night-mares.

I sat with my back up against the headboard, legs outstretched in front of me, my mother's journal unopened on my lap. In the dim lamplight, my finger and thumb hovered in the bottom right corner of the leather-bound cover, itching to turn it over.

I didn't know what compelled me to open it. It was as though my hands were being guided by a puppeteer, unable to resist the biological pull toward the woman who birthed me.

The Devil was uncharacteristically silent as my eyes fell upon the very first entry, my mother's handwriting causing a lump to form in my throat.

January 7, 2001

My baby is due in two months. Marcus and I are so excited. I am a little nervous too. I don't know the first thing about being a mother. It is what I am called to be, as a child of God and a woman, but sometimes I don't feel ready. Everyone thinks I am being ridiculous. And maybe I am. Being a mother is what I am supposed to do. There is no greater calling in the world. Marcus and I have been discussing baby names. For a girl, we were thinking Elizabeth or Claire, though I really like Evie. For a boy, we're not sure. I guess

he will have to tell us once he is born. Either way, I can't wait to welcome God's
precious gift.

I released a shaky breath as I turned the page, my mother's fears and hopes circling my mind alongside my own anger and guilt. She would have been nineteen when she wrote that entry—I could not imagine preparing to be a parent so young. She must have been so scared. I shook my head and continued reading.

April 9, 2001

Augustus is one month today. He's such a sweet boy. Not smiling yet, but Father Andrej says he'll be smiling in no time.
He's very clingy. He cries when I'm not in the room. He likes to be held. I am exhausted, but I am happy. Being a mother is every woman's dream, is it not? I am so lucky to have a child of my own.
Marcus went back to work straight away, so it's just been Augustus and me at home. I am scared to sleep in case he needs me, so I'm awake for twenty-two hours a day. Is this motherhood? I miss sleep. I miss peace and quiet. But I love Augustus. I wouldn't trade him for the world. I just wish I still felt like me. Thank you, God, for making me a mother. I hope I can make you proud and raise Augustus to be a good, loving and obedient child. I have so much to learn, but with your guidance, I believe I can be the perfect mother. I have so much love to give.

I slammed the journal shut, throwing it onto my bedside table as I curled up beneath my sheets, blinking away tears before they could fall.
I missed her.
I hated her.

I missed her.

I blamed her.

I missed her.

I was glad she was gone.

*****

The coach pulled up in the visitor car park of Framlingham Castle, students spilling out, eager to stretch their legs.

I stood with Ava and Eden, all three of us hugging our arms around ourselves as the November air sent a breeze of ice shards along our skin.

Mr Singh did a headcount before guiding us toward the entrance where we were met by an enthusiastic tour guide who looked as old as the castle itself.

"Castles have like...no central heating, we're going to be freezing in there," Ava complained, teeth chattering.

"I know," Eden sighed, reaching to adjust Ava's scarf. "Could it have really hurt to have organised this excursion during the spring or something?"

"I think it's cheaper this time of year," I said.

"Fuck cheaper," Ava said. "We go to an expensive ass school."

The tour guide led us inside the former fortress, recounting historical events that took place within its towering walls.

"It was here," he said, lowering his voice as if revealing a secret, "that Mary Tudor was proclaimed the Queen of England."

I dragged my fingers along the rough, patched brickwork worn with age, my eyes drifting over the cobwebs lining the arched ceiling.

History was Auden's favourite subject, and I thought about how much he would enjoy wandering the same halls as a former Queen of England. I pulled out my phone to snap some photos for him, Ava and Eden walking ahead as they giggled amongst themselves.

"It's really cool, huh?"

I lifted my head and scowled as Alexander leaned against an arched entryway, arms folded over his chest. His dark green eyes flickered between my face and my throat that swallowed thickly.

Without uttering a word, I slipped my phone away and stepped past him, shoulder knocking his.

"Wow. Mute again, Saint?"

I turned a corner to follow the group, jaw clenched as Alexander walked beside me, hands shoved into his pockets.

"I think I want to be an historian," he said casually, as if we were just two friends conversing about a shared interest. It was some kind of game—a game I had not yet learned to play.

"I'd write books and stuff," he went on, "maybe teach at a university. That would be cool."

"Good for you," I mumbled.

"What about you?"

"What about me?"

"What do you want to do? After school?" he clarified. "Something with art?"

"Artists don't make a lot of money," I replied.

"True, not unless you're super mainstream and famous," he sighed. "What, then?"

"I don't know," I admitted. "Haven't thought about it."

"Really?"

"Really."

"We've got two more years so...you have time."

I said nothing.

"Listen, Augustus...I...."

"What?"

"I'm sorry. For being an asshole to you all these years."

I looked around for a hidden camera, convinced I was the subject of a prank.

Alexander's laugh resounded along the concrete walls, reclaiming my attention. "What are you looking for?"

"You're messing with me," I said.

"I'm not," he insisted. "I swear I'm not. I'm being serious."

"Why now, then?"

"Why apologise, you mean?"

I nodded.

"I don't know. I guess I just...want to be friends with good people and...you are someone I should have befriended back in year seven."

"I thought you *were* going to befriend me," I admitted. "And then you turned on me. Why?"

Alexander ran his fingers through his hair, averting his gaze. "I...was threatened by you."

"Threatened by me? Why?"

"Come on, Augustus. You're smart. Haven't you figured it out?"

I shook my head.

"You got a higher score than me in that test. The one that decides what level class you're in," he explained, shaking his head. "Until you came along, I was the smartest in the room. And I was scared. Rightfully so. You're one smart motherfucker."

"I'm not. Not *naturally*. I work hard for my grades. And besides, you're smart too," I said. "You've beaten me loads of times."

"You've beaten me more."

I scratched the back of my neck, not knowing what to say. An apology was on the tip of my tongue, but that didn't feel right. Why should I apologise for my success? I worked hard. I deserved every good grade I received. And yet...the crestfallen look on his face tugged at something in my chest. Guilt.

"Listen...it was never my intention to...threaten you in any way," I said, carefully, "I just wanted to do well. My aunt paid a lot of money for this school, and I owe it to her to do my absolute best."

"Yeah, of course, I get it," he nodded, lifting his gaze to give me a sad smile, "my parents want me to be the best, too. They think I don't try. And then they get angry and..."

He trailed off, the unspoken words heavy in the air. I chewed on the inside of my mouth, chest tightening at the memories of walking past Alexander in the school corridors, his blue and black bruises blinding.

"Regardless," he spoke up again, shaking his head, "I shouldn't have been such an asshole to you."

"Thank you," I breathed out. "I uh...I appreciate that."

He gave me a smile—not a grin, not a smirk—a genuine smile. It softened his features, made him look younger, boyish.

Light poured in from an arched window as we paused at the top of a staircase overlooking the view of the fortress grounds. We stood, shoulder to shoulder, hands almost touching on the stone railing.

"Can you imagine being here, hundreds of years ago, guarding the Queen of England within these very walls?" he breathed out. "We're standing where young men like ourselves would have once stood, willing to die for Queen and Country."

I smiled at his enthusiasm. While Alexander was indeed studious, I would have never guessed his passion for history. It was clear that within this fortress, I was privy to a side of Alexander he kept concealed.

While he studied the view, I studied his face. His skin was a shade lighter than mine, a single mole beneath the right side of his bottom lip. And those lips...they were a pale pink, curved like a long bow. I was imagining how soft they would feel against my fingers when he looked up, catching me eyeing him like a ghost eyeing the living.

I immediately dropped my gaze, heart thundering wildly in my chest. What the hell was wrong with me?

"Boys!" Mr Singh called out from the bottom of the staircase. "Stay with the group!"

Without a word, I hurried down the staircase and rejoined Ava and Eden who hadn't seemed to notice my absence. They were chatting amongst themselves, barely paying attention to the history all around us.

We continued the tour and once it was over, Mr Singh gave us thirty minutes to explore the grounds before we had to meet up again for an educational video presentation.

I followed Ava and Eden to a wide, stone staircase. They sat close together, practically intertwined, ignoring my entire existence.

Not wanting to endure their flirting, I ventured off on my own, returning to the darkness of the fortress.

The heavy oak doors creaked open, the light behind me casting a shadow across the worn stone floor, moss and lichen growing between the cracks. I wandered down the narrow corridors, smoke lingering in the royal tapestries lining the walls.

It was quiet, the only sound the echo of my footsteps as I turned a corner, almost colliding with Elysse Martina. Her hands clutched around my forearms as she steadied herself, a breathless gasp pulsing through the hall.

"I'm sorry," I said, taking a step back to grant her space.

"No, no, it's okay," she assured me with a smile.

I nodded and made to step past her when she stopped me, fingers gripped around my wrist. "Want to explore together? I'm kind of scared."

I glanced down at her hand, lip curling in displeasure. "Scared of what?"

"Ghosts," she said.

"Ghosts can't hurt you. They're dead."

She laughed as if I had made a joke, head thrown back so that her blonde strands fell down her shoulders.

"Come on, let's go," she giggled, dragging me down the hall.

I had only spoken to Elysse twice in my life.

The first was in year eight when we were assigned seats in French. She was quite popular, even back then. A dancer, a swimmer, a gymnast. We never really spoke until one lesson when she asked, in a panic, if she could copy my homework.

We hadn't spoken again until a few weeks ago, when we passed one another in the hall and she complimented my new haircut. Ava, who had been beside me, snorted and made a comment about how Elysse had dated all the boys in her 'social status', so she was now branching out to the 'losers'.

"We shouldn't go too far," I told her as the air grew thick, a cold dampness following our every move.

"Here is nice," she said, pulling me into a small, windowless room with a wooden chest tucked in the corner, the only light coming from the flickering lanterns in the corridor.

By the door stood an armoured guard, traditionally decked out in iron, steel and chainmail. There was no person behind the helmet, but the figure was so tall and life-like that you could almost be fooled.

"I thought you said you were scared," I murmured, taking in the small space. "This is a bit creepy."

"But I'm safe now," she beamed, shifting closer, "with you."

I raised an eyebrow, backing away until the stone wall pressed into my shoulder blades. "I won't exactly be able to protect you from ghosts."

She giggled and shook her head. "Do you believe in ghosts, Augustus?"

I shrugged. "I have never really thought about it."

"What do you think about instead?" she asked.

I think about throwing you off the side of this fortress, watching your skull crack open so you can never touch me again.

"Why are we in here, Elysse?"

"Because," she said, placing both hands on my chest, "I thought we could have some fun on this boring ass trip."

I opened my mouth to tell her it wasn't boring, that we were standing amongst historical artefacts from the Middle Ages, when her lips suddenly connected with mine.

I froze.

I had never shared a kiss with anyone, yet alone a pretty girl like Elysse who anyone would have kissed back. But I didn't.

I stood there, locked in a tense stance, as Elysse ran her tongue along my bottom lip.

My eyes locked with Alexander; his lips parted and eyes wide as he stood in the hallway, watching Elysse press her body into mine.

The expression that crossed his face—anger, hurt, something in between—unlocked the chains holding me in place, my body returning to life to push her away.

"What? What's wrong?" Elysse frowned.

"You...you shouldn't do that," I stammered.

"Do what?"

"Kiss people with–without asking!"

"Don't you want to kiss me?"

I shook my head.

"What, are you gay or something?"

Blood ceased running through my veins, all warmth evaporating to leave a cold empty shell of a boy, standing in front of a girl seething with rejection.

"No," I said, forcing my voice to remain calm, "I just don't want to kiss you."

"You're so gay," she scoffed, sauntering toward the door.

"I'm not gay!"

"Augustus the Gay," she laughed, throwing her head back. "Roman Emperor of the Queers!"

Untamed rage possessed my body, an overwhelming tremor that sent my hand toward her neck, slamming her head against the concrete wall with a deafening crunch.

She screamed, blood pouring from the gash on her temple as she crumbled to the floor, blonde hair stained red.

I stood over her sobbing body; leather shoe pressed against her pale throat. Beneath the sole, her pulse fluttered.

"Please," she whispered.

I pressed my foot down harder, watching the blood vessels in her eyes burst one after the other. She choked, gasping for air, hands clawing uselessly at my feet. Pleasure flooded through me, her struggle placating the anger that soared through my veins. I was in control. She was at my mercy.

Colour fled her warm skin as Death crouched down beside her. She stopped moving, stopped gasping—hands dropping to the concrete floor, eyes vacant.

"Hello?" Elysse waved a hand in front of my face, shaking her head. "Oh my god, you're gay *and* crazy."

I watched her leave the room, not one drop of blood falling from her flawless skin. She was breathing. She was *alive*.

My shoulders sagged in relief.

I was not a monster. I was not the Devil.

CHAPTER FIFTEEN

"Oh, come on, it's not that bad," Ava assured me on our way to our visual arts class. "Augustus the Gay kind of has a nice ring to it."

I shot her a look. "But I'm not gay."

She shrugged.

"What?"

"You're not gay."

"Yes, I'm not gay, that's what I said."

"But if you were, there's nothing wrong with that," she pointed out.

"Obviously," I said. "I'm not saying there *is* anything wrong with that."

"You're kind of acting like there is," she said, gaze resting on my father's crucifix dangling from my neck.

"I just don't want to be called something I'm not," I said defensively. "Is that so wrong?"

Ava said nothing, which meant it *was* wrong, and she was annoyed.

The truth was, I knew I couldn't really talk about this with her. For one, she was a lesbian. Being insecure about my new nickname sounded like I thought being queer was wrong, which wasn't how I felt at all. And two, when Ava first came out, she'd endured a lot worse than a stupid nickname. The boys in our year made jokes about 'turning her straight' while the girls distanced themselves, telling her not to flirt with them.

Now, she wore her badge proudly, the lesbian flag all over her social media. But I'd been there during her struggles. And now here I was, practically making a scene because I was labelled gay for not hooking up with a girl the second I had a chance. She probably thought I was such an asshole.

"Look," I broke the silence, "I'm sorry. You're right. There's nothing wrong with being gay and I shouldn't care if people call me some stupid nickname. I just..." I ran my fingers through my hair, searching for the right words to accurately explain the thoughts and feelings fluttering wildly in my head. It was hard to voice the things I usually buried deep down. "...I'm just not."

"That's fine. I get it." She smiled, though it seemed forced. "I mean, I'd be horrified if someone called me straight."

She entered the classroom ahead of me and I followed, hoping that I could amend the rift I'd caused between us. During our lesson, I tried to think of a way to start up a conversation, but every time I opened my mouth, words lodged in my throat, silencing me.

At lunch, Ava told me she was going to study in the library with Eden. She invited me to join her, but I knew she didn't really want me there.

Eden and Ava were officially dating—Ava had asked her out on the school excursion—and they'd gone out to dinner over the weekend. They were keeping things on the down low, but Ava had updated me every step of the way. I could tell Eden made her happy, but I wasn't thrilled about sharing my best friend.

For the first time since Ava and I met in the art studio in year seven, I was eating alone amongst the scent of wet paint and damp brushes.

This is it, the Devil drawled, *she left you. Just like your mother did.*

***

Augustus the Gay. Roman Emperor of the Queers. These titles chased me through crowded corridors, narrow staircases, and across the vast school yard. There was nowhere the whispers did not follow.

Elysse and her friends were going out of their way to make my life miserable, to punish me for fracturing Elysse's ego. But they weren't the only ones. Alexander seemed intent on punishing me too, but I had the sense it was for an entirely different reason.

He found me in the art block, snatching my paintbrush out of my hands to wave in front of me like a wand. Dark circles decorated his green eyes, his expression empty despite the laugh that poured from his lips.

My lack of response seemed to anger him more than any word I could utter. He wanted something from me. I just wasn't sure what.

"Are you gay, then, Saint?" he drawled.

I resisted the urge to slam my fist into his face. It seemed our temporary truce was over.

"No," I said.

"You were looking at me when you were kissing her," he murmured, "did you want to kiss me instead?"

Heat flamed my cheeks, mouth void of all saliva when I swallowed. "No."

He leaned closer, fingers playing with the crucifix hanging from my neck, my breath catching in my throat when he flicked it back in my face.

"Too catholic to be queer, too queer to be catholic," he spat as he backed away, leaving me alone in the empty art room.

***

The Am I Gay Quiz glared up at me from my laptop screen, the only source of light in my dark bedroom. It was nearing midnight, and despite having an English exam the following morning, I could not bring myself to sleep or study.

The quiz waited with question one staring at me expectantly, my fingers hovering over the mouse. I was nervous, as though my answers would determine my entire future.

The first question was already a difficult one: *Are you physically attracted to a person of the same sex?* I hadn't really experienced any kind of physical attraction, so I selected unsure.

The second question asked if I'd ever wanted to kiss someone of the same gender. I selected no, not interested.

Alexander's lips crossed my vision, calling me a liar. Did I want to kiss him? No. He was an asshole. And when I looked at his lips, it wasn't with sexual desire. It was...different. He was beautiful in a way I wanted to capture with a paint brush. You could think someone beautiful without wanting to have sex with them. Mountains were beautiful, but you wouldn't kiss them.

I continued through the questions, pausing at *Has anyone ever asked you if you were gay?* I reluctantly selected yes.

I answered the remaining questions and waited, anxiously, as a loading screen prepared my results.

In the centre of the screen, it said, *You may be bisexual or on the LGBTQ+ spectrum.*

I immediately closed my laptop and reached for my phone. Without even thinking, I messaged Ava and asked: 'How did you know you liked girls?'

Three dots appeared immediately, indicating Ava was awake and typing up a response. 'You okay?' she wrote.

I sighed and left her on read, rolling over to bury my face in my pillow. I didn't want to think about it. I was just confused. There were more important things to worry about, like exams.

Sleep eventually lured me into a nightmare-fuelled slumber, one without my mother and without any flames. But the Devil remained, as always, hiding in the shadows.

In the dream, I emerged from my bedroom and stepped out into the hallway, pausing as I recognised the familiar mold-covered walls of the House on North Lane.

Cobwebs decorated the ceiling, the pale glow of a lantern illuminating the blood stains on the floor.

On the other end of the hallway, a small boy sat on the edge of a mattress that seemed to disappear into the wall. His body was facing sideways; head completely turned the other way. His brown curls were the only feature I could make out in the darkness.

As soon as I stepped forward, I was once more inside my bedroom. Confused, I reemerged out into the hallway and the boy was still there, though this time his head had turned slightly, his pale ear and jawline now visible.

I stepped forward and returned to the bedroom once more.

Shaking my head, I re-entered the hallway, the boy's head now facing the same direction as his body, the whole left side of his face now visible. He looked a bit like Auden, but the curls were all mine.

"Hello?" I called out.

The boy did not turn. I stepped forward and immediately returned to the bedroom.

Frustrated, I burst from the door and once inside the hallway, glanced toward the boy. His head had turned more in my direction, the curve of his lips drawing attention to the blood dripping down his chin. A single curl fell over his left eye, shielding it from view, though I could have sworn I saw something crawl out from it.

This time, I made sure to remain perfectly still.

One step and I would be back in my bedroom.

"Hello?" I called out again.

There was no response. No sound, other than the gentle pitter patter of rain falling on the roof.

The boy was draped in shadow, expression hidden. I risked a step forward and was immediately punished. Taking a deep breath, I opened my bedroom door and calmly stepped out into the hallway once more.

This time, the boy was facing me, his entire, terrible face illuminated by the light.

Spidery veins crawled up his pale neck and over his cheeks, curving around his eyeless sockets. Dark blood spilled from his mouth and nose, a crimson tide barrelling toward me. I backed away, but with each retreating step, the closer I seemed to get.

The boy's lips parted slowly; a dirt covered vine protruding from his mouth, slithering toward me like a snake. It found my ankle, cold and damp, crawling higher as a piercing wail erupted from the boy. It shook the room, fungi growing from the boy's rotting flesh as the vines pulled me closer and closer. The boy reached out a hand and–

I woke with a jolt, lungs gasping for air as I sat upright, a puddle of sweat dampening the sheets underneath me. Running a hand over my face, I reassured myself that it was all just a bad dream, but the taste of iron lingered on my tongue.

***

It was the last week of school before summer break. Assignments handed in; exams completed.

Since Eden only shared one of our classes, I did not have to compete for Ava's attention as often as I would at recess and lunch. We watched news bloopers on her laptop, sharing earphones, laughing hysterically until our stomachs ached.

It felt like the old days again—the days before Eden.

"Hey, are we still seeing The Conjuring 2 tomorrow night?" I asked on our way to PE, our gym uniforms conveniently 'forgotten' at home.

"Oh, shit, sorry, I forgot to tell you," Ava said. "I went to see it with Eden on Sunday night. It was so good! You'll love it!"

A lump formed in my throat, her words stunning me into silence. I swallowed my hurt, afraid of what I might say as anger, confusion and disappointment fought for dominance over my racing thoughts.

We'd been preparing to see this movie for months. We talked about it non-stop, watching promotional interviews in class when we should have been doing work. I'd been so excited.

Ava must have sensed the betrayal piercing my heart, for she added, "I can still watch it with you if you want."

"No, no, it's fine," I mumbled.

"I'm sorry," Ava said. "Eden wanted to see it and I just completely forgot."

"Completely forgot?" I repeated. "Are you serious? We've been talking about it for months!"

Ava sighed. "I know. But she's my girlfriend, okay? I got excited that she was interested in horror and wanted to watch a movie with me."

"Oh, so now that you have a girlfriend, I mean nothing to you?" I scoffed.

Careful, Augustus. Rein it in.

"That's not what I said!" Ava snapped.

"Well it's how it feels!" I snapped back.

"You're just jealous," she scoffed, shaking her head, "you're jealous because I have a girlfriend and you don't."

"Are you fucking serious?"

"Yes, I'm damn serious!"

"Ava, you're not fucking special for having a girlfriend," I said, a laugh eerily similar to the Devil's escaping my throat. "You know what you are? A bad fucking friend."

"A bad friend?" she echoed, pausing in the hallway to stand in front of me, tears swimming in her eyes. "I am the bad friend? You're the one who has been miserable and rude ever since I got a girlfriend. You don't want me to be happy unless it is with you!"

"That's not true."

Isn't it?

"Why, then? Tell me why you hate Eden so much!"

"I don't."

"Don't lie to me, Augustus!"

I ran a trembling hand over my face, swallowing back my honesty in the hope that I could repair this situation before I worsened it. The last thing I wanted was to lose Ava. I would rather be forgotten accidentally than abandoned on purpose.

"I'm sorry," I whispered. "You're not a bad friend. I'm just...disappointed."

"I know," Ava nodded, shoulders dropping. "And I'm sorry to have disappointed you. I didn't mean to. I'm just...I love Eden."

"I understand."

Liar.

"Come on," Ava said, wiping at her eyes, "We're going to be late."

CHAPTER SIXTEEN

I had always been my own worst enemy.

The moment I entered the world, loneliness haunted me like a ghost summoned to a Ouija board—only there because I allowed it. And so, I pulled out my mother's journal, knowing all that it would bring me was pain.

There were nights I contemplated burning it, watching it transform to nothing but ash and dust. But then there were nights where I was drawn to the memories of my mother, craving her presence even if only through words.

September 19, 2007

Augustus is a nightmare.
Meals he loved only a week ago now lay untouched on his plate, his stub-bornness wasting Marcus' hard-earned money. He talks back, questioning everything...even God. The other night, as we sat cuddled on the couch, he asked how to know whether he was awake or dreaming. There is something wrong with him.
And there is a violence in him when he doesn't get his way. Doors slam, holes appear in walls, hateful words spill from his lips.
He draws pictures of monsters and lies in an attempt to manipulate me. Just the other night, when I took away his crayons and pencils, he looked me in the eye and said, 'You act like you've never been bad, too.'

Nightmares plague him every night, the Devil invoking such fear that he calls out my name. When I come to him, he is asleep with his eyes wide open, eyes as black as night.

I love my son more than anything, but the Devil is fighting for his soul, and I must fight back.

I will not give up on him. I will fight until the very end to bring him with me into the Kingdom of Heaven with the Lord, our God.

I slammed the book shut. My own worst enemy—inviting pain I should have long since buried.

People like my mother lied. They made promises they didn't keep. I didn't blame them. It was only a matter of time before they uncovered the truth, before they realised I was a snake wearing the wrong skin, an actor behind a mask.

You must understand that everything was—is—my own fault. I had opportunities to cease being alone, but I was incapable of grasping onto them. Maybe, deep down, I wanted to be on my own. It was easier than being disappointed, let down.

Summer came and went. I spent all of it alone, in my room, ignoring messages from Ava asking if I wanted to go to the beach with her and Eden, or join them on a camping trip, or come over for a horror movie marathon. I did not want to be a sympathy invite, so I pushed her away.

Auden insisted on keeping me company, face buried in a book on one side of the bed while I curled up on the other, staring blankly at my bedroom wall.

I couldn't move. I could barely eat. Nothing convinced me to leave my bed. I just had no energy.

And then summer ended, and fear enveloped me in a cage only I had the key to. But I never unlocked it.

My own worst enemy.

***

I walked through the school gates with Auden by my side. Pushing his glasses up the bridge of his nose, he looked around with wide eyes, no doubt in awe at how much larger this school was compared to his former one.

With a gentle hand on his upper back, I guided him toward his form room, answering all his questions along the way. His hands were fluttering wildly in front of his chest as we neared his classmates. When I caught them staring, I moved to shield him from their judgemental gazes.

"You remember where to find me at recess and lunch if you need me?" I asked just as the bell rang.

Auden nodded enthusiastically, eyes darting in between me and his classroom. "The art block!"

My heart ached. Despite everything we had both been through, we had made it to this moment. My baby brother, all grown up. He was in secondary school, he was using his words confidently, and he was excited to learn. I was proud of him, like a father might be proud of their own son.

"I have to go inside now," he said, jerking his head toward his peers who were piling inside the classroom.

With a quick nod, I let him go. But it was hard, letting him face the world alone. Maybe I clung onto Auden so much because I wanted him to be everything I wasn't. Maybe I saw a future for him that I knew I could never have. I was afraid that if I wasn't there to guide him, he would fall and never get up. But Auden was strong—much stronger than I had ever been—and I needed to trust him.

I was late to my own form room, but I wasn't the only one. Alexander and I almost collided as we stepped through the door. His elbow pressed against my ribs, and I shot him a look. He returned it with a smirk.

Ava was in her usual seat, though it took me a moment to recognise her. Her black hair was up in two braids leading to a low bun, the strands of curls framing her face dyed a pale purple, which was against school rules. Not to mention the nose and lip piercing.

I sat down beside her with a quiet 'hello' of which she returned without looking up from her phone.

We had barely spoken over the summer, and I knew that if we had any chance of rekindling our friendship, I needed to let go of my grudge and act like nothing was wrong.

"You got piercings," I said, "they look good."

Ava seemed to brighten enough to look up. "Thanks. I already have a detention because of them."

I snorted. "That's when you know you look good."

"Damn straight," she grinned.

Throughout the day, Ava and I exchanged brief conversations in between classes, and for a while, I had hope that things would improve between us. But then...there was Eden. Always hovering. Always a thorn in my side, piercing through flesh until it bit into bone.

Within seconds of the bell ringing for recess, Eden appeared out of nowhere and threw her arms around Ava, smothering her with kisses.

Rolling my eyes, I announced that I was heading to the art rooms, but neither of them followed. They were, most likely, going to have lunch with Eden's friends.

I tried to convince myself it didn't matter now that I had Auden—now that I wasn't alone. But the hurt remained. It was hard being so easily dismissed by someone who had once made you feel like the centre of their world.

Auden was waiting by the door when I arrived, and everything in me crumbled at the tears that stained his cheeks, his shattered lenses clutched to his chest. My biggest fear had come to fruition. I wasn't there for him, and he had fallen.

"Who did this to you?!" I demanded as I crouched down in front of him, wiping away his tears with the sleeve of my blazer.

"I did."

I turned, slowly, rage reddening my vision as I settled my gaze on Alexander. Not too long ago he had said he wanted to be friends, even apologising for being an 'asshole'. And yet here he was, proudly declaring he'd laid a hand on my brother.

"What the fuck did you do to him?!" I snapped as I advanced toward him.

"We played a little game," Alexander grinned.

I punched him square in the jaw without hesitation, my knuckles groaning at the impact.

Auden inhaled sharply behind me and called my name, but the Devil had taken hold, and I let him.

The Lord said to turn the other cheek, and so I did. I gave Alexander half a second to recover from the first, unexpected blow before my fist met the left, untouched side of his face.

Not sure that is what the Lord meant, but I approve.

He staggered backwards, a string of curse words rolling off his blood-spattered tongue. Auden sniffled behind me, fuelling my rage.

"Apologise," I demanded, fingers curling around the collar of his shirt. "Apologise. Now."

Alexander opened his mouth as I forced him to his knees, the loud crunch of bone replacing what words he might have spoken. Tears filled his eyes. I smiled.

"Go to Hell," he spat.

I gripped either side of his face, tilting his head up to look at me. Seeing him so helpless at my feet brought a level of satisfaction I'd never quite felt before. "If I'm going to Hell," I whispered, leaning down so my face was mere inches from his. "I'll be taking you with me."

I released hold of his face and threw him to the ground, the Devil urging me to slam my foot into his skull.

"Go on," I encouraged, slowly stepping aside so that Alexander could look Auden in the eye. "Don't make me ask again."

Blood dribbling down his chin, Alexander looked up at Auden, pure hatred in his deep-sea green eyes. He looked like a fallen Angel, cast out of Heaven and condemned to the fires of Hell.

I waited, patience growing thin.

"I'm sorry," Alexander forced out, voice low. "It won't happen again."

"No, it won't," I agreed. "Because if you dare lay a hand on him again, I will kill you."

***

Principal Reid's office looked the same as it had five years ago, when I sat in the same chair I did now.

She had changed, though. Her hair had streaks of grey, the skin around her eyes and mouth loosening. The gentle expression she had worn back then was long gone, her anger and disappointment now lethal.

"Why did you do it?"

"I did not do it for me," I said.

A pause. "For who, then?"

"For Auden."

Principal Reid frowned and leaned back in her seat, her eyebrows furrowed as she watched me. "Why?" she repeated.

"Excuse me?"

"Why for *Auden*?"

My gaze fell to my bruised knuckles, remembering how it had felt to bring Alexander to his knees. I had failed to protect Auden once before, and I intended to never fail him again.

"He's been through enough as it is," I answered. "If Alexander had just left him—us—alone, I wouldn't have hit him."

Principal Reid clicked her tongue. "You're suspended, Mr Saint. For a week. I suggest you use this time to reflect on what your priorities are. You're a high achiever, your marks are exceptional, and I can see you doing exceptionally well. But your behaviour is a hindrance to both yourself, and the school." She pinned me with a look. "Think carefully about how you wish to proceed when you return."

I met her gaze unflinchingly. "And Alexander? What is his punishment?"

"You should concern yourself with your own punishment," she said. "You're dismissed."

***

Ava messaged me that night, asking what happened. I recounted everything whilst my body soaked in a vanilla scented bathtub, heat fogging up the mirror so I wouldn't have to endure my devilish reflection.

'You should have just walked away,' Ava replied, 'now you're suspended during an important academic year.'

'He hurt Auden,' I wrote back, 'I wasn't just going to let that go. I'm not sorry for what I did.'

'How about next time you just come to me?' Ava asked. 'I could have helped without getting you suspended.'

'Lol. How can I come to you when you're always with Eden?' I added a laughing emoji to indicate it was a joke, though I would be lying if I said there was no truth to it.

'I'm not?'

'You are.'

'You can spend time with us too.'

'And be a third wheel? No thanks.'

At this stage, I knew I should have put my phone away before things escalated beyond my control, but I was already heated with everything that happened with Alexander that I just had to release all my bottled emotions.

'No one said you had to be a third wheel,' Ava replied, 'Eden has friends you could get to know.'

'I'd rather die than be friends with sports people.'

'Wow.'

'What?'

'It's kind of fucked that you're insulting my girlfriend and her friends.'

'It's actually more fucked that your whole world revolves around Eden and you completely forget everyone else.'

Ava responded with a simple 'k' and I released a frustrated sigh as I shut off my phone and closed my eyes, surrendering to the warmth of the water. I sunk lower, and lower, until my head submerged completely under.

A crushing weight pinned me down, the smell of rotting meat and decay infiltrating my nostrils.

My eyes snapped open, the Devil's face inches from mine. His shadowed limbs macerated my chest, the bathroom light flickering to the rhythm of his manic laughter.

Snakes slithered in the water, tangling themselves around my arms and legs. Their fangs pierced my flesh, blood seeping into the soap caressing my skin.

Be still, Augustus.

Rodents crawled over the Devil's shoulders, dropping one by one to land on my chest. Pain exploded as teeth tore into my skin, claws shedding through muscle and tissue without restraint.

I screamed, but all I produced were soundless bubbles. The Devil's fingers caressed my face almost tenderly as more rats spilled over his shoulders to gnaw at my flesh. They swarmed my torso, burrowing beneath my rib cage as my organs spilled into the water.

Don't fight it, the Devil whispered as bloodied water clouded my vision, *this is your baptism.*

CHAPTER SEVENTEEN

The Devil's voice followed me every hour of every day.

It was difficult to concentrate on schoolwork with him whispering in my ear, reminding me what awaited me after death because of the demon festering in my soul.

You're feeling sorry for yourself, he whispered on the walk between ancient history to mathematics, *but it is all your fault. You drove them all away because you are not good enough. You will never be good enough.*

I tightened my grip on my bag strap and tried to shut him out, but my silence only encouraged him further.

You will always be alone. Even Auden will leave you one day. And it will just be you. And me. Forever.

I dropped my bag outside the classroom and carried my workbook and laptop inside, dumping it into my usual seat near the back window. Alexander watched me, his dark green eyes menacing. I dismissed him, as I usually did, and waited for the lesson to begin, ignoring the way the Devil described all the ways he'd dismember my classmates, starting with Alexander.

"Good afternoon, everyone," Mrs Nguyen greeted us in her usual, clipped tone. She set her laptop down beside a tall pile of papers on her desk. "As promised, I have your exam results. Overall, a good effort, though some of you appear to be neglecting your studies."

Chatter filled the room as students received their results. There were gasps, high fives, groans and curses. Alexander whooped loudly, his mark no doubt one of the higher ones in the class.

As Mrs Nguyen approached me, her usual warm smile and quiet congratulations was notably absent, the paper placed on my desk in silence.

The fifty-five percent blinked up at me in a glaring red, my ears ringing and head burning as I tried to process what I was seeing. Not once had I received anything below eighty percent. Not even in mathematics, which was definitively my worst subject. While other students may have been relieved to have passed, I felt as though the world was crumbling all around me. This could not be real.

I rummaged through the paper, reading the provided feedback, drinking it all in like a wild animal while chatter continued all around me. I overheard students comparing their marks: sixty-seven, eighty-one, seventy-nine. Alexander bragged about his ninety-six, the highest in the class, no doubt. He must have been surprised I hadn't contested him, for he whirled around in his seat and pinned me with a questioning look. I scowled and avoided his gaze, biting down on the inside of my mouth to avoid the tears that threatened to fall.

"Do you have an explanation for these results, Augustus?" Aunt Vera asked later that evening. We sat across from one another at the dining table, empty plates of food collected by Mrs Brighton as I shifted uncomfortably in my seat. I hadn't intended on informing her of my failure, but she'd caught me staring at my exam papers instead of studying at my desk.

"I...haven't been sleeping well," I murmured, which wasn't entirely a lie.

"There will be no more drawing or painting in your art studio until your marks improve," she said, "and no screen time past seven."

"But—"

"And," she cut me off, eyes narrowing, "you will complete your homework in the library where I can supervise you. Not your bedroom."

I swallowed. "You don't trust me to study?"

"I have invested far too much money in your education to risk your failure in these critical years," she replied. "You're not my child. This is not charity. You *will* improve, do you understand?"

"Yes, ma'am."

I wished I could say that my fifty-five percent was a one off, that it was a freak incident that had not repeated itself. Unfortunately, it was only the beginning.

My English essay was handed back to me with a sixty percent, my ancient history assignment a fifty-nine, and my visual arts project a sixty-five. Instead of improving, I only seemed to be getting worse.

Wow, the Devil said as I stared down at yet another low scoring assessment result, *you're not even good at school anymore. Even good grades are running away from you.*

The fifty in biology—my lowest mark yet—was a gut wound that could not be mended. I would bleed out, my body swimming in its own pool of blood.

Pathetic, really, the Devil went on, *what good are you if you're, you know, not any good? And Aunt Vera paid all this money...*

My hands curled into fists at my side, knuckles whiter than clean snow as I breathed through my racing heartbeat and nausea.

You're such a disappointment, Augustus. Really. You let Alexander win. And without even putting up a fight.

"Shut. Up," I whispered.

I can't believe you're failing everything. No, wait, I can. You ruin everything.

"I said shut up."

If you can't even maintain good grades, what can you do? You're a failure. A failure, a failure, a fail—

"SHUT UP!"

The room went silent.

Heads swivelled in my direction, some bewildered and some annoyed. Alexander stared at me as though I had grown a second head and Ava frowned, studying me like a confusing piece of art.

"Augustus?" Mr Han approached me, his eyebrows furrowed and his lips pulled down. "What's the matter?"

My cheeks warmed, leg bouncing up and down uncontrollably as I picked at my nails. I wanted to run. I wanted to run far, far away until I couldn't run anymore. And so, I did.

Without taking any of my things, I launched to my feet and sprinted out of the room.

Mr Han called out to me, but no one followed as I fled the building and travelled across the school yard. My feet guided me to the only place nearby where I felt safe. The art block. I found the empty art studio, slipped inside, and slammed the door shut behind me. As soon as I did, I pressed my back against the door and slid to the ground, my whole body trembling as ugly sobs burst from my mouth.

I cried, and cried, and cried until exhaustion took over and I merely sat with my head hung low, the Devil finally quiet.

***

The window in Principal Reid's office was open, a cool breeze wafting through to brush my curls out of my eyes. She was seated behind her desk, elbows resting on the dark oak wood while I sat in the chair across from her, my restless hands busying themselves with a piece of lint I'd torn off my sweater.

It had been a few days since my outburst in Mr Han's biology classroom, a few days since I'd deigned to attend school.

Mrs Brighton hadn't really believed I was sick, so she'd called Aunt Vera who was visiting theatres in Paris. She warned me that if I didn't resume classes, she would withdraw access to my art studio *permanently*.

And so here I was, in Principal Reid's office.

"I know year eleven can be...an adjustment," she was saying, her voice blending in with the Devil who sang church songs from the chair beside me. "But the drastic drop in your marks, your absences, your outburst...we're all very concerned for you, Augustus. Can you tell me what is going on?"

Tell her about me, I dare you.

"I'm fine." The lie slipped out of me before I could catch it. I knew I wasn't fine—far from it, actually—but I dreaded the consequences of admitting the truth. The last time I'd shared my real feelings, Ava had stopped talking to me. And although I didn't believe Principal Reid would grant me that same silent treatment, I did fear what she would force me to do.

"Do you have an explanation for what happened in Mr Han's classroom?" she asked.

"I was overstimulated," I told her, and that wasn't necessarily a lie. "I was disappointed in my results and...I lashed out. It was wrong. I'm sorry. It won't happen again."

"And your four-day absence?" she pushed on.

Tell her how you spent all day in bed. You didn't even shower, you dirty freak.

"Unwell," I forced out. "And much better now."

A quiet sigh escaped Principal Reid's throat as she leaned back in her seat, watching me.

I kept my head down, afraid that if she glimpsed my red-rimmed eyes, she'd see right through me.

"I had high hopes for you, Mr Saint," she said after an agonising moment of silence. "You're an intelligent young man. If you'd asked me who would be school Dux a month ago, I would have said you." She shook her head, disappointment darkening her features. "I don't know what is going on. And I have known you long enough to know you won't tell me what it is. But it is important you get yourself together for these final years, Augustus. Don't throw your future away. If you put your head down, and work hard, I truly believe you'll get into a university of your choosing, in any field you desire."

I swallowed hard, a heavy weight sinking into my chest. She was right. I needed to put myself back together. I owed it to myself, and Auden, to secure a good future for us. The Devil was a test I could not fail. I'd let him drive my mother away, and Ava too, but I would not let him drive away my future.

***

Sleepless nights with my face buried in a book chased the nightmares away.

My marks returned to eighty percent and above as I slipped into my final year, though the fear of failure never left, haunting me down every corridor and down every staircase.

Success was not easy to obtain, it required hours of study, exams often finding me in my dreams, where I had five minutes left to complete a one-thousand-word essay. I would wake up, in a cold sweat, the Devil on the bed beside me, laughing at the stress that had its tight grip around me.

Although Ava and Eden had separated over the summer between year twelve and thirteen, there was no attempt at rekindling our friendship. We hadn't messaged at all over our break, and upon returning to school, I only discovered their breakup when I caught Ava with a group of girls from her photography class and not Eden. Instead of approaching, I watched happiness leak from her from a distance.

My absence in her life didn't seem to weigh on her at all, but I missed her every day.

Auden kept me company at recess and lunch in the art rooms. While I worked on my final art project, he completed his homework. He still hadn't made any friends, and since final exams were fast approaching, I was growing nervous about leaving him all alone. Who would be there to protect him when I was gone? All I wanted was to amend the sins of my past. It was my fault he grew up without parents, and I wanted to give him the best chance at being a teenager and adult that I could. After all he suffered, he deserved happiness.

In between studies, I researched university courses to answer the one question everyone, including myself, had begun asking: What do you want to do after school?

University was the logical answer. I was studious, so pursuing academia made sense. I wasn't good with my hands, so a trade was out of the question. And while I enjoyed art, and received praise from my teacher often, I could not see a future where I could live off my art. The world did not respect the arts, and while it was a nice dream to pursue your passion, I knew that I needed something stable, something I could live off.

But, apart from art, there was nothing I was particularly passionate about. I liked reading, history, and writing—but the only options before me were being a teacher, a librarian, or a museum collections manager. None of those screamed at me with enthusiasm.

All around me, my classmates seemed to know exactly what they wanted to do. Teacher, nurse, doctor, lawyer, news presenter, pilot, photographer, event planner. One by one, they enrolled in courses designed to aid them in their future career, and I was left with no idea of what I wanted to do.

It was not until one night, alone in my room, that a spark ignited. A small spark, not enough to light a fire, but enough to form an idea.

My mother's journal was in my hands, her panicked handwriting staring up at me with startling clarity.

February 27, 2009

God speaks to me in my dreams. He tells me my son is possessed by the Devil. He gives me instructions on what to do, and I feel his presence when I tighten the restraints around Augustus' wrists, withholding food until he apologises for misbehaving.

Marcus says I am insane, but he doesn't understand. Everything I do...I do for our family. Jesus was accused of being crazy too. The son of God! If I am crazy, then crazy I am. I will not give up on my family.

To kill the Devil, my son must die. And that is a sacrifice I am prepared to make.

The words should have stung. But instead, relief loosened my shoulders, gently cascading over muscles that had known nothing but tension. My mother did not hate *me*. She hated the Devil.

God spoke to her, just like the Devil spoke to me. But while God made her lock me in dark rooms and paint me with bruises, the Devil merely conjured violence in my head. I saw him, and heard him, but was he really there? Why didn't he just make me kill Elysse, instead of merely making me *believe* I did?

You fight me because I am the Devil. Your mother would not have fought God, for he is good. She let him in.

My eyes locked on the words 'insane' and 'crazy', the letters around them blurring until they were the only two words on the page. My father thought my mother was crazy...Elysse had called me crazy too.

I flicked through the remaining pages of the journal, the words 'insane' and 'crazy' jumping out at me in big, bold letters. They danced atop the pages, mocking me, daring me to confront them.

Was my mother crazy? And if she was, did that mean *I* was crazy too?

I slammed the journal shut and glanced toward my desk where my biology textbook lay open, a diagram of a brain and all its different systems luring me closer until I was at my chair, reading about the frontal lobe and how it controlled decision-making, judgement and behaviour. I vaguely remembered Mr Han talking about the different functions of the brain in class, and how the frontal lobe didn't fully develop until humans reached their mid-to-late twenties. That was why, he said, teenagers often engaged in risk-taking activities without processing the consequences.

Chin resting on my hand, I read through the entire chapter specifically focused on the brain, the words 'insane' and 'crazy' still roaming my head. Maybe there was a physiological explanation for my mother's behaviour, a *psychological* reason. It would explain why everyone else around us—including my father—didn't hear or see the Devil. Maybe my mother was unwell. Maybe I was too.

I wanted to know what was real and what wasn't. I wanted to know the truth. And maybe...there was a way to figure all that out.

CHAPTER EIGHTEEN

"I want to study Psychology," I announced at breakfast.

Auden nodded enthusiastically while he chewed on dry toast, ever the supportive little shadow.

"Psychology is quite a broad field," Aunt Vera said as she lowered her teacup. "What would you like to do with a psychology degree? Become a psychiatrist?"

"Yes, I think so," I answered, reaching for my glass of water.

"What spurred that decision?" she asked. She was watching me, closely, as if searching for something.

"I have an interest in the human mind and behaviour," I said, avoiding her gaze. "I have a lot of questions I want to answer."

"Well, there is good money to be made in Psychiatry. Society is...increasingly unwell."

"So, do you approve?"

"I do."

Relief flooded through me, shoulders dropping as a long breath escaped my throat. "I'll start applying, then."

***

University applications were a nightmare. They were several pages long, littered with repetitive questions, and required a personalised letter alongside my current grades, and infuriatingly, my work experience—that of which I didn't have.

Final exams were approaching, and the stress was building. The fear of failure was a ghoul clawing through my chest. My memory, which had once been so clear, was failing me with every practice question I slaved away at. It became a very *real* possibility that I would fail and not be accepted into *any* university, prestigious or not.

The anxiety had me crying myself to sleep, the idea of failing after years of success more traumatic than having my own mother try to exorcise me. I knew that compared to some of my classmates, I had no reason to cry. My grades were high, and I'd basically secured full marks for my final visual arts project. Yet that self-doubt remained.

"You need to eat," Auden said from my bedroom doorway the night before my first exam. He was in his dressing gown, headphones around his neck and a book tucked under his arm. "There is food downstairs. Mrs Brighton says it will go cold soon."

"I'm not hungry," I murmured.

"But you have an exam tomorrow," Auden frowned, entering the room to stand behind my desk, his shadow darkening the pages of my notebook. "You can't go into the exam hungry."

"I can't stomach food right now," I sighed.

"How about a drink, then? I can make you some chocolate milk."

I knew Auden just wanted to help, so even though I didn't particularly feel like a hot chocolate, I nodded, watching him hurry out of the room with purpose.

When he returned, I gave him a grateful smile and took a small sip while he made himself comfortable on my bed, a book open on his lap. I didn't mind his company. In fact, it seemed to settle my racing heartbeat and ease the choir of self-doubt corrupting my mind.

That night, no tears followed me into my dreams.

***

Silence swallowed the examination hall, the only sound the tap, tap, tap of an examiner's heels as she walked up and down the rows of desks, students with their heads down, hands curled around their pens.

English literature was my second-best subject behind visual arts, and despite my lack of confidence going in, the questions aroused a mountain of knowledge that spilled onto the page with ease. I quoted the metaphors, analysed their meaning, and linked the overall themes back to the question.

By the time the exam was over, my wrist ached and my head pounded with exhaustion.

As we all emerged from the hall, chaos ensued. Students compared their answers, chatting about how ridiculous the stimuli were, and cheered because their first exam was over.

I had no one to celebrate with. My eyes drifted toward Ava who was in a circle of girls, all talking loudly about the Macbeth quotes they used for the second essay. I wanted to ask Ava how she did, but I couldn't bring myself to walk over knowing that she had not once looked for me in the crowd.

The next exam was the same. I finished fifteen minutes early, read over everything twice, and left the hall without a word to anyone. No one asked me how I did, no one asked me to compare answers, no one acknowledged me at all.

***

Summer came and went in a flash. I worked part time at a local grocery store, stocking shelves and serving at the counter. It was boring, and I was often subjected to unnecessary verbal abuse, but it helped me save up money for university.

As soon as I received my exam results, the offers came flooding in. Some with scholarships, some without. I decided on Dawnridge University, a reputable school with a thoroughly funded Psychology department. My first year would be covered by a scholarship, the second year dependent on my overall grade. But, like most things in life, there was a downside. I'd have to leave Cambridge.

"You can stay on campus," Great Aunt Vera told me. "Or you can rent a unit nearby and commute to school."

"But what about Auden?"

Aunt Vera looked puzzled for a moment and when she opened her mouth to speak, she was cut off by her phone ringing.

I sighed, returning to my laptop to search for affordable accommodation while the Devil hovered behind me, sharp claws digging into my shoulders. He made no comments about my acceptance into Dawnridge's psychology degree, nor had he seemed panicked about the move. There was an unusual sense of calm about him. It was suspicious.

My phone lit up, eyes drifting from an overpriced two-bedroom apartment to a notification from Alexander Parsons. A friend request. I scoffed. The audacity. Curious, I clicked on his profile and scoured through his most recent posts, finger hovering above a photo of him with his acceptance letter from Oxford University. I slumped back in my chair, disappointment and envy wrapping around me as I stared at the Oxford logo.

I had been rejected, of course. Oxford had been a dream of mine, but it would be Alexander's reality. He beat me—and that was a wound I wasn't sure I could stitch up. It felt like I would be bleeding for eternity.

You just weren't good enough.

✳✳✳

A week before I was set to leave Cambridge, Auden and I walked along the luscious green grass separating the River Cam from the city's gothic architecture, the summer sun warming our cheeks. We shared a box of chips, chewing quietly while children flew kites around us.

Auden was not thrilled about the move. He was a creature of habit, thriving in the familiar, and a change in environment challenged his sense of safety. I proposed, even though it pained me, that he stayed with Aunt Vera. He refused.

"Your new school looks nice," I said, glancing down at him with a chip raised to my lips.

"Really?"

"Mhm. I looked up some photos." I pulled out my phone to let him swipe through. "The library is huge."

"What about our new place?" he asked.

"It's...nice enough," I said. "Close to public transport. And a bookstore! Isn't that cool?"

Auden brightened at that. "Can we visit the bookstore every day?"

"Of course we can!" I grinned, wrapping an arm around his shoulders, shaking him gently. "I'll even let you buy a book our first day!"

"Thank you, Guses!" he beamed.

I opened my mouth to respond when out of the corner of my eye, I recognised a group of girls from my school year who were seated on a beige picnic rug, plates of food in their hands as they laughed at something one of them had said. Ava was amongst them, head on Eden's shoulder, giggling. They must have been talking again.

Walk away, Augustus, she doesn't care about you.

Knowing this was probably the last time I would ever see her, I disregarded the Devil's advice and slowly made my way toward her, hands trembling at my sides.

Ava looked up, and when her eyes met mine, her smile faded and she turned away, pulling Eden in closer.

The rejection was clear. I couldn't even be angry; it was all my fault.

Averting my gaze, I returned to Auden, leaving behind Ava and all our shared memories.

No one cares about you, little monster. Everyone leaves. At least you understand that now.

PART III

CHAPTER NINETEEN

As a boy, I feared the voices.

They nested inside my skull, feasting on the terror and revulsion born from the Devil's merciless embrace. His voice led the assault, his demons never far behind. When they spoke, when they taunted, I did everything I could to drown them out.

As a boy, I feared the voices.

As a man, I welcomed them.

It was all about mastering control. Once I realised the voices lived, and died, with me, there was nothing left to fear.

When they spoke, when they taunted, I listened.

Maybe that was my downfall.

I waited for the moment they stepped out of line, cutting deep into my pale flesh, blood falling freely as a reminder of just who was in control. And like clockwork, the voices scattered, hiding in the crevices of my mind I dared not touch. One thing was clear: they could not survive without me.

The only voice that did not fear my death was the Devil. He would follow me anywhere, dragging me into the fires of Hell with his sharp talons and crooked grin.

He was the only voice that challenged my control, stealing the reins when reality became distorted.

Here in the House on North Lane, though, he wasn't the only voice whispering in my ear.

A candle flickered to announce her presence. The ghost of North Lane. My mother.

I stood by the splintered window of my old bedroom, breathing in the only ounce of freedom the House would allow.

Smothered by swirling black clouds, the moon's pale glow vanished beneath a cloak of darkness, the trees surrounding North Lane transforming into monsters of bark and leaves.

"Augustus."

The candle flickered out, plunging the room in darkness. I breathed in slowly, steadying my racing heart.

The voice was barely a whisper, easily mistaken as a sigh. Too soft to be the Devil. Too gentle.

I turned, slowly, an eerie emptiness staring back.

"Augustus."

The voice came from the hallway, and I followed, as though in a trance.

"Augustus."

The hallway was empty, dark—a thick dampness tainting the air. A dead rat rotted in the centre of the wooden floorboards, cobwebs spilling across the ceiling. A wooden beam groaned above me, the House and I once more at odds with one another.

"Show yourself!" I demanded.

I was sick of the games. I wanted her to face me; to confront the monstrous demon she'd always claimed me to be.

"Or are you too afraid?" It was my turn to taunt, voice mirroring the Devil's. "You know I can't kill you twice, right?"

A flicker of white flew past me, a barely visible apparition that descended the staircase before I could process what I had seen. I followed, quickly, floorboards grunting with every step.

In the centre of the living room stood a figure, a white mist emanating from within the faded chalk pentagram.

"Mother?"

"Augustus."

The voice did not come from the figure standing in the circle. It came from behind me, urgent. Pleading.

I peeled my eyes away from the faceless mist and turned. The second my eyes landed on the solid figure standing at the top of the staircase, everything in me crumbled.

"You..." I breathed out, hand reaching to steady myself on the cold, dust-drenched railing. "It's you."

CHAPTER TWENTY

Rain chased me up the wide, uneven steps of Dawnridge University, brown locks glued to my forehead. Wet leaves clung to my shoes. Water soaked through my backpack. And, most gratingly, my brown woollen sweater had begun to secrete the distinct, earthy scent of lanolin.

I released a long sigh, gaze drifting up toward Dawnridge's towering spires, grey stone adorned with moss. Deep green vines crawled along the sculpted scholars that lined its walls, small cracks birthing hints of lichen.

A heavy wooden door, framed in a detailed arch, guided me inside. It groaned shut, condemning me to a damp chill that poured from its ancient walls.

Wet footprints coated the marble floor. They darted in all different directions as students and teachers flocked to their respective classes.

It was day one of a three-year bachelor's degree in Psychological and Behavioural Science. A two-year post-graduate degree to follow, and then a doctorate—the end goal to be a clinical psychiatrist. It was a long and arduous journey, but I had one goal. To understand what happened to my mother, and what was happening to me. I was going to prove to myself that I was *good,* and that I could achieve *good* things. I was not the Devil, and he was not me.

Nervous anticipation clawed through my insides, nausea bubbling up the closer I got to the lecture hall. I was early—half an hour, to be exact—so I found an unoccupied bench and sat down, legs bouncing wildly.

Wanting a distraction, I pulled out my phone and logged on to social media. Ava and I had not unfollowed each other *yet*, so her post was the first to appear on my screen. She was standing in front of the Birmingham University entrance. According to her caption, she was studying Art and Design. Her smile was wide, joy pouring from her in endless waves. I debated liking the photo but continued scrolling instead.

We were both too stubborn to apologise, neither one of us willing to be the first to break. Perhaps we meant less to each other than we initially thought. It didn't matter. I didn't need her. I didn't need *anyone*. I had Auden, and that was enough.

A notification from my manager, Edith Browning, lit up my screen. I clicked on the message, sighing as she asked whether I could work that afternoon. Knowing I had a full schedule of classes, I replied apologetically, explaining that my semester had begun and my availability had changed. When she didn't respond, my stomach cramped with guilt.

Two weeks prior, when Auden and I first moved to Guildford, I applied for a job at *Browning Books*, a small family-owned business selling second-hand books donated or sold by members of the community. It was only a ten-minute walk from the unit I rented, convenient since I had not gotten my driver's licence and did not want to spend what little money I had on public transport more than necessary. Aunt Vera made it clear she would not be a bank.

Mr Browning, an elderly man dressed in suspenders over a white collared shirt and brown trousers, wanted to retire. His daughter, Edith, worked at the bookstore six days a week and required some part-time work now that her father would no longer be working alongside her.

She was a cheerful woman, with mid-length strawberry blonde hair that she often wore in a loose ponytail, her bright blue eyes always scouring for things that needed tending to in store.

A high school student named Penny could only work weekends and school holidays, so I was hired to offer Edith extra support.

It was a good job. On most days, it was just Edith and me in the store, sorting through recent donations and choosing which books to prioritise on the shelves. The store was not a large one. It had a small wooden counter near the entrance with a cash register as old as Mr Browning and a grandfather clock from the early nineteenth century. There were four aisles, with tall dark oak bookshelves on either side. General fiction, romance and literary classics were in aisle one, fantasy and science fiction in aisle two, young adult and children's fiction in aisle three, and non-fiction in aisle four. Books that did not fit into these categories were scattered throughout.

Auden loved the bookstore. He visited often when I worked, not wanting to be in our new unit alone. Edith didn't seem to mind when he took a book off the shelf and read it quietly at the counter while I served customers and repriced stock. He hadn't been thrilled about the move, so having somewhere he grew to love like *Browning Books* was a good start to getting him adjusted.

Prior to the start of university, I was working every day from Wednesday to Sunday, but with university starting, my work hours were limited. I could only work Mondays, Fridays, Saturdays and Sundays. This was made clear to Edith prior to my being hired, but still, guilt ate away at me the longer I went without a reply. I hated the idea of disappointing someone, especially with my history of doing so. I wanted Guildford to be a fresh start. A new beginning.

As it neared nine am, I rose from the bench and approached the lecture hall, teeth chattering, though not from the cold.

The outdoor gothic architecture had creeped inside, grotesque sculptures of bats and the undead hung above images of saints on the smooth, stone pillars holding up the arched ceiling.

Dawnridge University had not always been a school. In the early sixteenth century, it had been a Cathedral and home to hundreds of monks, priests and important Christian figures. The campus had of course expanded since then, with many modern buildings adjoining the original architecture, but its religious history was evident everywhere in the lecture hall. It was a reminder that God was watching me from the stained-glass windows.

Rows upon rows of brown pews lined the first floor of the lecture hall, students scattered throughout; some in groups, some seated alone. I debated heading upstairs to the second floor but stopped when I heard laughter from above. I didn't want to risk distraction. Deciding to take the last row on the first floor, I sat at the very end with my laptop open, fingers drumming against the flimsily attached desk with my knee bobbing to the same rhythm.

Students flooded in the closer it got to 9am. At 8:55, the projector on stage flickered on and the words *An Introduction to Psychological Studies* lit the screen.

There were dozens of students in the hall by the time a tall, slim man with short white hair and a trimmed white beard stepped up onto the stage, a book under his arm and a takeaway coffee cup in his hand. He wore brown trousers and a brown, grey and black plaid jacket over a tan collared shirt. His glasses slipped down his narrow nose, thin lips tugged up into a polite smile as he looked out at the students flooding the hall.

"Ah, so many fresh, young faces," he said, book and coffee cup discarded onto his lectern. "Many of you still have light in your eyes. Welcome to Dawnridge! And to those of you without that light in your eye, welcome back to Hell!"

He laughed at his own attempt at humour while everyone else shifted uncomfortably in their seats, my legs bouncing more wildly than ever. If anyone had sat in my pew, they would have certainly felt it. Thankfully, no one even looked my way.

"My name is Doctor Elijah Graham, and I was a practicing psychiatrist for..." he stroked his chin in thought, "...nearly fifty years. I went into academia to further my research on trauma and the brain. My research days are nearing an end, but I am thrilled to be here with you all, passing my knowledge down to every brilliant mind here."

He went through some introductory slides with definitions of terms that would be used throughout our course. Biopsychology, behavioural neuroscience, empirical evidence, cognitive perspectives, nature versus nurture. I noted everything, determined to memorise every word in order to secure a scholarship for my second year. According to email correspondence with the university's student advisory team, I required a High Distinction in all eight subjects that I completed over the first two semesters. One slip up would mean I would have to *beg* Aunt Vera for financial aid or apply for government assistance—an undesirable debt either way. My *only* option—succeed.

"Since it is only your first day," Professor Graham said as he switched off the projector, "I don't want to spend the whole hour *lecturing* you. I want to engage you all in a...friendly competition."

I closed my laptop wearily as whispers echoed through the hall.

"I want you all to divide into two groups," Professor Graham went on, "one group form a line to my left...and the other my right."

No one moved.

"Come on," Graham waved his hands enthusiastically, "get up! get up!"

I reluctantly approached the left side of the room since it was closer, many students doing the same.

No one quite knew what was going on, but there was a hum of anticipation in the air.

"Now," Graham smiled, "one by one in the order you've lined up in, you will come on stage and compete in a simple game of trivia. The winner of each round will remain on the stage and compete against the next person until there is only one person standing in the end. One student could win every round and make it to the end or lose to their final opponent who is the last to compete, stealing the victory. It is all about luck and intelligence."

There was a collective groan. I, myself, debated fleeing before I had the chance to get up on stage. There were eleven students in front of me. If I left at that very moment, no one would know. But something gave me pause.

"The winner," Dr Graham said, "will earn a personal recommendation for the Dean's Merit Award. This will open *many* opportunities for you, including scholarships, paid fieldwork, and extra credit. Not to mention an exclusive dinner with the Dean and Dawnridge's Psychology Board."

A personal recommendation. For the Dean's Merit Award. For the scholarship. This could be my ticket in. If I had a recommendation, *and* my grades were good, how could they possibly refuse? I would have security. I would be able to breathe, knowing I was set on the right path.

Interest flooded the room as many students became more enthusiastic about the challenge.

One by one, students from both teams were called up to the stage to answer a question. Topics ranged from popular culture, animals, history, science, politics, sport, and, of course, psychology.

The first five players on my team had lost to a tall, dark-skinned male with short black hair, his lips pulled up into a polite smile with every correct answer that rolled off his tongue. That same smile faded, however, when the sixth player on my team beat him, only to last one round before she too was booted off the stage.

As my turn neared, my stomach flipped erratically. Sweat moistened my hands. Heat flamed my cheeks. I needed a bathroom, desperately. Taking deep breaths, hands fluttering at my sides, I focused on my end goal and what winning would mean for me. I needed to do this. For myself. And for Auden's future.

Player eleven was eliminated and it was my turn to grace the stage. I approached on shaky legs, doing my best to focus on my opponent and no one else. She was a tall young woman with long black waves that rolled down to her elbows, black-framed glasses magnifying her brown eyes. She had surpassed the last six players on my team, and she looked me up and down like she would surpass me too.

"Your question is…" Dr Graham started, reading from a card in his hands. "…how many ribs does a human skeleton have?"

"Twenty-four!" I answered instantly, my voice louder than I intended due to the adrenaline hammering through my veins.

"Correct!" Graham boomed, satisfaction flooding through me at the glower on my opponent's face.

I watched her walk off, one leg shifting from the other. This was it. If I could make it through every question thrown at me, I really could win that recommendation.

Each student from the right side came up and then went back down. The questions seemed to be in my favour, answers pouring from my tongue before my opponent could even part their lips. The recommendation was within my grasp. I was going to win. I had almost dethroned every member of the right team when *he* stepped up.

He approached with an air of confidence I hadn't seen in any of my previous opponents. Hands tucked into his grey trousers, a sage knitted vest over the top of his white collared shirt, he stepped up onto the stage, his tall frame towering over mine. His black hair flopped over his forehead, parting in the middle to reveal clear, smooth skin above his chestnut, oval brown eyes. Bow-shaped lips pulled into a smile, he held out his hand to me and wished me luck.

Caught a little off guard, I shook his hand silently before averting my gaze.

"The question is...which planet in our solar system has the most volcanoes?"

My mind blanked and my opponent answered with a carefree, "Venus, Sir."

"Correct!"

Heat climbed to my cheeks, every cell in my body forming a protest as I glared at my opponent—glared at the one responsible for snatching my win. He gave me a wink and a smirk as I walked off stage, and my body only burned hotter. I wanted to gouge out his eyeballs and slice the smirk right off his face. Instead, I dumped myself into my seat with a scowl and watched my opponent beat every single person from my team as though the questions were designed purely for him.

"Well, it seems we have a clear winner," Dr Graham announced with a pleased smile as he gestured to my tall, smiling opponent. "Can I get a round of applause for my first recommendation, Nathaniel Carrington!"

***

The first semester at Dawnridge was overwhelming. Late nights cramming for exams. Early mornings skim reading the required articles for a nine am class. Assignments submitted seconds before the midnight deadline. Between work and study, I rarely had time for my art. Sketchbooks lay abandoned on my bedroom floor; paint brushes dry from disuse.

But the intense study load was worth it. I was at the top of every class—except one. In *Introduction to Psychological Studies,* I was ranked second. Ranks were exclusive to Dawnridge University. To 'encourage competitiveness' that would lead to 'patterns of success.' It only made me anxious. I needed to be number one, but there was one student who bested me in every assignment. One student who buzzed around like a fly I could not squash.

Nathaniel Carrington.

And to make matters worse, he wasn't even a psychology student. He was in his second year of *medicine* and had selected *Introduction to Psychological Studies* as an elective. He was *electively* beating me.

His hand was always raised to answer a question—a long, over-explained response that should have been five words at most—shifting in his chair to face the rest of us as though *he* were our teacher.

I often had the urge to tear his arm from his socket and slap him right across the face with it. Instead, I took notes of every word that rolled off his tongue, underlining words I intended to find the definitions of so I could reassure myself I wasn't all that far behind. I could be his equal, if I tried hard enough. No, I could be *better*.

You couldn't even best Alexander, and Nathaniel is smarter than him.

He laughed at Professor Graham's jokes, insisted on calling him *doctor*, and requested further reading material at the end of every class. I remained behind, pretending to take extra time packing my bag, when I was really recording every title that Professor Graham recommended Nathaniel. I couldn't let him get ahead.

No one else seemed to share my disdain. He was popular, a swarm of wasps he called friends always around him as though he were a rare flower they needed to pollinate. Even those who weren't a part of his friend group seemed to worship him, congratulating him on every success.

As part of our second assignment, we were required to respond to at least three students' discussion posts. And, of course, he chose *mine* to interrogate.

His condescending, and incorrect response contradicted every statement I made. It wasn't a requirement to defend ourselves in the comments, but I did anyway, dismissing all his counter arguments with evidence from multiple peer-reviewed articles. If there was one thing I always insisted on being, it was right.

Unfortunately, Nathaniel appeared to share this mindset, for he responded once more, using his own 'evidence' to support his incorrect claims. This back-and-forth continued all night, the discussion board flooded with our repeated arguments. In the end, Nathaniel ended our debate with: 'Let's agree to disagree.'

We hadn't spoken in person, not since he won Professor Graham's personal recommendation. I doubted he even realised that the *Augustus Saint* he had argued with on the discussion board was the same one he'd faced that very first day. I probably never even crossed his mind, just a dark cloud being chased out of his sunlight.

He had certainly crossed mine, though. And it wasn't even just about securing the Dean's Merit Award or the scholarship. It was about knocking him off his golden throne; about making him sweat. I wanted him to have to *fight* for that number one ranking, for everything else seemed to come to him so easily.

I watched him sit in the front row of every class, friends circling him like birds waiting to be thrown a bite of bread. They craved his attention, waiting for a smile or a laugh, or even just a glance.

A permanent scowl on my face deterred anyone from sitting near me. I did not care. I was used to not having friends. And the friends I did make were only temporary, so what was the point? I was not like Nathaniel. I did not need an ensemble of adoring fans.

I built a cage around my heart and gave no one the key.

CHAPTER TWENTY-ONE

The second semester at Dawnridge brought with it endless rain and merciless deadlines. Students splashed through puddles, black coats and flimsy umbrellas raised above their heads as they sprinted between classes. Some mornings, there was snow—a blanket of white draped over the grass. By the afternoon, it had melted.

I was enrolled in four new classes, one of which was an elective subject where I was once again competing against Nathaniel Carrington. For someone enrolled in a medical degree, he sure seemed invested in psychology. And good at it, too.

Psychological Manipulation proved to be a rather difficult subject. A surprise to me, really, considering the course outline listed seemingly simple topics such as ethical versus unethical psychological tactics, human vulnerability to manipulation, the Milgram study, gaslighting, cult psychology, propaganda and psychological manipulation theories, to name a few. Science and statistical analysis—which I found somewhat more challenging in other subjects—were not required. And yet, I received a disappointing seventy-six percent on my essay: Foundations of Manipulation. A Distinction. It was a blow to the gut. I needed to secure a High Distinction for the remainder of the semester, or my second-year scholarship was as good as gone.

Despite the low mark, there was only *one* student ahead of me. Nathaniel, of course. He'd received an eighty percent, just falling short of a High Distinction. Clearly, I wasn't the only one struggling.

We were warned *Psychological Manipulation* would be a challenging subject during our very first lecture, but it was obvious Nathaniel had never received such a low mark before. His fingers raked through his black hair until it was sticking up in all different directions, teeth nibbling on his bottom lip until he tore skin, blood staining his teeth. He didn't relax until our Professor, Helen Haywood, announced the course ranking—as was the Dawnridge way—and he was crowned first place. My name followed his, and when it did, Nathaniel glanced over his shoulder to look at me.

I met his gaze, unflinching. We had two more assessments until our final grade was etched in stone. Two more opportunities to replace him at the top and secure the scholarship for myself.

Or he will defeat you, like Alexander did.

The Devil's voice slithered into my thoughts, but I ignored it. Nathaniel wasn't Alexander. And Dawnridge wasn't Trinity College. I was going to succeed. I was finally going to be *good* at something.

***

Sunlight poured in through the stained-glass windows of the lecture hall, heat radiating off the wooden pews as spring chased away winter. I rolled up the sleeves of my black-buttoned shirt, my jacket discarded on the back of my chair as Professor Haywood entered with a stack of books and a joke about the psychological manipulation she underwent to make it to class on time.

Haywood was young compared to most of the teaching staff I had encountered thus far. She couldn't have been beyond thirty-five, her dark brown hair always tied neatly into a mid-length ponytail, her high-waisted trousers matching the colour of her blazer. She was nearing the end of her doctorate, specialising in, you guessed it, psychological manipulation. Her research focus was the criminal mind. And this week's topic: The Psychology of Cults.

I opened my laptop and created a new word document, fingers hovering over the keyboard as the Devil whispered, *speaking of cults, remember when you were briefly part of one?*

I swallowed my retort, gaze flicking toward the empty front row. Where was Nathaniel? The door opened. And there he was—Mr top-of-the-class know-it-all with his band of loyal kiss-ups.

The large group shuffled into their seats, filling up the entire first row. Their incessant laughter echoed along the walls, the Devil and I scowling with displeasure. University required a level of sophistication and professionalism that Nathaniel and his friends seemed to lack. This was not high school. And yet they smiled and kicked back in their chairs as though none of this really mattered. Except Nathaniel, I observed, who sat up straight with his attention on Professor Haywood like a magnet to iron.

I studied the back of Nathaniel's rustic knitted vest and the white collared shirt he wore underneath. His sleeves had been rolled up to his elbows, the silver chain around his wrist dangling every time he lifted his arm. He always dressed the same. Brown, black or grey trousers. A knitted vest of various colours. A white collared shirt. I had never seen him in a hoodie and sweats like most students who had morning classes, arriving in whatever they had worn to bed.

"Cults are the shared beliefs and practices of a small group, often religious or spiritual in nature, that is directed toward a particular figure or object," Professor Haywood began her lecture. "There have been many famous cults throughout history, you may have heard of the Manson family, the Peoples Temple, or the Fundamentalist Church of Jesus Christ of Latter-Day Saints."

As Professor Haywood went through her slides, my mind wandered to the God's Soldiers Church. It had been a long time ago, and yet it was hard to forget. There were many attributes of a cult that I could apply to Joe and his devout congregation.

1) Social isolation. Outside of our immediate family and the Church, my mother didn't interact with anyone. Uncle Brady was banned from the house. And I didn't even know Great Aunt Vera existed until long after my mother had left.

2) Leadership control. Joe was God's 'special soldier', a leader who claimed to have had frequent communication with Him. This gave him authority over his members.

3) Unreasonable fears. My mother believed Auden and I were possessed by the Devil. And Joe only perpetuated this belief.

4) A belief that the leader was always right. My mother hung off every word Joe said. Without question.

Throughout the lecture, it was becoming increasingly apparent that I had, very briefly, been a member of a cult. And my mother most likely underwent significant psychological manipulation that led to that fateful night in North Lane.

Do you feel guilty for hating her now?

The Devil's voice was mocking, as though he enjoyed the questions and doubts circling my mind, unable to find purchase.

I did not know how to feel. She was convinced of my possession long before we joined the cult. Even if she was manipulated into conducting the exorcism, it didn't change the abuse she inflicted on me prior to meeting Joe.

But maybe we should have tried harder to find her. To help her escape Joe's grasp. Why hadn't we ever found her? Did she want to leave, or was it all manipulation?

"What makes a cult so appealing?" Haywood's question cut through my spiralling thoughts, returning me to the present.

A raised hand caught her attention, and Nathaniel answered, voice as smooth as a slow current, "Cults provide a sense of community."

"Yes," Haywood nodded, flicking over to the next slide. "Cults often appeal to people who are lonely, a victim, an outcast, part of a minority, etcetera. They want a community of like-minded individuals because humans, at our very core, crave belonging."

"And," Haywood went on, "people are easier to manipulate when they're desperate to belong."

I raised my hand, a question burning my tongue. It wasn't like me to speak up in class, but this topic had piqued my interest enough to overpower my anxiety.

"Yes, Mr Saint?"

"Many religious groups fall under the definition of a cult," I said, "are we categorising *all* cults as dangerous organisations that prey on the vulnerable?"

"That is a good question," Haywood said. "The word 'cult' does have negative connotations and there are indeed many harmless religious organisations that fall under the broad definition, but when *we* discuss cults in this class, we're referring to groups that display the attributes we discussed earlier. Leadership control, social isolation, etcetera."

Nathaniel raised his hand. "What is the difference between religious institutions like...the Catholic Church, for example, and your local deranged cult?"

"The Catholic Church doesn't socially isolate you," I answered before Haywood could. "That would be one difference, for starters."

Heads swivelled in my direction, but my gaze was on Nathaniel whose eyebrows shot up with interest. "That is debatable. What is your definition of social isolation?"

"Oh, that's easy. An absence of belonging, engagement with others, and social contact."

"The Catholic Church fails to create a sense of belonging when you're, I don't know, *gay*, for example," Nathaniel said, and I could have sworn his jaw clenched.

"But that's not what we're discussing," I said, "a cult would isolate you from friends, family, and coworkers because they have a different worldview. The Catholic Church might not accept you into the community, but they won't keep you from *yours*."

Nathaniel shook his head. "The lines blur when your family places significant value on the church."

He's got you there.

"It's not the same," I said.

"How is it not?" Nathaniel challenged.

"By definition, cults are typically *small* groups," I defended my stance calmly. "The Catholic Church is a large institution. It is not a cult."

"You make an excellent point," Haywood cut in before Nathaniel could respond. "There are over one billion Catholics in the world. By definition, it is not a cult but a religious institution."

I smiled, satisfied with my small win.

The remainder of the lecture went as it usually did. Nathaniel answered all the questions and received praise that lit up his face when he turned to his friend beside him, probably to brag. I knew all the answers too, but my fear of drawing attention to myself yet again kept me from raising my hand. I had already debated in front of the class and that alone had made me want to crawl out of my skin.

Toward the end of the lecture, Professor Haywood began discussing the requirements for our second assessment: a literature review on the theories regarding the types of people more at risk of being psychologically manipulated.

A stress headache pounded against my skull. I had other assessments due around the same time, and between work, classes, and Auden, I was struggling to manage my time effectively. But literature reviews were quite simple—all I had to do was compare theories from other academics and determine common themes or common variances. And yet, the pressure remained. This was my chance to overthrow Nathaniel and take his crown. I didn't want to waste it.

Why bother? He'll just win like Alexander did.

The second Professor Haywood ended the lecture, I fled the hall. A warm breeze caressed my curls, brushing them off my forehead as I made the short trek to the library. I was looking forward to an hour of solitude before my next class. Unfortunately, however, fate wrapped its cold hands around me and tugged me back.

"Saint!"

I came to an abrupt halt. No one called out to me. Ever. For a full minute, I thought that maybe it was just the Devil in my ear playing a trick on me, but then I heard quiet panting, and I turned, slowly, gaze resting on Nathaniel, his cheeks red from running to catch up with me.

"Hey! I'm Nathaniel." A flash of white teeth blinded me when he smiled, his hand outstretched towards mine. Black ink decorated the inside of his wrist, the number eleven etched in small roman numerals above his bulging blue veins.

"I know," I said, leaving his hand untouched between us.

The smile never left his face as he lowered his hand and slipped it into the pocket of his grey trousers, brown eyes radiating warmth like honey being poured into tea.

"I look forward to working with you again this semester," he said, tilting his head slightly to avoid the sunlight kissing his warm, golden skin. "You are doing well in this module. Second place, right?"

A sharp exhale erupted from me. He *knew* I was second to him. He *knew* and yet he phrased it like a question. My hand twitched with the need to slap the smile right off his stupid face and bury it where no one would ever find it.

Why does he make you so angry?

"Far below your level, I expect," I drawled sarcastically, ignoring the Devil's question, "you wouldn't want to work with someone like me."

Nathaniel shook his head. "On the contrary, you are quite literally the only one I would even dare to work with. This class is...quite difficult compared to my others. I think if we work together, pick each other's brains a bit, we can both walk away with High Distinctions."

I do not praise myself often, and certainly not over trivial things, but a round of applause would suffice to compensate for the laughter I swallowed down as I listened to Nathaniel speak. Did he really believe I would work with my competition just so that *he* could maintain his perfect grades? I was many things, but an idiot was not one of them.

"If you're finding this module difficult," I said, perfectly calm, "I suggest you take advantage of the affordable tutoring sessions the university offers."

Nathaniel opened his mouth, closed it, and then opened it again. A brush of wind flattened the mess of black hair over his forehead in a way that made him look almost boyish. I did my best to hide my amusement. *This* was how I liked to see him. Confidence knocked out of him like a bat to a pinata.

He watched me for a moment before a wide smile returned to his face. "If you change your mind," he pulled out his phone and held up a screenshot of his social media notifications, "you clearly know how to contact me."

Words abandoned me amid my horror. A week prior, I had been scrolling social media when Nathaniel's account was recommended on my feed. Curious, I clicked on his profile, scrolling through the many photos of award ceremonies and voluntary competitions, lingering on one photo of a pride parade in London. I must have accidentally liked the post whilst I was stalking his account. And he had known *all this time*. Humiliation was too light of a word for what I experienced in that moment.

Without uttering another word, Nathaniel returned to his friends who had been waiting by a bench beneath a large oak tree, fallen leaves decorating the pale green grass. He disappeared into the endless crowd of students while I hurried to the library, itching to disappear and drown myself in a pool of my own embarrassment.

Now, more than ever, it became an absolute necessity that I outranked him in the next assignment.

***

A requirement for *all* students enrolled in the Bachelor of Psychological Studies was to undergo six sessions with one of Dawnridge's experienced psychologists within the first academic year.

It was ridiculous, really. But I could hold off on it no longer, so I booked my first session with Dr. Valerie Rosewood. The expectation was that by undergoing a session for ourselves, we would be able to empathise with our future patients. I personally believe it was a way to snap off all the unstable students and throw them to the wind.

I knocked on the door to Dr. Rosewood's office and was met with a woman in her early thirties, short black hair that brushed her shoulders and piercing blue eyes that you only read about in books. She smiled in greeting and extended her hand before inviting me inside.

It was a small office, with four white walls decorated with motel art, the right one home to a window overlooking campus while the left contained two tall bookshelves.

"It's nice to meet you, Augustus," she said as the door fell shut behind me. "How are you finding your second semester at Dawnridge?"

She settled into a mustard-coloured armchair by the window and gestured for me to take the small, identical armchair across from her. With a notepad and pen in hand, one leg crossed over the other, she waited for my answer with an expectant smile.

"Yeah, uh, it's been good," I answered, shifting nervously in my seat as my gaze drifted toward the several objects on her desk, eyes gliding over the mountain of paperwork and a framed photo of three women throwing their graduation caps into the air.

"Well, thank you for coming to see me. I'm looking forward to our six sessions together," she said, drawing my attention back to the pen she fiddled with as she watched me. "Have you ever had a session with a psychologist before?"

I had, once. A month after my mother disappeared, Uncle Brady drove me to a children's clinic in the city while my father stayed home with Auden. I suppose it was an attempt to get me to open up about what I experienced in North Lane, or to unpack my feelings about my mother leaving, but I didn't say a word the entire hour. Uncle Brady didn't make me go again after that.

"No," I lied.

Dr. Rosewood nodded. "We're just going to have a conversation. Is that okay?"

She's acting like you have a choice, the Devil complained.

"That's fine," I forced out.

"If you feel uncomfortable at any point, let me know and we can discuss something else," she said, "but, you should know, discomfort is a sign of progress."

I nodded without a word, my eyes drifting toward the clock hanging above the window. Barely any time had passed since I sat down.

"Why have you chosen to study psychology, Augustus?"

My palms grew slippery with sweat as I shifted in my seat, leg bouncing up and down with little control. It felt like a job interview. And I did not do well under pressure. The only reason *Browning Books* hired me was because they hadn't received many applicants, and my living nearby worked in my favour.

"I...uh...I..." I cleared my throat and made a second attempt. "I guess I want to understand how the mind works."

"Ah," Dr. Rosewood hummed, "I think a lot of us are driven to psychology due to a desire to understand what makes people think and act the way they do."

I nodded my assent.

"And what are you hoping to do with this degree?"

"I want to be an accredited psychiatrist," I answered, though it was a practiced response. Despite my interest in psychology, I wasn't yet convinced that I wanted to spend nearly eight years studying to be a psychiatrist. It was a big commitment, and what if I changed my mind four years into it?

"A clear goal. That's good." Silence hung between us after my wordless nod. And then, "Tell me more about yourself."

I loathed this question. On the surface, it was simple, but at its core, you were required to pick yourself apart and choose what you thought the other person wanted to hear. In this situation, I wasn't quite sure what Dr. Rosewood expected, so I went with a universal sample response I had lined up. I told her I was from the small town of Rose Chapel but now lived alone with my younger brother, I worked part-time at *Browing Books* and spent my free time painting.

"Oh, what do you like to paint?" she asked, resting an elbow on her thigh as she leaned forward, seemingly interested.

I knew she was feigning curiosity, so I answered in a bored tone, "Random things."

"Random things like what?" she pushed.

"Does it really matter?" I challenged.

She sighed. "Augustus, one day you are going to be in my position, trying to get to know someone you'll be working with. Wouldn't you want them to answer your questions?"

"Of course," I said, slowly drawing my gaze toward the window. "But that's different. They will need help. I don't. This is just to pass."

"You will be evaluated, Augustus. And in order for me to evaluate you, you must be compliant and willing to engage in conversation. If I cannot evaluate you, you cannot pass."

And there it was. My crushing defeat. I could not simply get through these sessions with a stubborn attitude and dishonest answers.

"Okay," I sighed, "I'm sorry."

Dr. Rosewood's gaze softened. "There's no need to apologise, Augustus. Let's talk about your art then, shall we?"

***

"Augustus?"

I was at my desk, the pale glow of my computer screen the only light in a room swallowed by darkness. Auden stood in the doorway, still in his school uniform, headphones secured around his neck.

"What is it?" I asked gently, gesturing for Auden to switch on my light.

The room erupted in colour, my bedroom walls decorated with art I had accumulated over the years, some of my own, some purchased. Although my new room was much smaller than the one at Aunt Vera's, there was enough space for a single bed, a wooden wardrobe, a single bookcase and a desk. I hadn't purchased a set of drawers yet, so the clothes that weren't in my wardrobe were still in boxes, scattered across the carpeted floor.

"Can we watch a movie?"

I opened my mouth to tell him that I was too busy, that my university work was piling up and I didn't have time, but when I saw the hopeful look in his bright blue eyes and the nervous chewing of his lip, guilt barrelled through me. It had been quite some time since I'd dedicated time for Auden. We hardly saw each other outside of mealtimes. I missed him. And it was clear he missed me too.

"Yeah, of course we can," I breathed out. "Go pick a movie and I'll meet you in a few minutes, okay?"

His face lit up and he sprinted toward the living room, my heart aching at the thought of him spending these past few months alone, in a new city, without any ounce of attention. I was a bad brother. It was because of me we had to move, and yet I was selfish, failing to dedicate time to ensuring he was comfortable.

Slamming my laptop shut, I rose to my feet and met Auden in the living room, lips pulled upward at the bowl of snacks he'd gathered on the coffee table. Two sodas, a shared bowl of popcorn, and two chocolate bars.

"Where'd you get these from?" I asked.

"I bought them after school," Auden said.

"You planned to have a movie night?"

"Yes, I bought snacks as an incentive. But you agreed before I had to beg."

My breath hitched as if physically wounded. "I would never make you beg, Audie."

Auden shrugged and reached for the remote, avoiding my gaze as he flicked through available movies on our watch list.

I watched him, the way he chewed on the inside of his mouth and drummed his fingers against his thigh.

"Auden. Look at me for a second." He slowly turned his head. "What's going on?"

"Nothing."

"Bullshit."

"I just...feel like you don't need me anymore."

"What? Why would you think that?"

Auden shrugged, but I knew he had an answer, he was just too hesitant to say it.

I sighed and leaned forward, desperate to catch his gaze as I said, "I will always need you, okay? I know I've been busy with work and my studies, but I will never not need you. We're in this together, always."

"Promise?"

"I promise."

With a satisfied smile, Auden selected a movie while I reached for the popcorn. It broke my heart to know that Auden thought I didn't need him. I needed him more than he realised. He was the light anchoring me to my humanity, the salvation to my sin. Without him, I had no idea who I would be.

CHAPTER TWENTY-TWO

The House on North Lane was on fire.

Smoke crawled through every crack, smothering the rodents that lived in the walls, their cries of agony drowned out by the boy on his knees, trapped within a circle of flames. He gasped for air, choking, tears rolling down his cheeks as he kneeled over his brother, shielding him from the heat.

Flames engulfed the walls, the ceiling, devouring everything it touched.

A woman stood outside the circle, a crucifix in her trembling hands as she watched her children succumb to the flames. Tears dried her pale cheeks, one foot inching forward as though she'd walk through the fire to save her boys or die trying. But a man appeared at her side, strange words tumbling from his lips with a veracity empowered by his Holy book. He kept her in place without having to lift a finger, his power stronger than her desire to protect her children.

The older boy looked up at the man, defiance in his eyes. Too weak to stand, his breathing strained, he collapsed, arms still secured around his brother.

"Is it done?" the woman asked the man.

"I cannot be certain," the man replied, "the Devil is too strong."

"They're dying!"

"And so too is the Devil!"

Timber snapped, the roof threatening to cave in.

The boy's chest no longer rose and fell, his curls white with ash, smoke blackening his pale cheeks.

The woman broke free of her spell, throwing herself into the Devil's cage, crouching down to gather her son in her arms. She shook him, called his name, sobbed over his lifeless corpse.

"I'm sorry, I'm so sorry," she said, the world collapsing around them. "I'm sorry. Wake up, just wake up. I'm sorry."

She pulled him to her chest, rocking their bodies back and forth as a beam collapsed behind them, a loud snap that pulled the boy from Death's slumber.

His eyelids fluttered open, but it was the Devil who looked through his eyes, who used his body to crawl his way out of the flames.

When he looked in the mirror, I looked back.

***

Browning Books was quiet, as it usually was on a Thursday morning. Edith was in the back room putting new stock into the system while I stood at the counter, re-pricing books that were going into our small 'sale' section.

A bell chimed as the door swung open, and an old lady with a walking frame and a service dog stepped inside. The dog was quite large—a white labrador wearing a blue vest—yet it did well not to knock into any shelves.

"Good morning, dear," the lady greeted me, a smile on her thin lips as she approached the counter. She had short white hair combed neatly in gentle waves, a lavender cardigan draped over a plain white top and a long grey skirt. The dog followed beside her, attention focused on her small steps.

I lowered my pricing gun and returned the smile with a polite 'good morning' that sounded a little rough with disuse.

"Oh, darling, I'm looking for a book my grandson recently donated and I am hoping it hasn't been sold yet," the woman said, pulling out a receipt to place on the counter. "He gave you a rare special edition of Pride and Prejudice that has an inscription inside of it. It was a gift from my late husband, and I wasn't meant to part with it. Is there any way I can re-purchase it?"

I glanced down at the receipt briefly before nodding my head. "Of course. Just give me one second. I think it may still be out the back."

She thanked me profusely as I made my way to the back room and asked Edith about the recent acquisition. Since it was a donation, Edith told me to return the book free of charge. I did so, earning myself more praise.

"You're such an angel," she said, tears of relief swelling in her eyes as she held the book close to her chest, as if she wanted to bury it inside her, never to be parted again. "This book means the world to me."

Angel, she called you. If only she knew...

I forced a polite smile and watched as she slowly exited the store. My hands trembled at my sides, and I hid them behind my back as I tried to steady the unease contaminating my veins. It seemed my body didn't know the difference between being caged inside a circle of flames and receiving praise.

Liar. Liar. Liar.

I was no angel. My mask was just crafted so expertly that no one saw through the cracks I painted over every day.

After reciting this encounter with Dr. Rosewood, she set down her notepad and studied me with a mix of curiosity and pity. I had left out the Devil's voice in my head, but I may as well have mentioned it, for his thoughts mirrored my own.

"During this exchange with the customer, did you have any negative thoughts about *her*?" Dr. Rosewood asked.

"Negative thoughts?" I echoed, blinking. "Like what?"

"Like...'she smells awful', 'her hair is a mess', 'her voice is too shrill,'" she provided examples.

"What?" I shook my head. "Of course not!"

"Okay," Dr. Rosewood wrote something down quickly before looking back up at me. "Then why do you think you didn't deserve the praise she was giving you?"

"I was just doing my job," I answered, shifting uncomfortably beneath her gaze.

"Yes," Dr. Rosewood nodded, "but you mentioned feeling a sense of panic. And that you felt like a liar. You were being nice to this lady, and she was being nice to you. Why did you panic?"

"Because she called me an angel," I breathed out.

"And what's wrong with that?"

"I'm *not* an angel."

Dr. Rosewood pressed her lips together for a long moment before speaking again. "She did not mean a literal angel. And I think you know that. Why did you panic at being called an angel as a comparison to being called *good*?"

"Because I'm *not* good."

"Why don't you think you're good?"

I opened my mouth, closed it, and averted my gaze. How could I explain to her that I had the Devil inside my head, wanting to be unleashed? How could I explain that I was the reason my whole family fell apart? How could I explain all that had happened without being admitted straight into a Psych Ward?

"Augustus?" Rosewood prompted gently. "Why don't you think you're good?"

I swallowed thickly, hands clenching and unclenching in my lap as I scoured my brain for an answer that was honest yet *safe*.

"I was...a bad kid," I admitted reluctantly, gaze locked on a dust ball beneath Dr. Rosewood's desk. "I didn't do as I was told, I talked back, I had violent outbursts. At home, I was a little monster. Yet at school or at church, I was quiet, well behaved, an *angel*. And if anyone commented on how *good* I was, my parents would make a joke about how 'I wasn't like that at home', reminding me of what was *real*."

Dr. Rosewood nodded along as she made notes, gaze sympathetic when she lifted her eyes to meet mine. "I see. And because your parents brought up these differences in behaviour, you felt like you were somehow faking it when you were good?"

I nodded.

"Are you parents still in your life, Augustus?"

"No."

"May I ask the circumstances?"

"My father died when I was twelve. Cancer. And my mother...left when I was nine."

"I'm sorry for your loss, Augustus," she said gently.

"It was a long time ago," I shrugged.

"I want you to work on something for me before our next session," she said in an optimistic tone that indicated our hour had come to an end. "From now until next week, I want you to write down every good thing you do."

I raised both eyebrows up. "Huh?"

"It can be anything from picking up a piece of rubbish to helping a duck cross the road," she went on. "Anything good you do, write it down."

"Why?" I asked.

"I have a feeling you'll be surprised by what that list will show."

***

The first good thing I did that week was not brag when success was delivered with a ninety-eight percent on my second assignment in *Psychological Manipulation.* Nathaniel Carrington received a ninety-five.

I could tell he was disappointed by the slump of his shoulders and the way he hung his head. He was gripping the edge of his desk for so long that his knuckles had gone white.

A satisfied smile tugged at my lips as Professor Haywood congratulated me on my first-place ranking.

Nathaniel's head whipped around to find me, but I pretended not to notice, ignoring him as if I didn't even care that I *finally* beat him—as if I wasn't fighting a wide smile and pleasant hum.

We were even. Each of us had outperformed the other in one assignment, Nathaniel the first, I the second. The third would determine our final ranking. And it was going to be me. It had to be. I would not lose again.

The second good thing I did that week was not punch Nathaniel in the face when he approached me after class, laptop clutched in one hand while the other slipped inside his long, charcoal coat.

"Congratulations on your results," he said smoothly, matching my pace as he walked beside me. "You must be pleased."

And you must be devastated.

"I am," I said. "Are you?"

Nathaniel's lips spread into a tight smile that didn't reach his eyes. "I can do better. I know I can do better."

"Good for you."

"I have a question."

"Make it quick."

"You didn't get full marks. What was your feedback?"

I came to an abrupt halt, eyes narrowing until Nathaniel was barely visible beneath my long lashes. "Why would you want *my* feedback? You didn't get full marks either. Shouldn't you be focusing on your own failure?"

Nathaniel inhaled sharply at the word failure. "I just want to know if we're having the same problem. We both improved a lot in this assignment but we're clearly lacking *something.*"

"Why do you care if we have the *same* problem?"

"Because if we *do,* we can work together to fix it."

A cold laugh escaped my throat before I had the chance to rein it in. "I already told you I have no interest in working with you."

"Why not?"

I didn't answer. I simply started walking again, hoping he would get the hint and leave me alone.

"Is it because I won that trivia contest last semester?" Nathaniel asked as he followed. "I feel like you've hated me since then."

"I don't hate you. I don't even think about you."

Liar.

Nathaniel sighed. "Then why do you refuse to collaborate?"

"Because you're only interested in collaborating to benefit *yourself,*" I snapped. "You would have paid me no attention if I wasn't a threat to your ranking. And I have no interest in wasting time with someone so selfish."

In hindsight, my harsh words were not *good.* But at least I didn't punch him.

He didn't follow me the rest of the way to the library, and I didn't look back to see if my words had wounded him.

The third good thing I did that week was attend church with Auden.

It hadn't been something I planned on doing. I hadn't been inside a church since my father's funeral, yet Auden had requested it, and I suppose I was curious to know how it would feel being inside one again.

There was a Catholic church two streets down from Auden's school, so we caught the bus and walked to the front gates with a sign that said, 'All are Welcome'.

The Devil inside me quietened as we stepped inside, holy water anointed to our temples as we bowed before God.

There were a few scattered elderly people, a young family, and us. It was quiet. I glanced sideways at Auden whose gaze was fixed on the sculpture behind the altar. It was of Mary and a young Jesus, Mary's arm wrapped around her small son, a soft smile on her face.

"Why did you want to come here?" I whispered.

"I wanted to talk to God," Auden answered softly.

I suppressed a scoff as I looked away. God abandoned *us*. What kind of God demanded worship and offered nothing in return?

Careful, the Devil warned, *we're in His house now.*

I swallowed back my retort and bowed my head, feigning devout reverence while we waited for the mass to begin.

A hymn filled the church as a middle-aged priest with raven black hair and dark eyes walked down the aisle toward the altar. Everyone stood.

I struggled to pay attention throughout the mass, my mind wandering to thoughts of what work I still had to do for university, and when my next shift at the bookstore was.

Auden, on the other hand, looked entirely focused. I wasn't sure what this new desire to reignite his faith was, but I had to support it. If Auden wanted God in his life, who was I to stop him?

I, personally, was starting to believe there was no God at all. Or at least not the one from the Holy Bible.

All these people had faith in something they could not see. Yet I had seen God, standing behind my mother, while the flames crawled closer. He had done nothing to save me. If anything, he was more like the Devil. But he wasn't real. None of it was real.

My Father is a proud being. He will not take your insults lightly.

I scoffed. What more could God do to me that he hadn't done already?

I had seen Hell. And I came out with the Devil on my side.

CHAPTER TWENTY-THREE

If there was a God, he certainly had a sense of humour, for despite my adamant refusal to work with Nathaniel Carrington, we were paired together for our third and final assignment.

How did Nathaniel and I get paired together, you ask? Well, that asshole *requested* me. And because Professor Haywood absolutely adored him, his request was approved and I was left sitting there, mouth agape in horror, while Nathaniel swivelled in his chair to face me, grinning from ear-to-ear.

"Professor," I started toward Haywood just as Nathaniel stepped in front of me, blocking my path.

"Thank you for today's lecture, Professor," he said, all charm, "I am looking forward to getting started on this final assignment."

"I too am looking forward to it," Haywood said, sliding her laptop into its leather case. "I am sure you two will produce a well-researched presentation. You are my top students, so I expect great results."

"We will not disappoint," Nathaniel assured her.

Haywood gave each of us a polite nod before leaving the hall, students departing one by one to attend their next class or sprint toward the campus shuttle bus before it filled up.

"Why the fuck would you do that?!" I rounded on Nathaniel.

This pairing completely derailed my plan to replace his number one ranking. We had won an assignment each, and the third was meant to be the decider. How could I defeat him when we'd be working together to achieve the same mark? It would be a draw. And I was certain that Nathaniel's request to work with me was a tactic to save his own skin from humiliation.

"Do what?" Nathaniel feigned innocence.

"You know what."

"Why did I make the strategic decision to choose the only other person in this class that *actually* wants to succeed?"

"There are others," I insisted.

He shook his head, hands sliding easily into his pockets as he advanced closer, the scent of his floral cologne infiltrating my senses. "They aren't you."

"What the fuck is that supposed to mean?"

"It means you're the only one I believe will give me the best chance of attaining full marks," he said, "and I think you know I am your best chance too."

He has a point, you know.

"Maybe you're right," I relented. "But you're an asshole for not giving me a choice."

"Who would you have chosen, then?"

"I..." My mouth fell shut as I failed to conjure a single classmate who I would have been happy to work with.

Nathaniel smiled knowingly before moving to step past me. "I'll be in touch, Augustus. I am looking forward to working together."

***

I received an email notification during my study break the following day. It was from Nathaniel. I wanted to ignore it, of course, but fate would not allow it. I had been condemned to collaborate with him, my success aligned with his. I had no choice but to respond.

This is Hell, the Devil complained as I opened the email and read through his unnaturally polite message.

Dear Augustus,
I hope you are doing well on this fine morning. As discussed yesterday, I am looking forward to working together and would like to arrange a study session as soon as possible.
I prepared a research proposal and an outline of my arguments last night but since this is a group task, I would like your input and feedback before we proceed.
Please let me know your availability.
Kind regards, Nate.

Of course he already had an outline. It was his way of asserting dominance. But how could he possibly have an outline when we hadn't even discussed a topic? I would not reward his arrogance with compliance.

I responded to his email without a greeting, suggesting we share a google document and collaborate online rather than meeting up in-person.

His response entered my inbox minutes later.

Dear Augustus,
I believe it would be far more beneficial to work together in person as it is easier to brainstorm and debate ideas. Please let me know what day and time works best for you.
Kind regards, Nate.

A study session with Nathaniel Carrington—what day and time worked best for me? Perhaps the Friday after *never?*

You're being dramatic, the Devil scolded me, *you're acting as though he is the Devil incarnate.*

"Is that supposed to be some kind of joke?" I muttered under my breath.

Irony, perhaps?

"I hate you."

You hate everyone.

I rolled my eyes and forced myself to respond to his email with my availability. What choice did I have? I couldn't risk failing. If I had to endure Nathaniel for a few study sessions to succeed, then so be it.

***

Nathaniel reserved a study room tucked away on the third floor of the university library, an arched oak door with 'room 044' inscribed on the rusted plaque dangling from the worn wood. A curved window stained with dirt and grime offered a pale glow illuminating the dark oak desk in the centre of the room, the lantern in the right-hand corner barely adding any light.

I lowered myself onto one of four wooden chairs crowded around the table, dust coating my fingertips as I drummed them against the creaking wood. My leg bounced up and down to the same rhythm until the door screeched open and Nathaniel entered with twelve pages of research, his laptop, and two books on criminal psychology.

Within seconds, he launched into a presentation to convince me his chosen topic was the one we should pursue.

I sat in silence, arms folded over my chest as he rattled on with statistics and research. He paced up and down the small space as though he were a professor lecturing his students. I was bored out of my mind. And I did *not* want to do our essay and presentation on the topic he'd chosen.

"In conclusion," Nathaniel finished his argument with a charming smile that screamed *punch me in the face*, "I believe our research should focus on how serial killers manipulate their victims, detectives and members of the jury to convey innocence."

"I disagree."

Nathaniel frowned in a childish pout as a single strand of hair fell over his deep brown eyes. "You...disagree?"

"*Everyone* is going to choose psychopaths and serial killers. We did three weeks on 'the criminal mind' alone. And it's clearly what everyone is most interested in," I explained, "we should try and stand out by doing something *different*."

To my surprise, Nathaniel did not argue. "Okay," he murmured, picking at his bottom lip absentmindedly as he sat down, "what did *you* have in mind?"

I slid my laptop toward him so he could read the three pages of research and brainstorming I had prepared prior to our meeting. It was not as thorough as Nathaniel's—but it had all the information he needed to make a decision.

"Why did you choose this topic?" he asked once he'd finished reading. "I mean, we could have done *anything*. And you chose..." He squinted as he peered down at my laptop screen, "... religious fanaticism, an investigation into how cults manipulate its members to produce religious psychosis?"

My shoulders deflated. He didn't sound impressed. "I chose it because no one else will. Haywood is probably sick of psychopaths. Let's at least make grading our assignment interesting for her, hm?"

"It certainly is interesting..." Nathaniel hummed.

"But?"

"But nothing."

I gave him a look.

"I'm serious!" he insisted with a laugh as he returned my laptop. "It's interesting. I'm all in."

"But you're...a med student," I blurted out.

"And?"

"And this seems...vastly out of your..."

"Circle of interests?" Nathaniel offered.

I nodded.

A quiet chuckle escaped his throat. "You don't even know me, Augustus. How would you know what my interests are? What do you think I do in my spare time? Stare at medicine cabinets?"

"I don't know, do you?"

He returned the look I gave him earlier.

"Whatever," I rolled my eyes. "I just don't want to be blamed if we do poorly."

"Are you worried about doing poorly?"

"Of course."

"You shouldn't. You're paired with *me*."

God, he really was infuriating. "That does not reassure me."

"Liar," he teased.

I scoffed. "Are we in agreement then? Or do you have another PowerPoint presentation you need to get through?"

"I told you I'm interested!"

"Fine!"

"Good!"

"So, it's agreed then?"

"Yes!"

"Good!"

A long silence drifted between us as we glared at one another. Nathaniel's ears were red, and my jaw was clenched so hard that when I finally opened it to take a sip of water, it ached.

"Do you have a hypothesis?" Nathaniel finally broke the silence.

"Yes," I breathed out, "cults facilitate an environment of religious fanaticism that breeds psychosis."

Nathaniel nodded as he opened up a new page in his notebook. "Okay, then, we need a minimum of ten scholarly articles. You've already found some, right?"

"I have four," I shrugged.

"Alright. I'll find the other six," he replied.

"We also need a case study."

Nathaniel nodded and we spent the next few hours working in silence, only exchanging a few words to answer questions or resolve any concerns.

I had almost forgotten Nathaniel was there until a quiet 'holy shit' escaped his throat. I lifted my head and watched as he leaned closer to his laptop screen, lips parted and eyes wide.

"What is it?" I asked.

"Come take a look at this."

I moved around to stand behind him, leaning down to read the news article lighting up his screen.

"There was this Doctor in the United States who wanted to see if he could withstand the psychological manipulation of some cult leader," Nathaniel summarised, "and he joined with the intention of studying the members and providing tips on how to avoid being manipulated. It was originally only meant to be a one-month trial, but according to his family, he went missing for over a year."

"Holy shit," I repeated Nathaniel's words. "So what, he joined the cult, then?"

"Yeah, they found him after a year, thinking maybe the cult leader found out and had forced him there against his will," Nathaniel said, scrolling down to show a photograph from a police conference. "But he insists he decided to stay because he believed it was the right place for him. He didn't even *want* to return to his family. He had three children. Who leaves their children for a cult?"

I thought of my mother leaving Auden and I in North Lane, and muttered, "You'd be surprised."

Nathaniel tilted his head up to look at me. "Do you think we could use this as a case study? To show that psychological manipulation can occur to *anyone*, religious or not?"

"Yeah," I nodded. "And we can compare it to those who already have religious inclinations, see if there are any differences. Does the article talk about what this Doctor experienced inside the cult?"

Nathaniel hummed. "A little. It's mostly just information that his family provided after their brief encounter. I don't know how reliable it is."

"It's still useful," I said, returning to my own seat. "I'm going to try and find a case study to compare it to. Can you make notes on that one?"

"Already on it."

We worked tirelessly on our case studies and supporting literature, our track of time fleeting as we buried ourselves in article after article.

Neither of us knew the sun had set and that the library was closing until the lights suddenly flickered off, draping us in darkness.

"What the hell?"

"Oh, shit," Nathaniel said, pulling out his phone, "it's nine."

"Nine?!"

"The library is closing."

We gathered our laptops and books in a mad dash to leave the study room and bolt toward the doors. Nathaniel went to open them, but the doors merely shook. He tried again. They were locked.

"You're kidding," I breathed out.

"It's okay," Nathaniel said, voice calm despite the rapid rise and fall of his chest, "campus security will come around soon. They'll let us out."

I shot him a look. "Why were there no announcements?"

"I don't know," he said, running a hand over his face, "there usually are! Maybe they weren't working today!"

I groaned and tugged at the door as if it would magically open.

"There's no use," Nathaniel sighed. "Let's just sit down and wait for security. I'll try give them a call."

He approached the cushioned booth near the entrance, dumping himself down to spread out lazily, his lips tugging up into a grin once he caught me watching.

Scowling, I sat down at the table across from him. It was less comfortable than the booth, but I did *not* want to sit with him. I could feel him watching me, so I turned away, hiding my face beneath my thick waves.

"Are we just going to sit in silence?" Nathaniel asked.

"Yes."

"Aw, come on! We spent so long studying, I'm ready to socialise now!"

"I can think of nothing worse."

Nathaniel laughed as if I were joking. "Are you always this grumpy?"

I whirled on him. "I'm not grumpy!"

"Are you sure?"

"Yes."

"If you say so."

"Why are you being so annoying?" I complained.

Nathaniel lifted a dramatic hand to his chest. "You think I'm annoying?"

"No," I said. "I don't *think*, I *know*."

A playful gasp escaped his throat. This was all a game to him but I was being entirely serious. I glanced toward the doors, praying campus security showed up so I wouldn't have to spend another second with Nathaniel's crooked grin.

"You still haven't told me why you hate me," Nathaniel mused.

"I told you already…I don't hate you," I said.

"Okay, well you certainly don't like me," he pointed out.

"Does it matter?" I asked, slowly returning my attention to him.

"To me? Yes."

"Why?"

"I don't like being disliked," he said.

"Not many people do," I shrugged.

"Yes," he agreed, "but if there is something I do that upsets you, I'd like to know so I can stop."

"You can't live like that," I scoffed.

Nathaniel tilted his head to the side. "Like what?"

"Being a people pleaser," I said, waving a hand dismissively. "People are going to dislike you no matter what. You can't please *everyone*. What does it matter if *I* dislike you when you have so many people that *do* like you?"

Nathaniel straightened in the booth, elbows resting on the table. "Are you saying that you'll dislike me no matter what?"

I thought about it for a moment before nodding. "Yes."

"Why?"

"Because you are my competition."

A frown pulled at his lips. "Competition?"

"For first place," I said. "You are the barrier keeping me from coming first in *every* class. I want the scholarship for next year and *you* are the only thing getting in my way."

Nathaniel studied me as if I were a night creature crawling into the sunlight for the first time. "You do realise you can get the scholarship without ranking first in *every* subject, right? It's more about your marks."

"Yes, obviously," I said through gritted teeth. "But the teaching staff base their recommendations on ranking. That's why there is such a big focus on it."

Nathaniel sighed. "It's just one class."

"I know. But I'm not going to risk it."

"Well, at least *this* makes sense. Danny said I must have wronged you in my past life."

"Who the fuck is Danny?"

"Just some guy I've been talking to," Nathaniel chuckled.

"You've been telling some random guy about me?" I asked, gobsmacked.

"I told you I don't like being disliked!" Nathaniel defended himself. "And he asked me how my day was!"

"So this random guy thinks I'm an asshole?"

"Don't worry, I'll tell him you just hate me cause I'm smarter than you!"

Without thinking, I threw my pen lid at him. Nathaniel caught it with lightning reflexes, his eyes wide as he looked at me. "Did you just throw this pen lid at me?" He looked like he was trying not to laugh, and for some reason, that brought a faint smile to my lips, rage dimming.

"Oh my god!" he gasped as he threw the lid back at me.

I dodged it easily, laughing as it sailed past my head to land on the carpeted floor behind me.

Nathaniel chuckled and ran his fingers through his hair, combing it back away from his forehead. "I can't believe you threw a pen lid at me!"

"You threw it back!" I defended myself.

"It was return fire!"

"You're an idiot."

"Thank you."

I snorted. "It was not a compliment."

"Really? I could never have guessed."

"Sarcasm?"

"Mhm."

Rolling my eyes, I wiped a hand over my mouth to smother the smile that threatened to linger on my lips. Maybe Nathaniel wasn't so bad. He wasn't Alexander. In fact, in this situation, *I* was being Alexander.

"Why is it so important for you to be first?" I decided to ask after a long, comfortable silence.

He didn't need the scholarship, surely. Based on what little I had seen on his social media, his family were wealthy. He lived in a large house, wore expensive brand clothes, and travelled all around the world. But maybe his parents were like Aunt Vera—they had money but no interest in sharing it with their children once they reached eighteen.

Nathaniel's expression sobered, but he didn't object to answering the question. "I'm the oldest of seven children," he said, "and both my parents are surgeons. My mum moved here from South Korea to study medicine as a young woman and she sacrificed so much. She left behind her parents and her two younger sisters. It was hard for her...being in a foreign country, striving for success."

"And my dad was adopted as a toddler and brought here from South Korea to be raised in an English family. They were good to him but...it was transactional. And anyway..." He shook his head, slowly bringing his gaze up to look at me. "I'm expected to be the best of the best. They have worked so hard for the lives they have now, and the life they have given my brothers and me, and I feel like I owe them my success. Nothing is good enough, you know?"

I said nothing, words failing me as I digested the truth laced in every word.

"I have always been number one," Nathaniel went on. "And it's been something my parents tell their friends and colleagues proudly. If I fail...I'm an embarrassment."

"One failure surely wouldn't..." my voice trailed off at the look on his face.

"This subject...I'm doing poorly. My dad is disappointed. He says he understands now why Oxford declined my application...I *must* do well in this final assignment. There's no other option other than success."

"Oxford didn't accept you?" I asked, surprised.

Nathaniel released a bitter chuckle. "Yeah. It's my greatest shame."

I bit my lip, debating my next words. Nathaniel was the smartest person I knew, I had always assumed Dawnridge had been his first choice. To know that he too had experienced failure...it humanised him.

"I'm sorry you didn't get accepted into Oxford, but Dawnridge is an incredible university," I tried to comfort him. "You're not a failure."

Nathaniel smiled, though it didn't quite reach his eyes. "Thank you."

"And your dad may be disappointed, but *you* shouldn't be," I went on, "you're at the top of your course regardless of your one slip up in this subject. It's okay to not be at your best all the time."

"I know, I just...not all my brothers are as academic as I am," he sighed, leaning back against the cushioned booth. "I don't want them to experience the same pressure that I have. I don't want them to kill themselves trying to live up to my parents' expectations. If I am successful, if I make them proud, maybe my brothers will have more room to chase their own dreams."

"You're protecting them," I said.

"I guess so," Nathaniel shrugged. "But I'm also doing it for myself. What good am I if not the best?"

I swallowed hard. That sounded an awful lot like the question circling around my own head. Perhaps Nathaniel and I were not so different after all.

Biting my lip hard enough to draw blood, I glanced toward the unopened doors and released a frustrated sigh. "Can we call security again?"

"I'll try, but they haven't been answering," Nathaniel sighed.

I nodded, waiting patiently as he found the number and called it, his previous words replaying in my head. Guilt ensnared me. I'd treated him like the enemy, but he was just like me, a young man striving for success.

"No one is answering," he said, the slight narrowing of his eyes the only sign of his frustration. "God, they're absolutely useless."

I stood up and began pacing, trying to think of a way out of this situation. It was getting late and...my heart stopped.

Auden.

I pulled out my phone, a string of curse words rolling off my tongue at the flat battery. With no charger, I had no way to contact Auden and explain where I was.

"My phone is dead," I said in between curses. "We need to get out of here. There must be some alarm we can set off or something."

Nathaniel pursed his lips. "Maybe a fire alarm? You go look for it, I'll keep trying security's number."

With a nod, I hurried off in search of the fire alarm, the darkened library creating monsters out of bookcases. They towered on either side of me, whispering amongst themselves as I felt their wooden frames for guidance.

You forgot about Auden, the Devil whispered, *what kind of brother are you?*

I didn't answer, though that same question had speared through my chest moments earlier. I prayed Auden was okay and that he would forgive me for my unexplained disappearance. I had to get to him. And soon.

"Why did you abandon me, Guses?" a voice called out. "Why did you leave me all alone? Like Mumma did."

I slowed to a halt, the air torn from my lungs. "Auden...?"

"You're just like Mumma. Just like Mumma. Just like Mumma."

Bookshelves stretched toward me, inching closer as I turned to face my brother, dark eyes locking with mine. Only it wasn't Auden. It was the Devil, smiling from ear-to-ear, sharp teeth drenched in blood. Snakes slithered at his feet, hissing, forked tongues flicking wildly. Spiders poured from his eyeless sockets, his nose, his widening mouth.

I backed away.

The Devil followed.

"Why are you doing this?" I whispered.

To remind you, the Devil's voice growled inside my head.

"Remind me of what?"

Of who you are.

Shaking my head, I blinked away the grinning Devil wearing mine and Auden's distorted face, turning back around to resume my search.

I found the emergency exit and activated the fire alarm, the library erupting in a loud siren that burst my eardrums. Covering my ears, I sprinted back toward Nathaniel who waited by the door.

Security were there minutes later, unlocking the door to release us and turn off the alarm. We were questioned briefly, and once Nathaniel explained the situation, we were released.

"Let me drive you home," Nathaniel offered.

"It's fine, I'll find my own way," I mumbled, distracted.

"Augustus," he sighed. "It's late."

I studied him for a long moment. In the pale moonlight, his skin glistened, shadows casting wings behind him as though he were a guardian angel.

"Fine," I breathed out. "I would appreciate that, thank you."

Nathaniel's car was not what I had been expecting. Since he was 'Mr rich kid' in my mind, I had anticipated a 'Mr rich kid' kind of car. And while I had no doubt his car *was* expensive, I had not expected to climb into a 1950s Bentley.

"What decade do you think we're in?" I asked as I settled into the front passenger seat.

"Time is a man-made concept," Nathaniel replied.

"Actually..." I started, but my words trailed off as Nathaniel started the car and music reached my ears. "What the hell is this?"

"What?"

"The music."

Nathaniel grinned. "You don't like St. Elmo's Fire?"

I rolled my eyes and refused to give him a response, opting instead to look out the window, watching the blur of red lights and streetlamps.

"Did you always know you wanted to study psychology?"

The unexpected question hung in the air between us as I tried to concoct an appropriate response. To admit that I had no direct ambition, no idea what I really wanted to be, was not something I was ready for. Especially not with my rival. But Nathaniel glanced sideways at me at the traffic lights, brown eyes soft and curious, and I felt compelled to answer honestly.

"I don't know. I've always wanted to...understand the way the mind works," I said.

It was not a lie. I wanted to understand why my mother had treated me the way she had, and what had caused her to make the decision to abandon her family. There were so many complexities of the human mind, and I wanted to uncover each one.

"Ah," Nathaniel clicked his tongue, "you and I are not so different after all."

I had already drawn that same conclusion but enlightened him anyway. "What do you mean?"

"I mean..." he drummed his fingers against the steering wheel, gaze briefly flickering to mine, "...we both want to understand everything there is to know about the brain. You want to be a psychologist or psychiatrist, I'm assuming, and I want to be a brain surgeon. Sure, you are going about it psychologically while I am physically, but together, we could understand it *all*. A brain surgeon and a clinical psychologist. A powerful team, right?"

A team. I almost scoffed. What did Nathaniel, top-of-the-class Nathaniel, want with me when I had made it clear, on numerous occasions, that I wanted nothing to do with him?

You know the saying, the Devil hummed, *keep your enemies close.*

"What about you?" I asked instead before the Devil's voice could taunt me further. "Did you always want to be a brain surgeon?"

"Not at all," Nathaniel answered, "I actually wanted to work in a museum archive or be a music teacher. I love history. And I play the piano."

His words reminded me of Auden. He loved history and museums. I always imagined that one day he would be working in the archives or giving tours, spilling out facts he knew about an ancient civilisation or historical figure.

"So why medicine?" I asked.

"It was...always expected of me," he said, less enthusiastic. "My dad is a heart surgeon and my mum is a lung specialist."

"My mother was a religious fanatic who abandoned her family for a cult and my dad an alcoholic who didn't see his kids worth living for," I blurted out, "we don't have to follow the same path as our parents."

There was a long, uncomfortable silence before Nathaniel whispered, "Your mother..."

I shook my head. I did not want to talk about her. In fact, I didn't even know why I brought her up. There was just something about Nathaniel that made it so easy to spill all your secrets. It was dangerous. *He* was dangerous.

"Is she...the reason you wanted to do our assignment on cults?" Nathaniel asked.

"No."

"But–"

"I said no."

"You're back to hating me again, huh?"

"Yes."

We sat in silence until Nathaniel pulled up in front of my apartment complex and I opened the door to climb out. I was halfway out of the seat when I felt Nathaniel's fingers around my elbow, grip strong enough to bring me to a halt. I slowly turned to look at him.

"Augustus." He said my name like a prayer, summoning my omniscience from a golden throne above the clouds, imploring me to listen to his earthly concerns. "I want to be friends."

But I was no god. And I did not answer prayers.

CHAPTER TWENTY-FOUR

Weeping. Quiet, strangled weeping.

It greeted me within seconds of entering the apartment, my bag dropping to the carpeted floor as I followed the sound. I knocked on my bedroom door, silence swallowing the soft sniffles from inside. There was a pause, and then a barely audible 'come in' that granted me entry.

My heart shattered. Auden was curled up in my bed, knees drawn to his chest, rocking back and forth as silent tears trailed down his cheeks. He was trembling, uncontrollably, and I pulled him into my arms, whispering soothing words that failed to silence the sobs racking through his thin frame.

You did this to him.

"I'm sorry," I whispered, voice cracking. "I didn't realise the time and…and I got trapped in the library and my phone died and–"

"You forgot about me," Auden cut me off.

I lifted his chin, expecting to see anger or hurt, only to be met with resignation. He looked as though he had been *waiting* for this moment, as if it were inevitable.

"No," I shook my head. "I didn't. I could *never* forget you. I tried to call you but my phone died and I didn't have a charger and security took forever to let us out."

"Us?" Auden sniffled.

"I was trapped with…another student," I explained. "I would never abandon you, Auden. It was an accident. It will never happen again."

With tears glistening in his bright blue eyes, Auden studied me for a long, long moment before nodding his head and wiping at the tears that flowed down his cheeks.

"I'm sorry," I whispered, "I didn't mean to scare you."

"I was just wo–worried," Auden hiccupped. "I thought maybe…you didn't need me anymore."

"What? How can you think that?" I asked. "Auden…I'll always need you. You're my brother. You're…my everything. Don't ever think that, okay?"

Auden shook his head. "One day you won't need me anymore. I know that. But I just didn't want it to be today."

"That's not true."

A sniffle was Auden's only response as he adjusted his glasses.

"Come on," I sighed, rising to my feet and pulling him up with me. "I'm starving. Let's have some noodles, yeah?"

He nodded.

We ate. We talked. We went to bed.

Everything was okay. But I couldn't get his words out of my head: *One day you won't need me anymore.* Why would he think that?

***

With what little sleep I managed to acquire the night before, I stumbled into the lecture hall with a yawn and slow, tired blinks. My head throbbed. All I wanted to do was curl up in bed and forget about the world, but attendance was mandatory, and I did not want to risk falling behind.

Dr. Elsbeth Lay bid us all a good morning before proceeding with her lecture. Each week focused on a particular psychological disorder—symptoms, the diagnosis process, and treatments. According to the PowerPoint slides, this week's disorder was schizophrenia.

"What is schizophrenia?" Dr. Lay read off the first slide, her long black hair swaying as she moved from one end of the platform to the other. "It is a serious mental health condition that can change the way people think, feel, and act."

I rested my chin on my hand, gaze resting on the projector. The words on screen all seemed to blend together—a mere blur of black text. I blinked. Once. Twice. Three times. The words were moving, letters abandoning their post in favour of a word three paragraphs over.

"One of the most common symptoms of this disorder are hallucinations—such as seeing things that nobody else can, hearing voices that only you can hear. This is what is usually portrayed in film and television," Dr. Lay explained.

My throat went dry. The mirror, the Devil's voice in my head, the words moving around on screen—these were hallucinations, were they not? Nobody else had seen the mirror and no one else seemed to hear the Devil's taunts. I straightened in my chair.

"There may be delusions," Dr. Lay went on. "These are false beliefs that a person may feel are undoubtedly true."

My mind then shifted to my mother. She believed that Auden and I were possessed by the Devil, and that the only way to save us was an exorcism that ended in flames.

Nausea danced in my stomach, and I wrapped one arm around myself as I listened to Dr. Lay go on to list disorganised thinking, lack of emotional expression, agitation, memory problems, disordered behaviour, and inappropriate reactions as other symptoms of schizophrenia.

"There is a lot of debate around what causes schizophrenia," she said. "CT scans sometimes find abnormal functioning of neurotransmitters, like dopamine, can cause these symptoms. There have also been cases where brain shrinkage or circuitry can cause the disorder. One of the big ones is heredity.

It tends to run in families. If a parent has the disorder, their offspring are more susceptible."

I almost brought up my insides then and there. My mother exhibited symptoms of schizophrenia. As did I.

"To be diagnosed with schizophrenia, you will undergo a physical exam, blood tests, an MRI or CT scan, and a mental health evaluation. Since drugs may also cause similar symptoms, you'll need to be tested for those as well. If you have symptoms of delusions, hallucinations, or any of the other symptoms mentioned previously for a minimum of six months, you can be diagnosed with schizophrenia."

I needed air. I gathered up my laptop, swung my bag over my shoulder and stumbled out of the lecture hall with an arm around my stomach. The cool breeze did little to ease the panic spreading through me.

My hands trembled, vision nothing but a static screen as I swayed, losing control of my own bodily movements. A siren went off in my head, ears ringing violently as I heard a muffled 'you okay?' by a faceless student who stood a little to my left. I opened my mouth to respond, but the darkness swallowed me as I collapsed to the ground.

***

I couldn't remember how long I was blacked out for. One minute I was struggling to breathe and the next I was seated upright, back pressed against the trunk of a tree as I chewed on a banana handed to me by a student First Aid Officer.

"Are you sure you don't need me to call a paramedic?" she asked as she crouched in front of me, worry lines creasing her forehead.

"I'm fine," I assured her in between bites. "I didn't eat breakfast and I think my blood pressure just dropped. The banana is helping."

She nodded, satisfied with my answer. "Take it easy now, okay? Go home, eat, drink plenty of water, and if you continue feeling weak, go to the hospital."

I gave her my assurances and waited until she walked away before climbing to my feet, a little unsteady but strong enough to walk toward the bus stop.

Just realised you're crazy, huh?

A lump lodged itself in my throat and I swallowed it down quickly. It wasn't real. The voice wasn't real. The Devil wasn't real. It was all a figment of my overly active imagination.

I am real, the Devil corrected me with a playful chuckle, *you have never questioned my existence before, so why now?*

He was right. I never questioned it. Why? Did I think everyone had the Devil whispering in their ear? No, of course not. So why then did I never ask myself *why* I heard his voice? When had I just accepted that the Devil spoke to me, taunted me, and that there were no explanations?

Work Song by Hozier hummed in my ear as I slipped into a window seat on the bus and watched the world pass by. I blocked out all thoughts of my mother, of the Devil, of the symptoms of schizophrenia. Instead, my mind wandered to Nathaniel Carrington and the assignment we had to work on. I ended our last encounter rather...coldly.

Disordered behaviour.

I shoved the Devil to the back of my mind, imprisoning him in a cell along with my mother. There was nothing wrong with me. My mother traumatised me with thoughts that the Devil was inside of me, and I conjured him from that trauma. He wasn't real. But I wasn't insane.

You don't really *believe that do you?*

The prison was not strong enough to hold him, and I turned my music up louder, managing to drown out the world but not the cruel chaos in my head.

CHAPTER TWENTY-FIVE

"Professor, may I have a word to discuss the final assignment?"

Nathaniel's voice cut through the chatter echoing along the long, marbled corridor between the lecture hall and the staircase leading to the classrooms above.

My eyes snapped toward him within seconds, pausing mid-step as I glanced in between his dark green knitted vest and Professor Haywood's long brown coat.

"You may," she answered without glancing his way, "but I'm heading to my next class, so you'll have to walk with me."

"Of course," Nathaniel said, "here, let me help you with those." He reached for her tall pile of books, securing them in his arms so that her hands were free to hold her laptop and coffee cup without the risk of spillage.

And that's the man we're supposed to hate?

"Yes," I mumbled under my breath, following them at a distance as they ascended the wide, wooden staircase. "He's a teacher's pet. I doubt he's holding her books because he *wants* to."

I see. And why, pray tell, are we now following him?

The answer was simple. Nathaniel was discussing *our* assignment with *our* professor. Without me. He was up to something and, since I've never been fond of surprises, I was determined to find out what he was planning.

"...and I was just wondering if there were any opportunities to earn extra credit?" Nathaniel asked, voice drifting down the staircase where I waited in the shadows, following only when Haywood's muffled reply was too quiet to hear.

"...field work?" Nathaniel asked.

I needed to get closer. If Nathaniel was asking for extra credit, he may be trying to secure the number one ranking after all. And I couldn't, under any circumstances, allow that to happen.

"Observation is an effective primary research method you could employ," Professor Haywood said. "It would certainly validate your hypothesis and research results. In the psychological field, observation *is* most of the research, so I wouldn't be opposed to it."

"And this would...?"

"Yes, Mr Carrington. It would earn you extra credit." She paused in front of a door, indicating she had reached her next class. "However, given your topic, I would strongly advise against joining a cult for your observation."

Nathaniel laughed. "Strongly advising against it is not forbidding it, Professor."

"No," she agreed, "but you will do well to remember that I advised against it if you do find yourself in...trouble."

"Of course, Professor."

"Be careful, Carrington," she said, tone more firm than it had been previously, "I don't want you taking unnecessary risks for something as small as a few extra marks."

"Knowledge cannot be pursued without risk, Professor," Nathaniel said, "but I will be careful, I promise."

***

Nathaniel contacted me over the weekend to request that for our next study session, we meet at his house to avoid library imprisonment.

He picked me up from *Browning Books*, my black trousers speckled with dust and an orange price tag dangling off the sleeve of my black jacket.

"Busy morning?" he asked once I climbed inside the car.

"We were doing stocktake," I answered.

"Sounds fun," he mused, reaching over to snatch the price tag off me. "Oh, look, you're only three pounds!"

I rolled my eyes playfully.

We made small talk to fill the silence, discussing the gloomy weather, upcoming exams, the traffic.

I didn't apologise for the ending of our last encounter, and he didn't bring it up. I preferred it that way. Growing up, there were never apologies. There was an argument, silence, and after a few days, everyone returned to normal as though nothing had happened. He seemed to work the same way.

"My parents are at work," he announced as we passed through an iron gate, its sharp spires the first to feel the light rain drops falling from the grey clouds circling above. "My brothers are at school. James and Luca are home, though. And Marianne. She's our nanny." His cheeks reddened. "Not *my* nanny. Luca's nanny."

The gate opened with a mechanical grunt, granting access to a long, curved driveaway with freshly manicured green lawns on either side. A garage door opened to reveal white marble floor and polished black furniture, garden tools and boxes lining the shelves.

"How old is Luca?" I asked curiously.

"Three," he answered, parking the car to the right of the garage, leaving space for another three cars, if necessary. "He's the youngest."

"Wow. That is one hell of an age gap. How old are you?"

"Twenty," he chuckled. "But there's only a three year gap between Luca and Rio."

"I can't imagine having that many brothers," I said as we climbed out of the car.

"You just have the one, right?"

"Yeah. Auden."

"How old is he?"

"Fifteen."

"Oh nice, so like…four years between you?"

I nodded.

"James and I are two years apart. I don't even remember life before him."

"It must have been fun, though," I said, following him inside through the back door, shoes discarded at the entrance. "Growing up with all those brothers to play with, I mean."

"Yeah, of course. I love my brothers. But the fights were *crazy*."

"Really?"

"Yeah," he grinned, "James once tried to drown me."

I blinked in alarm. "*What?*"

Nathaniel laughed at the memory. "Yeah, yeah, we were…what, nine and eleven? We'd been fighting over a pool toy. I dove down to grab it and James stood on my back. Back then, we were nearly the same size, so it wasn't easy to get him off me."

"That's terrifying."

"It was at the time," he chuckled. "You never fought like that with Auden?"

I shook my head.

"Oh, well, you're probably a better big brother than me, then," he mused.

He led me down a long hall, a crystal chandelier hanging from the ceiling and photo frames decorating the cream-coloured walls. My eyes fell upon a photo of Nathaniel, no older than fourteen, sitting at a piano with a proud gleam in his eye and a dimpled smile.

"That was taken after I won a music composition contest," Nathaniel said, elbow brushing mine as he stood beside me.

"You look very pleased," I observed.

"I was."

"Do you still play?"

"Not as often as I would like to. Med school takes up most of my time."

I followed him further down the hall until we reached a laundry room where a middle-aged woman stood folding clothes, a little boy playing with building blocks inside a washing basket.

"Marianne," Nathaniel greeted. "This is Augustus. We'll be working on an assignment together in the study. Augustus, this is Marianne and Luca."

I gave the woman and child a polite nod, hovering in the doorway awkwardly while Nathaniel and Marianne discussed dinner arrangements.

My gaze landed on Luca who shared the same soft brown eyes as Nathaniel, the same black hair. While Nathaniel's was straight and combed neatly over his forehead, Luca's waves were wild and untamed. He didn't much care for my presence, playing happily on his own, and I looked away as Nathaniel guided me down another hall and up a large, carpeted staircase.

"How many brothers did you say you have again?" I asked.

"Six," Nathaniel chuckled. "Luc was my parents' last attempt for a girl."

"Ah, so definitely no more?"

"God no."

I snorted, shaking my head.. "And you said James was here too?"

"Yeah, he's sick at the moment, so he'll stay in his room," Nathaniel said, leading me down another long hallway.

"Is he like you?" I asked.

"Hm?"

"Is he going to study Medicine?"

Nathaniel shook his head. "Oh, no, James wants to go to business school."

"Oh, cool."

My gaze locked on a photo of the whole family in front of an altar, a baby who I assumed to be Luca draped in white in his mother's arms. I found Nathaniel's tall frame easily. He was standing beside his father, their identical smiles almost unnerving.

"That's us," Nathaniel mused, following my gaze. He pointed to the boy beside him, who he said was James. Unlike Luca, James did not resemble Nathaniel. His face was all sharp edges whereas Nathaniel's was soft. Beside James was Rio, the second youngest, who shared Luca's waves and Nathaniel's dimpled smile. He was taller than his older brother Avery, which was amusing to Nathaniel since Rio was a year younger. Then there were the twins—Kaleb and Kian—their identical wavy curls crawling down to their shoulders.

"Must be a loud house," I commented.

"Oh, yeah, definitely," Nathaniel grinned as he pushed open a heavy wooden door and invited me inside. "This is the study. Make yourself comfortable."

The 'study' was the size of my bedroom, living room, and bathroom combined. Dark oak bookshelves lined the wall to my left and the wall straight ahead of me. Books of all kinds littered the shelves, most stacked upright, though some had been shoved on top of the others horizontally.

Two large round wooden desks sat in the centre of the room beneath a large golden chandelier and atop a large rustic fur rug. Each desk had its own lamp in the centre with a power point switch beside it for laptops or phone chargers. A long, rectangular desk of the same colour was pressed against the wall to my right, seated comfortably below a window overlooking the back garden which housed a large swimming pool. I should have been used to grandiose homes since living with Aunt Vera, but Nathaniel's was on another level.

I sat by the closest round desk, the cushioned chair welcoming me with a warmth that one would not usually expect from an inanimate object.

I must have released a satisfied sigh, for Nathaniel glanced my way, lips tugged upright in an amused smile.

"Marianne will bring us some water and some snacks once she's done with the laundry," he said, fiddling with the cord to connect his laptop with the projector slowly falling from the ceiling.

My gaze fell upon the bulging veins crawling along his forearms and knuckles, the sight oddly alluring. I wanted to trace my fingers over the blue lines, following them until they disappeared beneath his sleeves.

The sound of the projector connecting with Nathaniel's computer snapped my attention away from his hands and onto my laptop which I had yet to open.

"What's the uh...plan for today?" I asked.

We had finished the bulk of our secondary research, but our report still needed to be written.

"Let's work on the structure and maybe writing our introduction and first paragraph," Nathaniel said. He gestured to the screen which illustrated a suggested structure he must have set up prior to this session. "Our introduction will list these points which will make up our four paragraphs."

I read through the four paragraph topics. 1) Cults as a breeding ground for psychological manipulation, 2) Vulnerable members of society more susceptible to the psychological manipulation of cults, 3) People with psychological disorders more susceptible to the psychological manipulation of cults, 4) Anyone is susceptible to psychological manipulation.

"Is there anything you want to add or change?" Nathaniel asked.

"Are we including any evidence of people not falling for the psychological manipulation of cults?" I asked.

Nathaniel paused. "Oh, I thought we were arguing that *anyone* is suscep-tible."

"We are," I said. "But I thought you wanted to earn extra credit and observe some cults for yourself. Unless you think you *will* be manipulated?"

A long silence hung in the air.

"How did you know about that?"

I shrugged. "You're obnoxiously loud in hallways."

"Listen, I–"

"It's whatever," I cut him off. "Do what you want."

"You're mad at me."

"I'm not."

"Are you sure?"

"Positive."

Nathaniel nodded. "You mentioned the other day something about a cult with your mother..." he said. "...were you part of it too?"

"No," I scoffed. "I mean...*yes*. But it wasn't really...I don't know. I didn't experience the manipulation, if that's what you're asking."

Nathaniel nodded, and I thought he would drop it, but unfortunately his curiosity was unmasked. "Could she still be with the cult? Your mother, that is. You said she went missing. I'm assuming the police already checked with them and everything...?"

"Yes, of course," I said, though I didn't really know the details. My father kept me in the dark regarding the police investigation, he didn't even want me talking to the detectives. "She mustn't have been there."

Nathaniel nodded, and this time, he dropped it.

As promised, Marianne entered with a tray of fruits, biscuits and cheese as well as two glasses of water. We thanked her before proceeding with our introduction and first paragraph. I allocated myself the introduction and research while Nathaniel tackled paragraph one. We exchanged brief comments here and there, but mostly we worked in silence.

Once we'd finished our first draft, we took a ten-minute break to eat the rest of the snacks. Nathaniel's curiosity flared up again.

"What was the cult called? The one your mum moved to?" he asked.

"God's Soldiers Church," I answered, mouth souring at the taste of that name on my lips.

"Do you remember much about it?"

I shrugged. "Not really. I remember a little about the leader...Joe. He and my mother got close and...I guess he kind of fed her delusions."

"Delusions?"

"She uh...she thought my brother and I were possessed by demons," I said. *But that wasn't because of Joe.*

Nathaniel's lips parted, words failing him as he blinked, repeatedly, a grape frozen halfway to his mouth.

"Basically," I went on before I had to endure any sympathy, "Joe validated her delusions and made it worse. My mother believed in everything he said."

Nathaniel shifted in his seat, grape returning to his small plate of untouched food. "Did she tell you...why she believed you and your brother were...possessed?"

"I was a bad kid," I shrugged. "I was disobedient, disrespectful...occasionally violent. And Auden...he was mute. He never said a word until my mother left. His silence unnerved her, I think. His tantrums, too. I think she believed that because we weren't angels, we were devils."

"Did you believe it?"

"What?"

"That you were possessed by the Devil?"

I waited, expectantly, for the Devil's voice in my head. His taunts. His laughter. But he was silent, his absence more unnerving than his presence.

"No, of course not," I lied. "That would be crazy."

"You were a kid, though. It would have been understandable if you did start to believe it."

"I'm not crazy," I said defensively.

Nathaniel threw his hands up in the air. "I never said you were."

I fell silent and reached for my glass of water, swallowing it all in one go to avoid further commentary on my history with my mother and the Devil.

I wanted to blame my mother, and the cult, for the Devil inside my head. But he was there long before the God's Soldiers Church, long before my mother's psychological manipulation. The truth was that he had always been there. And my mother had always known. She'd seen him, too.

Nathaniel typed something on his laptop, scrolling for a few minutes before he turned his screen around to face me. "Is this him?"

I stared at the photo of Joe. He looked just as I remembered, only older. A shiver spread from the top of my neck down to my tailbone, the memory of Joe standing beside my mother, speaking in tongues, one I had not wanted to revisit. "Yes."

"He looks like a politician," Nathaniel commented.

I snorted.

Nathaniel proceeded to scroll through the God's Soldiers social media account until he found a group photo. "Come look at this," he said. I moved around to stand behind him, peering over his shoulder. "Can you see your mum?"

I studied the photo, scanning faces for my mother. There was a woman with long brown hair flowing down her dark green cardigan and a taller woman with blonde hair wearing a pink floral dress. Three men in suits, nearly identical in their balding scalps and their lifeless eyes, stood behind them, one woman with dark curls and pale lips in between them.

"No," I sighed. "She's either just not in this photo or not there at all."

"Perhaps she doesn't want an online presence," Nathaniel suggested, "you know, since she disappeared and…"

His voice trailed off, my discomfort evident in the way I peeled myself away from the computer.

"Have you ever tried to contact him?" Nathaniel asked, gesturing to the photograph of a smiling Joe. "To find your mum?"

I shook my head. "No. My dad must have when she first went missing but he didn't really talk about it so it mustn't have led to anything."

"Weird."

"Hm?"

"You said he validated her delusions. If she ran away, leaving everything she has ever known, wouldn't it have made sense to go with the one person telling her she is right?" Nathaniel shook his head. "It's weird. I think he knows something. He probably lied to your dad."

Not surprising, the Devil spoke up, *considering he was sleeping with his wife.*

I grimaced at the memory.

"You should contact him. Even if she wasn't there at the time, she might be there now," Nathaniel said.

"They both think I have the Devil in me," I reminded him. "And I won't put Auden through that again. She almost killed us during that exorcism. I want nothing to do with her."

"Wait, *exorcism*?" Nathaniel asked in alarm.

"*Attempted* exorcism."

"Look," Nathaniel breathed out, "obviously she had dangerous delusions, but she's your mother, don't you want to find her and finally understand what happened?"

You have to tell him, the Devil said, *you have to tell him her delusions were right.*

"I want nothing to do with her," I said coldly.

Nathaniel opened his mouth only to close it when I returned my attention to my laptop and the assignment we were *supposed* to be working on. I knew he wanted to observe a cult for extra credit, and I wasn't going to sacrifice my own wellbeing for it, nor was I going to risk him obtaining a higher grade from my trauma.

***

Nathaniel drove me home as promised and I prepared dinner for Auden who was studying in the living room. A low hum of music drifted from his headphones, and I turned on the television to watch the news.

A stabbing in London, a terror plot thwarted, the world crumbling all around us. God had abandoned everyone, it seemed.

I switched off the news and approached Auden, peeling off his headphones as I placed a plate of food down in front of him. It was his favourite. His safe food. Chicken schnitzel and salad.

"What are you working on?" I asked, moving his homework aside so he didn't spill food all over it.

"Macbeth," he answered as he reached for his knife and fork.

I sat down beside him with my own plate. "Macbeth, huh? That's my favourite Shakespeare play."

"Why?"

"All the death," I joked.

Auden did not share my sense of humour, though he did say, "I am enjoying it."

"What are you up to?" I asked.

"Banquo's ghost."

"Oh yeah, I remember that part."

"It's not really a ghost, though. It's a metaphor."

"A metaphor, huh? For what?"

"For Macbeth's guilt and descent into madness."

I shifted uncomfortably and reached for my fork, hand trembling. Guilt. Madness. Insanity. Like Banquo's ghost, the Devil wasn't real. He was a metaphor. But he'd been with me since I was four, stranded outside in the cold, waiting to be forgiven for not eating my dinner. What sins of mine did he represent?

"What are *you* working on?" Auden broke through my thoughts, his question catching me off guard.

"Hm?"

"For university," he said, "you were working on an assignment today, weren't you?"

"Oh, uh...yeah. It's nothing interesting," I shrugged, "but last week I took a personality test, that was cool."

"What'd you get?"

"INFJ."

"That's my one too!" he beamed.

I chuckled quietly and ruffled his hair, affection sweeping over me at the wide smile on his face. I wanted to ask him about our mother—what he remembered of that final night in North Lane—but I didn't want to invoke that trauma. Auden and I rarely talked about it and it seemed better that way. I didn't want to remind him of that pain. My job was to protect him. So I didn't ask him about whether he thought our mother had schizophrenia or whether he thought maybe I did too. It was my burden to carry, not his.

Later that night, as I lay awake in bed at insomnia's mercy, I heard a scratching from within the wall behind my bed. It was nearing 3am, and in my exhaustion, I slammed my fist against the wall to scare away the rats or possums scurrying across the wooden beams.

For a beat, there was a silence, and then the rats knocked back.

It was a single knock, so I didn't think much of it.

Barely a minute passed before there was another single thump. Annoyed, I sat up and thumped the wall back.

Fighting with rats at 3am was not something I wanted to be doing, and yet there I was, nostrils flaring at the knock that returned to me. In a sleepless rage, I knocked back twice, hard, and buried myself under the covers, hoping the rats got the hint and left. I had just closed my eyes when I heard it.

Knock. Knock.

That wasn't possible. I sat up, slowly, and stared at my wall.

Knock. Knock.

I stumbled out of bed, almost tripping over the sheets that had tangled around my legs. There must have been something wrong with the pipes. The bathroom shared a wall with my room, so I trudged out, heart racing, and pushed the bathroom door open with my foot as my fingers flicked on the light.

The tiled walls remained intact. There was no leaking, or any notable signs of damage. It was a relief, given I didn't have the money to fix any issues, but it was unnerving. What had caused the knocking inside my wall?

I approached the wall connected to my bedroom and knocked, once. Nothing. The rats had scattered. And whatever plumbing issue might have caused it must have resolved itself.

Shaking my head, I turned to leave when the bathroom light flickered, the door slamming shut before I had the chance to flee.

Darkness enveloped the room. It devoured all warmth, leaving an ice-cold chill that settled deep into my bones.

I knew what awaited me in the clothed mirror—I knew who would be staring back if I turned around and removed the sheet. I had to leave. I had to get out. I tried to open the door, but it wouldn't budge.

"Let me go!" I demanded.

Not until you make me a promise.

"What promise?"

You must promise not to go looking for your mother.

I swallowed the lump in my throat, arms wrapped around my body to fend off the cold.

I had no interest in finding my mother, but it was strange the Devil would demand such a promise. Was it because I was right about her? Did she have schizophrenia or some other kind of mental disorder? And if I was right about her, did that mean I was right about myself, too? Hell, I had to be right, for who was I talking to right now?

"Why?" I challenged.

She has only ever caused us pain. Why bring that pain back into our lives? Think of Auden. Do you really want to hurt him again?

"You don't care about Auden. You don't care about us being in pain," I scoffed. "You're scared. You're scared that if I seek out my mother, she might be able to rid me of you once and for all."

Laughter burned my ears. The Devil's gentleness all but evaporated as fear crawled through my veins, goosebumps dancing along every inch of exposed flesh.

There is no Devil, Augustus. I am you. You are me. For your mother to rid you of me, you would have to die.

"No," I shook my head, "we are *not* the same."

You sound like your mother. Delusional. I am the voice in your head. Literally. You make me out to be somebody else—the Devil, the villain—so you don't have to face the truth of what you are. A monster.

"No."

Look at me.

I didn't move an inch.

Look at me.

I shook my head.

Look at me.

I turned, slowly, raising my head to look at the mirror. The white sheet had fallen, my reflection in the mirror uncorrupted, undistorted.

I am you. You are me. There is no Devil.

It was my brown curls, my hazel eyes, my sharp cheekbones and thin lips. There was no Devil.

My shoulders dropped, a breath of air escaping the confines of my chest. I was alright. Everything was alright. The Devil wasn't real and–

Shadowed claws burst from the mirror, shattered glass raining over me as darkness seeped into my skin. Talons tore at my shirt, burying into my chest.

I screamed, but my reflection only laughed. It laughed, and laughed, and laughed.

The room spun, glass shards flying toward me like bullets. They pierced my skin, swimming through flesh and bone. I tried to scramble away, to escape this torture chamber, but my reflection ruptured from the mirror, pinning me to the tiled wall, eyes as black as death.

It smiled; fanged teeth stained with blood, hungry for a taste of my flesh. The metallic tang of iron and rot poured from its breath as it inched closer to take a fatal bite, pain blinding my vision as everything–

"AUGUSTUS!"

My eyes snapped open, the bedroom light glaring down at my sweat-drenched body huddled in the corner of my bedroom, bed sheets twisted around my ankles. Auden's arms were tight around me, securing me to his chest.

"It was a nightmare," Auden said calmly, hand moving up and down my back the way I used to do it for him. "Just a nightmare. You're okay, now. You're okay."

I had always tried to hold back tears in Auden's presence, but they flowed freely now. I couldn't contain them any longer. "I think I'm going crazy."

"You're not crazy," Auden soothed me, rocking us both back and forth.

I cried myself to exhaustion in Auden's arms. I would never forgive myself for displaying such weakness in front of him, but he was my brother, and he understood me more than anyone else ever could.

As I closed my eyes, surrendering to sleep's warm embrace, the Devil's voice whispered in my ear, *Keep your promise, or your brother is mine.*

CHAPTER TWENTY-SIX

"How long have you been having these nightmares?"

Dr. Rosewood leaned back in her chair, one leg crossed over the other as she eyed me over the top of her laptop. I had booked an appointment to discuss my mental health, something I never thought I would do, but after the night before, I'd grown concerned.

I hadn't been able to determine what was real and what was a dream. And it frightened me. I did not want to turn out like my mother.

I hadn't told Dr. Rosewood about the hallucinations out of fear I would immediately be sent for testing and assigned a psychiatrist. So, instead, to test the waters, I told her about my nightmares.

"I've had them for as long as I can remember," I answered, gaze falling to the carpeted floor. "But I guess they got worse after everything that led to my mother leaving."

Dr. Rosewood had been alarmed to hear the story of North Lane, but she'd done well to maintain professional curiosity and not press me for answers I was not willing to give. Though I feared if I evaded any more questions, she would give me a poor evaluation.

"I see." Dr. Rosewood typed something briefly before returning her attention to me. "Sometimes, after a particularly traumatic event, our brain holds onto the memories to relive them, often through dreams or nightmares. It is not uncommon to experience the same recurring nightmare or nightmares with recurring themes."

"How do I stop it?" I asked. "I am losing sleep. I'm always exhausted. I don't know how much longer I can continue like this." My voice cracked. I hated how desperate I sounded.

"There is therapy," Dr. Rosewood answered. "And there are also some medications that can assist you in having a more restful sleep."

"I'd have to see a doctor for those, right?"

"I can refer you to a psychiatrist."

"What? Why not a GP?"

"You may have Post Traumatic Stress Disorder, Augustus. A GP can give you medication for general sleep issues, but a psychiatrist will be able to prescribe you stronger medications, if necessary," she explained.

"Will they do tests? Like scan my brain?"

"Most likely. There could be physiological causes for the nightmares and insomnia, and it is always important to rule them out."

I suppose that made sense, but the fear of someone looking at my brain and finding the Devil was overwhelming. What if they discovered a chemical imbalance that led them to believe I had schizophrenia? This could completely alter my life.

"I don't know...I might just get meds off a GP," I said.

"It is your decision to make," Dr. Rosewood said. "But I will write up the referral in case you change your mind."

I nodded, hands fidgeting on my lap as I watched her move around her desk, type something on her computer and then print a piece of paper. She handed it to me with a soft smile. "Let me know how it goes."

***

On my way to the library, I heard a word I hadn't heard since high school. It was such a hateful word, one that made me pause, turning my head expecting

to see Alexander hurtling it at his latest victim. It wasn't Alexander, however,
I wouldn't have been surprised to see him.

What did surprise me, though, was *who* the word was directed at.

Nathaniel stood with his friends, lips turned down and his eyebrows
furrowed, arms raised to placate the man who spat the word at him.

One of Nathaniel's friends approached the man, but Nate pulled him
back, mouthing 'it's not worth it.'

The man repeated the three-letter word amidst other insults while
Nathaniel's friends dragged him away. I watched, in silence, my jaw clenched
as I remembered the word being thrown at me when 'Augustus the Gay'
became my infamous nickname.

The other man, voice slurred, stumbled away as though drunk. I didn't
care whether he was intoxicated or not, he knew better than to throw harm-
ful words around. And for what? What could Nathaniel have done?

I followed the man, sticking to the shadows, my hands curling and uncurl-
ing at my sides. The urge to slam him to the ground, gouge out his eyes, and
tear him limb from limb was so strong I had to draw in a sharp breath to
wipe the grotesque imagery from my mind.

A hand on my shoulder ended my plan to confront him. I turned, slowly,
and groaned at the sight of Nathaniel. His collar had been ruffled. The man
had gotten physical with him, and the urge to end his life became even more
powerful.

"You should punch him," I blurted out.

"I'm not going to punch him," Nathaniel sighed.

I shrugged and turned to follow the man. "Fine, I will."

Nathaniel's fingers wrapped around my wrist, holding me back. "You're
like an angry cat."

"Excuse me?!"

"You know…when cats are angry, all claws and hisses, but they look really cute…" Nathaniel explained.

"You think I'm *cute*?" I asked, bewildered.

"Adorably so." He released hold of my wrist and calmly pressed his shoulder to the tree beside him, arms folded over his chest as he studied me from head to toe, no doubt registering the dark circles under my eyes and the pale colour of my skin. "You okay?"

"What happened with that guy?" I asked instead.

Nathaniel's small smile faded. "I met him last night while my friends and I were clubbing. We got around to talking and I thought we were having a nice time. I slipped him my number before I left but he must not have noticed it until I was already gone. And then when he saw me today…he blew up."

I swallowed hard. "Because…you slipped him your number?"

"Guess so," Nathaniel shrugged.

"I think you dodged a bullet there anyway," I said. "He's a jerk."

Nathaniel let out a breathless chuckle. "Yeah, I think so too. Where are you headed? Do you have class?"

I shook my head.

"Want to entertain me for an hour, then?" he asked casually, though by the look in his eye, I could tell he didn't want to be alone. "All my friends have class or are headed home. I don't feel like studying now before my next class. Just…thought maybe I'd wander around campus or something."

Under normal circumstances, I would have refused. I valued my alone time. But I knew Nathaniel could use the distraction, so I nodded and let him guide me through the old church grounds toward the field of grass where students liked to picnic on sunny days.

We found a small footbridge above a creek and sat down, legs swinging over the edge, our thighs brushing.

Nathaniel pulled out a cigar and offered me one. Although I'd never smoked before, I accepted, not sure what I was supposed to do with it.

"How did you know I was following that guy?" I asked once he'd lit both of our cigars.

"I turned around to make sure he was gone when I saw you," he said.

"How did you know I wasn't just...walking in the same direction?"

Nathaniel raised the cigar to his lips, releasing a puff of smoke before answering, "I don't know...you looked tense."

I coughed abruptly when I breathed in the smoke, throat and nostrils burning unpleasantly.

Nathaniel grinned, slapping me on the back to clear my airways. "First time?" he asked.

I lowered the cigar, no longer interested in smoking. "Yeah."

"It's a bad habit anyway," he said, "best not to start."

"Then why do you do it, Mr Med school?" I asked.

Nathaniel chuckled. "It's the only thing that calms me down when I'm upset."

A stab of guilt pierced into me. "I'm sorry for what that guy called you. It's...an awful word."

"Yeah, it is," Nathaniel agreed, "but it's okay. I'm used to it."

"That doesn't make it okay," I said.

"Yeah."

"Are you...okay?"

Nathaniel let out another breath of smoke as he nodded. "I'm fine. I just don't want to think about it anymore."

"What would you like to talk about instead?" I asked.

"You," Nathaniel answered without hesitation.

I raised an eyebrow. "Me?"

"Mhm." Nathaniel shifted his body to face me, one leg crossed while the other continued swinging off the edge of the bridge. "Tell me more about yourself."

I chuckled nervously. "I don't really like talking about myself."

"Oh come on," Nathaniel pouted. "If you tell me one thing about yourself, I'll tell you one thing about *me.* "

I opened my mouth to make a sarcastic remark about how I didn't really care to know more about him, but that was a lie. I *did* want to know more about Nathaniel Carrington—my rival.

"Fine," I mumbled, "let me try and think of something to tell you."

I must have been taking far too long, for Nathaniel leaned closer to whisper, "Would it be easier if we just asked each other questions?"

"Yeah," I breathed out, "probably."

"Okay," Nathaniel grinned, "You work in a bookstore so...what's your favourite book?"

I pinned him with a glare. "Just one?"

"Just one," he confirmed before taking another drag.

I scowled. "Since I can only choose *one,* I'll say *Frankenstein* by Mary Shelley."

"Ah, I haven't read that yet."

"What?! It's a classic. You must read it!"

"I will, definitely." Nathaniel stubbed out his cigar and grinned. "Okay, okay, ask me something!"

"Why are you so excited?"

"Is that your question?"

I shook my head. "No, no, wait no!"

He laughed, dimpled cheeks glistening in the warm sunlight as I searched my brain for a question I wanted to know the answer to.

"Why Dawnridge?" I decided. "I know you...didn't get into Oxford. But there's Cambridge and Edinburgh...why Dawnridge?"

Nathaniel clicked his tongue. "Oh, that's easy. I didn't want to be too far away from my friends and family. A lot of my school friends enrolled here and it's still a prestigious university, so I thought, why not? And I'm happy with my choice."

"So it wasn't out of fear that everyone at Cambridge would be smarter?" I teased.

Nathaniel gasped and poked my chest playfully. "Absolutely *not*! I would be at the top of every class there just as I am here!"

I grinned, feeling lightheaded from how easy it was to laugh with and tease Nathaniel. Maybe it was the lack of sleep, but everything just felt *good. Easy.*

We moved to the other side of the bridge, sheltering under the shade when the sun became too harsh for my pale skin.

"What's your favourite colour?" he asked.

"Guess."

Silence. And then, "Green!"

I didn't have a favourite colour. But the moment he said green, his smile wide and his head thrown back, green was suddenly all I could think about. The green of his tie, the green grass seeping through the rocks below our feet, the green vest he wore the first day I laid eyes on him. Everything was green.

"How did you know?!" I gasped playfully.

His laugh—a heavenly, euphoric sound—sent the butterflies in my stomach wild. "I was actually going to guess black," he said, slowly turning his head to face me, gaze locking on mine, "but then I thought about the small specks of green in your eyes and I just knew."

Heat crawled to my cheeks and I looked away, my mind screaming *what the fuck* while my heart did backflips and somersaults as though competing in a gymnastics competition.

Nathaniel was, quite possibly, the most beautiful human to ever walk upon this earth. And, I might add, the most infuriating. How could he say such things and then turn back around to face the water with a carefree smile while I was struggling to breathe?

I wanted to carve out his heart, bit by bit, and slice it into tiny pieces, scattering them like rose petals.

"What about you?" I cleared my throat. "What is your favourite colour?"

"Guess."

I rolled my eyes playfully and cocked my head to the side in thought. "Yellow?"

Nathaniel pulled a face that resembled horror, disgust and offence all at once. "Yellow?! Yellow?! Why yellow?"

"Why *not* yellow? What have you got against yellow?"

"Do you promise not to laugh?"

I shook my head. "No."

An elbow to the ribs was his response before he opened his mouth to speak, "When I was about eight or nine, I was painting outside with my brothers and the yellow paint I needed wouldn't come out of the tube. It was stuck. I really needed it, though. So, being the clever problem solver I am, I bit down on the bottom of the tube in the hopes that it would send the paint up. Just like toothpaste."

"Oh no," I whispered.

"Oh yes," Nathaniel sighed. "I bit down too hard and yellow paint splattered into my mouth. It was awful."

I laughed. It was an unfamiliar sound, almost unnatural coming from my lips, but I couldn't stop. "Let me get this straight...you hate the colour yellow, because you got yellow paint in your mouth?"

"Precisely."

I laughed again, unable to help myself. "That is ridiculous."

"Yeah, well, I'm book smart, not street smart."

"That's just a lack of common sense."

"Yeah, yeah, whatever."

"Alright, alright, what *is* your favourite colour then?"

"Brown."

"Brown?" I repeated, surprised. "Why brown?"

"It reminds me of autumn," he said, "of cosy days reading under a tree, fallen leaves all around me."

"And you look good in brown too," I added, gaze falling to his brown trousers and brown coat. I had said it without thinking, and when Nathaniel whirled to look at me, I immediately looked away.

"Thank you," he smiled.

"Is it…" I cleared my throat. "Is it almost time for your class?"

Nathaniel pulled out his phone and groaned. "Yes. Unfortunately."

Relief and disappointment washed over me all at once. "I'll walk you to class, then."

"You're not still worried about that guy, are you?" he mused as he slowly stood up.

Yes. "No."

Nathaniel chuckled as if he sensed my lie. I rolled my eyes, swung my bag over my shoulder, and led him to his class. It was strange, but at that moment, the Devil had no influence on me at all. He remained in his cage. Nathaniel, it seemed, was the lock that kept him imprisoned.

CHAPTER TWENTY-SEVEN

Sleep evaded me, even with the medication the doctor had prescribed. Dr. Rosewood was right. I needed something stronger, which meant I needed to see a psychiatrist.

But you're insane. They'll lock you up and throw away the key.

I splashed water on my face to drown out the Devil's words. He was right. I couldn't risk seeing a psychiatrist. What I needed to do was focus on my studies and eventually, things would settle down. I was just stressed.

And that stress was building due to approaching deadlines. Nathaniel requested two more study sessions, and I had an investigation report for another subject that was due by the end of the week, and I'd only gotten through the introduction. De-stressing seemed nearly impossible.

I must have resembled death when Nathaniel came to pick me up, for he immediately bombarded me with questions about my health.

"You're not a licensed medical professional yet," I pointed out tiredly.

"I am a First Aid Officer, though," he argued.

I shot him a look.

Nathaniel returned the look as he pulled up at the traffic lights. "I know something is wrong."

Feeling cornered, I opened the window and let out a long sigh of relief as the cool air kissed my skin. "I'm fine. I'm just stressed."

"With assignments?"

I nodded.

"Let's do something fun, then," Nathaniel suggested when the traffic light turned green, attention back on the road, "to de-stress and take your mind off things."

"What? No! We have to work on our assignment…you know, one of the things *stressing* me out," I said, exasperated.

"You're working with *me*, Augustus, we're going to get it done. Don't worry. We can afford to take some time off to relax," he said calmly.

"I'm not thrilled about this," I mumbled, head nearly all the way out the window to chase the wind.

"Where do you want to go?"

"I don't want to go anywhere."

"You have to choose."

"Nathaniel–"

"Choose!"

"I don't care, anywhere, just…" I let my eyelids flutter shut against the wind, "…just don't stop the car yet."

"Shall I play some music?"

I slowly opened my eyes, head turning to give Nathaniel my best 'are you fucking kidding' glare. He grinned, dimpled cheeks glaring back. It was hard to hate him when he smiled—the promise of Heaven in his eyes.

He connected his phone to the Bluetooth and turned up the music as he began to sing, voice cracking at the high notes.

"What the hell are you singing?"

Nathaniel raised his voice louder, body swaying from side to side as he continued to sing. "But we'll get together then!" He finished the chorus with a cheer. "You know we'll have a good time then!"

My lips betrayed me, spreading into a small smile as my hand shot out to nudge him.

"What?" Nathaniel laughed. "Don't tell me you don't know this song! It's in Shrek!"

"I never watched Shrek."

Nathaniel gasped and almost ran the car off the road. "WHAT?"

"Kidding," I smirked, just as the chorus started up again.

We sang for a while until Nathaniel pulled up in front of an art gallery.

"What are we doing here?" I asked, slowly rolling up the window.

"I know you like art," Nathaniel said, almost shyly, "and I haven't been to this gallery before, so I thought we'd check it out."

I ducked my head to hide the heat that rose to my cheeks. I wasn't used to anyone paying any interest to what I liked, nor making any effort to cheer me up. Nathaniel was an angel. And I was afraid of him, in a way. What was his end goal? Why was he being so nice to me? Was this a form of distraction so that he could discard me and claim the group assignment to be his own work?

You have to stay away from him.

"Come, there are some unique sculptures here," Nathaniel said as he started toward the entrance.

I followed, wearily, studying the back of Nathaniel's head as if it would answer the questions racing through my mind.

Inside, an employee greeted us and made sure we didn't bring any water or large bags into the gallery. Nathaniel took a pamphlet with information about the exhibitions and then guided me through a door to the left which led to the galleries on the first floor.

I slipped my hands into my pockets as I studied the artwork displayed on perfectly lit white walls, some framed in golden arches while others sat unframed on a canvas. These works were contemporary, with little descriptions underneath to add context to the artwork. Nathaniel pulled out his phone and snapped some photos of artwork he liked while I read descriptions.

Out of the corner of my eye, I noticed Nathaniel attempting a selfie in front of a large artwork which was supposed to be an optical illusion. The horizontal lines looked like they were moving side to side, even though they weren't.

"Would you like me to take a photo?" I offered.

Nathaniel beamed. "Yes, please!"

With a nod, I took the phone and stepped back, waiting for him to pose. He made it seem so effortless as he slipped his hands into the pockets of his long brown coat and began walking back and forth in front of the artwork. I tapped the camera repeatedly to capture him mid-step. In some shots, he leaned forward, others he leaned back, some he looked at the artwork, others he stood with his back turned.

Once done, I handed the phone back to him and he didn't even look through, as though confident there would be a good shot there.

"Would you like me to take any photos for you?" Nathaniel asked.

I shook my head. I didn't like the way I looked on camera, and I avoided any form of mirroring, never quite knowing when the Devil would break through.

Nathaniel didn't push. We made our way up to the second floor which was filled with classic, western artworks of biblical and royal nature, some including the English wilderness and architecture. I stood in front of one artwork that was as tall as the floor to the high ceiling. It had lighting all around the frame so you could take in every inch of it.

"This is unreal," Nathaniel breathed out from behind me.

He was right. It was unreal. The way the artist captured the feeling of descending into Hell, the fear, the uncertainty, the horror. The artwork reminded me of Dante's *Inferno,* though the description said it was inspired by the artist's personal nightmares of waking in Hell surrounded by the screams of tortured souls.

"Do you believe in Hell?" I asked curiously.

"Yes."

"Are you afraid of it?"

"Yes."

I nodded. "Me too."

"But I don't think we'll ever end up there," Nathaniel said, though he didn't sound as confident as he probably intended. There were doubts in his mind, and I wanted to analyse those doubts, pull them apart until I saw a crack.

"You probably won't," I said. "You won't even punch someone who upsets you. I think you're one of the good ones."

"But I'm gay."

I turned to look at him, head whipping around so fast that a sharp pain lanced through my neck. I ignored it as I studied the pools of sadness in his eyes. "You don't really believe God sends you to Hell for who you love, do you?"

"No," he sighed, "the God I believe in would never do that. But sometimes I do fear I am wrong. My friends say I should just abandon my faith. That being Catholic and gay doesn't make sense, but my faith has nothing to do with what is written in some old book—an old book written by other humans. But there's still a chance I'm wrong and...that scares me."

I remembered Father Andrej's words: *Sin is sin no matter how great.* But what did he know? He wasn't God.

"Bad people go to Hell, Nathaniel. And you're not bad. I promise."

A small smile lit up his face. "You're probably right. And I'm sure you won't end up there, either."

I scoffed.

"What? You're not a bad person."

"You don't know me."

"I know enough to know that a bad person wouldn't have spent the last two minutes trying to reassure me I won't go to Hell for being gay."

I shrugged. "I think that just means I'm not homophobic."

"Why do you think you're a bad person?"

Do you have all day? There's a very long list of reasons.

"Come on, what did you do that was so bad?" Nathaniel asked. "Did you kill animals or something? Did you hurt your brother? Did you set things on fire? What did you do?"

I hadn't expected the sudden interrogation, nor the way Nathaniel's jaw tightened, his eyebrows furrowed. He looked angry. And I panicked. I didn't want him to be angry with me.

"No...I...I didn't kill anything. I would never hurt my brother. And I didn't set things on fire."

"Well? What did you do, then?" Nathaniel pushed.

I hesitated before telling him the same thing I told Dr. Rosewood—that I was disobedient, disrespectful, that I drew on walls and punched holes through windows. I couldn't tell him the truth, so whatever words he conjured to console me would mean nothing.

Nathaniel's gaze softened and he shifted closer, raising a hand as if to touch me but decided against it before our skin could connect. "Augustus," he said, "you were a *child.* And children do those things sometimes. I'm pretty sure I did all those things at some stage, too. Does that make me a bad person too?"

"No," I said quietly.

"Then neither are you," Nathaniel bumped me with his elbow. "You're too hard on yourself. You're not some wicked demon for talking back a few times and smashing things when you're angry. You're not even that same kid anymore."

"Yes, but..."

"But what?"

Tell him, the Devil urged, *watch him run.*

I shook my head. "I just...I have this awful feeling that I..."

"What?"

The Devil's smile was all teeth. I couldn't see it, but I could hear it in his voice as he said, *Tell him. Tell him. Tell him.*

I closed my eyes, drowning out the voice with several deep breaths, and when I opened them, Nathaniel was gone, the gallery shrouded in darkness.

Panic consumed me. It pounded against my ribcage, the cracks echoing loudly inside the now empty gallery. The Devil's laughter sent me to my knees, hands over my ears in a pathetic attempt to shut him out. I struggled to breathe, as if smoke were infiltrating my lungs, and that was when I heard the crackling flames. They slithered toward me, inch by inch, heat drawing sweat from my pores.

"No," I whispered, trying to stand up, "no, no, no, no."

I whirled around in search of the exit, but there were only flickering flames surrounded by an endless void. Where was Nathaniel? Had he gotten to safety?

Struggling to capture enough air in my lungs, I stumbled forward, hoping the exit would appear as I ventured through the darkness. But there was no end in sight. I was going to die. This was real. It had to be. Surely hallucinations couldn't kill you. Not like this. Coughing, I collapsed to my knees and hunched over, tears burning down my cheeks.

You better get used to the heat...there's a lot more of it in Hell, the Devil cackled.

The flames crawled closer and, with no other way to process my fear, I screamed.

Hands clasped my shoulders and shook me, a voice that was not the Devil's calling my name. I opened my eyes, slowly, and blinked as the white walls of the gallery and the classic artworks filled my vision, brown eyes locking on mine with concern.

"Breathe," Nathaniel whispered, both his hands on my shoulders as he crouched down in front of me. "Breathe, Augustus. In and out. Just like that."

I inhaled when Nathaniel inhaled, exhaled when he exhaled. A security guard approached with a plastic cup of water, and I drowned it in one go to cool my burning throat. The gallery had been emptied of people, no doubt frightened from the screaming mad man. What was happening to me? It had never gotten this bad before. Was I completely losing my mind?

"Are you sure you don't want me to call someone?" I heard the security guard ask Nathaniel.

"No, it's okay, I'll take care of him," Nathaniel replied. "We'll leave now so we don't cause any more disruptions. I apologise for the inconvenience."

I let Nathaniel pull me to my feet and guide me back out into the carpark. He was speaking as he helped me into the car, but his words formed a string of nonsense I could not decipher. It wasn't until we were pulling into the hospital car park that I snapped out of my daze and finally registered the words he was saying.

"...and we'll just get you checked out in case maybe you've taken something that's making you unwell..."

"I haven't taken any drugs!" I snapped.

Nathaniel blinked, whether surprised by my snap or simply that I'd finally spoken, I didn't know. "Okay," he said, calmly, "but I still think we should let a doctor take a look at you."

He unbuckled his seatbelt while I sat, unmoving.

There was no way I was going inside a hospital. All I wanted to do was go home, sleep, and then have dinner with Auden. If I went inside the hospital, I wasn't sure who would come back out.

"Augustus," Nathaniel sighed. "I don't know what happened back there. It was like...like you were somewhere else entirely."

"It was a panic attack," I said, glaring straight ahead of me as my hands curled and uncurled on my lap.

"Okay...but you couldn't even *see* me. I was right in front of you and you–"

"I'm sorry if I scared you but I was having a panic attack that obstructed my vision and hearing," I interrupted.

"You were hallucinating," Nathaniel said, voice more firm now. "You were seeing something that scared you. You were *screaming*."

My hands trembled uncontrollably. I moved them under my thighs, my bottom lip caught between my teeth as tears pooled in my eyes. I didn't want to cry. Not again.

"I'm not going to force you," Nathaniel whispered, his hand resting on my knee. "But I really think you should. The doctors can organise an MRI or a CT scan and–"

I pushed his hand off my knee and climbed out of the car, slamming the door shut behind me. Nathaniel followed, his own door clicking shut quietly.

"Augustus–"

I didn't wait to hear what he had to say—I ran. I ran until I reached a park bench and dumped myself down onto it, face buried in my hands. Nathaniel must have lost track of me, or given up, for I remained alone.

Never alone, little monster.

A quiet sob escaped the back of my throat, the Devil's clawed hands sliding over my shoulders, piercing through flesh. I still didn't know the truth. Was he real? Or was it all just in my head?

I didn't remember how I got back home, only that when I did, Auden was reading a book on the couch, headphones on and uniform discarded for sweatpants and an oversized t-shirt. He looked up when I entered, and his eyes widened in a way that indicated I must have looked as bad as I felt. Not wanting him to see me in such a state, I shook my head and told him I was going to shower.

He was waiting in the hallway when I emerged from the bathroom in only a pair of black shorts, my wet curls slicked back away from my forehead.

"Are you okay?" he asked, following me into my bedroom.

"I'm fine, Audie," I tried to give him a reassuring smile, "just tired."

"Are you going to have dinner?"

"I think I'm just going to go to sleep. Are you okay to eat leftovers?"

"Yes, but–"

"Goodnight," I announced as I flopped down on my bed.

In a matter of minutes, sleep lured me into what I had anticipated to be a nightmare, only for it to be a dream I'd never had before.

I was inside the House on North Lane, seated at the dining table, sun pouring in from the kitchen window as I finger-painted with Auden. He looked only around three or four, which meant I must have been around eight or nine. We wore identical Spider-man aprons, our fingers stained a mix of green, red and purple.

My father was mowing the lawn out the front, the sound echoing through the entire first floor while my mother dusted the living room. She was asking Auden and I what we were painting when she accidentally knocked a candle from the bookcase, smashing it to pieces. With a yelp, she stepped back and in distress, called for me.

"Help me clean this up," she said, hands shaking.

I reached for a dustpan and broom and began cleaning up the shattered glass and wax.

"Help me, help me, help me," she kept repeating.

I was confused, given the fact that I *was* helping her. And then her words changed to *find me, find me, find me.* And those quickly became *save me, save me, save me.*

I turned to face her, dustpan falling from my hands as I instinctively backed away. Her hair was dishevelled and tearing from her scalp, her skin deathly pale. She was wearing the same white gown she'd worn that last night in North Lane, ash and dust clinging to the material.

Her hands found my wrists, holding me in place as she whispered, "Help me. Find me. Save me."

"You're right here, Mumma," I said, desperately trying to unshackle myself from her firm grip.

"Help me. Find me. Save me."

Her face twisted and her jaw snapped open, an inhuman scream escaping her throat as the floor trembled beneath us. Small critters poured from her mouth, falling to the wooden floorboards like a raging river. They crawled up my legs, slipping beneath my shirt and under my skin. She leaned closer, the stench of death and decay massacring my nostrils, and repeated her phrase. *Help me. Find me. Save me.*

The nightmare ended with heavy breathing and a pool of sweat. I sat up, glancing toward my alarm clock and the blearing red 3:33am. Running a hand over my face, I focused on my breathing and blindly reached for my phone. I had dozens of messages and missed calls from Nathaniel, and the memory of the day before came crashing back to me.

Guilt weighed heavy on my chest as I read through each one of Nathaniel's messages asking if I was okay, apologising, begging me to let him know where I was.

I didn't understand why he cared so much, and although I was still weary of whether any of it was real, I knew I'd hate myself if I let him worry a moment longer.

'Hey, sorry, I'm okay', I wrote back, 'I'm home.'

I didn't expect a response until a reasonable hour, but Nathaniel's message came in under a minute.

'Thank God. I'm sorry for today. I'm here if you need anything.'

I didn't have the energy to assure him I was fine, so I liked his message and put my phone away, my mind returning to the dream.

Help me. Find me. Save me.

It was no doubt a crazy thought, but what if my mother was trying to reach me? She needed help, she wanted me to find and save her. Maybe after all this time, she realised she was in a cult and couldn't get out on her own. I had no evidence to back up this absurd claim, but it was the only reasonable explanation for why she never came back. She needed saving and my father had failed. And I, too, would fail if I didn't try to find her.

CHAPTER TWENTY-EIGHT

Auden was eating cereal at the dining table when I finally emerged from my bedroom, a National Geographic documentary playing on his laptop. His headphones lay abandoned atop his scattered schoolbooks, the narrator's voice following me into the kitchen as I opened the refrigerator to an absence of groceries. A long sigh escaped my throat.

"What are you watching?" I asked, squinting to catch the title of the documentary on his screen. "Oh, is that Pompeii?"

"Herculaneum," he corrected.

"Oh, the Pompeii wannabe," I joked, letting the refrigerator door fall shut. "I'm going to go the cafe to get some banana bread and–"

"Herculaneum is not the Pompeii wannabe," Auden interjected.

"What?"

"You said Herculaneum is the Pompeii wannabe but it was its own town with its own unique features and history. The only things they share is that they're Roman and victims of Mount Vesuvius."

"Alright..."

"And Pompeii is only more famous because more of it has been uncovered since most of Herculaneum is buried under the modern city."

"Okay, you think you're so clever and–"

"I *am* clever," Auden interrupted calmly.

I closed my mouth, opened it, and then closed it again. Yes, he was clever. I could not deny that. And so, I brought up something *he* could not deny in return. "I'm older."

Auden blinked, as if unsure whether he'd heard me correctly. He waited a beat and then, with a small frown, said, "Yes. But that does not make you right."

"You're annoying."

He nodded, unsurprised by my childish retort.

"I'm going to the cafe," I mumbled.

"Will you bring me a chocolate drink on the way back?" he asked.

"No."

"But–"

"Auden, I'd burn the world for you," I said impatiently as I snatched my keys off its hook. "I'm obviously going to bring you back hot chocolate."

"Okay but it wasn't obvious–"

"Just finish your homework or whatever it is you were doing before you corrected me," I said and slammed the door shut behind me.

The cafe was crowded with business suits, school uniforms, nursing scrubs and high visual shirts as workers lined up for their morning coffee. Quiet chatter blended in with the sound of coffee machines and paper cups, Billie Eilish's voice pouring from the speakers.

I ordered a hot chocolate for Auden and some banana bread to share, shifting from one foot to the other while I waited. The Devil stood beside me, a silent, faceless shadow. His presence was not unwanted. Yes, he was my enemy. But he was familiar. And familiarity was a comfort. As long as I didn't look in the mirror, I could pretend he wasn't the Devil at all and more...a guardian angel, of sorts.

My phone vibrated in my pocket, drawing my attention to a message from Nathaniel regarding our assignment. We still had so much work to do. The previous day had been a complete disaster, because of *me*, and so I had little choice but to respond. Chewing on the inside of my mouth, I told him I was free for a few hours before my afternoon shift at *Browning Books*, and we agreed to meet at the library.

"Augustus!"

The cafe quietened. Lights dimmed. Several pairs of eyes followed me to the counter where my order waited. I reached for the hot chocolate, wincing as my fingers connected with the red liquid spilling down the sides of the paper cup.

"Uh..." I lifted my head, searching for a napkin and a staff member to question. But there were no napkins. Nor any staff members to assist me. The cafe had been completely emptied, an eerie silence hanging in the air as my gaze dropped to the sliced banana bread inside a paper bag.

White, blue and green splotches of mold invaded the aged bread, a single worm crawling out of a hole in the dough. It slithered toward me, multiplying, worms of all shapes and colours littering the counter.

I backed away, heart racing.

What's the matter?

"This isn't real," I whispered.

If it isn't real, what are you so afraid of? Eat the bread.

"What?!"

Eat the bread. Prove it isn't real.

Swallowing back the bile that threatened to escape my throat, I reached toward the bread, hands trembling. It wasn't real, and yet I felt the worms beneath my fingertips. It wasn't real, and yet the bread's sour, musty odour burned my nostrils. It wasn't real, and yet I tossed the bread to the floor, shaking my head. It wasn't real. But I couldn't eat it.

That's what I thought, little monster.

An hour later, I reached the study room Nathaniel had secured us on the third floor. He was seated at the long, dark brown desk, the collar of his white shirt unbuttoned to reveal soft, golden skin. His long black coat hung off the chair behind him like a shadow, his brown knitted sweater the same shade as his eyes.

I averted my gaze as I stepped inside, Nathaniel peering up at me with a small, almost nervous smile.

"Hi," he said.

I greeted him with a nod and what I hoped to be a polite smile as I stepped inside and placed my laptop down across from his, the desk already cluttered with annotated articles. An empty takeaway cup had tipped over, a drop of coffee soaking through Nathaniel's opened notebook.

"I was just working on paragraph two," he said, fingers drumming against his laptop as he updated me on the progress he'd made. "I found several articles analysing the isolation tactics cult leaders employ during recruitment stages. It's a way to maintain control. By severing a person's connection with the outside world...they have the power to determine what they think, feel and do."

"The perfect way to have their power unquestioned," I murmured.

"I want to know your thoughts on this," he said, sliding a book toward me, "there's a section on emotional control. It explores how guilt and fear are used to enforce isolation. Should I elaborate on this in my paragraph?"

I opened the book to the bookmarked section and skimmed through it before raising my eyes to meet his. "Yeah, definitely. It's a good way to detail how the manipulation process works."

"Perfect."

"I'll start on paragraph three," I said, "Religious psychosis, right?"

"Definitely," Nathaniel nodded, "but make sure you reference *how* cults facilitate an environment that breeds psychosis, with examples."

"Obviously," I said, suppressing an eye roll, "cults breed psychosis by telling their members they're special, chosen. That will be my main point."

"Good, good. Just checking we're on the same page."

We divided our tasks and worked in a comfortable silence, with only the soft rhythm of typing and the occasional scratch of pen on paper. But my mind wandered. The Devil seeped inside my head like spilled ink, darkening all my thoughts.

My mother's face appeared behind my eyelids with every blink, the words *help me, find me, save me* repeating in my head like a broken record. It meant something, it *had* to. Maybe she was speaking to me through God, and this was her means of communication—of asking for help. For over ten years I had been ignoring her, trying to forget her, but maybe it was time I finally found her and solved the mystery of why she disappeared. Of why she left me to succumb to Hell's fire.

Maybe you are *insane. You really think she is able to find you in your dreams?*

The God's Soldiers website lit up my screen before I even processed what I was doing, Joe's smiling face in the left-hand corner as I exited the pop-up ad asking for donations for their church.

I clicked the 'contact us' section and found an email address. I wanted to reach out to Joe, ask where to find him, but my email had my name in it, and I feared he would recognise it. There probably weren't a lot of Augustus Saints around.

Nathaniel clicked his pen, instantly snatching my attention. *He* was my solution. Joe would have no reason to recognise a Nathaniel Carrington email address. It was the perfect plan...except that I would have to *involve* Nathaniel. And he already knew too much about me already.

You could just kill him afterwards, you know.

"Nathaniel," I spoke up, forcing my voice to remain steady despite the anxiety coursing through my veins. "Can I use your email?"

Nathaniel ceased chewing on his pen lid and raised a perfectly arched eyebrow. "My email? Why?"

"I want to contact the God's Soldiers to find an address," I explained. "I want to find my mother. But I'm afraid that Joe will recognise my name and not help me. He won't recognise your name, though."

Nathaniel leaned forward with interest. "You're going to look for your mother?"

I nodded.

"Well shit, yeah, of course you can," he said, sliding his laptop toward me, his email open. "What brought this on?"

I didn't answer. My fingers, as if controlled by an invisible puppeteer, typed in Joe's email address and began to form the body of the email. Nathaniel moved to sit beside me, his shoulder pressed against mine.

"You sound too urgent," he said, shoving me aside to take his laptop. "You'll scare him away."

"How is 'I am looking for a like-minded community' too urgent?" I complained.

"No normal person talks like that," Nathaniel said.

"You just think everyone is stupid."

"I do not."

I gave him a look and snatched the laptop off him. "Just let me write what I need to write, okay?"

"Yeah, yeah," Nathaniel waved a dismissive hand.

I finished up the email, and once it received Nathaniel's approval, I sent it and leaned back in my chair with a long sigh.

"You will let me know when he responds, right?"

"The very second," he assured me.

"I hope he doesn't take too long."

"I'm sure he's not overflowing with emails," Nathaniel mused.

I nodded.

"What are you going to do? If you find her?"

I hadn't really thought about it. Of course, my intention was to help her. If she really was haunted by delusions and hallucinations, she needed help beyond what the cult could provide. But facing her again, after years of hating her and trying to forget...I hadn't really figured out how to do such a thing.

"I guess...I'd try and find out why everything happened the way it did," I whispered.

Nathaniel nodded. "And what happened? I know you mentioned an...exorcism?"

My throat dried up, making each swallow excruciatingly painful. "It's a long story."

"We still have..." Nathaniel lifted his wrist to read his watch. "...thirty minutes."

I chuckled bitterly. "We're not even friends."

"We could be."

"I don't think so."

"Why not?"

"I'm not a good friend," I said.

"Why do you think that?"

"Because I've only ever had one friend and I..."

Nathaniel waited, patiently, his eyes never leaving mine.

"...I fucked up," I finished.

"How?"

"It doesn't matter."

"I don't think you are a bad friend, Augustus," he said gently, "I just think you are scared of opening up."

"I'm not."

"Prove it," he challenged.

I raised an eyebrow. "Prove it?"

"Prove you're not scared." He closed his laptop, swivelled in his chair to face me and crossed his arms over his chest. "Tell me about the exorcism."

Prove it, prove it, prove it.

The Devil had challenged me in the cafe, and I failed. I could not fail again.

"Do you really want to know?" I asked.

Nathaniel nodded.

And so, I told him. I told him everything—the rope around my wrists, the linen cupboard, the mirrored room, the night I found Auden trapped in a circle of flames. I recounted it all as though the memories weren't mine, as though I had merely watched it all unfold through a screen or on a page.

"And then what happened?" Nathaniel asked.

I shrugged. "I don't know. I passed out and when I woke up...my father told me my mother was gone."

"Shit," Nathaniel whispered, "I can't believe you went through all that."

"It was a long time ago."

Nathaniel shook his head, the look in his eye a blend of sympathy and determination. "That's not something you can just...forget."

He was right. Over ten years had passed and yet I still carried the memory of that night as though it were yesterday. And it wasn't just that night that haunted me. It was the years building up to it—the years of being told I wasn't *good.* That I had the Devil inside of me.

"I want to help you," Nathaniel went on. "Find her, that is. If Joe responds to the email with an address, let me come with you."

"What?"

"Let me come with you," he repeated.

"Why? This has...nothing to do with you and–"

"I know. But I can be there to support you. To be a...friend."

"You're not my friend."

A flicker of hurt crossed his face. "I could be...if you let me."

"I told you I–"

"–am not a good friend. I don't care. I'm not letting you return to that monster alone."

I averted my gaze, shifting in my chair so there was more space between us. The room suddenly felt too crowded. Too hot. I rationalised that Nathaniel didn't *really* care about me. He just wanted to use the God's Soldiers Church for his extra credit.

"What are you so afraid of?" Nathaniel pushed. "Why won't you let us be friends when we clearly get along pretty well?"

"I don't want to get hurt."

Nathaniel frowned. "You think I will hurt you?"

I shook my head. "No, I'll...I'll ruin it. It'll be my fault. And I just..." I stood up abruptly, gathering my things. I didn't want to talk about this. It was bad enough reliving one period of my life, I didn't want to revisit another.

"Augustus." Nathaniel's fingers caught my wrist, his body towering over mine as he rose from his chair. "Sit. Please."

My breath caught in my throat.

"I won't force you to talk about it," he said, "just don't leave, okay?"

I raised my eyes to meet his, fear vanishing the moment a soft smile graced his features. I was safe. I didn't need to run. I was okay.

With a nod, I sat down and ran a hand over my face, steadying my racing heart so that we could resume our assignment.

That was close, Augustus. You can't let him in.

Not letting Nathaniel in proved to be a challenging task. He was not only unflinchingly curious, asking questions no one else would bother to ask, but he was warm, inviting, tempting me to spill all my secrets.

In my attempts to keep him at an arm's distance, he'd somehow shifted closer. Over the course of our study sessions, I learned a lot about him. Involuntarily, of course.

I learned that he spoke four languages: English, Korean, Japanese, and French. He was most fluent in English and Korean, but his favourite was Japanese because he loved reading manga and watching anime.

I learned that Halloween was his favourite holiday because he would take his brothers trick-or-treating and get a sugar high. They all dressed up in matching costumes. One year; the Adams Family, another year; shipwrecked sailors, his favourite year; fungi infected zombies from his favourite video game.

Speaking of video games, I learned that when he wasn't studying or writing music, he was lounging on a beanbag, PlayStation controller in hand as he battled monsters and gunned down criminals. His favourite game was The Last of Us, but he was also *very* passionate about Nathan Drake from Uncharted. I was pretty sure he had a crush on him. He neither confirmed nor denied it.

I learned that friendship was important to him. He had five friends from high school, three of whom studied medicine alongside him at Dawnridge. They were his world. Makayla was a makeup artist and moved to London to further her career. Her boyfriend Xander moved there with her to study gaming development. Nathaniel texted them every day, sometimes playing with Xander online. Jae-Hwa, Wes and Paige were the three he spent the most time with. All studied medicine. All wanted to be surgeons.

He'd also made several friends from university, though he referred to them as 'clubbing friends' and not 'crying in their arms friends'.

"What type do you want *me* to be?" I'd asked him teasingly in between classes.

"I thought we weren't friends," he said.

"Well, since you keep begging me–"

Nathaniel nudged me with a laugh, his dimples deepening the wider he smiled. I dedicated more time than I should have drawing out those dimples, the sight spreading warmth through my veins.

I learned that Nathaniel was stubborn, determined to retrieve answers I refused to give. But he was a masterful manipulator, softening me up so it was harder for my walls to stand tall.

"What happened?" Nathaniel asked one evening after a long four-hour study session to finalise our essay. He was asking about Ava, again, and for some reason, the gentle tone, the softness around his round, brown eyes, infiltrated my guarded walls.

"I don't know," I admitted. "It all just...crumbled so quickly. We were happy. Inseparable. And then...Eden...." I closed my laptop to save power since it was clear we wouldn't be resuming any study with the allocated time we had left. "Eden and Ava grew close and Ava liked her a lot. She wanted to spend every second of every day with her and I felt...replaced. I tried not to bring it up because I didn't want to fight but when I did...Ava just accused me of being jealous."

"Were you?" Nathaniel asked.

"Not in the way she thought," I answered. "She thought I was just jealous because I liked her or because I wasn't in a relationship. But that wasn't true. I didn't care about that. I cared that I was losing my best friend, and she didn't even seem to notice."

"Oh, you didn't like her?"

"What? Of course not," I said, shaking my head. "Ava liked girls and I…"

Nathaniel leaned forward. "Yes?"

"I don't think I'm capable of liking anybody." My mind flashed to Alexander and the day we shared at Framlingham castle. I shook the memory away instantly, not wanting to dwell on the way he'd looked at me when I had my lips locked with Elysse.

"What do you mean?" he asked, brow pinched with a mix of curiosity and confusion.

"I don't know…" I mumbled.

Nathaniel waited, patient.

"There was a time…in high school…where I thought maybe…I was gay." It was the first time I'd admitted it out loud. The first time I audibly acknowledged it. The words tasted like poison on my tongue, as though I had fallen victim to an assassin's attempt on my life.

Nathaniel straightened in his chair, but he didn't interrupt me as I went on.

"I didn't have a lot to go on, so I did a few 'am I gay' quizzes but I found the questions difficult to answer."

"In what way?"

I shrugged. "They were questions about whether I was physically attracted to men or women…whether I wanted to kiss them and…you know…" I waved my hand in a vague, uncomfortable gesture. "But the truth is…I don't feel physically attracted to either…so the test results were always inconclusive."

"Ah, yeah, I've done a few of those quizzes," Nathaniel mused. "Most really focus on physical attraction. Maybe you're asexual."

"A sexual what?"

There was a long pause as Nathaniel stared at me as if I'd grown two heads. "No," he said slowly. "Asexual. A person who does not experience sexual attraction. It's a sexual orientation, like being gay or straight."

"Oh," I said, embarrassed. "I've never heard of that. I thought I was just weird or broken."

"You're not weird or broken," Nathaniel assured me. "There is a whole community of people just like you. But there's a spectrum. Some might be completely sex repulsed, some might be okay with kissing, and others might be okay with having sex, it's just not something that they need."

"Wow," I breathed out. "You sure know a lot about this stuff."

Nathaniel chuckled. "See? I *am* smarter than you."

I elbowed him in the side. His laughter only grew, my own lips tugging upwards in response. I hated how easy it was for Nathaniel to make me smile, but oh how I loved it at the same time. I had never felt so free.

"Out of curiosity, though," Nathaniel said, "have you ever felt romantically attracted to someone? Like had a crush?"

Alexander's dark green eyes flashed behind my eyelids. "Maybe. I don't know. But I didn't feel that way about Ava. I just missed our friendship. It felt like Eden had taken her away from me. And we fought about it and we just...never spoke again."

"I'm sorry that you lost such a close friend."

I shook my head, no longer wanting to dwell on Ava or Alexander or anything from my past. "What about you?" I asked, diverting the conversation. "You ever had a crush?"

"Oh, yeah, plenty," Nathaniel chuckled.

"And have you..." I waved my hand and added, "...been in a relationship?"

Nathaniel's amusement faded and he shifted uncomfortably in his seat. I opened my mouth to tell him he didn't have to answer when he said, "Yes. One."

"What happened?" I asked.

"We were in high school. All boys private school. He was captain of the cricket team, and I was school captain. In retrospect, we were nothing alike. He was smart, though. We could debate about anything and everything." He drummed his fingers against the table as he spoke, the only indication of his nerves. "But he...wasn't out yet. As gay. He hadn't told a soul. Only me. And so, we were...a secret. For a while, I didn't mind. I wasn't out either, so I respected it. But eventually I *did* come out. To my parents. To my friends. But he just...couldn't."

I bit my lip, hands itching to reach out and hold Nathaniel's restless ones. "Did he have...strict parents or something?" I asked.

"I don't think so," Nathaniel said. "I only met them once but...they didn't seem religious or old fashioned or anything. But maybe they were homophobic, I don't know. I think it was more...the sporting culture. I think he was afraid of being seen as weak or as a...predator, of some kind."

"So what happened?" I pushed.

"He grew distant when I came out," he answered, sorrow painting every line of his face, "he probably didn't want to risk being accused of dating me. I was...bullied by some of his friends. And he did...nothing. He just watched."

My jaw clenched. "That's fucked, Nathaniel."

"Yeah," he chuckled bitterly, "but I don't hate him. He was...a scared kid. I hope he has accepted himself now. And that he's happy."

"Do you still...?"

"Have feelings for him?" Nathaniel finished. "No. Not at all. I've moved on. Been trying to find someone new for a while."

"And no luck?"

Nathaniel studied me for a long moment before shrugging, "We'll see." He clicked his tongue and leaned back in his seat. "What about you? I know you're not *physically* attracted to anyone, but could you see yourself being *romantically* interested in anyone?"

I shook my head. It would be nice, I supposed, to have someone I could call my partner, someone to come with me to an art gallery, or museum, or to picnic with me in long grass by the water. But no one could love me. I was hard to love. My own mother had failed, what chance did I have with anyone else? I'd be lucky to even maintain a friendship.

"Maybe one day," Nathaniel hummed.

I nodded, gaze falling onto my lap.

"I'd still like to be friends, you know," Nathaniel said.

At my silence, disappointment etched across his furrowed brows, lips pulling down in a heartbreaking frown.

I needed to adjust to being on my own. And that meant my walls had never been higher. But Nathaniel, somehow, always seemed to find a ladder tall enough to climb over.

"I'm not going to hurt you like Ava did," he said.

"You can't promise that."

"I can." He slowly rose to his feet, a look of determination sharpening his features. "I, Nathaniel Carrington, promise to never break your heart."

I fought valiantly to suppress an eyeroll as he ever so dramatically crossed a hand over his chest. He looked like a knight swearing allegiance to his monarch the way he stood with his back straight, feet together, expression serious.

"And I, Augustus Saint, promise to never break *your* heart," I played along, mimicking his stance with my own hand splayed across my chest.

I never kept that promise.

CHAPTER TWENTY-NINE

An unreliable narrator is an untrustworthy storyteller, deliberately deceptive or misguided.

Do you trust me?

You shouldn't.

I murdered my mother.

I am the villain of this story.

I have lied to you.

Repeat it to yourself, like a mantra. You cannot trust me. What is real? You are being fed a lie.

Nathaniel ate the lie, devoured it, worshipped it. And you don't want to share his fate, do you?

Nathaniel had always loved the villain. They were tragically misunderstood, he'd declare in between study sessions, seated on the couch inside his study, popcorn between us while he forced me through hours of television. There was goodness in their hearts. Buried deep, deep down. Trauma shaped their hard shells, built their guarded walls. It wasn't their fault, he insisted.

I disagreed. Villains had always been given a choice. Judas chose to betray Jesus of Nazareth for coin, Macbeth chose to commit treason for power, and I chose to evade happiness as though it were the plague. There is always a choice. And the wrong one can tear at your soul, steal your humanity, and lock it up in a cold cellar.

The ghost of North Lane knew that all too well, something we bonded over in the darkness, imprisoned with only haunting memories of our sin. We were both awaiting a salvation that would never come—a salvation that we had both chased away.

Nathaniel had been my salvation before I abandoned him, driven by the fear of being unravelled and a hunger to understand my past.

And I had been my mother's, before the truth barrelled toward us in frightening waves. Now she was dead, and I was a prisoner in her House, forced to roam the dark halls like a long-forgotten phantom. And maybe I was, for who knew how much time had passed?

A floorboard creaked on the staircase, drawing my attention away from the scorched living room—a room reduced to nothing but a grey memory. Instead, my gaze drifted toward the staircase where I had once stood, gazing out at my brother shivering in a circle of flames.

On the third step from the bottom, a faceless shadow stood, its slender fingers curled around the wooden railing. It was too tall to have been my mother, and so I wearily stepped forward, searching the darkness for a face. Perhaps there was more than one prisoner trapped in North Lane.

The shadow turned and ascended the staircase, each step groaning from its weight. I followed, anxious, chasing an alliance that could buy our freedom. But no matter how quickly I ran, I never caught up. The shadow was faster, waltzing down the hall with an air of ease I could not imagine belonging to a prisoner.

"Wait!" I called, stumbling through the darkness, nails dragging along the torn wallpaper to feel my way toward the back of the House.

There was a room at the end of the long upstairs hallway. It had always been boarded up. My parents never told me what was in there, except that it was locked, and no one knew where to find the key. I had never really paid much attention to the room as a boy, but as I watched the shadow figure disappear inside, I racked my brain for answers.

My fingers curled around the door handle and twisted, but the door remained locked. I tugged, pulled, and shook the handle. But still, the door remained impenetrable.

Why did the shadow lead me here? What was inside? What secret was the House on North Lane keeping from me?

CHAPTER THIRTY

A week passed without a response from the God's Soldiers Church.

Nathaniel assured me that the email had been sent, but I grew anxious. What if my plan to find my mother unravelled before it even began? What if I never found her? What if I never uncovered the truth?

That would be for the best, little monster.

Our assignment was near completion. The essay had gone through several drafts, and all that remained was a summary to be presented in PowerPoint slides. I had no other upcoming deadlines—aside from one online exam that I wasn't really worried about—so the stress that had plagued me weeks prior had gradually evaporated. It found Nathaniel, though.

Approaching deadlines had him picking at his lips obsessively and peeling off the skin around his nails until they bled. He didn't raise his hand to answer questions, nor did he follow Professor Haywood after a lecture in order to bombard her with psychological manipulation theories.

I'd asked him if he was okay, and he'd given me a dashing smile that should have lit up his eyes. But it didn't. He was overwhelmed with three upcoming medical exams and two research papers due on the same day. In order to ease some of his stress, I took the responsibility of finishing our presentation. We'd argued about it until I convinced him that I could easily put the slides together in between customers at work. If it meant Nathaniel would have one less thing to worry about, I was happy to do it.

And here I thought he was our rival...

The morning of the presentation, Auden and I walked to the bus stop together. Although we caught different buses with different routes, we stood side-by-side amongst a small crowd of school students and workers downing their morning coffee. I had flash cards in my hands, mouthing my speech under my breath as I shifted from one leg to the other.

"Are you nervous about your presentation?" Auden asked.

"Yes."

"Why?"

"I am not entirely fond of public speaking," I answered, "and since Nathaniel is, well, *Nathaniel*...my poor public speaking abilities will be even more noticeable."

"I don't like public speaking either," Auden sighed, reaching for my hand. He squeezed my fingers gently before adding, "But I am sure you will do well. You're just as good as Nathaniel. Don't overthink it."

I glanced down at our hands and squeezed back, lips spreading into a small smile. "Thanks, Audie."

You never thank me like that.

By the time I reached Dawnridge, the lecture hall was already crowded with students. I scanned the room for Nathaniel's floppy black hair and dimpled smile, shoulders relaxing when I found him near the platformed stage, head tipped back as he laughed at something one of his friends said. The sound brought a smile to my face, but an unexpected pang of jealousy followed. What did *I* have to do to make him laugh like that?

I shook the thought away and forced my legs forward.

Nathaniel's eyes found mine within seconds, and he paused mid-sentence, words vanishing in his throat. For a moment, I was confused by the way his lips parted, gaze darting in between my gelled hair and my freshly ironed clothes. And then I remembered the effort I had put into my appearance that morning. I'd trimmed my curls, coating them in just enough gel to keep them in place, whilst the small stubble I had been growing was cleanly shaven, my bare face moisturised with aloe vera to avoid an acne breakout. My usual black attire was replaced with a pair of white trousers, a brown belt, and a slim-fitting forest green sweater, knitted and thrown atop a white collared shirt. Knowing I was to present in front of the entire class, I intended to appear welcoming and trustworthy as opposed to moody and unapproachable. Nathaniel's own fashion and sense of style may have been an inspiration, but I'd never admit that out loud.

"Hey," he greeted me, hands casually sliding into his brown trousers, "you cut your hair."

"Only a little," I shrugged.

"I like it," he said, "and your outfit too."

Heat flamed my cheeks, the compliment catching me off guard. "Thank you."

"I am running on caffeine and caffeine alone, could not get a wink of sleep last night. How are *you*?"

"Wait, you're nervous?" I gaped at him.

"It appears so. I am not thrilled about having to present in front of all these people...but I'll be fine."

"What do you mean? You...present all the time! You're always raising your hand and bragging about how much you know!"

"I don't brag—"

"You're always so confident! You debate, you answer questions, you volunteer and—"

"That's different."

"How?!"

Nathaniel opened his mouth to answer but Professor Haywood's voice cut him off, announcing the start of the presentations.

We moved to our seats silently, flash cards trembling in my hands as I glanced toward the projector which listed the order we would present in. Nathaniel and I were the sixth.

My legs bounced up and down as the first pair made their way on stage. They introduced their topic—the psychological manipulation of serial killers—and proceeded to summarise the main points of their essay. I could barely concentrate, my stomach cramping to the point I feared I would bring up last night's dinner.

Nathaniel's hand rested on my thigh, momentarily distracting me from the anxious beast coursing through my veins. My knees ceased bouncing. Heart rate slowed. Heat crawled up my neck, ears no doubt reddening.

"You were right," he confessed in a whisper, "everyone chose criminals."

The second and third pair, like the first, focused on the psychological manipulation of criminals whilst the fourth pair focused on psychological manipulation in relationships. As our turn neared, Nathaniel began picking at his bottom lip, his grip on my thigh tightening. Wanting to ease his nerves as he had eased mine, I placed my hand on top of his, interlocking our fingers without uttering a word. The art of comfort was a stranger to me, but I remembered the way Auden had squeezed my hand at the bus stop—the way it chased away some of my fear. I hoped it would do the same for Nathaniel. But I didn't dare look at him, even as I felt his piercing gaze.

The fifth pair explored the psychological manipulation employed by detectives to catch criminals, a unique approach that Nathaniel insisted Dr. Haywood would reward with a high mark. Envy crawled beneath my skin, burying itself amongst all my anxiety and self-doubt. What if they outranked us? What if we hadn't done enough to secure a High Distinction?

It will be your fault. This topic was your *idea.*

Nathaniel will hate you. He'll never talk to you again.

You won't get a scholarship. You'll be in debt for years.

You'll ruin everything. Just like you always do.

You're a failure. You're a monster. You're—

"We're up," Nathaniel whispered, snatching me from my spiralling thoughts.

I followed him toward the stage, head down and eyes glued to the flashcards clenched tight in my hands. I inhaled sharply. The world tilted. Stomach cramps threatened to send me to my knees. I swayed involuntarily, the nausea overwhelming.

Once Nathaniel plugged in his laptop, and our PowerPoint slides lit the screen, I cleared my throat and recited the words I'd been practicing all morning. I want to tell you it all went smoothly, but my voice cracked. Trembled. Words poured from my mouth in a stutter. Swallowing hard, my eyes briefly flickered toward our classmates only for my gaze to lock with the Devil's, his smile revealing sharp fangs glinting in the dimming light. He didn't need a mirror to find me here.

Professor Haywood vanished. My classmates too. It was just me and the Devil, alone in a room cloaked in shadow.

I opened my mouth to speak, to question his presence, but something crawled up my oesophagus—a sharp, insectile movement tickling my throat, choking me. I coughed violently, folding in on myself.

On the topic of cults, the Devil said, leaning forward in his seat, *I think this is the perfect opportunity to remind you what happened the last time you were subjected to the God's Soldiers Church.*

Smoke thickened the air. Flames devoured every exit. I dropped to my hands and knees, body convulsing in a desperate attempt to expel the foreign object trapping my airways. Tears blurred my vision. Blood filled my mouth. A sharp edge tore through my throat, a silver crucifix landing on the stage coated in blood and saliva.

Don't go looking for them, little monster. You won't like what you find.

"Augustus?"

Nathaniel's voice banished the Devil, students returning to their seats. They exchanged glances with one another, an uncomfortable silence filling the room.

I straightened up, massaged my throat, and resumed the presentation as though nothing had happened. There was no Devil. No smoke. No blood-slicked crucifix on the stage. None of it was real.

The atmosphere shifted when it was Nathaniel's turn to speak. His voice was calm, confident. No one would have guessed how nervous he'd been by the way he moved across the stage with ease, cracking unscripted jokes in between significant talking points. He had the entire hall in a trance. A captivating, commanding presence. Even I struggled to look away.

"Therefore," he finished, pausing in place to address the crowd of students leaning forward in their seats, "it is evidently clear that cults employ various manipulation techniques, such as isolation, fear and guilt, trauma bonding and information control to facilitate psychosis, often religious in nature."

A round of applause announced the end of our presentation and the nausea that had twisted my insides vanished, replaced with an adrenaline rush that had me ready to take on the world. It was only relief, I knew, but it was a feeling I would chase forever.

Nathaniel received several claps on the back as we returned to our seats, smiling from ear-to-ear as he tossed his flashcards into his satchel without reverence. He leaned back, shoulders slumped, clearly as relieved as I was that it was all over.

"You did great," I whispered as the next pair stepped up onto the stage.

"You too," he whispered back.

He's lying.

I swallowed hard and shifted in my seat, forcing my gaze forward. The Devil was right. If Nathaniel hadn't completely captivated the room, my poor performance would have cost us a high mark. It would have been all my fault.

It doesn't matter. You won't see him again anyway. What reason will you have to spend time together now that your assignment is over?

I hadn't considered that until now. But it was true. Nathaniel and I had only spent time together because of the assignment. But now...there was no reason for us to see each other outside of lectures. I would return to being alone.

You will always *be alone, little monster. You should know that by now.*

***

Miserable. That was how I felt all the way home, Nathaniel appearing behind my closed eyelids every time I blinked. His dimpled smile, his brown doe-like eyes, his long lashes, his ensemble of knitted vests. I had no right to feel this way when I was the one who refused his offer of friendship, but it hit me, with the threat of never seeing him again, that I'd already considered him a friend. And now...I had no reason to reach out to him. No excuse to worm my way into his life.

As if I'd summoned him with my thoughts, my phone rang, Nathaniel's name lighting up the screen.

"Hello?"

"Hey, what are you doing tomorrow?"

I blinked, slowly, debating my answer. "Why?"

"Are you working?"

"Why?"

"Let's do something."

"What—"

"Just us."

My stomach flipped at those two words. *Just us.* I bit my lip, fighting back a smile that threatened to chase away my scowl. He *wanted* to spend time with me. Just *us.*

"Augustus? You there?"

"Uh, yeah, yeah." I cleared my throat, running a hand over my face as I tried to ease my fluttering heart. "I'm free. To do something. Tomorrow. Free to do something tomorrow."

"Great!"

"What uh...what were you thinking?"

"It's a surprise."

"A surprise?"

"I can't wait!"

"Nathaniel, what are we–"

"I'll pick you up at twelve," he spoke over me. "We'll be outside so don't forget sunscreen."

"O–Okay."

"Perfect! It's a date!"

***

It's a date, it's a date, it's a date.

I stood in front of the free-standing mirror in my bedroom, a towel over the top to hide my face, leaving my body open to inspection. Adjusting the dark grey collared shirt I'd finished buttoning, sleeves rolled up to my elbows, I debated removing my silver crucifix and instead opted to tuck it beneath my shirt, the top button undone to provide a glimpse of silver chain.

"Where are you going?" Auden asked from the doorway.

It was Saturday, and on the Saturdays I wasn't working at *Browning Books*, Auden and I usually watched movies or binged through British crime dramas.

"I'm going out with...a friend," I said, leaning down to tie my shoelaces and adjust the belt on my loose black trousers.

"Nathaniel?" Auden guessed.

I nodded.

"He's your friend?"

"Mhm," I murmured, trying not to take offense to his surprised tone.

"Where are you going?"

"I don't know, but I'll be home for dinner," I promised him.

"You don't know where you're going?"

"No idea." I stepped around him to walk down the hallway, his footsteps trailing after me. "It's a surprise."

"A surprise? Why?"

A frustrated sigh nearly escaped my throat until I reminded myself this was Auden, and he was just trying to understand why my Saturday off work would not be spent with him. "I will tell you everything when I get back, okay?"

"Okay."

I cupped the back of his neck and leaned down to kiss the top of his head. "I'll see you later."

Auden gave me a small, weary smile before returning to the living room to watch television alone. Guilt wrapped its familiar fingers around my throat, clenching my airways as I watched him flick through channels without his usual 'how about this one?' and 'this sounds great.' I almost cancelled then and there, but as I opened the door to leave, I nearly collided with Nathaniel who had his hand raised to knock on the door.

"Oh, sorry!" we both said at the same time, followed by nervous laughter.

Nathaniel wore a long black coat—one he often wore on the cold days at Dawnridge. A beige knitted sweater was underneath, atop a white collared shirt. His black trousers were nearly identical to mine, though his were more slim fitting while mine were loose.

"You look…" we both started at the same time, paused, and then tried again.

"…lovely," Nathaniel finished.

"…warm," I said.

A nervous laugh bubbled up inside of me as I reached for my black jacket that hung by the door, doing my best not to study his red cheeks or dark pink lips kissed by the cold. He stepped aside and I shut the door behind me before following him to his car.

"So…where are we going?" I asked, trying to steady my wildly beating heart as Nathaniel opened the passenger door for me.

"It's a surprise."

"Still?"

"Yes."

With a playful eye roll, I sat down and watched as Nathaniel moved around to the driver's seat.

The drive was a rather long one—thirty-five minutes, mostly open road, with green fields and tall trees on either side. Music blasted through the stereo speakers, wind blowing through our hair with the windows rolled down.

"Are you not going to tell me where we're going?" I asked in between the silence between songs.

"All I'll say is there will be wine, paint, and the open air," Nathaniel said.

I wasn't one to indulge in wine—the mere smell had me pulling faces—but I did love painting and the open air. "Consider me intrigued."

"Thank God for that," Nathaniel grinned.

Why do people always thank God for things he didn't do?

Alarmed at the Devil's appearance, I swallowed hard and tried to block him out. I didn't want him to spoil my first date.

Is that what this is? Or was it just a phrase?

Not now. Not now. Not now.

"We're almost there," Nathaniel announced, drawing my attention back to him.

I nodded, realised Nathaniel's eyes were on the road, and said, "Cool."

"You okay?"

"Yeah, just nervous."

"Nervous?"

"Nervous that you're taking me to the middle of nowhere to kill me," I joked.

A surprised chuckle escaped Nathaniel's throat. "I'm flattered to be considered a potential killer."

"Why would you be flattered by that?" I laughed.

"Because no one ever thinks of me as a *bad boy.*"

"Oh my god."

"What? Is it not true that bad boys get more attention?"

I clutched my stomach as I cringed, unable to fend off a grin when Nathaniel laughed along with me, the sound a sweet melody I could replay forever.

Minutes later, Nathaniel pulled up on the side of the road, twigs crunching beneath the tires as a grass field appeared before us. There was a broken wooden fence, an empty bottle, and nothing but open road.

"So you really are going to kill me, huh?" I breathed out, only half-joking.

Nathaniel merely grinned as he climbed out of the car and waited for me to do the same. Despite Nathaniel being taller, I was confident I could overpower him in a fight. He was slim, lean, and I was wider, with a little muscle.

I approached the fence and peered out at the well-maintained grass field, white flowers blossoming amongst the weeds. In the distance, I could make out a lake, and even further, grass mounds.

"Is this someone's property?" I asked, glancing sideways at Nathaniel who stood beside me, hands on the fencing.

"It's my grandfather's," he answered, "he owns a large estate and this land, while his, is far from his home. He has granted me permission to enter, so don't worry about being shot."

"Lovely."

Without a word of warning, Nathaniel climbed over the fence and landed on the other side, a grin brightening his face. "You coming?"

With less grace than I would have liked, I hopped over the fence and followed him through the grass, still not completely convinced he wasn't going to kill me.

Our hands accidentally collided as we walked side-by-side, though neither of us commented on it as we discreetly created more distance between ourselves.

Not far from the lake, I slowed to a halt.

Nathaniel kept walking until he reached the brown, white and grey checked picnic blanket set out atop the grass, four brown cushions circling a picnic basket with a bottle of wine standing beside it. There were two small easels with a clean canvas perched on each, an empty paint palette and a tub of paint and brushes to share.

A real date.

I slowly dragged my gaze from the picnic spread to Nathaniel who looked nervous all of a sudden, one hand raised to pick at his lip while he shifted from one leg to the other, unable to stand still under my gaze.

"You...set this up?" I asked quietly.

Nathaniel nodded. "Yeah. Our own little...paint and sip. They do these classes you can join but I figured it'd be better with just...us."

I said nothing, unable to process what I was seeing or hearing. Nathaniel had set this all up...for me? I didn't deserve it. Not at all. I had only ever been cold to him, and distant.

"But I warn you," Nathaniel rambled on, "I am *not* good at painting. And with wine in my system...I'll be even worse. So don't expect a masterpiece."

Biting my lip, I approached the blanket and sat down in front of one of the easels, slipping off my shoes so I didn't dirty the rug. I watched Nathaniel do the same, his eyes fixed on me as though afraid that if he looked away, I would disappear.

"If this isn't something you want to do we can always go and–"

"Nathaniel," I interrupted, voice steady despite the nerves gushing through my body, "this is perfect."

His face lit up, shoulders dropping with relief. I watched as he opened the basket and retrieved two wine glasses, the intense, fruity aroma filtering through my nostrils as he poured us each a glass.

Nathaniel handed me the wine, and I took it gratefully despite my initial trepidation. Alcohol had never appealed to me. The scent alone turned me off. But I raised the glass to my lips anyway, tension locking my body as though I was being held at gunpoint.

Watching me over the rim of his glass, Nathaniel raised both eyebrows and shook his head, the corner of his lips pulling up into an amused smile. "Augustus...don't drink the wine if you don't want to."

"No, no, I want to," I lied, tipping my head back slightly as the wine trickled down my throat. I coughed, lowering the glass as my eyes watered from the foul taste.

Nathaniel laughed and leaned forward to snatch the glass out of my hands. "We can paint and sip without the wine."

"But–"

"It's fine," Nathaniel waved a dismissive hand at me. "I was only going to have a little bit anyway…since I have to drive back and everything."

I nodded, a little embarrassed, and turned my attention to the paint and blank canvases. "What should we paint?"

"Hm." Nathaniel looked around, no doubt searching for inspiration, when his eyes returned to me. "I was thinking of painting you."

"Me?"

"I'm not very good so you'll probably look like a weird blob, but it gives me a chance to stare at you without being weird."

"Oh, and telling me all that definitely makes you sound less weird," I said sarcastically.

A laugh, soft and delicate, escaped his throat as he reached for two empty yogurt cartons and filled them with water. "What can I say? I'm an honest guy."

"Too honest," I mused as I took one of the cartons and selected a paint brush. "I guess I shall paint you, then."

Playfulness glistened in Nathaniel's honey-brown eyes as he leaned down, elbow propped up on a cushion as he flashed me a smirk. "Shall I model for you?"

"You look ridiculous," I said.

With a pout, he sat up and opened the paint tubes, pouring them onto his palette before I did the same with mine. "Well, if you do need me to pose," he played along, "just let me know."

I dipped my brush in green paint, using gentle brush strokes to create the green field of grass behind him. To lighten the dark green, I used another brush to dip into the white paint, the blend of colours creating the perfect shade to match the grass.

Nathaniel and I shared glances as we worked on our artwork, my tongue in between my teeth as I outlined the shape of Nathaniel's seated body. He was all lean angles, though I tried to capture the soft edges of his face beneath his dark hair.

I didn't know how Nathaniel was doing, but when a string of curses escaped his throat and wet paint splashed onto his trousers, I assumed he wasn't doing too well.

Biting back a smile, I gently lowered my paint brush and fixed my gaze on him as he tried to clean the paint, smearing it all up his thigh.

"Bloody yellow paint," he hissed.

"Instead of fighting with the paint," I mused, "how about we do something you *actually* enjoy."

"No, no, I'm having fun," he tried to assure me despite his clear frustration.

"*Nathaniel.*"

"I swear I am! I'm just having some issues with cleaning myself up."

Barely suppressing a chuckle, I crawled towards him and peeled off my jacket, sacrificing the material to try and savour some of his. This close, I could smell the rich scent of his floral cologne and vanilla shampoo. I could also make out his attempted artwork—it was human, though it didn't look like me.

"Your jacket..." Nathaniel frowned.

"A small sacrifice for your dignity," I teased.

"It'll stain..."

"Definitely."

"I'm sorry."

I gave him a look. "You're sorry that I *chose* to help clean you with my jacket?"

He nodded, bottom lip jutted out like a child. I nudged him playfully, with perhaps a little more force than necessary, sending him lying back on the rug, head landing on the grass. In an attempt to prevent the fall, his arm snaked around my waist, dragging me down with him. I barely had time to cushion my fall, hands braced on either side of his head.

Grass tangled in between black strands of hair, white teeth glistening as his lips spread into a dimpled smile, he looked at me as though I was exactly where he wanted me to be.

Heat simmered in the pit of my stomach, rising to inflame my cheeks as I struggled to *breathe* at the sight of Nathaniel underneath me.

This is wrong, the Devil said in a singsong tone.

If the Devil thought it wrong, then it must have been *right.*

Nathaniel's gaze danced between my eyes and my lips, my heart skipping a beat at the realisation that he wanted to *kiss* me. Did *I* want him to kiss me? Did I want to kiss *him?* These questions soared through my brain, one after the other, and before I had the chance to process a single one, his hand was cupping my neck, the tips of his fingers tangled in my brown curls.

"Augustus," he whispered my name like he was down on his knees, worshipping me like one would a God. "I really want to kiss you."

I swallowed, my heart pounding so loud that it thundered in my ears. My tongue moved to wet my lip, an involuntary expression of my desire. I had never *wanted* to kiss anyone before. And yet here I was, mouth-watering at the mere thought of Nathaniel's lips against mine.

"I think I want you to kiss me too," I whispered.

Nathaniel smiled, hand tightening in my hair as he brought me closer to the curve of his perfect mouth. My eyelids fluttered shut the moment our lips connected. It was a gentle press of lips, both asking the other for permission. His lips were soft, inviting, and warm. I had no desire to pull away, not even as

Nathaniel's other hand slid up to my chest. Could he feel my wildly beating heart?

Unable to hold myself atop him without crushing his body, I rolled to the side, Nathaniel following me, his tongue sliding along my bottom lip as my lips parted to grant him entry. It felt good. Intoxicating.

A quiet, whisper of a moan escaped Nathaniel's throat, and he deepened the kiss. His hands grew more adventurous, sliding underneath my shirt, his hands burning my cool skin.

It was then I pulled away, panting as I fought to catch my breath and create as much distance between us as possible.

Nathaniel sat up, his lips red and swollen, eyes dark beneath his long, slow blinking lashes. He adjusted his trousers discreetly, his gaze apologetic as it settled on my trembling hands.

"I'm sorry," he breathed out, "I...didn't mean to...make you uncomfortable."

I shook my head, embarrassed, scared and guilty.

I *wanted* him to kiss me. I *loved* the feeling of his lips against mine, but the idea of *more* sent violent shockwaves through my body. I didn't want *that.* And I knew Nathaniel would not have pressured me to do so, but knowing he *wanted* to was a wake up call. I could not give him what he wanted. I could not string him along.

"You...you didn't do anything wrong," I said, scrambling to my feet. "I'm sorry. I just don't think we should..."

"Should what?"

"Do that again."

Nathaniel frowned as he climbed to his feet. "Was I that bad of a kisser?" He asked it jokingly, but I could tell by his wounded expression that there was some genuine insecurity there.

"No, of course not." I wanted to bury myself in a hole and lay there until death enveloped me into its arms.

"What is it then?" he asked, voice gentle.

"I don't want to have sex."

"We don't have to have sex."

"But you *want* to."

Nathaniel infiltrated the space between us, hand raised toward my cheek, his expression softening as he looked deep into my eyes. "I *want* to be with you. I want to be with you in any way *you* want to be with *me.*"

I must have had doubt written all over my face for he added, "I am not here to change you, Augustus. I am not here to wait until you are ready. If you one day decide you want to take that step, then great, I'll be with you. And if you decide you *never* want to go beyond kissing, that's great too!"

"I just don't want you to miss out on anything," I whispered.

Nathaniel tilted my head up to look at him. "All I want is what we have now. Art galleries and flowery fields and late-night study sessions locked in a library."

My vision blurred. "Really?"

"Really," he confirmed, pressing a feather-light kiss to the top of my head. "Now, let's finish up your painting, hm?" He pulled away and lowered himself back down onto a cushion. "I can't wait to see what masterpiece you've created."

CHAPTER THIRTY-ONE

Days with Nathaniel were picnics in grass meadows, movie nights snuggled underneath blankets, and after-hours tours of *Browning Books* when it was my turn to close up shop. It was stolen kisses between classes, longer kisses in silk sheets, with no pressure for anything more.

The Devil quieted in his presence. Nightmares transitioned to dreams. Permanent scowls were replaced with permanent smiles. I was, in every sense of the word, *happy*. It was strange, unfamiliar, but I clung to it, afraid of it being snatched from my hands, never to be found again.

We received our results for *Psychological Manipulation*— ninety-eight percent, the highest in our class. Prior to our being forced to work together, we would have glanced around the room in search of the other's reaction, but this time, we were seated side by side, grinning from ear to ear.

Nathaniel's friends wanted to celebrate the end of the semester with a night of bar hopping, but Nathaniel declined, informing them he'd already made plans with me. His friends wriggled their eyebrows and made suggestive noises before Nate managed to shew them away with a laugh.

"We don't have plans," I pointed out as we walked away.

"I know," Nathaniel chuckled, "but we *should* do something. You're the only one I want to celebrate with."

"What should we do, then?"

"I don't know. It's your turn to surprise me, don't you think?"

"You want *me* to decide?"

"My love language is quality time and acts of service," he hummed, reaching for my hand, "so yes, Augustus, I would love it if *you* planned our next date. Make it a *surprise*."

Planning a date was hard. Not only because I had not one romantic bone in my body, but because it was for *Nathaniel*—and it was *his* heart on the line. What if I let him down? What if he realised I wasn't good enough for him?

To combat my self-doubts, I made a list of all of Nathaniel's favourite things—most of which I learned involuntarily during our study sessions. Music, the piano, video games, horror movies, his family, museums, reading. I considered forcing him to read Frankenstein by Mary Shelley on our surprise date—he'd promised to read it weeks ago and *still* hadn't—but I wanted to prove I could be selfless, that I had paid attention to his interests and wanted to share them.

And so, our date began with dinner. I know what you're thinking, but don't worry, the date didn't *end* with dinner. What little faith you have in me...

We dined at his favourite Korean restaurant, sharing a large bowl of tteokbokki with cheese and noodles, the red sauce bringing tears to my eyes. I had to scull two glasses of water before braving the sticky fried chicken, Nathaniel laughing at my low spice tolerance.

There was a photobooth next door and even though I despised the way I looked on camera, I dragged Nathaniel inside and put on whatever silly hat he wanted me to. The silly hat he selected was a strawberry that he clasped under my chin, a single curl falling over my forehead while the others remained confined beneath the red and green head piece.

"Cute," he grinned, snapping a photo of me with his phone before slipping on an identical strawberry that was, indeed, quite cute.

We posed for several photos, with and without props, but the old lady minding the store watched us with narrowed eyes and pursed lips, so we only paid for two sessions before fleeing with our photo prints.

"How are you so damn photogenic?" I complained, glancing down at the four poses Nathaniel nailed whilst I looked like a fish that had fallen into a shark tank.

"Shut up, you look adorable," he nudged me, "I'm hanging these up in my room."

"Gay."

"Don't pretend like you're not obsessed with me," he teased, "I've seen the photo you set as your home screen."

A cool breeze caressed the back of my neck as I reached for his hand, snuggling closer to escape the cold. In a matter of seconds, his coat was around my shoulders, not a word exchanged. We walked in comfortable silence, hand-in-hand, until we reached his car, Nathaniel opening the door for me with a warm smile brightening his rosy cheeks.

"Here," I said, returning his coat, "you're cold too."

"I don't mind the cold," he insisted.

"It's fine, I promise."

"Augustus Saint." His tone was firm, though his hands were gentle as they cupped either side of my face. "I would rather freeze to death than have you uncomfortable for even one millisecond. Wear the damn coat."

And wear the damn coat I did before climbing into the passenger seat, smiling to myself as the scent of his vanilla cologne infiltrated my nostrils.

"Where to now? The night is still young."

"It's a surprise," I grinned before giving him the address to an eighteenth-century building owned by an elderly woman named Beverely White.

Mrs White did not live in the two-storey house with brown bricks smothered in ivy, front steps warped by decay, and tall windows stained with centuries of soot, mold and neglect. It was too haunted, she claimed in a BBC interview six years prior, she didn't want to live alongside the dead. The home was rented out to ghost hunters and television programs, as well as people like me who wanted to take their horror-loving boyfriend to a 'real' haunted house.

"What is this place?" Nathaniel asked as we pulled onto the driveway, gravel crunching beneath the tires. The house glared down at us, a welcome sign swaying weakly from a single hinge as though waving us to come in or run away.

"The most haunted house in the United Kingdom," I recited from the booking website, "where the living meet the dead."

"For real?" Nathaniel asked, eyes widening.

"I guess we're going to find out."

We climbed out of the car and ascended the front steps, wood wincing beneath our feet. A maroon door with a rusted '109' awaited us at the top, a blackened window on either side watching us like a predator watching its prey. The instructions stated the key was under the pot plant on the right of the door, which I made Nathaniel retrieve since my gaze was locked on my reflection staring back at me in the window to the left. The Devil winked. And then he was gone. But the damage was done, his presence tormenting me even at my happiest.

"So, what's the story with this place?" Nathaniel asked as he unlocked the door and stepped inside, reaching blindly for a light switch.

"The lights don't work," I sighed as I moved to step past him, "Mrs White doesn't want to pay for electricity. There are supposed to be torches on the—oh, yep, here they are."

Handing him a torch, I flicked on my own, its light cutting a narrow path through the suffocating darkness of the first floor, crumbling wallpaper unveiling cracks along the walls. A thick dampness smothered the air, dust crawling into my nostrils, a set of sneezes drowning out the darkness. Cob-webs dangled like curtains from the high ceiling, exposed beams crawling with spiders.

"The story," I sniffled, clearing my throat, "is that in the mid-eighteen hun-dreds, two young women were murdered. One body found on the staircase, the other on the second floor, both covered in blood."

"Are you making this up?" Nathaniel asked as he shone his light into the living room, floral wallpaper looming behind dust-covered furniture and crooked photo frames.

"No." Oak floorboards creaked with every step, a symphony of the aches and pains of an old house. "I read about it on the website."

"Oh. Well, carry on."

"The young women—Emelia Bath and Violet Vaccari—moved into the house along with Emelia's older brother Henry," I said. "The nature of their relationship is unknown, though some theorise they were lovers, whilst others believe Violet was a friend of the family set to marry Henry. All three lived here for nearly a year before tragedy struck."

"Let me guess, Henry murdered them," Nathaniel said, torch fixed on a portrait of Mr Bath hung above the fireplace.

"Henry travelled a lot for work. Reports say he'd been away for several weeks when the women's bodies were found."

"Who found them?"

"Julian Walsh," I answered. "A fifteen-year-old boy who lived next door. He knocked on the door on September seventeen intending to ask Emelia if he could pick a rose from their garden for his mother. But the door was open. He went inside and found Violet sprawled halfway down the staircase."

"And Emilia?"

I cast my torch toward the staircase, the moth-eaten carpet torn from the wood, leaving patches where a body once stained it with blood. "Upstairs. Just before the first step."

"Who was it, then? Who killed them? And why?" Nathaniel asked.

"No one knows," I sighed, "the murder remains unsolved to this day."

We ascended the staircase, wood protesting under our weight as shadows danced around the edges of our torches, dust floating across our light beams. A cold chill crept along the back of my neck, the darkness menacing.

Upon reaching the second floor, our torchlights extinguished, the house enveloping us in darkness. I reached for Nathaniel, but my fingers met only air.

"Nate?" I whispered.

Silence.

You're alone again, little monster.

Dread carved a blade through my chest, the Devil's fingers curled around the hilt to drive it in deeper as blood filled my mouth, trickling down my chin. Breath evaded my lungs. Knees fell to the floor. Laughter rained down on me as death inched closer.

And then a pale glow illuminated the room, an indistinct shape holding a flickering candle. It hovered in a familiar hallway, a cold draft brushing the curls from my forehead, delivering a breath of fresh air that swam toward my lungs.

I had returned inside the House on North Lane, the door to my bedroom to my left, the strange figure lingering at the end of the hall. I stepped forward, the floorboards beneath my feet shooting upward like wooden stakes waiting to impale me. Swallowing a scream, I turned to descend the stairs, only for the Devil's face to appear inches from mine, beetles pouring from his mouth.

I staggered backwards, elbows landing on the jagged floorboards with a crack. The walls towered over me, the floor beneath me shaking as though an earthquake had struck. The Devil placed his foot on my chest and pressed down, teeth razor sharp.

This is where you belong. And where you will stay if you try to find your mother.

"Augustus!"

Fingers tugged at my hair, forcing my head up to meet a pair of big brown eyes wide with concern. Nathaniel held me, his warm body trembling against my own.

We were on the staircase where Violet's body had been discovered, my knees against the wood whilst Nathaniel crouched down to hold me, to stop me from falling.

"What happened?" he breathed out.

I didn't answer. *Couldn't* answer. The Devil was there. The House on North Lane had found me.

I trembled like a leaf, Nathaniel's words muffled as the Devil rattled around in my brain.

"Augustus?"

"Let's go. Let's just go."

I grew distant once I returned home, not replying to Nathaniel's messages or answering his calls. I wish I could say that I didn't let this drag on for too long, but who was I if not one to ruin something good? I had happiness in the grasp of my hand, and I was willing to let it crumble and drift off in the wind. All because of the Devil—a Devil I had failed to shut out.

Guilt weighed heavy on my shoulders, but I convinced myself I was doing the right thing. For Nathaniel's sake. He deserved better than the burden I brought him. He deserved someone who could take him on a date without hallucinating—someone who didn't shut down the second things crumbled all around him. I thought I had made the right decision, but the nightmares returned in Nathaniel's absence. Sleepless nights, miserable days.

A week had passed before Nathaniel cornered me on campus. I thought I could successfully avoid him since classes were over, but he found me on my way to the library, dark circles under his eyes, his lips cracked and peeling.

"What's going on?" he asked, the tone of his voice sending an ache through my chest. "You've just...ghosted me. Why?"

How could I tell him about the Devil? How could I explain that I was trying to protect him? How could I make him understand that I would only bring him pain, and that it would be easier for the both of us to pretend the other didn't exist?

"Please," he begged, reaching for my hand, "just tell me what it is so I can fix it."

"You...can't," I said.

His eyebrows furrowed. "I don't understand..."

"I just..." I fought for words. "...please, just leave me."

"No." Nathaniel said. Final. He gripped my hand tighter. "Talk to me, Augustus."

I closed my eyes, fighting back the tears threatening to fall.

"We were good," Nathaniel went on, urgency drenched in his tone. He wanted this to work. Badly. "We were good, right? I wasn't imagining it?"

I shook my head.

"Then what happened?"

The Devil happened. *I* happened.

"Augustus? Please..."

"I don't want to hurt you..." I whispered.

"You're hurting me every second of every day," Nathaniel whispered back. "It hurts so fucking bad. But I want you to hurt me. I want you to look me in the eye and tell me you hate me, if only so that you will look at me."

I raised my eyes to look at him, and every single one of my defences crumbled. There was nowhere I wanted to be other than his arms. I'd made a mistake. "I'm sorry," I breathed out, throwing my arms around him, face buried in his chest. "I'm sorry. I got scared and..."

Nathaniel's own arms snaked around my waist, holding me close as he whispered soothing words into my ear. "It's okay, Augustus. It's okay. I'm here. I'm never leaving you."

I am here too, little monster. And I am never *leaving you.*

***

The God's Soldiers Church had yet to respond. My mission to find my mother was on hold, and although the Devil had barricaded himself in a dark cell within my mind in rebellion, my own conscience demanded I save her.

There wasn't a lot to go on, though. My research resulted in one single article from when my mother first went missing, the Rose Chapel Police Force pleading with the public for any information. No one knew where she was. And no one cared enough to keep looking.

"Why are you searching for mum?"

Auden stood behind me, eyes glued to my computer screen as he adjusted his glasses, lips pursed in displeasure. I hadn't heard him come in, his bare feet silent against the carpeted floor.

"Auddie, I thought you were asleep," I said, "are you okay?"

"Why are you searching for mum?" he repeated.

"I...was just curious."

"About what?"

"What the search was like..." I half-lied, "...you know, when she first went missing."

"Why?" His voice lowered a fraction, eyebrows furrowed. A flash of anger darkened his eyes—a flash of fear parting his lips. It made sense, really. He'd been alone with our mother before I'd arrived, trapped within a circle of flames, smoke crawling into his lungs. He had more reason than I to fear her.

"Because dad never told us anything," I answered, frustration creeping into my voice. In those early days, I had a lot of questions. Auden too. If our father had answered them, perhaps I wouldn't be here now, typing her name in a search engine as though she were a mere case study and not my mother.

"Are you trying to find her?" Auden asked.

Without answering his question, I closed my laptop, launched to my feet, and steered Auden out of my bedroom. He opened his mouth to protest, but I cut him off before he had the chance. "Do you want to meet Nathaniel tonight?"

The question seemed to have caught him off guard. "What?"

"Nathaniel. My boyfriend. Do you want to meet him?"

"I can't," he said, stunned.

I knew he was shy, especially around new people, but I hadn't expected a flat-out *no.* "Why not? Nathaniel has been dying to meet you. You can just say hello. I won't make you talk for long."

"I can't," Auden said, hands fluttering anxiously at his sides.

I didn't want to cause him any more anxiety, so I merely nodded and ruffled his hair. "Okay, not tonight then. But soon, alright?"

"Okay," Auden whispered, face pale.

That night, Auden remained locked up in his room when Nathaniel came over. We played video games on my couch, a shared blanket draped over us as we competed for the first-place trophy in Mario Kart. Nathaniel had been disappointed not to meet Auden, but he didn't push. He said two of his brothers were shy too, so he understood.

In between competitive shouting and teasing, there were long kisses, our fingers intertwined as we melted into each other's arms. He kept his promise, of never asking for more, but I still felt guilty, as though I were withholding something from him. And there was insecurity, too, a fear that he would seek physical intimacy elsewhere. It would cause me to grow distant, and Nathaniel, through no fault of his own, became a potential enemy in my mind. I fought through it, knowing jealousy had jeopardised my friendship with Ava and I didn't want it to do the same with Nathaniel.

The following day, Nathaniel invited me inside his favourite place in the world—other than my arms, of course. His words, not mine. He seemed nervous, words pouring from his lips twice as fast as he explained that he'd never shown anyone outside of his family this room before. It was his treasure, his safe space.

Biting his lip, he paused in front of a tall, dark oak door, fingers curled around the golden handle. I waited, patiently, as the door creaked open and Nathaniel gestured for me to step inside, his eyes wide and vulnerable.

It was his music room—soundproof walls lined with charcoal padding, a large classical piano in the left-hand corner, black paint polished, shining in the room's dim light. Beside the piano, a long wooden cabinet displayed several trophies and awards, Nathaniel's musical achievements starting from the age of five. Three violins and a cello hung on stands by the right-hand corner, a glass table littered with music books and instrument cleaning products beside it. As he approached the piano, I realised this was his equivalent of my art studio. He was showing his canvases, letting me into his art.

"I wrote you something," he said. His fingers found their assigned keys, stool groaning as he shifted to make room beside him. "I started writing it before we even..."

"Even what?"

"Started dating," he chuckled breathlessly.

I lowered myself down next to him, our thighs pressed together. He tested one of the many white keys beneath his fingers, and then, with one last inhale, music spilled into the air.

It was soft, a gentle caress against my cheek, a private kiss under the moonlight. And then it was wild, as though we were running barefoot in the woods, the meadow, the galleries.

Nathaniel's fingers moved effortlessly along the keyboard, his bottom lip caught between his teeth as he chased the music that poured from his soul.

I closed my eyes as the music grew louder, chaotic, more intense. It was circling me, surrounding me, consuming me.

My heart thundered against my chest, and behind my closed eyelids, I was running. I was running from Nathaniel, ducking under tree branches and leaping over moss-covered logs. But Nathaniel was too fast. He caught me, arms wrapped around my waist, holding me in a firm, warm embrace.

The music calmed. It was quiet, almost shy. It was asking a question—a question I hadn't known the answer to until this very moment.

Nathaniel—the one behind my closed eyelids—held me. He held me and he calmed me and he loved me. He infiltrated my guarded walls and conquered the caged monster of my heart.

I tasted salt on my lips as my eyelids fluttered open, a thumb on my cheek, wiping the tear away before I could process the music had ended.

"What do you think?" he asked quietly.

"I think that was beautiful," I whispered, "And I think I love you."

CHAPTER THIRTY-TWO

It was 3am the following morning when Nathaniel sent me three messages that would change my life.

The first: 'The God's Soldiers Church got back to me.'

The second: 'We've been invited.'

And the third: 'It's in Essex.'

It was finally happening. I was going to find my mother.

Why do you even want to find that woman? We're better off without her.

The Devil's hatred for my mother went deeper than mine. I suspected it had a lot to do with her attempt to exorcise him from me all those years ago. In his eyes, she was the villain of this story. But perhaps things weren't so black and white.

In the passenger seat of Nathaniel's car, I reread the emailed response from the God's Soldiers Church, scoffing at the phrase *righteous path* which had been repeated numerous times alongside *God's calling* and *holy war*. Had Joe been following a *righteous path* when he bedded a married woman? Was it *God's calling* to lock said married woman's son up in a dark mirrored room with only a pool of water and the Devil for company?

"Do you think he knows he is being manipulative?" I asked, returning Nathaniel's phone. "Or do you think he genuinely believes in what he is saying?"

"Based on what we learned last semester...I'd say yeah, he knows he's being manipulative," he mused, fingers drumming against the steering wheel as we waited at a traffic light. "But he probably believes in it, too. I'd pay to be a fly on the wall—or I guess universe—when people like him die and wake up in Hell instead of Heaven."

I snorted. "Me too."

We reached Essex in just over an hour, travelling down unmaintained roads ravaged by weeds, scattered twigs snapping beneath our tires. Trees lined either side of the dirt, their twisted limbs shrouding us in darkness. The car's headlights were our only source of light, streetlamps a luxury reserved for the city.

The GPS led us down a narrow road, Nathaniel and I swaying back and forth as his tires rolled over dips and cracks.

Up ahead, a one-story building was tucked in between tall oak trees, its grey bricks crawling with moss and ivy. A large pale blue banner hung across the front entrance reading *The Church of God's Soldiers*. Trees crowded the dirt covered driveway; fallen leaves scattered along the dry grass. It reminded me of the House on North Lane and the woods that guarded it.

Nathaniel parked the car and climbed out with no hesitation. I, on the other hand, grew weary. As soon as Joe laid eyes on me, our cover would be blown. Although it had been over ten years since he'd seen me, on my knees and gasping for air, I had no doubt he'd recognise the devil within. Not to mention I had the same mess of brown curls and a permanent scowl that only Nathaniel and Auden seemed able to chase away.

I remained frozen inside the car until Nathaniel moved around to my side and opened the door, his long legs bending as he crouched down and reached for my hand. "This is the moment you've been waiting for, right? Your mother could be in there."

That evil witch? We should leave immediately.

I swallowed hard. If my mother *was* inside, would she recognise me? Would she still think I was possessed by the Devil, or would she finally see her son? All these questions raced through my mind, sending my heart beating a million miles per hour.

"Augustus..." Nathaniel said soothingly, "...I'll be with you the whole time. I promise."

I allowed him to pull me to my feet and guide me toward the door, his hand warm in mine. There was no doorbell, so Nathaniel raised his fist and knocked. I inhaled sharply and held my breath, anticipating recognition crossing Joe's face before he banished me without hearing a word I had to say. Only it wasn't Joe who answered the door, it was a thin young woman in a long, brown linen skirt and a beige crochet cardigan over a plain beige tank top. Her long brown hair was tied back in a single fish-tail braid, her raven-coloured eyes darting from Nathaniel and I with confusion.

"Hi!" Nathaniel greeted the woman with a flash of his disarming smile. The woman brightened to him immediately as he said, "My name is Nathaniel. I was invited here by Joseph Kade."

"Oh, yes, Nathaniel," she smiled with yellow teeth, the front two chipped and crooked, "Joe is expecting you." Her gaze drifted to me, her smile fading, "Only...you."

"Ah, yes, this is my...boyfriend," Nathaniel said.

My heart fluttered at the word boyfriend, only to immediately crumble when the woman narrowed her eyes.

"You are both men," she said.

I was about to grab Nathaniel's arm to leave when he opened his mouth to speak, his voice smooth and steady as he said, "Yes, well, that's kind of why we've sought out a community that will help us...be sinners no more."

It hurt to be called a sinner, but I knew Nathaniel was just trying to grant us entry. And it was working. The woman's suspicions vanished, and she nodded, opening the door wider to let us in. "Of course. We welcome *anyone* who wants to be saved."

We followed the woman down an empty hallway with cracked, floral wallpaper, the green, red and brown colours desaturated with age. At the end of the hallway, there were plastic chairs scattered across the wooden floor, dark stains almost resembling blood.

A large statue of the cross hung in the centre of the back wall, a small black table in front of it with a Bible, a candle, and a framed photo of Joe. It was unclear whether the God's Soldiers used this room to worship God or their leader.

As we entered a second hallway—this one decorated with religious memorabilia—we heard the faint sound of church hymns from outside. I glanced out the window overlooking the backyard just as the woman said, "That's our choir. They're practicing for tonight's sermon."

There were a group of six women and three men of various ages standing barefoot in the grass, one bald headed man standing across from them, moving his hands like a conductor. I searched the faces for my mother, but none belonged to her.

The woman knocked on a door at the end of the hall. It had a small plaque hanging eye level that read 'Captain'. I rolled my eyes. Did he really think they were God's Soldiers, and he was some kind of Captain? It was deranged. Utterly delusional.

"Enter."

Run. Now. Run.

The familiar voice set the Devil wild inside of me. He thrashed against my walls, begging to take control of my body so we could flee. I hadn't expected such a violent response, but then the mirrored room flashed behind my eyelids with every blink—the water, the chains, the isolation. I took an involuntary step back from the door, but Nathaniel reached for my hand, squeezing it gently before I could run.

Words were exchanged between Joe and the woman before the door opened wider and Nathaniel and I were allowed inside. The 'Captain's' office had been invaded by mold, black blotches crawling along the peeling wallpaper like bruises on a decaying corpse. It was small, with only enough space for one tall bookshelf pressed up against the left corner and a desk, the wooden floorboards speckled with dust. An earthy dampness thickened the air, every inhale poison. I tried to hold my breath, but the sight of Joe knocked it out of me.

He was seated behind the desk, a framed photo of him and his followers hanging on the wall behind him. His hair had greyed, but his eyes maintained the cold menace I remembered when he locked me in that mirrored room.

He rose to his feet to shake Nathaniel's hand, but when his eyes landed on me, he paused, hand slowly dropping to his side.

Run! Run! Run!

I met his gaze, daring him to throw me out, banish me, create a scene in front of all his devoted followers. I wasn't that same scared little boy anymore. There was no way he would have the power to lock me inside a dark room ever again.

"You've grown," were his first words to me as he slowly sunk down into his chair.

"You've aged," was my response.

Joe seemed to forget all about Nathaniel as he assessed me. "What are you doing here?"

"Where is my mother?" I demanded.

A flicker of confusion crossed his wrinkled face, his lips parting as if to speak, only to hang open without a word. I didn't understand what he expected. Why else would I have visited this wicked hell hole?

"My mother," I repeated, frustrated at his lack of response, "where is she?"

"Not here."

"Then you won't mind if we look around and–" Nathaniel started, but I cut him off by taking a step forward, hands pressed flat against the dust covered desk.

"Where. Is. She?"

Joe leaned back in his seat, hands falling comfortably to his lap. "Why now? It's been what...ten years?"

"Answer the damn question!"

"As I said, she's not here," Joe said, jaw clenched. "Have you tried North Lane?"

Run!

"What?"

"North Lane." It was Joe's turn to repeat himself now. "Have you looked there?"

No. I had not. I had sworn never to return to that place and had assumed my mother would have done the same. The memories were unpleasant. For both of us. "Why would she be there?"

Joe opened his mouth to answer when the door to his office burst open, and three women entered, not at all surprised to see that Nathaniel and I were standing in front of them.

"It's time, Captain!" one of the women announced.

With a plastered smile, Joe nodded and rose to his feet. With a dismissive glance my way, he said, "Don't come here again."

I stared after him, mouth agape. Nathaniel reached for my hand once we were alone in the office, his thumb brushing my knuckles gently. "Should we...visit North Lane, then?"

"No," I said immediately, yanking my hand back. "No, he's lying! Or keeping something from me! That house is...it's abandoned."

"Why would he lie?"

"To draw me away," I said, my feet guiding me out of the office and down the hall before I could hear Nathaniel's response.

He's hiding something. He's hiding something. He's hiding something.

The light in the hallway flickered violently and followed me toward the back garden where Joe and the women had disappeared.

"Joe!" I yelled.

Every head turned my way, a blend of bewilderment, confusion and anger. Joe's eyes narrowed to slits as he trailed his eyes up and down my body.

"It's still in you, isn't it?" he asked quietly.

I paused, my resolve fading at the realisation that Nathaniel would bear witness to this—would learn about the Devil inside of me. Up until now, it was a mere metaphor. But if he heard any more of this conversation, he would know the truth.

"I don't know what you're talking about," I lied. "Where is my mother?"

"I already told you, dear boy," he said, his followers parting like the red sea as he moved toward me. "She's in North Lane. But I can't let you return to her...not with the Devil eating at your soul."

"Oh, save him!" one of the women said. Her bronze hair was tied up in a bun, loose strands decorating the side of her freckled cheeks. "Save his soul!"

"He doesn't need saving." It was Nathaniel. He stood beside me, one hand on my shoulder as he stared Joe down. "There is no Devil."

Joe titled his head to the side. "Has he told you, boy? Has he told you about–"

"ENOUGH!" I shouted. Dark clouds swallowed the sun, the back garden shrouded in a grey gloom. I could feel the Devil stirring, threatening to come out. I held him back, not wanting Nathaniel to see.

"Let's go, Augustus," Nathaniel whispered gently in my ear. "There is nothing more for us here."

Trembling, I turned to follow Nathaniel—turned to leave Joe and this quest to find my mother behind. But Joe's voice made me halt. He recited familiar words—words I could not understand but recognised from that night in North Lane.

The exorcism, the demon hissed.

Alarmed, I reached for Nathaniel's hand. I heard him shout something, a warning, and then everything went black.

***

I awoke to the sound of my name. It was soft, gentle—an angelic hymn that silenced the Devil, though my head still pounded as though his fists were slamming against my skull.

"What...happened?"

Nathaniel tucked a curl behind my ear, expression grim. "You were drugged." He turned his head to reveal a trickle of dry blood on the side of his neck. "Me too."

My fingers traced the red line of blood along his neck, a flood of anger cascading through my veins. He'd gotten hurt. Because of me. Who knew what else they would do?

You know. You know what they will do.

The Devil hovered behind Nathaniel, black eyes wet with unshed tears. He blinked, slowly, lips pressed together as though he were in pain. I averted my gaze, only for the Devil to appear to my left. And then again to my right. I inhaled sharply.

Mirrors.

Memories of the mirrored room flashed behind my closed eyelids as I buried my face in my hands, hiding from the mirror's cruel torment. The Devil and I were inseparable here. There was nowhere for me to hide.

"The door is locked," Nathaniel spoke up. "I heard voices outside a few minutes ago, but I couldn't make out what they were saying."

"We need to get out of here," I said, voice muffled. I refused to lift my head in case Nathaniel caught my reflection in the mirror.

"There are no windows. No other exits other than the locked door."

"We need to get out of here," I repeated.

"We will," Nathaniel assured me, his fingers finding my chin, tilting my head up to look at him. "But we'll need to wait."

"Wait?"

"Someone will open the door eventually," he said, "and when they do, it'll be our chance to escape."

"There's just one problem," I said, slowly glancing down at my feet which were chained to the shallow pool of water at our feet.

Nathaniel followed my gaze. "Fuck." He tugged at the chains, the iron slicing at my flesh. "FUCK!"

A droplet of blood danced through the dark water. "You're not restrained," I observed. "You can leave. If we create a distraction and–"

"No," he cut me off, shaking his head, "I'm not leaving you."

"You have to," I said, "it's my fault you're even in this mess. Joe doesn't want you. He wants me."

"I don't give a fuck," Nathaniel said. "I'm not leaving you. We're going to get out of here. Together."

"And how do you propose we do that?"

"We wait."

"That's what you said before."

"I know, I'm pretty consistent, aren't I?" he teased.

"Nathaniel–"

"Just trust me, okay?"

"I do trust you but–"

"We're going to get out of here," Nathaniel said, cupping either side of my face. "Just follow my lead, okay? We spent a whole term learning about the psychological manipulation of cults. I think I may have picked up a thing or two."

"What are you saying?"

"I'm saying..." he turned his head toward the door, "...I'm going to manipulate Joe into letting us go."

I shook my head. "He wouldn't do that."

"He would...if he believed it was God's will."

CHAPTER THIRTY-THREE

I had been drifting in and out of sleep when the door creaked open, a faint yellow glow following Joe inside the room. He was dressed in a long priestly gown, white robes fluttering behind him as he clutched the gold crucifix hanging from his neck. He raised it to his lips and kissed it, slowly, eyelids fluttered shut as though in prayer. A small Bible was tucked under his arm, several pages notably absent, no doubt torn out so as not to contradict his teachings.

"You look ridiculous," I said in greeting. Nathaniel had allocated me the role of arrogant demon—a role I played easily since Joe really did look pathetic. "For someone who spits on Catholicism, you do resemble Father Andrej a lot with your costume."

"It is not a costume," Nathaniel defended him, playing the role of devoted believer, "he is a messenger of God. A soldier."

"Not a very good one," I mumbled.

"What would you know, *demon*?" Nathaniel hissed.

"I thought you said there was no demon," Joe said, glancing in between us, a mixture of amusement and confusion fighting for dominance on his old, wrinkled face.

"That was before I saw it inside him," Nathaniel spat, lips curled in disgust. "I didn't want to believe it. But...it's why I brought him here. I sensed...something evil. I want the demon gone."

Joe arched an eyebrow.

"You can do it, can't you?" Nathaniel asked. "He mentioned you tried before...when he was a boy. Do you think...you can banish him for good this time?"

I laughed—a low, guttural sound, foreign to my own ears. "Too weak," I said, shaking my head. "Too weak to succeed."

"I am much stronger than I was ten years ago," Joe told Nathaniel, taking the bait.

"I bet the Devil is stronger too," Nathaniel said.

Joe's lips spread into a confident smile. "No one is stronger than God."

"You'll help him, then?" Hope softened Nathaniel's narrowed eyes and un-furrowed his brows. If he were a stranger, I would have believed he really was trying to save me. "I just want my friend back."

"I fear your friend has always been the Devil," Joe sighed, one hand resting on Nathaniel's shoulder. "Once the Devil is gone...Augustus will be a mere stranger."

A raging fire ignited within my soul. It burned through me, heat flaming my cheeks as I thrashed against my chains. "Get your hands off him!"

Joe shot me a look—a blend of boredom and annoyance—as he pulled away from Nathaniel and sauntered toward the door. I glowered at him, our eyes locking in a silent standoff.

"I will return at midnight for the exorcism," he said. "Say your prayers. You will need them."

***

The plan was simple. At midnight, Joe would return to perform the exorcism. Whether he came alone or with his loyal followers, Nathaniel and I would play along until we had an opportunity to flee. And in that time, I just had to ignore the Devil snarling in the mirrors all around me.

"During the exorcism, you should act like...the Devil is resisting," Nathaniel said, pacing back and forth. "Don't speak, though. Maybe just...wrestle with your chains? Groan?"

"For how long?"

"I don't know. Just long enough to be convincing."

"Do you really think he'd fall for it?"

Nathaniel scratched the back of his neck. "He's delusional, isn't he? He'll see whatever he wants to see."

"I guess."

"And once you're no longer possessed by the Devil, he'll unchain you. That's when we flee."

"What if he's not alone? His followers could overpower us."

"If he's not alone, we'll have to keep up appearances a little longer," Nathaniel sighed. "You'll need to act...I don't know...upset and scared and confused. Once you're deemed no longer a threat, we should be able to just...leave."

"Or they'll try and recruit us," I mumbled.

"We'll adapt," Nathaniel assured me. "We'll get out of here, I promise."

Food was delivered to us in two white bowls atop a plastic tray, a single jug of water beside it. The scent of herbs and simmering meat swallowed the damp rot that clung to the mirrored walls, my stomach grumbling with anticipation.

A dark-haired woman hovered in the doorway, her bare foot tapping against the floor as her grey eyes settled on Nathaniel. I recognised her from a photo posted on the God's Soldiers social media page, but the shift in her appearance was unnerving. Where there had once been colour in her cheeks, there was now only grey, as though she had been snatched right out of a black and white film. Her hair, which had been long and healthy, was now wild and untamed, patches of baldness littering her scalp. She'd grown thin, her dress sliding off her shoulders with every exhale. What was Joe doing to these people?

"Thank you," Nathaniel broke the silence as he crouched down to lift a bowl.

The woman said nothing as he carried it toward me, her fingers fiddling with the grey material of her creased dress, foot still tapping rhythmically against the damp floor.

I pinched the spoon beneath my trembling fingers, twirling the yellow soup around mindlessly while I waited for Nathaniel to retrieve his own bowl. Just as I raised the spoon to my lips, the woman cleared her throat, loudly, and I raised my eyes to look at her. A stern expression darkened her features as she pressed her hands together in prayer.

"Oh," Nathaniel breathed out, lowering his bowl to the floor.

I hesitated before doing the same.

"In the name of the Father, the Son and the Holy Spirit," the woman began, eyelids fluttering shut as she bowed her head. "Heavenly Father, we thank you for the food we are about to eat, for the hands that prepared it, and for your abundant provision. Bless this meal, nourish our bodies, and cleanse our souls. Amen."

"Amen," Nathaniel said.

"Amen," I forced out.

She nodded to our bowls, permitting us to eat.

I took small, hesitant sips while Nathaniel devoured his like a man starved for days instead of mere hours. The woman remained by the entrance, watching us.

"What's your name?" Nathaniel asked once he'd finished his soup and returned his bowl onto the tray.

"You may call me Agatha," the woman replied, lifting her chin.

"It's lovely to meet you, Agatha," Nathaniel said. "How long have you been with the God's Soldiers Church?"

"Three and a half years," she answered.

"That's a long time," Nathaniel hummed. "Is your family here with you?"

Her eye twitched at the word 'family', the tapping growing louder as she shook her head. "My family are non-believers. They are not welcome here."

"I see," Nathaniel said, softening his tone, "I am sorry to hear that."

Agatha shook her head and pinned her gaze on me. I wasn't sure why until she asked, "Have you almost finished your meal?"

I opened my mouth to respond when Nathaniel's next question cut me off, "Do you know Mary Saint?"

The sound of my mother's name on Nathaniel's tongue caught me completely off guard. I dropped my spoon, the splash of water as it sank to the bottom echoing along the walls as I glanced in between my boyfriend and the woman sending daggers in his direction.

"Mary Saint?" she repeated.

"Yes," Nathaniel nodded, "do you know her?"

"I've never heard of her," she said, stepping forward to retrieve my spoon whilst snatching the remainder of my soup from my hands.

"I don't think he's finished—" Nathaniel started, only to fall silent when Agatha fled the room, leaving only the jug of water behind as the door slammed shut.

"It wasn't that good anyway," I mumbled.

Nathaniel sighed. "Do you think she's lying? About not knowing your mother?"

"I don't know. What reason would she have to lie?"

"She's only been with the Church for three years," Nathaniel thought aloud, "your mother could have left before then. We need to speak with someone who has been here longer."

"And how do you propose we do that?" I asked. "It's not like we can just go around interviewing people."

"Well, no, but—"

"Look," I cut him off, "it doesn't matter anymore. We just need to get out of here. Let's just focus on the plan, alright?"

Nathaniel released a long, reluctant sigh. "Alright, yeah. Focus on the plan."

***

Midnight entered the mirrored room like spilled ink, its shadow carrying the nauseating scent of charred flesh and sulphur. Joe stood before me, priestly attire abandoned and replaced with a long black robe, a frayed rope tied around his middle.

Nathaniel stiffened beside me, his lips parting in silent protest as Joe raised a wooden crucifix in my direction, the end sharpened to a stake.

I reached for the Devil in the dark abyss, seeking his comfort in the face of our common enemy, but it was my own panicked voice repeating run, run, run.

"Carrington," Joe started, his voice low and reverent, "help me light the candles, will you?"

I flinched at the memory of the flames inside the House on North Lane, the smoke's suffocating grasp stealing my every breath.

Nathaniel obeyed, head bowed. He played the role of blind follower so well, he almost fooled me. Could I trust him? He was probably scared, terrified. If it came down to me or survival, what would he choose?

Once the candles lined every corner of the square room, their flames dancing menacingly in the mirror, I closed my eyes, calling for the Devil. The

Devil, who feared no one but God, feared the man standing in front of me, as though Joe really was a vessel of the Lord.

"Pray with me," Joe said, reaching inside his robe for a crystal blue rosary he handed to Nathaniel. "Don't stop no matter what happens."

Nathaniel nodded, clasping the rosary in between his hands as though it were a life raft keeping him from drifting out to sea.

Their voices echoed in unison, their prayer bouncing off the mirrored walls, growing louder and louder as candlelight painted distorted shadows on their reflections, faces warping into their own Devils.

I watched, fingernails clawing at the flesh of my arms, as Joe inched closer until he stood mere centimetres away, the crucifix close enough to bite. I did not have to act when I thrashed against the chains and spat at his feet. There was no one I hated more at that moment.

Latin rolled off his tongue, the Devil stirring at the resurrection of the dead language. I hadn't known it was Latin during my first exorcism, but schooling introduced me to the language that the Devil was so afraid of. His silence heightened the fear flooding through my body. I wasn't used to facing these horrors alone. The Devil had always been there. Taunting, yes. Mocking, of course. But he was there, protecting me when necessary.

I thrashed against the chains as Nathaniel had instructed, channelling the role of a demon fighting against God's divine power.

Joe raised his voice, but the flames did not rise at his command. Smoke did not smother me. I was not gasping for air, fighting to survive, like all those years ago in North Lane. It was not Joe, then, who had the power to expel the demon. It was my mother.

"Satan!" Joe called, droplets of holy water landing on my forehead. "You are banished from this boy's body! You are banished from his soul! You are banished from God's Kingdom! Be gone!"

I wrestled with the chains, spitting at Joe's feet.

"Be gone!" Joe repeated.

I screamed, the sound echoing along the walls, my reflection trembling as though a demon really were struggling to maintain possession. I gave my chains one last yank before collapsing with feigned exhaustion, eyelids fluttering shut.

A heavy silence followed, the flames drowning in wet wax.

"Did it work?" Nathaniel asked, voice laced with hope. "Is the Devil gone?"

Joe crouched down, fingers against my neck to feel for a pulse. "Augustus?" he called softly. "Can you hear me?"

I forced my eyes open with feigned confusion, groaning as though my muscles ached. "What's...what's going on?"

"Your soul has been freed," he said, a slow smile spreading across his face, "you have been saved. The Devil plagues you no more."

I will tear that smile off his face with my teeth.

The Devil had returned, his harsh tongue a welcome torment. I relaxed, shoulders slumping as though I were a man truly freed.

"What happens now?" Nathaniel asked.

Joe brushed the hair out of my eyes as he said, "Now we pray."

Nathaniel hovered by the door, picking at his lip as he watched Joe raise his hands in the air, prayer spilling from his lips in endless waves. I could tell he was growing impatient, as was I.

I sat, unblinking, head bowed in a mimicry of devotion. The Devil laughed behind my glassy eyes, hatred laced in each word that poured from his wicked tongue. I dared not look in the mirror, afraid of what I might see in the Devil's eyes.

"Augustus," Joe whispered. "I am going to unchain you. Rise slowly, your body may be weak."

The rustle of metal announced the removal of my shackles, the absence of iron a welcome relief.

Nathaniel was at my side in an instant, throwing one of my arms over his shoulder to steady me as my legs refused to cooperate. "We should go," he whispered, guiding me toward the door.

"Now hold on, just a second," Joe said, following us out into the hall, "come to my office. Let me dress those wounds."

Nathaniel and I exchanged a wordless glance. We had little choice but to resume our roles of obedient soldier and freed soul. We followed.

Joe sat at his desk, gesturing for Nathaniel and I to take the seats across from him. We did, the chairs groaning from our weight, as if on the verge of collapsing at any moment.

"That was a spectacular performance," Joe said, voice dripping with condescension.

Nathaniel straightened in his seat. I deflated.

"The Devil is still in there," he went on, shaking his head with disappointment, "I can feel him."

"Wait, the exorcism didn't work?" Nathaniel continued his act, lips parted in surprise.

Joe's gaze snapped to him. "Enough."

Nathaniel opened his mouth to prolong the act, but I cut him off, knowing the show had come to an end.

"Why let me go, then?" I asked.

"To give you a choice."

"A choice?" I scoffed.

"You can stay here and pray until the Devil is banished for good," he said, leaning forward in his seat. "Or, you can die."

I swallowed the lump in my throat as he withdrew a long blade from his desk drawer, the Devil unnaturally calm as he paced up and down the crowded corridors of my mind.

Nathaniel shielded me from the blade, rising to his feet, long limbs an easy target for an attack.

"We're leaving," he announced coldly. "We're not a part of your...deranged cult."

"That boy is possessed," Joe spat, pointing the blade toward me. "And that demon has lodged itself into your heart."

Nathaniel released a low, humourless chuckle. "Oh, so now I am possessed too?"

"Nate," I whispered, tugging at the hem of his shirt.

"I cannot allow the Devil to harm another soul," Joe said, "move aside, boy, or I will cut you down too."

Nathaniel was as still as a statue, defiance in every line of his body. I realised, with sickening clarity, that Nathaniel would die if I did nothing. He would choose *me*.

The Devil threw my body toward Nathaniel, knocking him to the side to avoid Joe's blade. He grunted as he hit the wall, but an apology had to wait, for Joe lunged toward me, blade aiming for my neck. It whistled over my head as I ducked, my hands reaching for his robes like a feral cat, nails cutting into the material to keep him from Nathaniel.

His blade swung in my direction, narrowly missing my chest.

I tackled him to the floor, a tangle of limbs battling for dominance. I kicked the weapon from his grasp and held him down with my entire body, knees on either side of his writhing torso, hands pinning him by the chest.

"Demon!" he spat.

I silenced him with an elbow to the throat, reaching out with one hand to retrieve the blade that had fallen from his tight grasp.

Joe gazed up at me, fear dancing in his eyes. I drank it in, absorbing the way his eyes widened, pupils dilating, lips parted in a breathless gasp. I watched him the way he watched me all those years ago, smothered by smoke, trapped in the flames, praying for a God that never came.

"You're the Devil," he hissed. "Soon they will all see just how monstrous you are!"

Let them.

Let them believe it. Let them tremble. Because the real monster was not the Devil. It was me.

"See you in Hell."

I drove the blade through his heart.

CHAPTER THIRTY-FOUR

The metallic scent of blood poisoned the air, red droplets staining the collar of Nathaniel's shirt as I clung onto him, air evading my lungs with every trembling inhale.

"He's dead," Nathaniel said in a detached tone, his arms stiffening around my waist.

Dead.

I glanced down at the fresh corpse, a river of blue veins cascading down his pale skin, a waterfall of blood pooling around him.

Dead.

"Police," I choked out. "We...we should...call–call the police."

Nathaniel's expression shifted, wide eyes narrowing as he shook his head. "What? No. They'll arrest you. Charge you with murder."

It's what you deserve.

"But I..." My voice trailed off, a numbing ache settling into every bone and muscle in my body. I swayed, blood drenched hands flickering across my vision, dancing in my mind—death, murder, blood.

I needed to sit down, needed to close my eyes, needed to fall asleep and never wake up.

"Augustus?"

Darkness welcomed me with open arms, Nathaniel's voice dissolving into a soft hum, a lullaby coaxing me into sleep.

***

I awoke in a bed that wasn't my own.

A news reporter detailed a recent flood on television, cars roared down the highway, a symphony of rhythmic chaos that lured me from my slumber.

I sat up, ran a hand through my sweat-drenched curls, head pounding as though I had been slammed over the head repeatedly. Blinking, I glanced down at my shirtless torso and–

Where the hell were my clothes?

Confusion. And then panic.

I stood, frantically searching for my clothes. All I found was a white bathrobe, wrapping it around my shivering body in seconds.

A door to my left creaked open. Nathaniel entered, an identical white robe around his slim frame, black hair dripping wet.

"You're awake," he breathed out, "how are you feeling?"

"I...what happened?"

"You fainted," he sighed, shifting closer. "You hit your head pretty hard but I've had a look at it...should be okay with some rest."

I nodded, relaxing at his touch. "Where are my clothes?"

"In the laundry room," he answered, "they'll be clean and dry soon."

I chewed on my bottom lip as fragments of the night returned to me. A sharp blade. Blood. The wet, slippery sound of steel piercing through flesh. Blue veins and decaying skin.

My knees gave out and I collapsed onto the mattress, horror sending ice shards down my spine. "Oh my god."

"What's wrong?" Nathaniel frowned.

"I...I...how did we get out?"

"Out?"

"Of the house...after what I..."

"Of Joe's house?"

I nodded, heart hammering in my chest like a wild animal desperate to escape an enclosure.

"We walked out the front door…"

"But the others…they would have seen…"

Nathaniel sat down beside me, hand clasping my knee gently. "Seen what?"

"The blood."

"The blood?" Nathaniel repeated, alarmed. "What blood?"

I glanced sideways at him, tears blurring my vision. Why was he acting like he didn't remember? He was right there. "*Joe's* blood. I killed him."

"*Killed* him?" Nathaniel repeated. "What are you talking about? You didn't kill him. Joe's fine. He let us go. Said your soul had been saved."

"What are *you* talking about?!" I snapped, voice cracking. "You were right there! You saw it! You said he was dead!"

Confusion and fear crossed Nathaniel's face as he studied me. "Augustus…that never happened. I promise you…you didn't kill anybody."

I glanced down at my hands. There was no blood, but I assumed Nathaniel had helped me clean it off.

"But the clothes…the blood…"

"There was no blood. You vomited a little as you passed out, that's all."

I stared at him, searching for the lie. I couldn't find it. "That…wasn't real? I really didn't kill him?"

"You didn't kill him," he confirmed, reaching for my hand to clasp firmly. "I promise…you didn't kill anybody."

"It felt so real," I whispered, peeling my hand from his grasp.

"Just a hallucination, perhaps?"

"I'm not crazy."

"I never said you were."

"But you think I'm hallucinating?"

"I'm just saying that is a potential explanation for what you experienced."

Don't act surprised, Augustus. You've been questioning your sanity for a while.

"No, no, no," I stood, pacing back and forth, fingers raking through my hair. "This can't be happening."

Nathaniel reached for my hands, but I flinched away from his touch. "Augustus..."

"Please just take me home. I need...I need to see Auden."

***

I stumbled into the kitchen and flicked on the kettle, gaze drifting toward the clock that read 6:45am. Auden's alarm was set for 7am on school days, but he usually showered and brushed his teeth thirty minutes before, slipping into his school uniform by the time the alarm screamed at him to wake up.

Pouring a hot chocolate for the both of us, I let my mind wander, replaying the memory of plunging a blade through Joe's heart.

Not real.

The Devil stood beside me, his eyeless sockets crawling with roaches that threatened to fall into my drink. Tendrils of smoke danced around him, snakes slithering up his legs as his clawed hand reached for my teaspoon. He stirred my drink wordlessly. I didn't realise why until I glanced down at my trembling hands, fingertips dripping with blood.

I told you not to go looking for her, he said, *look what has become of you.*

"I was already insane!" I snapped, rushing to the sink to wash away the blood stains. "I've seen you my whole life!"

Have you ever asked yourself why?

I fell silent, attention fixed on removing all evidence of blood, whether real or not.

The Devil watched on. There were no taunts. No laughter. It seemed the mirrored room had broken him just as much as it had broken me.

I waited ten minutes before venturing toward Auden's room, concerned his absence meant he was unwell.

There was no response when I knocked on the door, so I entered without an invitation, frowning at the sight of Auden still asleep in bed, glasses untouched on his bedside table.

"Audie?" His eyelids fluttered open, but he made no move to sit up. "Are you feeling okay?"

He shook his head weakly, cheeks pale and forehead glistening with sweat. Frown deepening, I placed a hand on his forehead and cursed. He was burning up.

"I'll be right back," I promised him before hurrying out of the room to find some medication to fight the fever, snatching a wet towel to cool his forehead.

I remained with him until he showed signs of improvement, taking slow sips of water and small bites of fruit.

"Where were you?" he asked, voice raspy.

"I was...with a friend," I answered.

"You were gone for *days*," he said. "I thought you left me again."

His words were a dagger to the heart—tearing through flesh until it embedded itself in my bones. I'd promised him I would never abandon him, and yet I had vanished without a word, leaving him all on his own.

You're just like your mother.

"I'm sorry, Auden, I'm so sorry."

"Why? Why did you leave?"

"It's...it's complicated," I breathed out, "but I never intended on leaving you. I was just trying to—"

"Please," Auden cut me off, "just tell me the truth."

Swallowing the lump in my throat, I raised a hand to tangle through his hair, caressing each strand away from his forehead. "I will," I lied, "but you need to get better first, okay?"

He coughed weakly before falling asleep in my arms, every cell in my body at war with each other as I fought between staying with Auden and figuring out what the hell was wrong with me.

***

Browning Books was empty when I arrived, with only Edith at the counter flicking through the weekly sale reports. She updated me on what was required for my shift before she left, handing me the keys to lock up.

For the first hour, I patrolled the shelves, using a cloth to wipe down dust whilst adjusting books that were out of place. In that time, I had one customer—an old man looking for World War II non-fiction. He bought two books and thanked me for my help. Once he was gone, I called Auden to check on how he was, and in a weak voice, he told me he was feeling up to eating, so I ordered him some food from my phone and hoped he'd be well enough to answer the door.

The second hour went by slowly. Not one customer entered the store. I scrubbed down the counter, swept the floor, and organised Edith's paperwork into neat piles.

During the third hour, the door opened and a figure in beige trousers and a short-sleeved white collared shirt tucked in, stepped inside. The aromatic scent of vanilla and citrus wafted through the air, and my shoulders dropped. It was Nathaniel.

Hands in his pockets, he pretended to scour the shelves while I stood behind the counter, our bodies only metres away while our hearts measured the distance of the Earth and stars. We hadn't spoken since he'd dropped me back home. He'd texted me, of course, but I hadn't responded.

Not a word was spoken as he walked up and down the aisles, his long fingers pulling books off the shelf only to return them minutes later as he browsed through row after row.

Are you just going to watch him like a creep?

I was surprised to hear the Devil's voice. It was calm, lacking its usual bite. I had grown comfortable with his silence—comfortable with my *own* thoughts. I did not flinch, though. His presence was not unwelcome.

"Are you looking for anything in particular?" I asked once Nathaniel returned a third book onto the shelf.

"No," he answered, slowly turning to face me, "I'm here for you."

"Why?"

"I want to ask you a question. Just one. And I want you to be honest with me."

"Okay."

"Do you believe there is a demon inside of you?"

He knows. He knows. He knows.

"Excuse me?"

"Answer the question, Augustus. Do you believe there is a demon inside of you?"

No, no, no.

"Yes."

I did not know what I expected from Nathaniel in that moment. Perhaps I expected him to gasp, scream, or flee from the store. But deep down, I knew he wouldn't do that. What I hadn't anticipated was for Nathaniel to lean back against the bookshelves comfortably, arms folded over his chest.

"Tell me about it," he said, "this...demon."

I shook my head, ready to tell him no, when he raised a hand to silence me.

"Don't," he said, voice soft, "just tell me."

I swallowed back my protests, lowering my gaze to the pile of books on the counter. "Well," I cleared my throat, "the first thing you should know is that...it's not just a demon."

His eyebrows shot up. "Oh?"

"It's the Devil."

Nathaniel didn't even flinch. "As in, Lucifer?"

Should I be flattered that he hasn't run away yet?

"Yes," I answered, weary. It almost felt like this was some sort of trap. A test.

"Do you see him?"

"Not often."

"So you *have* seen him?"

"In the mirror."

"You've seen him in the mirror?" he clarified. "What does he look like?"

An angel.

"What's with the interrogation?"

"I'm just curious."

"You think I'm crazy."

"Did I say that?"

"If you don't...then maybe you're crazier than me."

"Maybe I am."

I clenched my jaw and said nothing.

"Do you hear him?"

"Yes."

"Often?"

"Yes."

"What does he say?"

I say he'll die a slow and painful death.

"You don't want to know."

Nathaniel's eyebrows rose higher. "Is he talking to you right now?"

Why are you answering his questions? He's going to find out.

"Yes."

Nathaniel watched me for a long moment before pushing himself away from the shelves, crouching to pick a book off the floor that had fallen over. "The Devil...does he like me?" he asked.

"Is that what this is about?" I sighed, suppressing an eye roll. "Flattery?"

"Does he like me, Augustus?"

No.

"I don't...think he likes anyone. But he doesn't hate you. He's actually...quite calm in your presence."

"Good, good. I rather like him too. Always thought he made a lot of sense."

I always knew there would be someone out there who would appreciate me.

"The Devil is the villain," I pointed out.

"Only because the story is told from God's perspective." He settled the book back onto the shelf and turned to face me, the sun colouring his eyes gold. "And God, perhaps, is the greatest unreliable narrator of all."

"What do you mean by that?"

"The Bible is considered the word of God, is it not? Or at least divinely inspired?"

I nodded.

"There are many contradictions in the Bible," he explained, "and therefore these accounts are unreliable. For example, the death of Judas. The book of Matthew portrays Judas as remorseful after betraying Jesus, even returning the thirty pieces of silver to the temple before hanging himself."

"Did he not?" I frowned.

"How can we know for sure?" Nathaniel shrugged. "Acts 1:18 states that Judas purchased a field with the thirty pieces of silver and he falls head-first, dying in the Field of Blood."

"Okay, sure, but that's just...different memories," I defended the Bible. "These accounts were written years later. And by people, not God. It doesn't change the fact that Judas died an unhappy death as a result of betraying Jesus. It doesn't make God some kind of liar."

"I never said God was a liar," Nathaniel said. "Just unreliable. His rules keep changing."

I shook my head, unconvinced.

"Okay, tell me, does God love everyone?"

"Of course," I said.

Yet he abandoned you, little monster.

"Well, the book of John would agree with you," Nathaniel nodded, "but Leviticus? Psalms? Proverbs? They all indicate that God hates evildoers. Sinners."

Hence why he hates you.

I swallowed. "Well, that makes sense. God is good. Why would He love evil?"

"That's not the point, Augustus. The point is that when the Bible, and God Himself, is contradictory, how can we know the objective truth?"

"Careful," I said," you could be condemned to Hell for that."

"Maybe then I'll finally get the Devil's side of the story," he chuckled.

I crossed the space between us, reaching to adjust his collar which had tucked itself beneath his brown vest. "Nathaniel Carrington...I am starting to think you're worse than me."

"Is that a good thing or a bad thing?" he grinned.

"Bad," I leaned up to whisper in his ear, "but the Devil in me likes it."

Nathaniel smirked and reached for my waist, but I took a step back, his hand gliding through air. An audible sigh escaped his throat. "How long has the Devil been inside of you?"

"A long time."

"How long?"

"Since I was four."

"That's quite young," Nathaniel hummed. "Why do you think he chose you?"

"I'm the son of a crazy religious fanatic, who better to possess than me?"

"So your mother is crazy for being religious, but you're not for believing you're possessed by the Devil?"

Ah, so it was a trap. He does think we're crazy.

"My mother is crazy because she would have let me die that night in North Lane."

"Of course."

"Don't patronise me," I scoffed.

"I'm not," he said softly, "I'm just trying to understand."

"Now answer my question. Just the one. Do *you* believe I have the Devil inside of me?"

A look of defeat crossed his face, and I knew the answer before he even had to say it. "No," he whispered. "I don't."

With a bitter chuckle, I turned away and returned to the counter. I couldn't leave since I was at work, so I had to rely on Nathaniel being the one to walk away. But he didn't.

His footsteps stopped at the counter.

"Is there anything else I can do for you?" I forced out.

"Is that all you have to say to me?"

"There is nothing to say." I grew defensive, hands curling into fists at my side as my heart thundered wildly against my chest. Did he want me to apologise? *He* was the one who lied to me. He was the one who was always trying to fix me like I was his little broken project. He was the one who made me open up only to shut me down.

"So what, that's it then?" he asked, voice cracking. "We're just...done?"

I didn't answer.

Nathaniel scoffed and ran his fingers through his hair, messing up the neat styling he no doubt spent several minutes on. "God, Augustus, are you not sick of it? Are you not tired of being your own worst enemy? You think everybody is against you. Have you ever considered that I am just trying to help?"

"What do you want me to say?" I asked, voice cracking. "Because I genuinely don't know, Nate."

"I just want you to let me in."

"I did," I hissed, "and you called me crazy!"

"I never said that!"

"It was heavily implied!"

"I just want to help you, Augustus."

"You can't save me," I whispered.

"Then let me die *with* you."

Tears filled my eyes before I had the chance to fight them. What did he see in me? What could I possibly have to offer him? All I seemed to do was hurt him, and yet here he was, fighting for me. No one had ever fought for me before. Not my mother. Not my father. Not Ava. Only Nathaniel.

You could save every soul on Earth and never deserve him.

"I don't want to be with you," I said.

Nathaniel's shoulders dropped and he hung his head in defeat. His lips parted, as if to speak, only for a heavy silence to thicken the air. He nodded without a word, leaving me alone inside *Browning Books* with only books for company. My heart shattered like a glass cup smashed against a tiled floor. It hurt. It hurt more than anything I'd ever felt before.

You did this to yourself.

I slammed my fist against the counter, pain lancing through my knuckles. Blood fell to the wooden floorboards, trickling in between the small gaps to feed the darkness below.

In another universe, I was someone who could love Nathaniel. In this one, I was someone who only brought him pain.

CHAPTER THIRTY-FIVE

Heartbreak condemned me to my bed like a sickness, the soft mattress my only comfort. I hid under the covers, its hollow embrace failing to soothe the ache in my chest, the memories of Nathaniel and the way I ended things replaying mercilessly behind closed eyelids.

It's for the best, the Devil reminded me.

"Guses."

Auden, wrapped in a blanket, stood in my bedroom doorway, face pale and hair sticking up in all different directions. His glasses had fogged up, blurring his watery blue eyes.

"Are you still feeling sick?" I asked.

He nodded, feet shuffling toward the bed to sit beside me. I raised a hand to his head. Ice cold. No fever.

"Maybe we should go see a doctor," I said.

"Why do you always make *me* go to the doctor when you don't even go for yourself?" he complained, shaking his head.

"What are you talking about?"

"You don't take care of yourself."

"I'm fine, Auden," I said. "I'm not sick. Just tired."

You're always lying to him.

"Can we do something today, then?" he asked. "I never get to spend time with you anymore."

He's begging for your affection. Just like you used to beg for your mother's. You're more and more like her every day.

"Of course," I breathed out, massaging my forehead to silence the Devil's cruel truth. "What would you like to do?"

"Can we...go home?"

"We *are* home," I frowned, feeling his forehead again in case a fever had formed in the last minute or so.

"Not here," he said, gently smacking my hand away. "*Home.* North Lane."

The House on North Lane.

"Why...why would you want to go there?"

"I want to see," he said.

"See what?"

He didn't answer, his eyelids falling shut as a bead of sweat trickled down his forehead. Frown deepening, I carried him to his bedroom and tucked him in, stroking the hair out of his eyes as my mind wandered to the House on North Lane. It couldn't be a coincidence that the House was at the centre of all my dreams, that Joe suggested my mother was there, that Auden wanted to return. The House on North Lane held answers—answers I intended to uncover.

You can't go back there, the Devil warned. *Do not return to that House.*

***

Dawnridge library was practically empty, vacant seats stretching in all different directions. There were students scattered, heads bent in unison as they flipped through their summer textbooks, whispers echoing along the walls.

I lowered myself down onto the cushioned booth by the entry, the same one Nathaniel had claimed the night we unintentionally trapped ourselves in the library. Although I wasn't enrolled in any summer classes, I intended to use the library's resources to research schizophrenia. In particular, cases of hearing or seeing the Devil. I needed to understand what was real and what was in my head before I committed to venturing back to the House on North Lane.

An email notification brought my research to a halt. The final grade for *Psychological Manipulation* had been released, and my finger hovered over the mouse, heart thundering wildly inside my chest. Everything else in my life had crashed and burned. I just needed one thing to go right.

Clicking on 'view my results', my eyes locked on the loading wheel until my grade appeared on screen, the 'High Distinction' sending a wave of relief through my body. I did it. I secured a second-year scholarship.

A cacophony of laughter flooded the entryway, my gaze drifting from my grade toward Professor Haywood. She held a takeaway coffee cup in one hand while the other carried her laptop and books, her glasses sliding down her nose as she laughed at something the student beside her said.

My body stiffened as Nathaniel moved his hands expressively while he spoke, his lips spread into a smile and his head thrown back with laughter.

Look at him. Already much happier without you.

His smile was a dagger to the heart, his laugh the hand that tore it from my flesh, letting me bleed out alone on the floor.

You wanted him to be happy, didn't you?

No. I wanted him to be as miserable as I was without him. And that was the problem.

I averted my gaze and returned to my grade, clicking on a link to the class ranking without acknowledging the taste of venom on my tongue. Why did everyone else get to be happy? Why was I always left alone to dance with misery?

Because they let themselves be happy. You had your chance.

I didn't need him. I didn't need anyone. Loneliness and I were old friends.

Liar.

Equal first place. Tied with Nathaniel, of course. The class ranking listed his name first, followed by mine right by his side. If we were still together, we might have celebrated with another date night. Instead, my gaze drifted toward where he sat with Professor Haywood, discussing the summer class he'd told me he planned on taking. He didn't turn around. Not once. Not even when I heard Haywood announce we shared equal first in the course ranking.

Unable to stomach his presence any longer, I gathered my things and fled the library, desperate to escape before the Devil's words unravelled me once more.

"Augustus."

I paused in the doorway, glancing up at Nathaniel who peered down at me, expression unreadable. "Congratulations," I said, voice cold, "you secured the first-place ranking. Just as you wanted."

"As did you."

I shrugged. "Not an achievement for me. I wanted to surpass you. Not tie with you."

"Still?"

"Always."

Nathaniel sighed. "Can we talk? Please?"

"We're talking now."

"You know that's not what I meant."

I turned away, but Nathaniel's fingers found my wrist, holding me back.

"I'm sorry, okay? The interrogation was wrong and–"

"It doesn't change the fact that you think I'm crazy," I cut him off.

"I don't think you're crazy," he said, inching closer. "But I do think you need some medical attention that–"

I pulled my wrist free. "I'm leaving."

"Please don't go," he begged, voice cracking. "Just stop pushing me away. You always shut me out instead of letting me help you."

"I didn't ask for your help. I don't *want* your help."

"One day," he whispered, eyes saturated with unshed tears, "you're going to push too hard. And no one is going to be there when you realise you *do* want help."

"How hard will I have to push *you* until you leave me the fuck alone?" I asked.

A flicker of hurt cascaded down his face. "You don't want me to leave you. You don't. I know you don't."

The laugh that erupted from me was pure ice. "What makes you so damn sure?"

"I know you," he whispered, hand extended towards mine, warm gaze pleading, "and you are scared. Your whole world is crumbling. You are running away from something good because you're terrified to lose it. But Augustus...I am here. I am RIGHT HERE! Don't run from me. Please...not me."

My gaze dropped to his hand. A small part of me wanted to reach for him, to collapse in his arms and surrender to the warmth of his body. It would have been easy. It would have been safe. Nathaniel would have calmed the raging storm in my head, bringing me to safety like a lighthouse guiding a ship home from sea.

But I left his hand there, alone and untouched, shutting out the sound of his choked sob as I threw away my last chance of happiness.

CHAPTER THIRTY-SIX

The door to my apartment was open. It shouldn't have been, I'd locked it that morning before I left for Dawnridge. The keys were in my pocket, and the spare could only be accessed from inside where it sat tucked away in my bedside drawer. Perhaps Auden had ventured outside and forgot to close it in his fevered state. But there was an urgent voice in my head—a voice that wasn't the Devil's—that screamed *wrong, wrong, wrong!*

Greeted by an eerie, disorienting silence, I stepped inside and flicked on the light by the entry, listening for the familiar sound of the television from Auden's bedroom. There was only an unsettling quiet.

Wanting to check on his fever, I wandered towards his bedroom, the hallway seemingly never-ending. One step forward only seemed to send me seven steps back. I blinked, quickening my pace, hand outstretched to grip the wall as the floor began to rise and fall like waves beneath my feet.

"Auden?!"

His bedroom door hung wide open. I paused amidst the waves, barely able to hold myself upright as the voice repeated *wrong, wrong, wrong!* Auden always had his door closed. He preferred the apartment divided into 'separate spaces'.

I peered through the doorway, dread humming through me as the single voice became several, all chanting *wrong, wrong, wrong!*

The bed was empty.

Bed sheets were sprawled along the floor—twisted, tangled, like tree roots in a dense forest. Abandoned food wrappings lay crumbled beside a pair of glasses and headphones, my gaze whipping around wildly in search of a light switch.

As a pale-yellow glow chased away the darkness, a scream threatened to tear through my chest. Blood spatters—dark, dried blood—painted the floor beside Auden's bed. It creeped along the bed sheets, a red trail leading toward a silver crucifix by his pillow, the sharp edge dripping with blood. A bolt of recognition shot through me. Flames. My mother in her white gown. A silver crucifix pointed toward me. But how did...?

Not real, not real, not real.

"AUDEN?!"

I reached for the crucifix in a panic. It was the only evidence that proved my mother had come for Auden. Joe must have told her of the visit, helping her track us down.

Joe is dead. You killed him.

That wasn't real.

This *isn't real.*

My fingers trembled around the crucifix. It didn't matter what was real. Auden was gone, and I would *kill* to ensure he was returned to me.

CHAPTER THIRTY-SEVEN

A pool of white mist circled the House on North Lane, crawling up the front steps and onto the porch where I stood, my mother's crucifix trembling in my hands. The trees loomed closer, watching me, waiting.

Red bed sheets flashed behind my eyelids with every blink, my mind conjuring images of Auden's lifeless, blood-drenched corpse. I no longer cared about finding my mother. All I cared about was *him*. I had to find him. He had to be okay. I saved him once, and I would do so again.

The Devil wrestled for control as I unlocked the door, a damp rot greeting me with a cold embrace. He screamed, begged, negotiated for release, but I didn't need him. My rage was my own.

I covered a hand over my mouth and nose as I stepped inside, eyes watering from the smell. Dead animals, no doubt. Rotting corpses in the ceiling, under the floorboards, buried in the walls.

What if it's not animals? What if it's Auden?

"It's not Auden," I growled out, though fear had already embedded itself in my lungs, every breath a battle as I ventured deeper into the House.

You don't know that.

A light flickered on, illuminating the ash covered living room, a long wooden beam dangling from the charcoal ceiling. Rats scurried back into their hiding places, maggots crawling over dried blood that stained the floorboards. I released a shuddered breath.

Standing in the chalk pentagram in the centre of the room was my mother. She was dressed in the same white gown she'd worn the night of the exorcism, and every night since in my dreams, her hair a tangled nest of auburn curls and dust. Her skin had paled, as though she had spent all these years hiding from sunlight.

Let me out! Let me out! Let me out!

My breath hitched in my throat, conflicting emotions tearing through my heart and mind. I wanted to run to her; wanted to run *from* her. I wanted to burrow into her chest, be held the way I used to when I was a small boy, chasing my mother's love. I wanted to abandon her to the House's wicked whims. But I could not leave. Not without my brother.

Reuniting with her no longer had the desired effect. She had taken too much from me. Auden was all I had. And she took him; stole him from me. I had nothing if I didn't have my second half.

"Where is Auden?" I demanded.

She offered no response. Nothing but a blink.

"Where is he?!" I repeated.

Her lips parted, Latin rolling off her tongue. Even now, after all this time, she saw only the Devil and not her son.

"It doesn't work, Ma!" I shouted, arms sprawled out like an angel's wingspan. "You've tried it before! And guess what? The Devil is still in me!"

Her eyes widened, but she did not stop, nor back away. She was glued to the spot, trapped in the pentagram intended for me.

"Tell. Me. Where. Auden. Is!"

She refused to answer, voice rising as The Lord's Prayer spilled from her lips. There were no flames, but I could feel their heat. It burned through me until manic laughter erupted from deep inside of me, a dormant volcano no longer.

"...Hallowed Be Thy FUCKING Name!" I prayed with her, both hands wrapped around the crucifix in mock prayer. "What does that even mean, Ma?! Do you even know?!"

It means to make holy the name of God, the Devil answered my question, *and separate it from all that would dishonour it.*

"Well, this..." I said, gesturing to my mother, the pentagram, and the remnants of a House that no longer felt like a home. "...none of this honours God! You idolised Joe—a human—over your God, allowing him to corrupt your soul. I may be the Devil, but you are certainly no saint. Where is Auden?!"

The Latin, the prayers, they continued as if I had said nothing.

Shaking my head, I stepped forward to snap her out of her mania, to plead for whatever part of my mother was left in this empty shell, but my hands passed right through her.

I stumbled forward, the absence of a solid form sending me straight inside the pentagram. Glancing in between my hands and my mother, my momentary confusion prevented me from registering the circle of flames crawling toward me. It wasn't until thick smoke clouded my vision that it hit me. I was exactly where I had been all those years ago. Had this all been some kind of trap?

A tug on my shirt diverted my attention, gaze falling on Auden, an endless stream of tears cascading down his face. He was four years old again, and scared, rocking back and forth as he coughed, and coughed, and coughed. I really had returned to that night in North Lane. Had I ever left?

Joe sidled up to my mother, his dark eyes ablaze with flickering flames. They spoke in tongues, their voices rising louder in unison, the flames growing taller. I was succumbing to the smoke once more, just as I had as a boy.

Falling to my knees, I reached for Auden, desperate to shield him from the raging heat.

You will die. You have to let me in.

Curled up, gasping for air, I watched my mother through the orange glow. She smiled, warmth flooding back into her skin. I screamed. Her smile grew wider. How had I ever hoped to save her?

Let me in. The Devil's voice was urgent, pleading. *I can save us.*

My eyelids slammed shut. I couldn't hold on any longer. Auden was weakening in my arms. His breathing was shallow, ash clogging his airways. I cleared it with my fingers, rolling him onto his side as he coughed up black phlegm.

Let me in!

I was not the villain of this story. I was a hero. I would save my brother. I was not the monster my mother claimed me to be.

But the Devil *was*. And I let him in.

My eyelids snapped open as I rose to my feet, the Devil carrying Auden and I through the flames. He placed him down carefully, my mother's gasp stuttering her words as the crucifix she wielded like a weapon fell from her grasp.

The Devil crouched down to lift it, waiting for a burn that never came.

"See, ma?" I asked, voice crackling like wood around a campfire. "Your God has abandoned you. You didn't hallow His name well enough."

She lunged for me, sharp nails outstretched like daggers. I stepped to the side, the absence of my tall frame sending her to the floor, knees slamming against the wooden floorboards with a sickening crunch.

A quiet sob escaped her throat. "Our Father, who art in Heaven, Hallowed be..."

The Devil prowled forward, circling her like a predator preparing its kill.

All I could think about, as I gazed down at her trembling body, was stopping her from hurting Auden—hurting me—once and for all. I just wanted it all to end.

"Look at me," I said. A demand, not a request.

My mother slowly lifted her gaze, black tears pouring from her red-rimmed eyes.

"Why did you come for him?" I asked.

"For who?"

"Auden," I hissed.

"I did not come for him," she said. "He came to me. He wanted to come home."

I hesitated, Auden's words replaying in my head: 'I want to go home...to North Lane.'

"And instead of welcoming him, you what...continue what you started that night?" I asked.

She didn't answer.

I shook my head, disgusted at what she had become. Perhaps if she had been less critical of the Devil inside me, and looked in the mirror herself, she would have seen the evil within. *She* was the monster here. Not me.

There can always be more than one monster, Augustus.

My jaw clenched. Even now, the Devil was not entirely on my side. Even now, he tormented me.

"I want my son. Give me my son." My mother's nails slashed my cheek, a manic gleam in her eye as she watched me stumble, nearly losing hold of the crucifix.

"I *am* your son!" Blood rolled down my throbbing cheek, the taste of iron lingering on my tongue. "I want my *mother!*"

"You are no son of mine."

It hurt. Even after all this time, it hurt. I advanced forward, eyes locked on my mother, crucifix gripped firmly in my hand.

"I am God's soldier," she said, "armed to fight the Devil. And the Devil wears my baby boy's face to manipulate me. His deception will not win. *You* will not win."

She was sick, so very, very sick. My father should have gotten her help when he had the chance. It never had to be like this.

"Let Auden and I go," I said, softly, "I don't want to fight you anymore."

"I can't do that."

Her hand shot for my throat, but the Devil was faster. He seized control of my body, throwing me into the iron cage deep in the darkest corner of my mind while he stepped back, escaping her cold clutches.

In my mother's brief moment of hesitation, the Devil slammed my foot into her stomach, her knees reuniting with the floorboards once more with a choked gasp. This time, the Devil did not let her rise. He showed her the same mercy she had shown Auden and I—none.

"Tell me I am not the Devil," he said, using my voice as he twirled the crucifix in my hand, "and I will let you live."

My mother trembled, tears pooling in her wide, unblinking eyes. "You *are* the Devil!"

"It didn't have to be this way," he sighed, the floorboards cracking beneath my feet as he guided me forward, grip tightening on the crucifix. "But you've given me no choice."

My arm lifted without my permission, the crucifix raised high above my head.

Everything slowed.

My mother inhaled.

The Devil exhaled.

I slammed my fists against the iron bars of my cage, shouting for it all to end.

And it did.

The Devil brought the sharp end of the crucifix down on the top of my mother's head, her body crumbling to the floor. She was still, too still, blood spilling from her head like water tipping over a waterfall. It reddened the floor beneath her, a stark contrast to her pale flesh.

The crucifix fell to the floor in slow motion, my hands fluttering wildly at my sides.

I murdered my mother.

She was dead. Dead. I killed her.

Swallowing back the bile that rose in my throat, I turned toward Auden, only for my reflection to confront me inside the mirror that had started it all. Where had it come from? Why was it here? Who was I staring at?

The reflection was eight years old—brown curls shorter than they were now, hazel eyes wider, blood seeping from the clawed wound on his cheek. His hands, trembling like mine, were stained red, a pale corpse bleeding out behind him.

My mother's corpse.

Do you see?

"No," I whispered.

Yes, you do. But you refuse.

"It's not real."

You murdered your mother.

"It's not real."

You murdered her eleven years ago.

"It's not real."

You murdered her that night in North Lane.

"No, I saw her tonight."

You went right through her.

"A hallucination."

A ghost.

"I had to save Auden."

And you did.

"It's not real."

Your father told you she left. But he saw the body. He buried it.

"It's not real."

You've known the truth this whole time.

"It's not real."

You have to face what you have done.

"It's not real."

I'm not real.

"It's not real."

I've never been real.

"It's not real."

You are the monster.

"It's not real."

You need to face it, Augustus.

Auden. I needed to find Auden. He was the reason I was here—the reason I let in the Devil. I needed to save him and prove I wasn't the monster everyone thought I was.

"Auden?!" I choked out.

I scoured every inch of the first floor, the mirror following me into every room, a haunting reminder of what I had done.

"It's not real."

It's real.

"It's real."

It's not real.

"It's not real."

We can play this game all day.

"It's not real."

I ascended the staircase, shouting Auden's name into the endless void. There was no response. Every room was empty.

Breathing heavily, stomach threatening to bring up my last meal, I bolted downstairs to check the outside perimeter, but when my fingers wrapped around the door handle, it would not open. I tried again, and again, and again, even using my foot to kick it open, but it would not budge.

Frustrated, I hurried to a boarded-up window and attempted to yank off the planks of wood. An invisible force threw me backwards, pain shooting down my spine.

There was no way out. Not one door, window, or crack. The House would not let me leave. I was trapped—a prisoner of the House on North Lane.

CHAPTER THIRTY-EIGHT

I am made of neglected glass and abandoned iron—uncared for, forgotten, alone.

No, not alone. Never alone.

The ghost of North Lane hid in the shadows. Watching me. Taunting me. A harsh reminder of what I had become—of what I had always been. She was right. The Devil lived inside me. I was the monster haunting this tale. And now, I was condemned to an eternity with her ghost, trapped inside an endless loop—my own personal Hell.

I had long since given up hope of escaping, but I had not given up on Auden. I had to find him. He was the sole reason I returned to North Lane, the reason I murdered my mother, the reason I could not escape. But even if we were prisoners of the House, at least we'd be imprisoned together.

Days passed, and those days turned to weeks, and weeks turned to months. I thought I'd seen him one day, standing by the stairs, but he'd transformed into a mere shadow, vanishing before I could utter more than his name. He was gone. Nowhere to be found.

It was just me, the ghost, and the House on North Lane.

***

I stood in front of a door that would not open, an unyielding guard sealed at the very end of the upstairs hallway. It was here the shadowed figure led me, yet I could not follow it inside, the House barring me from its secrets.

"What are you trying to tell me?" I asked, fingers tracing over the splintered paint, small specks of dust drifting to the floor.

The Devil's clawed hand caressed my shoulder, the stench of rot gushing from his lips that parted to whisper, There is nothing for you in there.

"How do you know?" I asked, testing the doorknob I knew would not budge.

We are trying to escape this prison, *he said, claws digging deeper into my flesh,* not explore it.

"You know what?" I freed my shoulder from the Devil's grasp, shoving him backwards. "I don't need to listen to you anymore!"

Don't be stupid, little monster.

"I'm not a monster!"

Your mother's ghost says otherwise.

Rage tore through me, fist raised to strike the Devil. His lips spread into a grin. Wicked delight glistened in his eyes. He wore my face, yet I could hardly recognise myself. Who was I? Who had I become? Who did I want to be?

The Devil wanted me to strike him; to be the monster he believed me to be. I had no intention of proving him right.

"I don't care what you say," I said, lowering my fist. "I don't care what you think. You do not get to decide who I am."

Behind me, the door clicked open, and the Devil vanished. Inside the room, the shadowed figure stood facing a mirror. The mirror—its familiar golden arch outlining the ghost of its reflection. It was not my mother. Nor the Devil. There was one other prisoner inside the House on North Lane.

The figure was tall, dressed in black trousers and a plain black t-shirt, the long sleeves stained with blood. His dark brown hair was an untamed mess atop his head, skin pale, almost luminescent. And his eyes—as blue as a cloudless sky.

Auden.

"You," I whispered, "you are the ghost haunting the House on North Lane."

"You," Auden whispered back, "you are the ghost haunting the House on North Lane."

I blinked, startled. Auden blinked back.

I raised my hand. Auden followed.

My knees slammed down onto the wooden floorboards, a loud crack echoing along the walls. The ghost knelt in front of me—silent, waiting.

"I don't...understand."

"You are the ghost haunting the House on North Lane," he repeated.

"A ghost? But I'm not dead," I said. "Are...you?"

Auden shook his head. "I was never born."

If I hadn't already fallen to my knees, I certainly would have at those words. "What...what are you talking about?"

"I'm not real, Augustus," Auden said, "I never was."

"That doesn't make any sense. You're my brother. We've grown up together."

"Have we?" Auden asked.

And then he was gone, the mirror reflecting four-year-old me, curled up outside on the front porch, shivering from fear and the cold. I was praying to God, praying for my mother's forgiveness, praying for a sibling so that I would no longer be alone.

The image shifted and I was in the hospital room, only it wasn't Auden in my mother's arms, it was me. My mother whispered soothing words as I cradled my bruised wrist, but as soon as the nurses left the room, she handed me to my father as if she couldn't stand to look at me.

All those days in the woods—alone. Images of my childhood came and went, the mirror unveiling the truth. I had always been alone. Auden—the ghost of Auden—had been right. He never existed.

The mirror reflected that night in North Lane—trapped in a circle of flames as my mother spoke in tongues, waving her crucifix in front of her like a sword.

It wasn't Auden I was trying to save, but myself.

"You created me," Auden returned to the mirror, "so that you wouldn't be alone anymore. That's all you ever really wanted. To not be alone. And I became a reason for you to live, to aim for something better."

A choked sob escaped my throat as Auden's face shifted to mine, and the reality of my whole life came crashing down on me. Auden wasn't real. None of it was real.

Auden was the innocence I had lost and now I was alone, just as I had always been.

I screamed, I cried, I sobbed, until my tears dried up and I was nothing but an empty shell, laying in front of the mirror. Everyone I loved was dead. Or never existed.

What about Nathaniel?

Sniffling, I sat up and lifted the hem of my shirt to wipe my eyes. I had been trapped in this House for too long alongside ghosts and haunted memories. I needed to escape. I needed to move on. I needed to find Nathaniel. I had made a mistake—a huge, irredeemable mistake. But I wanted him in my life.

There was a knock on the front door as if I'd summoned him with just a thought. I staggered to my feet, heart and head aching, desperate to find him.

The knock grew louder, more urgent, as I descended the staircase, floorboards coming alive to gnaw at my feet, the House trembling with rage. It refused to let me leave—refused to let anyone in.

Did I dare hope to find Nathaniel on the other side of the door?

I raced toward the entrance in slow motion, the walls growing closer and closer in an attempt to suffocate and crush my bones. But I pushed through, the knock pounding inside my head, trembling fingers desperate to curl around the door handle.

The door hadn't opened in a long time, but maybe, with the ghosts gone and my memories resurfaced, the House would have no choice but to let me leave. Had I not been punished enough?

The door creaked open slowly, a blast of light chasing away the darkness that curled around me.

And there he was, standing in the doorway, his eyes glistening with tears, his perfect lips parted in surprise.

"Augustus," Nathaniel whispered, "you let me in."

ACKNOWLEDGEMENTS

In all honesty, I can't believe I am here, writing the acknowledgements at the end of my debut novel—a novel I never thought I would finish, yet alone publish. It feels surreal.

I have so many people to thank. To my mother—who I certainly do not want to murder—thank you for being excited to read my book. I remember when I was around nine or ten, I wrote my first book on your old computer and printed it off to show you. Even though it was absolutely terrible, your praise and encouragement has led me to this moment, publishing my very own book. Thank you. I love you more than words can say.

To my dad, thank you for showing an interest in my book even though you're not a reader and you dislike horror. When you asked me to read my prologue to you out loud, I was nervous, but your praise meant the world.

To Kaya and Sylvia, thank you for being Hallowed Be Thy Name's biggest cheerleaders. You inspired me to continue writing even when I felt like giving up. I hope it lived up to your expectations, and I am personally relieved I no longer have to endure your begging to read it. You're both amazing, I love you!

To Rin, my incredible cover artist and friend. You brought my story and characters to life in a way I had only ever dreamed of. Thank you for your patience, passion, and commitment to Hallowed Be Thy Name. I look forward to working with you on future projects.

To my editor, Kylah. Thank you for believing in Hallowed Be Thy Name. You made me realise I really could publish this silly little messed up project of mine, and I will be forever grateful for your support.

To my beta readers, I owe you a great debt. Your feedback and support helped shape Hallowed Be Thy Name into what it is today—a book I can be proud of. I am so grateful for your encouragement and honesty.

To my street team—the Hallowed Ones—thank you for all your excitement, encouragement and support leading up to release. I could have not done any of this without you.

And finally, to you, dear reader. By taking a chance on a debut Indie author, you have helped fulfil my wildest dreams. I hope you enjoyed Hallowed Be Thy Name and that some part of it resonated with you. Keep fighting those demons no one else can see.